GOLDEN SHIELD

J.R. ANDREWS

First Edition: December 2020

E-mail: jr@jrandrewsbooks.com
Website: http://jrandrewsbooks.com

Editor: Virge Buck at Red Adept Editing (https://redadeptediting.com/)
Cover and Formatting: Streetlight Graphics

Hardback ISBN: 978-1-7343958-3-9
Paperback ISBN: 978-1-7343958-4-6
eBook ISBN: 978-1-7343958-5-3

For Mom,
It probably ain't the Great American Novel,
but this one means a lot to me.

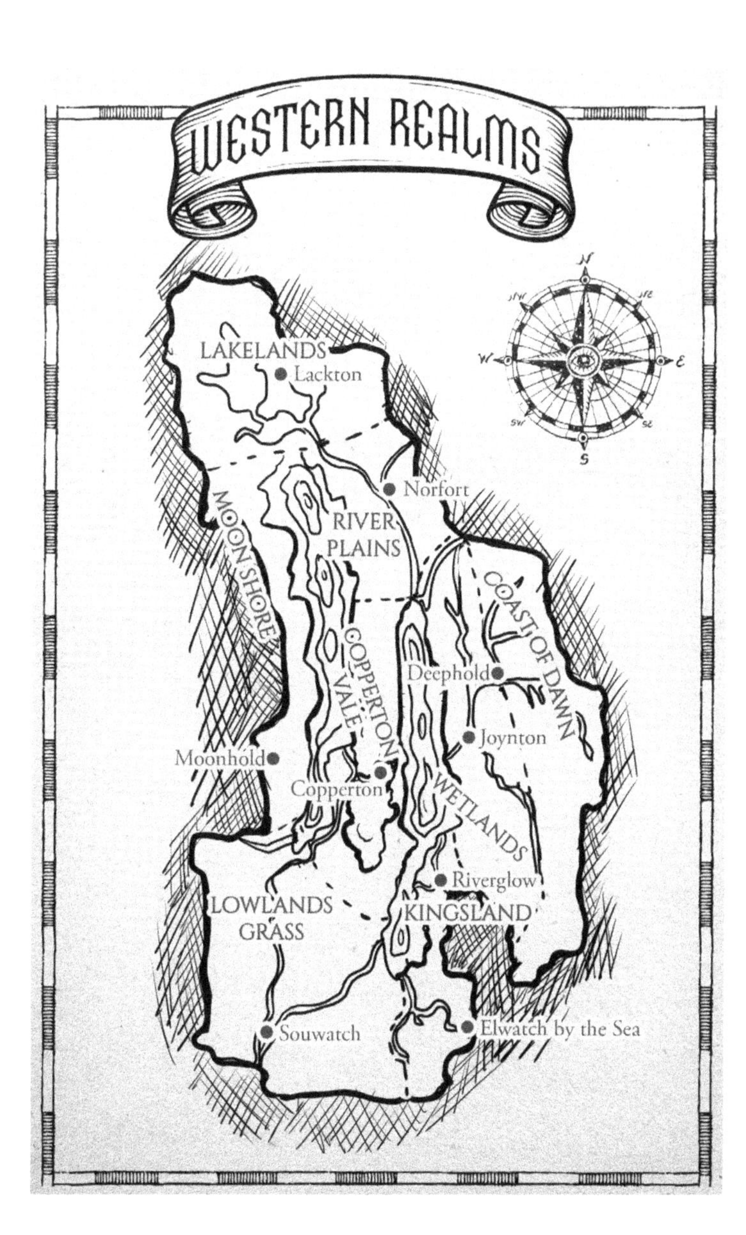

WESTERN REALMS
N
S
E
W
LAKELANDS
Lackton
Norfort
RIVER PLAINS
MOON SHORE
COPPERTON VALE
COAST OF DAWN
Deephold
Joynton
Moonhold
Copperton
WETLANDS
Riverglow
LOWLANDS GRASS
KINGSLAND
Souwatch
Elwatch by the Sea

BOOK ONE

NOVICE LESSONS

CHAPTER ONE

THE REAL WORLD

GERALD LAWSON WAS GOING TO die. Soon.

"Dammit, Zeke," he muttered into the mic of the headset hooked to the laptop beside him, "if you don't hurry up with that Rain of Fire cast, I'm going to be toast, and then these trolls will use you as a punching bag."

Raindrops spattered the driver's-side window of his Simmsville Township Police Department cruiser, reflecting pinpoints of the one hazy, yellowish bulb hanging over the parking lot of the town's only high school. Just a few more hours until this sodden, never-ending overnight shift ended. With luck, he'd get through it without even having to get out of the car. As soon as it ended, he was looking at seventy-two glorious hours to himself. His wallet was full of cash for the pizza delivery guy, and the fridge at the apartment was stocked with energy drinks. He was all ready to embark on an epic video game marathon.

The twenty-three-year-old, the town's youngest and newest police officer, shifted his weight in the driver's seat, trying to find a comfortable way to sit while focusing on his laptop screen.

"Shut up," said a voice through his headset. "I'm doing the best I can. I didn't design the game. The spell's cool-down phase is out of my hands, Ger."

Gerald rolled his eyes. Ezekiel Dahlberg was his roommate and had been his best friend since they were both seven. After more than fifteen years of friendship, though, that irritated whine Z used when he felt persecuted was like nails on a chalkboard.

Tired of waiting for his friend to cast that attack spell, Gerald tapped buttons on his keyboard in an ordered, well-timed succession. On screen, a figure in glowing, ornate armor surrounded by a trio of cave trolls roared and spun in a circle. An orange ring of light exploded outward, slamming through the monsters. Numbers drifted above them, showing how much damage the attack inflicted.

"You need a better rotation for multiples, then. Because these trolls are trying to hand me my ass while you stand around doing nothing, waiting for your spell to be ready or your pedicure to dry or whatever." Proving his point, one of the monsters launched a counterattack, slamming Gerald's rugged-looking avatar in the head with a spiked club. Stars circled over his Warrior, who staggered in place.

He sighed. "Great, now I'm stunned. One more hit and I'm dead. If I end up in the graveyard, we'll have to start this dungeon all over again."

"Don't wet your pants. I got it." A slender, robed figure, an elven Mage several paces behind the Warrior, raised his arms and launched a pillar of liquid flame into the sky. Half a second later, the three trolls were awash in a fiery downpour as a new string of numbers ticked into the air over them. One by one, they fell to the ground, charred and lifeless.

"See? No problem."

"No problem? Jesus, Z, I'm more than three-quarters dead, and we're barely halfway through this cavern. We're going to have to sit here for a good two minutes while I heal. At this rate, it'll be this time tomorrow before we reach the Ogre Chieftain."

"I told you, dude. We need a healer."

Gerald shifted in his seat again and scratched at the badge on his chest. Damn thing wasn't supposed to bother him, given the way his shirt was reinforced, but it still scraped him worse than any T-shirt tag he'd ever worn. The discomfort half made him wish he'd taken a job on some big-city police force where you had to wear a protective vest under your uniform shirt at all times. At least that would have kept him from constantly getting stabbed by his badge's pins. How did people spend thirty years as cops wearing the things that etched lines into their chests? Then again, he'd been out of school and on the job for only three months. Maybe he'd get used to it. Or just get old and stop caring.

"You say that every time we try this dungeon," Gerald replied. "'We need a healer. We need a healer.' Well, we need a damage dealer, too, which is you. We also need someone to take the brunt of the attacks we face so your delicate snowflake of an elf doesn't get smacked around. And that's me. The real problem here is we keep trying to tackle four-person dungeons with only two people."

"I'm telling you, Ger, people do it all the time. You can totally beat Basha'Un, Lord and Master of the Cave Ogres, with only two players. I spent all day reading about it in the *Realm Quest* forums."

"Fuck. Then we're doing it wrong or something, because we've already been at this an hour, and we'll be lucky to survive the next fight. And we haven't even gotten to the ogres yet. Are you sure Robby and Derek can't play?"

"Yes," Zeke replied. "I met Rob for happy hour last week, and he said he was letting his subscription go. He and Sharon are getting pretty serious, and he doesn't have time. He even talked about buying a ring soon. And Derek isn't doing much of anything, anywhere. The guy's been working twenty-hour days trying to get ahead. He said being a new broker is killing him."

"God, dude, remember when you could count on your friends?"

Zeke clucked his tongue. "Maybe you should just go back and roll a Paladin. Then you could take damage and heal yourself."

Gerald shook his head. "No way. You want me to bail on a level 36 character and start over? I've got months of time in my Warrior, most of it from before I started working. When would I find time to grind out a Paladin? As it is, I'm risking my job to be playing from my cruiser, overnight shift or not. I should be out patrolling right now. You know, that 'protect and serve' bullshit? If the chief ever finds out about this, I'll be stripped of this itchy-ass badge in about 30 seconds."

"You know you don't have to worry about that," Zeke assured him. "No one will ever find out. As the one and only member of the Systems Department for the Township of Simmsville, I promise you there's no evidence now and never will be that you were playing *Realm Quest* from your cruiser at one o'clock in the morning."

"You seem pretty sure, Z." With Gerald's luck—or rather, his lack of it—he'd get caught somehow anyway. As the new guy on the force, he was stuck with the overnight patrol duties nobody else wanted. That was fine with him; he was a night owl already. Plus, hardly anything ever happened in town at night, so he had a lot less paperwork to do than the day-shift guys. But since he'd signed onto the force, time for gaming had been hard to come by.

All his friends, or at least the ones that still played cooperative online games like *Realm Quest*, played them at night, after work. So Zeke, the town's IT guy, had come up with this as a solution. It wasn't perfect, but it beat not being able to play at all.

Occasionally, he felt a twinge of guilt over it. He really *should* be out on patrol. But he wasn't hurting anyone. Overnight calls in sleepy Simmsville were about as common as flying goats. The minimal work Gerald did do at night amounted to handing out speeding tickets and chasing teenagers away from the local make-out hot spots. Giving up his game time to do more of that was about as attractive as spring cleaning the dump of an apartment he shared with Zeke.

"My health is back to full. Let's see if we can get to the Ogre Chief boss before I have to make a lap around town."

"Awesome! I've got a great feeling about tonight. We're totally gonna kick some a—"

His sarcastic reply was cut off by the familiar click of someone new joining their voice chat group.

"Hey, nerds, what's up?"

"Oh, hey, uh, what's up, Brooke?" Gerald's voice cracked on her name. Jesus, would he *ever* not sound like a twelve-year-old around her?

"Hey, Brooke," Zeke said. "Perfect timing! You want to jump in here? We could use the help. I mean, we really need a Priest, but your Assassin's knives would come in handy, too."

"Not tonight, Z. I just needed to hear some friendly voices while I eat a pint of mocha chip. Dane and I broke up. For good this time."

Gerald's cheeks warmed. It was news he'd been waiting to hear.

"Bummer," Zeke went on. "What happened?"

"Oh, the usual bullshit. You know how it goes. I don't want to talk about it right now."

"Yeah, okay."

"Guy was a douche," Gerald added. "You're better off alone, anyway."

"Yeah, right, alone. Always alone." Her half-mumbled tone suggested she didn't believe him. "You know, I think maybe I'll just call it a night early. Talk to you guys later."

She was gone before either of them could reply.

"Great work, dumbass."

"What?"

"It doesn't take much sense to know you don't tell someone who just ended a relationship that they're better off alone."

"Why not? She is better off alone. Dane was a controlling scum nugget."

"First off, he wasn't that bad. You just didn't like him because he was going out with her. Same as you don't like *anyone* who goes out with her. Second off, when you say something like 'better off alone,' what the person hears is, 'you'll always be alone.' And the last thing someone wants to imagine after a breakup is that they're going to end up a creepy aunt or uncle with an apartment full of cats that smells like mothballs."

Gerald frowned. When you put it that way, he had kind of messed that up.

"God. She's never going to like me if I keep saying stupid things."

"Don't worry about it, Ger. She'll have forgotten about it tomorrow."

"I hope. This is it, Z. I'm not waiting around anymore. I'm going to tell her how I feel. Make my move."

"What? And ask her out? Ha! Sure you will. You've only said that, what? A hundred times? I'll believe it when I see it."

"Fuck off. I'm going to do it this time."

"Yeah, right. Whatever. I mean, I'll be happy for you if you do. God knows it's about fucking time. Let me know how it goes. In the meantime, can we get back to clearing this cavern? That Ogre Chief isn't going to kill himself for us."

"Right, yeah. Let's do it."

Not long after, they stumbled upon four snarling trolls, who took turns pounding Gerald's Warrior over the head with clubs. He fought back with a glowing war hammer and a shield as tall as the avatar holding it. Behind him, lightning sizzled from Zeke's Mage, knocking the unsuspecting monster back with each strike.

"Fifteen seconds and I'll have these punks down in a storm of fire," Zeke said over the headset.

"If I last that—" Gerald started just as the police radio on his shoulder squawked to life.

"Charlie three-two, come in."

"Oh, shit."

"Shit, what? We own these trolls."

"It's dispatch," he hissed. "Shut up."

With trembling fingers, he smacked the mute button on his headphones and squeezed the button on his radio. "This is Charlie three-two, over." A bead of sweat gathered at his temple. He struggled to keep a twinge of panic out of his voice.

"Sorry to bother you, Ger," replied an older man, his voice thick with sleep. "What's your location?"

"I'm just passing the high school, Phil. What's up?"

"We've gotten a couple of calls that something strange is

going on over at the Quik Mart. Both callers mentioned colored lights flashing inside the store and some loud noises. I figure that Chad, the new kid, probably just forgot to turn off all the beer displays before he closed up for the night. But I need you to swing by and check it out."

"Sure thing, Phil. I'll be right there."

"Copy that, Gerald. Like I said, I'm sure it's nothing. Let me know what's going on so I can clear the night log and get back to sleep."

"Roger. Charlie three-two, out."

He frowned at the game running on his laptop. The display had become a fuzzy, purple-gray, slow-motion version of the cavern. The message "You DIED" flashed in the center in big, angry letters.

"Dammit."

He toggled the mute button and was assaulted by a string of cursing that would have made a drill sergeant blush. "Holy bloody pumping fuck, Gerald, we were almost there!" Zeke shouted, the words ringing in Gerald's ears. "What the hell? You couldn't wait ten more seconds? Dammit, Ger, dammit, dammit, shit, cock, dammit!"

"Easy, Z. Calm down."

"Bullshit! You calm down! We had them! But then you disappeared and got killed like a chump. After that, the trolls turned to me, and I lasted about three seconds. Green fuckers clubbed me to death before I could do anything. I swear to God somebody better really be dying."

"Jesus. It's only a damn game. Listen to yourself. Shut up a take a deep breath."

"But—"

"*No*!" Gerald barked. "Take a breath and count to ten. Then we'll talk."

That cut through the rant. His friend inhaled and exhaled

twice and then counted to ten in a soft voice. As he did, Gerald put the car in gear and pulled out of the parking lot, slamming down the accelerator. The cruiser leapt up the road in the direction of the Quik Mart.

"Okay, Ger. I'm okay. Sorry, I lost my head."

"Sooner or later, you're going to have to learn to control that temper, Z." He'd been blowing his stack like that since middle school. Getting him to stop and count to ten was as familiar as brushing Gerald's teeth.

"I know, I know. I'm sorry. So what's going on?"

"A few people called in and complained about some funny colored lights and noise coming from the Quik Mart. It's probably just a beer display that didn't get turned off. Phil said they have a new kid closing up. But I have to drive by and check it out. Make sure nobody broke in or anything."

"Whoa, cool! You haven't had anything fun to check out since old Hal got so drunk he wouldn't leave Rita's Diner until she made him pancakes."

"You're messed up. None of what I just said is cool. It's just going to be a big, stupid hassle that I'll end up writing a pointless report about. Look, sit tight, and I'll check back in with you twenty minutes after I've made sure it's all okay. Maybe we can try the Ogre Chief again later."

"No way. I'm bored as hell, and I already drank two Monsters. I'm meeting you there."

"What? No, Jesus, Zeke, you can't do that."

"Arrest me when you get there," his friend laughed, and then the channel went dead.

Shit.

CHAPTER TWO

THE QUIK MART

GERALD WHIPPED HIS CRUISER INTO the Quik Mart's parking lot, his mind swirling with thoughts of Brooke. She was just like him and Zeke, and she didn't give a flying rat's ass what anyone else thought about it. She could quote *Star Wars*, *Star Trek*, and *Doctor Who* from memory, had a longer pull list of comics than Gerald, and took *Realm Quest* more seriously than Z. Gamer, geek, and a lover of science fiction and fantasy in any form, she was self-reliant and the kind of friend who would stand in line with you overnight in pouring rain without a second thought, just so you could score the latest new phone on release day.

In high school and college, the three of them played games together online every free moment, as if it was a religion. In fact, many of Gerald's favorite memories were of him, Zeke, and Brooke huddled together over laptops around a coffee shop table, clearing a dungeon full of rabid owlbears or vengeful kobolds.

Things had changed with age, though, and these days, her gaming schedule was even less dependable than his. When she wasn't dating someone, she popped online almost nightly. As soon as some new boy caught her eye, though, she'd disappear and stay away from the game world for weeks.

That prolonged absence from time to time made the burden of carrying his silent, intense crush on her almost unbearable, but he did it anyway. And while that might have been okay in middle school, when he first realized he had feelings for Brooke and had to be in the running for Most Awkward Adolescent in History, he was a grown man now. He had no excuse to have done nothing about his feelings.

That was not to say he hadn't tried. At times, he'd tried to pay for her pizza or sushi whenever they went out as a group (she invariably told him to stop being a tool and that she could and would pay her own way). On some holidays, he'd bought her an adorable stuffed thing from her favorite video game (she'd coo over it, briefly, and then forget it, just as she did with all the cute gifts of questionable use other guys gave her). And he made a point to never, ever have a good thing to say about any of the boyfriends with whom she had short-lived relationships (which, looking back, tended to strain his relationship with her more than strengthen it).

One year, he'd even sent her roses for her birthday—anonymously, though, for fear she might "take it the wrong way." Of course, that guaranteed she couldn't take it the right way, either, so instead, she puzzled over it for a minute, shrugged, and made potpourri a week later. These days, he still wasn't sure what he'd hoped to accomplish with the gesture.

Gerald told himself they'd never talked about it because the timing was always off. No way he could bring his feelings up while she was dating another one of her Mr. Forgettables, and when she wasn't, well, then she'd be back in the Realm, and he didn't want to risk messing that up either.

Deep down, Gerald knew it had nothing to do with timing and everything to do with being afraid of rejection. But that was all about to change. No more tiptoeing around in the dreaded "friend zone." Time to come clean with her.

As he slid to a stop on the wet asphalt, thoughts of his stagnant love life scattered. As promised, Zeke was waiting for him, leaning against a beat-up, thirteen-year-old Toyota, waving like a crazy person. His narrow, pale face was split with a fool's grin. The dude could get excited about an insurance seminar.

Throwing his door open, Gerald climbed out of his sedan, squinting against the colored lights still flashing from its roof. "Get back in the car and go home. You shouldn't be here. I could get in huge trouble, Z."

His friend shrugged. "Whatever. Like this is any worse than what we were doing ten minutes ago. Anyway, forget about me. What the hell is that?" He pointed at the store.

As he followed Zeke's finger, Gerald's jaw fell open.

"What the…"

Through the glass of the store front, an eye-searing white light reflected off every mirrored surface inside. Rather than a single steady beam, though, it flickered in constant motion, like moonlight on the ripples of a swimming pool. As if that wasn't strange enough, every few seconds, a burst of color would suffuse the light, cycling from sea green to royal blue to magenta.

"That doesn't look like any beer display I've ever seen." Zeke sounded like a kid seeing fireworks for the first time.

"No, it doesn't. Now go home."

"No way."

"Dammit, I don't have time to argue."

"Well, I'm not leaving."

"Gah! Fine. But stay out here. This could end up being a crime scene."

Zeke said nothing. Taking his silence for agreement, the young cop approached the store's door and grasped the handle. Expecting the door to be locked, he gave the handle a tentative tug. Instead of a lock catching on the frame, it flew at him. He yelped, let go, and jumped backward. His other hand dropped to the holstered revolver at his side.

"Holy shit." Inside the store, the colors continued to whirl like sci-fi movie effects.

Zeke snorted. "Yeah, that's a pretty scary door. You sure you don't want me to come in with you? Maybe hold your hand?"

"No, dumbass. It just startled me because it wasn't locked. Now let me do my job."

"Suit yourself."

Gerald took the door handle again and gave it a slow, consistent pull until it opened more than halfway, enough to let him through. He'd never been a small guy, and with the freedom to make bad decisions that came with new adulthood—like having ice cream for dinner and washing it down with a six-pack—he'd gotten increasingly stouter than was wise for someone who might need to chase down the criminals. That was probably why every time the chief saw him carrying around a soft drink or a bag of chips, he threatened to put him on desk leave until he dropped twenty pounds.

With a hand still on his gun holster, Gerald took an apprehensive step forward.

"Hello?"

No answer.

He crept a few wary feet into the store and released the door, letting it swing shut behind him. Whatever was going on in here, he had to deal with it on his own.

Based on the flashes of color on the floor, the light was

coming from the far back corner of the store, near the beer cooler. Tall shelving units blocked his line of sight, though.

Shuffling forward with as much stealth as he could muster, he inched toward the end of the first aisle. At the corner, he stopped, trying to control his breathing. Could anything be over there? Sure, the smart money was on this being some kind of teenage prank, but what if it wasn't? What if it was something crazy? Like an alien or a ghost or something? What if this was the start of the zombie apocalypse? None of that shit was real, right?

He took another few deep breaths while wrangling with his imagination, which was too used to playing video games and watching fantastic movies.

"Well, go on. What is it?"

Gerald jumped at the unexpected voice, nearly leaving his less-shiny-than-they-should-have-been standard-issue shoes empty. Standing in the now-open doorway, Zeke gave him a sheepish look.

"What the fuck is wrong with you?" he growled. "You're lucky I didn't just shoot you!"

His friend shrugged while giving him a half smirk.

"Idiot." After one more measured breath, Gerald popped the snap on his holster, the first time in his short career he'd done it.

Comforted by the grip of his gun, he leaned an inch into the aisle.

And then another inch.

And then one more.

At last, the opening to the beer cooler slid into view.

But it wasn't the beer cooler.

The heavy plastic strips usually separating the warm air of the store and the cold air of the beer cave were gone, replaced with some kind of… gel. It was greenish or grayish or greenish-gray, and it rippled like a pond during a soft spring rain. Whatever the hell it was, it was the source of the flickering reflection.

After a childhood spent watching science fiction movies and television shows, Gerald already knew the perfect words to describe it, even if saying it out loud would qualify him for a straitjacket and calm pills four times a day.

Without question, though, that was some kind of portal or gateway or something.

"Good Lord," he said, whistling.

Identifying it was only half the puzzle. Whatever the thing (portal) was, it didn't account for the cycling colors. Something else was causing that. And after a few tentative steps closer, he found it, lying on the ground beside a pair of very strange boots.

The boots were attached to legs. Legs covered in breeches—not pants, mind you, breeches—embroidered with hoops and whorls of golden thread.

After several more heart-pounding steps, Gerald was so close to the rippling cooler doorway (portal) that he could almost touch it. He eyed it as he passed but then put it out of his mind. It didn't matter as much as the bizarre figure of the man sprawled out on the floor halfway up the soft drink aisle. He was covered in armor that matched the breeches, and a coordinating helmet rested on the ground not far from his head. The helmet must have fallen off at some point, revealing shoulder-length, shock-white hair and a full beard.

Next to the man was a half-staff capped on one end with an orb swirling with colored lights. At least, it *looked* like a half-staff. Gerald had never seen a real one outside of the game, but the proportions were about right in reference to the man.

"Sir? Are you okay? Sir? Hello?" His voice leaked out in a bare whisper, and even then, it cracked.

"Oh my God, Ger!" Zeke sagged against the two-liter soda bottles at the far end of the aisle, hand over his mouth. "What the hell?"

Gerald found his voice. "I… I don't know. Just, Jesus, don't touch anything!"

"What am I going to touch?" his friend shot back. "I'm not stupid. Besides, grabbing at sleepy Admiral Anachronism there sounds like a good way to end up dead, in a way you'd only see in a horror flick."

"Just… just… shut up. Let me think!"

At the barked command, the old man groaned and shifted his boots.

"Oh, hell! Sir? Are you okay? Oh, Jesus! Can you hear me?"

He groaned again and opened one eye, peering at Gerald from beneath bushy white eyebrows. "Yes, I can hear you," he croaked. His voice was old, dry, and full of gravel, like the hero of a black-and-white western.

Grunting, he pushed himself up, rolled over into a sitting position, and leaned back on the snack chips. "And my name isn't Jesus." With his right hand, he grasped the staff and pulled it across his legs.

"Do you know where you are, sir?"

He began to answer but fell into a coughing fit instead, like he'd had a two-pack-a-day habit for twenty years. The spasm of hacking wracked the ancient man's entire body.

"Are you okay, sir? Do you need medical attention?" Gerald reached for his radio. "I'll call for a doctor."

Regaining control, the old man waved and shook his head. "No, no—healing. I'll be fine."

"What is your name, sir? I'm Officer Gerald Lawson of the Simmsville Police Department. What's going on here?"

At the mention of his name, the man on the floor cast a questioning look at him. "My name is… never mind. It doesn't matter who I am. Your name is Lawson? Blessed Thela, could I have been that fortunate? Are you a keeper of the law?"

Gerald frowned. "I'm a police officer here in Simmsville, yes. Listen, sir, do you want some kind of—"

The armored man's boots scraped on the cheap tile floor as he heaved himself up, changing the entire situation in a blink. A man with a glowing staff and full body armor was giving him a determined glare. Like he was about to do something he didn't want to do but had no choice.

"Hold on just a minute, gramps. Why don't you just sit back down before we all get nervous here."

"I'm sorry, son," he said, "but this is why I came." He squeezed the staff with the swirling colors in a gauntleted hand and set his feet into a familiar stance. His body was partially turned to offer a leaner profile, with his knees bent slightly and the left foot forward. The weapon in his right hand was drawn back at the ready.

Jesus, it was a Warrior's attack stance. From *Realm Quest*, the goddamn game.

Without hesitating—or even conscious thought—Gerald swung his revolver free of his holster and pointed the weapon at the strange old man's chest. Adrenaline raced through his arms and legs, filling him with a liquid heat and a jitter to match.

"Sir, I'm… I'm warning you. Drop that weapon and get down on the ground. I don't want to hurt you."

"Holy shit, Gerald, what are you doing?" Zeke gaped at him from behind the man.

The geezer twisted his head around. "You are a lawkeeper as well? Gerald Lawson's friend?"

"Yes. I mean, no. God, dude, what's your problem? Relax. We're just trying to help you."

"Lawkeeper, there is but one way you can help me, I am afraid. May you and Thela both forgive me."

With a quickness at odds with the old man's wizened appearance, he rushed at Zeke, raising the staff over his head.

"Wait. Stop! *Halt*!" Gerald screamed. Zeke crossed his arms and lifted them in defense, eyes wide and mouth open in surprise. With a flick of the man's wrist, the colored end of the staff dropped under his protective arms and struck him in the temple with a dull thud. Zeke crumpled to the ground.

"Don't even fucking twitch, old man!" Gerald shouted, flinging spit. Jesus, what just happened?

With a fluid heel-to-toe spin, the man brought his dark eyes back to Gerald. "Your friend will need your help."

"Shut up! Of course he needs help!"

"There's only one way you can help him now." Again, with that surprising speed, the man dashed forward, boots thumping on the ground.

He raised the staff again.

"*Freeze*!"

One single, ragged heartbeat, and the man kept coming. Gerald's training and instinct took over; he squeezed the trigger of his revolver three times in quick succession. At the same moment, greenish fire erupted from the orb at the end of the man's weapon, filling the space between them. Gerald threw an arm up to cover his face and turned away from the heat of the fireball. Beside him, cereal boxes, cookies, and snack chips burst into sea-green flames.

One second, he could feel the heat on his face, and the next, the fire disappeared. Swirling colors arced toward him.

Something at least as heavy as Zeke's beat-up old Toyota hit him in the head, and Gerald flew back into a shelf of tortilla chips. Sinking to the floor, the old man stood over him, again wracked with a fit of coughing.

Dozens of bags of snacks were burning now but with the regular, orange kind of fire, spreading fast.

The world got fuzzy around the edges.

Zeke? What about Z? At the far end of the aisle, there was no heap on the floor where his friend should have been.

"Where's Zeke?" Did he actually mumble that or just think it?

The old man coughed again and fell to one knee. Catching himself between fits, the hard, determined look melted away. His face becoming a mix of guilt and sorrow, he whispered, "Thela forgive me."

Gerald's vision spun in loopy circles. His arms, his hands, his eyelids all weighed a ton. Or more. Two tons, even. And so many colors. It was so much, too bright to look at.

And then the colors melted to black.

CHAPTER THREE

THE GAME

AT SOME POINT LATER—MINUTES? HOURS? days?—the blackness gave way to a dark, bleary orange.

Burning. Something was burning. The acrid smell of it filled his nose. But it wasn't quite right. The scent was charred and rich with sulfur but still… clean.

Gerald forced his eyes open and shrank back against the heat and fickle light of a building burning around him. With a groan, he rolled over onto his back, still on the floor.

Except.

The floor wasn't right. He *should* be lying on cheap tile. But instead, he was facedown on wooden planks. And they looked wrong just as the air smelled wrong. They were blurry, lacking the right level of detail, even though they were inches from his face. At this distance, every splinter, seam, and imperfection should be clear as day.

The hit to the head from the old man must have given him a concussion. Who'd have thought an old guy with a smoker's cough could whack someone that hard with a stick?

He coughed several times himself. To his surprise, it cleared his head.

"Z?" he called out.

No reply.

"*Zeke*!"

Still, nothing.

Muscles creaking at the effort, Gerald forced himself into a low crouch and squinted, taking stock of his surroundings. Zeke was missing, and this wasn't the familiar Quik Mart. There weren't enough shelves, they weren't tall enough, and everything in the place was made of wood, not cheap metal. The floor, the shelves, the long counter to his right, everything.

The place was on fire, though.

To his left was a closed door shrouded by the smoke blanketing the ceiling. To his right, a counter stood in front of an archway, two doors wide or more. He crossed the room on his hands and knees, raised himself to eye level with the counter, and peered over. Beyond the doors, he found a wide, empty space (a storeroom of some kind?) and another set of barn-like doors flung open to the night air. The smoke from the fire poured through them, pointing his way out.

Dropping back to his hands and knees, he skirted around the counter, past the archway, and into the empty room. The wood floor gave way to stone, and the ceiling rose several feet higher, affording him space to stand without being wreathed in smoke.

He staggered across the room on wobbly legs, likely from being unconscious for who knew how long. Closer to the doorway, his feet crunched on a sparse scattering of grain on the floor. The place was a warehouse or something. Or at least it had been.

By the time Gerald reached the cooler air outside, he felt a little less like a corpse. He stood in a dirt-path alley that ran away from him in both directions. He inhaled, filling his chest to capacity. The air was cool and fresh, a marked difference from the tang of the billowing smoke inside. Still, just as the smoke had smelled *cleaner* than it should, the night air, too, was *off*. Like being in a car with the air conditioning cranked up, it was light and artificial, synthetic. And now he could only just pick out hints of the burning building when it should have been heavy with moisture and thick with the stench of smoke.

Above him, the flames reached out from a window on the second floor, licking at the structure's roof. Even worse, the roof was made of straw. What were those roofs called? Thatched? Who had a thatched roof anymore? Where the hell was he? And where was the fire department? He should be hearing sirens or something from emergency vehicles.

Gerald grabbed his radio and pressed the talk button. "Dispatch? This is Charlie three-two, come in."

No response.

He tried again. "Charlie three-two for Dispatch. Come in? Phil?"

Still nothing. He frowned. The radio must have gotten busted up when he hit the tortilla chip shelf or the floor inside the store. He'd have to get to his cruiser to call this in. His cell phone or the backup radio, one, would work. He still didn't have the faintest clue where he was, but his car should be somewhere along the street at the mouth of the alley. Maybe he had a concussion and was hallucinating Simmsville as a Middle Earth–style village, but his whacked-out brain couldn't keep him from seeing his police cruiser. Could it?

Deep grooves in the dirt led away from the warehouse. That, too, made him crinkle his nose in confusion. It had rained cats and dogs earlier. The alley should have been a muddy, sloppy stew. Instead, the well-worn path was dry as a bone, although not dusty.

"At least a concussion will mean a few days off to recover," he muttered.

Shaking his head, he trudged up the alley. Exhausted by the effort—but not out of breath, which was puzzling—Gerald reached the archway at the end and stepped out into the street.

And had to catch himself.

With his mouth hanging open and eyes even wider, he slumped against the stone building beside him in disbelief. Along both sides of the cobblestone street stood similar-looking two-story buildings, each with a thatched roof and single wooden door. Some had painted wooden signs hanging over them, as still as death. The street curved up ahead of him, winding its way up a hill. The street, the curve, the hill, everything took his breath away.

He'd seen it a thousand times. But never quite like this. Never in three dimensions.

"Jesus Christ," he whispered. "It's… this is… Copperton. I must have taken a worse hit to the head than I thought." The burning building he'd left behind was MacHarrison's, one of two competing dry-goods stores in town, and that cobblestone path—if he followed it—would lead right to the steps of Copperton's Town Hall.

He knew because he'd spent hundreds of hours every week running back and forth through this town. It had been his starting point once and was his home city now, the hub of all his activity—specifically, the hub of all his *online* activity. Copperton was his second home, the place where he hung his hat. That particular hat, though, was a make-believe steel helmet with dragon wings.

This place wasn't real. It existed only digitally, as a setting in *Realm Quest*, the game he and Zeke were just playing.

He pressed the heels of his palms into his eyes and rubbed, but there was no familiar pressure and no burst of colored sparks inside his eyelids. When he stopped, nothing changed. The fictional, digital town of Copperton surrounded him. Him. Not an avatar but him in an actual physical body, although a much more fit version of it. He was still wearing his usual Simmsville Police Department uniform with the shiny gold badge and standard-issue revolver and leaned against a make-believe video game building that seemed as real and sturdy as the Quik Mart.

Gerald ran his fingers along the stone surface of the wall. Rough, hard, jagged, just like real masonry. But like everything else, it wasn't quite right. The texture, especially, was perplexing. Smooth to the touch yet rough at the same time. Almost as if his senses were processing everything into two separate sets of signals and his brain was trying to layer them together, with mixed results.

It all seemed too complicated—too detailed—for a concussion-borne hallucination. Could it be a dream? Possibly, especially considering the odd filter making everything seem synthetic.

"I've got to wake up. The Quik Mart is going to burn down on top of me if I don't."

Squeezing his eyes shut, he *willed* himself to come to.

He counted to ten, lingering over each number. Nothing felt like it changed. Peeking out from under one eyelid, he frowned. Copperton, still.

What did people say when they wanted to make sure they weren't dreaming? "Pinch me"? He pinched himself, hard, on the arm, but it might as well have been a gnat nibbling at him for all the pain it caused.

"Shit," he mumbled. "I've got to wake up somehow."

Considering other ways to force himself awake, he trudged up the street toward the center of town. The major game characters in town—the ones who handed out quests—

hung out there. Maybe his brain was so used to *Realm Quest*'s system of making everything you needed obtainable via a mission that he needed to accomplish some meaningless task before he could snap out of it.

Buried in his thoughts, he almost walked right past the Miner's Rest without looking up. But something—a bit of movement, maybe—caught his eye. The Miner's Rest was the town's most popular inn, in large part because it hosted the rowdiest tavern in Copperton. Players went there just to act like idiots in front of other idiot players while wrapped in the comfortable shroud of online anonymity.

Tonight, though, the place was idiot free and quiet as a tomb.

The doorway to the Rest's stable was open, and the light silhouetted a man in shadow. Maybe he needed to talk to that guy? It couldn't hurt. If there was one hard-and-fast rule for role-playing games, it was to talk to everyone in the town whenever possible.

Gerald trotted across the street and up to the stable. He came up behind the man and tapped him on the shoulder. "Hey, buddy, do you have a second?"

The man turned. He wore nondescript gray breeches and a matching shirt beneath a beaten leather breastplate. A pair of dark, angry eyes glared at him over a royal-blue kerchief covering the remainder of his face.

"I'm not your buddy," the man growled. "And who do you think you are? You should be cowering away like all the rest of the townsfolk until my brothers and I finish here." Looking Gerald up and down, he chuckled. "Especially since you look all dressed up for a Festus play. But it's not even Harvest. Festus isn't for four moons."

Looking over the man's shoulder, Gerald glimpsed three

dirty kids huddled by an old wooden cart. Whatever was going on here, it wasn't good.

"I'm not so interested in fashion advice from a man with a napkin over his mouth," Gerald snapped. "When did 'train robber circa Hollywood, 1965' become en vogue? Better yet, why don't you tell me what's going on here?" Normally, a suspicious-looking guy trying to corner kids in a barn would be facedown in the dirt already, but none of this was real. Why make a fuss in a dream? Was it even worth it?

"I don't think you need to worry about what's going on here, Festus," Robber replied. Then, faster than Gerald could react, the man hammered him across the chin with a right cross.

A burst of light flashed in Gerald's eyes like nothing he'd ever experienced. It was accompanied by the odd sensation of something clacking together five or six times in his head, like the beads from his first-grade teacher's old math tool sliding from one side of a row to another. The sharp stab of pain that should have exploded from his chin was instead a dull ache, and that was gone in seconds.

Gerald stumbled back a few steps and reached for his gun. Robber advanced on him, and after another flash, held a cudgel that appeared out of nowhere. "I'll teach you to interfere with the Exceptas Clan." Over his shoulder, he barked, "And when I get done here, I'm going to deal with you little snots. You're coming with me, one way or the other, and if I have to come in there and drag you out, you're not going to like it."

"Buddy, stop right…" Gerald started, raising his gun.

"What's going on here?" a woman said from behind.

He half turned and took a few more steps back, trying to keep both the woman and Robber in view at the same time. She was short, a head or more shorter than the man. They were dressed the same way, though, all in gray and with the same blue kerchief. Her eyes were familiar, but he couldn't put a finger on where he'd seen them.

"Who are you?" he demanded.

At the same time, Robber said, "Nothing to worry about, Jehnil—"

"Shut up, idiot!" she hissed. "And I'll be the judge of what's 'nothing.' Explain yourself."

"This man don't have the sense the rest of the townspeople do and came out to challenge me. So I was going to make an example out of him. Something for the others to remember the next time we come raiding."

"You were going to try, you mean," Gerald smirked.

As she eyed Gerald up and down, the woman's eyebrows rose in surprise. The expression disappeared quickly, though, and she scowled back at Robber. "What are you even doing here? Why aren't you with the rest of the Clan? They'll need help loading up the wagons."

Robber gestured to the stable. "I saw some kids running around. I thought Tristan would want me to bring them back."

"You really are stupid, aren't you?" she replied. "We're here for supplies. That's it, nothing else. By Thela, we don't steal children in the night!"

"But I..." he said, hanging his head.

"Save it. Get back to the group. They'll need you to help with loading. Go!"

Chastened, Robber shuffled away from the stable without a word. Passing Gerald, he sneered under his facial covering. "I'll remember you, Festus. Don't worry. You won't be protecting townies for long."

Gerald sighed. This nonsense couldn't end fast enough.

After the man left, the woman stood by the gate to the stable yard, staring at Gerald in silence.

"Um, excuse me? Lady? Jehn or whatever? Hi, anyone home?"

She kept staring but gave him no reply.

"Okay, then, whatever. Kids?" he shouted into the stable. "Mr. Creepy is gone. You can come out now."

Three uncertain faces materialized from the stables but didn't venture out.

"Oh, for the love… come on, come out of there. You need to get home. You're not going to object, are you?" he asked the woman.

Again, no response.

The three kids—two boys, one girl, all between eight and ten—inched their way outside with caution, as if walking on early-winter ice. They froze once again, seeing the Clan woman.

"It's okay," Gerald said. "She won't bother you. What are your names?"

The girl assumed the role of spokesperson. "I'm Frega. This is Blust and Daven."

"All right, Frega, Blust, and Daven. Do you all have homes? Parents?"

The boys nodded as Frega replied, "Yes."

"Solid. Then get outta here. Go home. Now. Stay out of sight. And the next time these guys"—he pointed at the woman—"come around, you stay inside. Got it?"

"Yes, my lord," Frega replied. The three of them raced off and ducked under the stable-yard fence. The boys didn't break stride once beyond it, but the girl stopped and turned back.

"Sir? Are you the new Sheriff?"

"What?" Gerald said.

"The new Sheriff of Copperton? Are you the king's replacement?"

The "my lord" and "sir" were bad enough, but this was

getting ridiculous. Jesus, just being the night cop of Simmsville was hard enough. Whatever being Sheriff of Copperton meant, he wanted that about as much as he wanted the plague.

"No," he replied, making his voice stern. "Now go on. Move!"

Frega scampered away, and not long afterward, all three of them were out of sight.

Satisfied, he turned back to the woman and stepped closer to her. "So, lady, you having a fit or what?"

"What?" she answered. "No, I just… was trying to make a decision. I… I didn't expect to find you here."

"That makes two of us. I didn't expect to find me here either."

"Thela truly does work in Her own time, I suppose. Let's hope you're not too late."

Gerald scratched his head. "Look, lady, you can start making sense whenever you want. And have you got a name? That other guy called you Jehn or something, right?"

"You'd do well to forget everything that lummox said. And I hope you'll accept my apology, but tonight is no time for you to be stumbling around town."

"What does that mean?" But he was talking to no one. The woman—Jehn—was gone. She went from solid and opaque to transparent and gone. In the span of two heartbeats, she'd disappeared.

"Lawkeeper?" she said, somehow from behind him. Gerald whirled around…

…in time to catch the fist streaking toward him.

A burst of light exploded again, followed by that odd *clacking* sensation in his head. Ten clacks, maybe? Or fifteen?

And then, black.

CHAPTER FOUR

THE RAID

GERALD COUGHED, INHALING A MOUTHFUL of dry, gritty particles that he hoped were dirt. He was face-down in a stable yard, after all.

Pushing himself up, he groaned. She'd whacked him pretty good, leaving a bit of sting to linger across his cheekbone. Much more memorable than the love tap Robber had given him.

He stood up and was, again, alone. How long had he been down? A minute? An hour? A week? Could be any of the above, but it didn't *feel* like that long. The night sky still loomed overhead, and the whole town was still quiet. Thelaroth's yellow moon hung in the same spot as before, but then, did video game moons ever move?

Now what? Continue toward Town Hall? Or go looking for that woman and find out what the hell she was talking about? She'd called him "Lawkeeper," just like the old man at the Quik Mart. Maybe she was a figment of his subconscious, trying to tell him something.

"Ah, fuck it," he muttered and started again for the center of town.

As he climbed the hill, the Miner's Rest and the stable faded behind him. He reached a cross street to his left. If he followed that, it would lead him out of the town and into the Ore Wood, the massive forest surrounding Copperton.

"I don't know what's more messed up," he muttered, "that I'm literally standing by this street and know right where it goes or that there's no one else around." Copperton normally teemed with people, both nonplayer characters and other players. He'd only ever seen it packed full and bustling. This was just plain weird.

"Hey, mister. Sheriff," a voice called from the forest road.

"Who's there?"

"Just me." The girl from the stable, Frega, stepped out from an alcove between two buildings.

Gerald sighed. "What are you doing? Didn't I tell you to go home? And I'm not anybody's Sheriff."

"Then why are you wearing that?" She pointed at the shiny badge on his chest, emblazoned with an eagle carrying a scroll in flight.

"That's—nothing. What do you care about that?"

"Are you dumb, mister? That's the Sheriff's shield. The real one's bigger, of course. Regular-sized, so you can use it, but yours looks the same as the one he carries."

"What? You're saying someone has a shield just like this?"

She drew closer and stepped up on her tiptoes. "Yep. Just like that one. The Sheriff does."

More and more ridiculous. "Fine, whatever. But I'm not the Sheriff. Got it?"

"If you say so. But are you gonna stop the Exceptas?"

"What the hell is an 'Exceptas'?"

"Did that lady Crit you over the head or something? She must have to make you forget them that fast."

"No, she didn't 'Crit' me. I—" He shook his head in disbelief. As if landing a "Critical Hit" was a real thing. "There's no such thing as a 'Crit.' Just… never mind."

"I'm sorry if you really can't Crit when you fight. Everyone else can. Are you an herb gatherer or something?" She chuckled, taking an obvious swipe at his fighting prowess or lack of it.

"Look, shorty, I can too—" He stopped. Arguing with a fictional kid in a dream about his martial prowess in a video game was The Official Line. He wasn't crossing it. "Whatever," he went on. "So those two are who you're talking about? They're the Exceptas or whatever?"

"Of course. Who else dresses in all gray and covers their faces?" She gave him a confused look, as if he should know that already. "They were just a couple of them, though. The Clan is huge and getting bigger."

"Ah, got it. Look, I'm sorry, but no, I'm not going to 'stop' them. Whatever they're doing that needs to be stopped, it's not my job. I just want to go home. Which is what you should be doing, like I told you. Before you get in trouble."

"I can't. They're at my house, stealing all our stuff. My family owns the armory. Or we did, up until tonight. After they take everything, we'll be broke."

Great. A kid giving him a guilt trip and a quest to stop thieves. When would it end?

"Fine," he said with a sigh, "show me."

The girl's whole face brightened, and she grabbed his hand. "I knew you were the Sheriff!"

"I'm not the Sheriff," he said. But by then, he was talking to her back.

He knew where she was taking him already. There was

one armor and weapon shop on Forest Road. It was the last shop before the town ended at the edge of the woods, set off a hundred yards or so from all the other buildings, which otherwise stood side by side. The armory, though, included a smithy, so additional space between buildings served to make the enormous heat of the forge less dangerous to the surrounding townspeople.

Gerald and Frega stopped and crouched beside the corner of the last house before the armory. In her yard, several hulking Exceptas raiders were loading a huge wagon, stacking it high with shields, swords, bows, axes, and weapons of all kinds. Near the wagon, that woman, Jehn, stood beside a barrel-chested man. He was dressed in the same gray clothes but wore an iron breastplate and no kerchief.

"Come on, boys," he boomed, fists resting at his waist. "Let's finish up and leave these kind people be." Behind him, three figures squatted in the shadows of a huge tree, bound together and gagged.

"Your family?" Gerald whispered.

Frega nodded.

Shit. Grim-faced, he slid his revolver from its holster.

The girl raised her eyebrows, expecting an explanation.

"Looks like ten guys just like Robber, plus that Jehn lady and the leader guy. But I've only got eight shots on me and no extra ammo."

"Ammo?" she asked, cocking her head.

"Just… never mind. When the big booms start, run to your family, cut them free, and get the hell out of here. Do you have a knife?"

A small dagger flashed into her hand from nowhere, glinting in the moonlight. She hadn't even moved.

"How did you—?" He shook his head. "Whatever. Are you ready?"

Frega nodded again.

"Okay, I'm going to start counting. When I hit three, I'll draw their attention and start shooting."

He took a deep breath, pushing aside the mountain of disbelief in the back of his head. Simmsville was a small, quiet place. He never expected to have any reason to shoot at someone in the line of duty. Yet here he was, weapon drawn, planning to do exactly that. This wasn't real, though. It was a dream. Or a video game. But, hey, when in Rome, you did as the Romans did. Even if Rome turned out to be Thelaroth.

"Okay. One… two…"

Before he could say "three," the ground shook, and fire rained down from the sky. Incandescent orange and yellow spheres, the size of small melons, fell among the Exceptas warriors. Chaos took over. The workers dove for the ground or under anything that might serve as cover. Several of the unfortunate bastards erupted into flames before they could reach safety. The leader spun toward town, and a huge two-handed axe appeared in his hands. "Mage!" he shouted, pointing. "Stop him!"

A stream of the fireballs lanced at one of the wagon's rear wheels. Three fireballs blasted it in quick succession, turning the spoked wooden ring into a pile of flaming debris. The wagon, suddenly lacking a quarter of its support, lurched backward and crashed into the ground. The neat stacks of weapons and armor the Clan had piled up slid off in a chorus of clanging metal.

Gerald shifted to the other side of the house they were crouching behind for a better look at where the Exceptas leader was pointing. He peeked out and gasped.

Whoa, was that Zeke?

Whoever it was, he was tall and thin and wore a wizard's robe with the hood up. His face protruded just enough to be recognizable, and it sure looked like Zeke. Either way, he was doing an awesome job of directing the shower of fiery destruction.

Whipping his hands up to shoulder level, the Mage shot the Exceptas leader a defiant sneer. "No more stealing from the innocent, Exceptas dog!" The voice, although magnified somehow to project strength, carried a pinched, nasal undercurrent as though the speaker was talking while blowing his nose. The guy sounded just like Zeke too.

Taking three fast strides, the Exceptas leader released a deafening war cry and slashed at the wizard with his massive axe. With a burst of light, colorful sparks flew as the weapon struck him across the chest. Zeke (or whoever) grunted and flew backward, landing in a heap of gangly arms and legs and violet robes.

"No!" Gerald screamed, "*Zeke*!" Jumping from behind the building, he positioned himself between the Clan leader and the puddle of groaning wizard a few feet behind him. He roared, and strength—no, more like some kind of Power—flooded through him, shooting tendrils of electric heat from deep in his chest through his arms and legs, hands and feet.

Four of the Exceptas workers also jumped into the battle and rushed at him. The first pair carried crude cudgels, and the next two held old, rusting war hammers. They were basic weapons, sure, but they'd do the trick.

The cudgels came first, arcing at Gerald's head. A voice in the back of his head shrieked that he was rushing to fight five, six, maybe more Warriors, each wearing some kind of armor, while he wore nothing more than a thin cotton police uniform. He shoved the voice away just as something cold and electrically charged washed over him. Whatever it was, the sensation clung to his tingling skin, shrinking and tightening against it like drying glue.

No time to think about it. Instinct took over, and he threw his left arm up to protect his head from the blunt weapons. They were going to break it—in several places, probably—but that was better than having his skull split like an egg.

The clubs struck with more force than he'd expected, but rather than causing the crack of breaking bones, they bounced off with a thud. He swung his pistol up, ready to fire.

But he didn't.

Somehow, firing it wasn't right. Unnatural. Instead, he smashed the barrel of the revolver into the bridge of the first guy's nose and hammered the butt of the gun on top of the second guy's head. With each strike, particles of color erupted between the weapon and its victim. Both attackers dropped to the ground.

The next pair of Exceptas screamed as they came at him, their wicked-looking war hammers curving through the air, singing with bone-cracking malice. Those definitely weren't going to bounce off his forearm. Panic catching in his throat, Gerald flexed his knees and dropped to the ground, hoping to duck under the attack.

Streaks of lightning flickered overhead. Sparks flew as electricity blasted both hammers, knocking them back. The crackling charge then raced up the length of the weapons, toward the warriors.

They wailed and threw the hammers, backing away while they rubbed stinging hands.

The Mage, back on his feet, nodded to Gerald in appreciation.

The massive leader with the telephone pole–sized axe was the only Exceptas Warrior remaining. The woman, Jehn, lounged against the now-lopsided wagon, watching them with narrowed eyes, like one judging produce at the grocery.

"The two of you have ruined a perfectly good night's

work," the man said. "We were expecting you townies to stay out of our way like good children. Especially without a Sheriff."

Gerald smirked. "See, there's your problem. I'm no townie."

Turning his axe to catch a sliver of moonlight, the man smiled. "Are you the new Sheriff, then? Is it possible that Dalor has chosen to act boldly and quickly for once rather than cower within the walls of his keep in Riverglow City, huddled in indecision?"

Gerald clucked his tongue. What was it with these people? "I don't know what you're talking about, but I'm not anyone's Sheriff. But I'm pretty sure my road home goes through you."

He felt the Mage step up next to him and stole a sideways glance. The guy was almost the spitting image of Zeke, but there was something not quite right.

"Get out of here, Tristan," the wizard said. "Scurry back to your hole in the woods and hide. And don't come back. We'll be waiting."

Gerald didn't so much plan to be waiting, but he wasn't about to say anything.

The leader—Tristan?—shrugged. "Well, Mage, we'll have to make do with the three loads of supplies we did manage to get tonight. As for the weapons"—he gestured at the heap of metal beside the broken wagon—"believe me, we will be back. The Legion of Guardians is coming, and we intend to be prepared." With that, his axe flickered and reappeared in a harness on his back.

The woman, Jehn, moved among the fallen Exceptas workers, crouching beside each. As she touched each one with glowing hands, the injured man would groan and stand back up.

As the last of them got to his feet, she nodded at Tristan. “I’m finished.”

“Good evening, gentlemen,” Tristan said, “I look forward to meeting you both again.” And then the Exceptas left, making for the forest at a dead sprint.

“Wait!” Gerald called. “My quest…!”

He still didn’t know how to get home.

CHAPTER FIVE

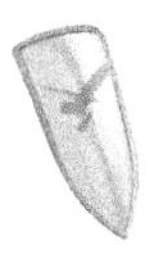

THE SMITHS

"DUDE, THAT WAS *AWESOME*!"

Gerald frowned. "Are you out of your mind? That was *not* awesome. Someone could have been killed. Hell, I don't know how you survived that axe to the chest. And who are you, anyway?"

"What do you mean? It's me, Zeke! Did you get amnesia or something? And what are you worried about? This is *Realm Quest*. It's a freaking video game. You can't die here. If you do, you just get rez'd. Plus, did you fail to notice? I can make fucking fireballs! That's the literal definition of awesome!"

Gerald crossed his arms, scrutinizing this Zeke's face. Something wasn't right about it. It was too smooth. Could it be that—? He raised his hand to his friend's cheek and squeezed. Rather than bunching between his fingers as he expected, the skin held its shape, flat and smooth. His fingers slid across the surface of it like some kind of plastic.

"Dude?" Zeke yelped, recoiling. "What the fuck? Did you just try to… pinch me or something? We're not that kind of friends. You're way too ugly for me, anyway."

"Jesus," Gerald said with a gasp. "We're rendered. That's why you look funny."

Zeke cocked his head. "Of course we're rendered. It's a video game. You have to expect to look a little more digital than in real life."

"What? Do you even hear yourself? That's… ridiculous. This isn't a video game. It's my subconscious or something. I'm just having a dream."

"No, you're not," Zeke replied, shaking his head. "If that was true, I wouldn't be here."

"Don't be stupid. I've known you forever. My brain can make up a fake Zeke."

"Doubt it. Your brain would make me as you want me to be. I wouldn't be half this cool. Now, if you ask me, I think that when the old guy at the Quik Mart hit us in the head with the color stick, he somehow sent us here."

"That doesn't even make sense. You don't get transported from the real world to a video game by a magic item in a convenience store."

"Dude, I'm telling you, Quik Mart staff and boom! Here we are. And I don't care what you say, it is awesome."

"Okay, smart guy, if that's the case, how come I'm in my uniform and you're dressed up in character?"

His friend winked, lifted his robe, and stuck out a denim-covered leg. "I was wearing my Pac-Man T-shirt and jeans when I woke up here. I didn't want to scare the locals, so I snagged a robe off someone's porch. Plus, I figured I should cover these bad boys." Pulling back the hood, he revealed a pair of pointed ears sticking up through strands of blond hair.

"You're an elf?"

"Right? Like I said, awesome!"

Gerald groaned. Could this get any worse?

"Hey, Lord Sheriff? Mister Goldenshield?"

Frega, the girl, was with her family. They stood near the tree they'd been tied to, rubbing their wrists where ropes had been moments earlier.

"Come on, really?" he shouted back. "I'm not any of those things. Gerald. Just call me Gerald."

She shot back a glare suggesting he had feral hedgehogs crawling out of his ears. "If you say so. Anyway, Lord Gerald, this is my dad, Bergan Smith, my mom, Fayn, and my stupid little brother, Pendtil."

"Hey, shut up!" the younger boy countered.

The father, Bergan, was a mountain of a man. Wider than a doorway at the shoulders and almost as tall as a bear, he bowed at the waist, showing a grace that belied his stature. "My lords, we are in your debt."

"We. Are. Not. Lor—" Gerald began, but Zeke cut him off.

"We are but humble pilgrims, Master Smith. Thank blessed Thela for bringing us to you in your moment of need."

"Indeed," the older man replied, lowering his eyes in respect. Looking back at them, he added, "If you don't mind my asking, where are you masters from? I've never seen such finery as that, Lord Goldensh—er, Master Gerald." The armorer gestured at Gerald's blue police uniform.

"I, uh," Gerald stammered.

Zeke, as usual, was thinking faster than his friend. "They're traveling clothes from a strange, faraway place, Master Smith. They come from a tiny village deep in the dark ashen inland of Venasier. They are lightweight, to make the journey easier, and they prove that one's faith in Thela is all the armor needed on the road."

"I see." The man scowled. As the town armorer, it seemed he wasn't much of a believer in faith as armor when he could have a solid piece of plate across the chest. "Forgive me, but the night is getting short, and we have quite a mess to clean up." He waved at the piles beside the wagon. "Will you be staying in Copperton long? The Exceptas raids have been getting worse and worse since our Sheriff disappeared. I worry they will continue until King Dalor sees fit to send a new one our way."

"I don't think we'll be here too long—" Gerald started.

Zeke cut him off. "Sure, yeah, it'd be awesome to hang around for a bit."

They shot irritated glances at each other. Zeke put up a hand to stall Gerald's argument.

"Come to think of it, Master Smith," he went on, "we don't have a place to sleep this evening and are short on coin. If we helped you get your merchandise sorted and back into the shop, might you have a place we could stay until morning?"

Bergan rubbed his chin and eyed them with suspicion. "Thela's truth, you fellas seem like decent folk, but then, you look and act a little strange. Not to mention that I do have my family's safety to consider. And no offense, Master Elf, but your kind isn't thought of very highly on this side of the ocean."

The situation was almost enough to make Gerald throw his arms up in frustration. Getting help from strangers when the family business was being cleaned out was all well and good. But it seemed that letting them stay the night in return was too much to ask.

"Bergan Smith!" his wife exclaimed. "That is no way to show your appreciation for the kindness these two gave us. At the very least, you will let them rest in the forge house if they feel they need sleep."

"I suppose," he said, nodding. "That agreeable?"

"That would be perfect." Zeke grinned.

Gerald sighed. Great, now they were camping. He hated camping.

They carried the equipment, a few pieces at a time, back inside the Smiths' shop, and then Fayn and Frega showed them to the smallish building behind the armory where Bergan managed the forge work. A huge pit for the fire dominated one side of the room, a large anvil and a workbench stood in the center, and various tools and half-made pieces of equipment were scattered throughout. An open doorway in the back led to a tiny room with a pair of straw-covered pallets on the floor.

"The room back there was set up for when we had apprentices. It's not a great deal of space, and I'm afraid to say it can be a bit drafty, my lor… that, is, masters, but it should do for the night."

"It's great," Zeke told them. "We appreciate you letting us burden you."

Gerald coughed but said nothing. A hard pallet in the drafty workhouse was a poor substitute for a cozy, warm bed, but maybe if he fell asleep, he'd wake back up in the real world.

"Nonsense," the woman replied. "My husband can be an overcautious horse's rear, but don't think for a moment we aren't thankful right down to our bones for what you did tonight. You saved our livelihood, and, I dare say, our very lives."

"It was our pleasure, madam. I'm only glad we were here when you needed us." Hard to believe Zeke could lay it on so thick with a straight face.

"'Twas Thela's mercy, truly, Master Elf. Now then, I'll send Frega out with a pile of blankets. That should keep you warm until morning. Good night, my lords."

For a moment, Gerald thought to correct her again, but it was late, and he'd done more than enough protesting all the things they'd called him tonight besides his name. If it got him a moment's peace to keep his mouth shut, that was what he'd do.

After Fayn and Frega left, he stepped outside to wait for the girl. Above him, in the star-filled, indigo sky, the full moon shone down from a different place than before. It did move after all. Gerald smirked. Real or not, it represented the same moon he'd wished on hundreds of times in his life. The same moon that was shining down on Simmsville and even hanging over Brooke, whatever she was doing at that very moment.

"I wish—" he whispered.

A glint of something caught his eye, moonlight reflecting off his badge. Frowning, he unclasped its pin and slipped it off his shirt. Damn thing had been a pain ever since he got it. This "Sheriff" business was just icing on the cake.

Goldenshield, they'd called him. He had to admit, the name had a nice ring to it. Of course, they also wanted to make a lord out of him or name him the town cop because of the stupid thing. At not even twenty-five years old, the last thing he wanted to be was a responsible adult, let alone some kind of local authority.

"That thing's pretty, you know," a stack of what looked to be animal pelts said, moving toward him.

He slid it into his pants pocket. "I suppose it is," he replied. The collection of blankets Frega was carrying shuffled past him. Somewhere in the depth of his consciousness, a few insubstantial words, light as fingers of fog, drifted through his mind:

Soft Blankets x 4.

He held out his hands to take the pile. This time, words flashed—rather than floated—in his head.

Take Soft Blankets x 4.

Half a heartbeat later, he was holding them. Gerald flinched in shock. What the hell?

"Are you okay?

"Uh, yeah. It just.... Well, never mind. What were we talking about?"

"Your shield medal thing."

Oh, right. "It might be pretty, but I'm not sure it's worth the trouble it causes."

The girl nodded in agreement. "Yeah, so you probably shouldn't wear it around if you don't want folks thinking you're the Sheriff."

"Frak, no, I don't want that," he said.

"Come to think of it, you need to get some new clothes too. Or people are going to think funny things about you anyway."

"Yeah, I get that, but this is all I got."

"Dad might have something you can wear until you get some coin. I'll ask Mom about it in the morning."

"Hey, thanks, kid. You're okay."

"You didn't have to come to my house when I told you those Exceptas were here. So you're okay too."

His face flushed with guilt. He'd bothered to come here only because he figured it might lead him home or out of the dream or whatever. Good thing they were outside in the dark so she couldn't see his cheeks. "I guess."

"Is the elf really a friend of yours?"

He smiled at the mention of Zeke the elf. The guy was wound up like a kid in a toy store here. A part of him hoped this *was* some kind of crazy alternate world and not just a dream. That way, at least, his friend's experiences would be real. Well, real for being in a video game.

"Yeah, he's my friend. I've known him for years. We grew up together."

"I've never seen an elf with a human before. He seems different. Not snotty like other elves. Kind of hyper, though."

"You could say that." Zeke was the kid in grade school who used to get so upset when something went wrong that his face would turn hot-rod red and he'd hyperventilate until someone shoved an empty lunch bag on his face. He didn't *react* to things as much as he *overreacted*. But he was a good counterpoint to Gerald, who figured there was no situation that couldn't be improved with a short—or long—nap.

"So, are you guys going to stick around?" He couldn't miss the gleam of hope in her eye.

"I… I don't know, Frega. We'll see what happens tomorrow."

With any luck, there'd be no tomorrow. Instead, he'd fall asleep soon and wake up back where he belonged, in his right mind and normal body. Or at least, that had better be the case. Because whatever this turned out to be, it was delaying his chance to talk with Brooke. Now that he'd made up his mind about her, he didn't want time to talk himself out of it.

"Oh, okay," the girl replied, crestfallen. She brightened quickly, though. "Hey, since you guys need some money, how 'bout we do a few hunter contracts tomorrow?"

"Hunter contracts?"

"Yeah, the forest around here is filled with dangerous critters. You can sign up for contracts at Town Hall to kill a set number of them in return for coin. Plus, you get experience for free."

Oh, God, she was talking about grinding. In the game, each kill earned experience, and when you got enough to reach a certain goal, your character advanced to the next level. Although leveling up often came with new skills and abilities, if you had a quest to kill twenty Venomous Adders for their skins, it was common to go half-crazy waiting for the nineteenth one to show. Tedium, combined with competition with other players for each snake skin, could make raising a character from Level 5 to Level 15 a soul-crushing grind. Hence the term.

"Ugh," he whispered to himself. Gerald wanted to grind out a character in person about as much as he wanted to be Sheriff. Going through it when all you had to do was click something on a screen was one thing. Actually walking out into the woods and doing it by hand sounded like medieval torture.

But… they didn't have any money, clothes, armor, or much experience with combat in this world. Maybe taking a few collection quests wouldn't be the worst idea.

"Come find me in the morning and we'll see. For now, get into the house before your mom or dad start wondering why you haven't come back yet."

"Okay. Goodnight, Goldenshield."

"Goodnight, Frega." The girl turned and ran toward the armor shop.

"Frega?" he called. She stopped at the back door and looked back.

"Yeah?"

"I'll pay you to call me Gerald."

She gave him a wide smile. "No way. Goldenshield is too cool. And you don't have any coin anyway."

With that, she slipped into the building, leaving him alone with the moon and a pile of animal-pelt blankets.

CHAPTER SIX

THE SITUATION

BLANKETS IN HAND, GERALD ENTERED the forge house and brushed past Zeke, who didn't even look up. He stared, instead, at the cold forge, mesmerized. Ignoring his friend, he walked through the doorway into the apprentice room in the back and turned to one of the pallets.

Again, he was struck by soft words drifting through his head, unbidden.

Sleeping Pallet

And then, as he moved to put the blankets down, others came.

Drop Soft Blankets x 4

He blinked, and the blankets were stacked neatly on one of the pallets.

"What the fuck?"

"Ger!" Zeke called, almost screaming, from the other room.

He raced back to the forge, expecting to find more Exceptas hammering at the door. Instead, Zeke held a hand up in front of his own face and waved that hand over a collection of various smithing tools.

"Jesus, Zeke, I thought we were under some kind of attack."

"This is so frakkin' cool! Have you tried it?"

Gerald gritted his teeth. After everything they'd been through, in the past—what? Hours? Half a day? Who could tell?—he needed to shut down. Recharge a little. He felt like one of those science project volcanos. If he had to deal with even one more thing tonight, it would be the vinegar that made the baking soda erupt. "Tried *what*?" he asked, trying to keep a lid on the irritation.

If Zeke noticed, he didn't let on. "Look at something and then place your hand over it. It's the coolest thing!"

Gerald sighed. Once Zeke got geeked up about something, though, he wouldn't let it go until you did what he wanted. With an enormous huff, Gerald looked at the closest tool and put his hand out.

Smithing hammer - 5 Dmg, 40% wear

"Holy shit."

"Right?"

Gerald shifted his focus to the next item, a pair of tongs for pulling hot metal from the blazing fire of the forge.

Forge Tongs

And then the next thing.

Forge Bellows

And the next.

Use Forge

"Okay, that's pretty damn cool. Does it work for anything, you think?"

"No, look at the wall."

He did, keeping his hand up as before. Literally, nothing came to mind.

"So?"

"Seems like it has to be something you can pick up or use," Zeke said, still moving his line of sight from one thing to the next.

"Have you tried picking anything up yet?"

"No."

"Try it," Gerald suggested.

Zeke twisted to his right, finding a half-finished dagger. He stretched his hand to it, but his fingers brushed smoothly against the metal. He frowned. "What the hell?"

Gerald couldn't help but smile. Between them, Zeke was without question the smarter of the two, which made him the one most often explaining how things worked. Having a turn at it for once was nice. "Don't try to grab it with your hand. Think about taking it."

"Duh, Ger! Of course!" When he turned back to the dagger, it flickered and appeared in his right hand. With a squeal of delight, he waved the small, gray weapon in the air in triumph. Then, extending it again over the now-empty spot on the rack, the surrounding air rippled. The dagger vanished and returned to its original place.

Zeke giggled like a child with a new toy and repeated the process six or seven times, taking the dagger and dropping it back into place. "My God! I love this place! What are we going to do tomorrow?"

Gerald's grin faded. In all likelihood, they'd fall asleep and wake up back in the real world, but he didn't have the heart to tell Zeke that. "Who knows," he said. "We should get some sleep, though. And then go from there."

With one last smiling glance at the dagger, the elf nodded and headed for the back room. Reaching the pallets, he turned to one stacked with blankets, and a pair of them shimmered into his outstretched hands. In a fluid motion, he twisted to the other, empty pallet and thought the blankets into place.

Zeke's Mage's robe flickered and disappeared, materializing again folded in his hands. He *Hung* the simple garment on a peg on the wall and laid himself down on the pallet. A moment later, the fur blankets covered him.

Facing the other pallet, Gerald unbuckled his equipment belt and detached all the accessories that went with being a police officer. He hung them all on a separate peg.

"So, wait," he said, face pinched in confusion.

"What?"

"If you didn't know to *Think* things on and off, how'd you get that robe on?"

Zeke made an embarrassed face. "You don't want to know. It wasn't easy."

Gerald raised an eyebrow but then let the subject drop.

Lie Down

In a few jerky motions, he kind of unfolded onto his pallet. Then he lifted a hand to the stack of fuzzy hides.

Cover Soft Blankets x2

Just like Zeke, he was covered in the blink of an eye. He rolled over on the makeshift bed, testing the arrangement. To his surprise, they were neither tight nor constraining but let him move beneath them just as a normal comforter would have on his own bed back in Simmsville.

"This place is weird," he muttered.

"Bullshit," Zeke argued, "it's awesome. Did you miss the part where I rained fire down on those Exceptas thugs?"

"Okay, yeah, I guess that was cool. But we got lucky. There were a ton of them. I can't believe we didn't get killed."

"Nah, they were nothing to worry about. I figure they had

to be several Experience Levels below us. Totally no problem for our wicked combo of fighting skills."

"What level do you think we're at?" He didn't know what to guess.

"Five or Six, probably," Zeke mused. "Rain of Fire is the first area spell pyro mages get, and we earn it at Level Five. Exceptas thugs are usually only Three. Sometimes Four."

"How do you know that? And how did you know their leader's name? Kristan, was that it?"

His friend chuckled. "How do you *not* know? Don't you remember when we started playing *Realm Quest*? One of the first big quest chains we had to complete was to clean the Exceptas out of the forest around Copperton."

"Really? I mean, I guess I kind of remember having to kill twenty outlaws or something. And then we had to do this whole big, long Instanced cavern expedition. That took forever." He grimaced at the reminder. Defeating an Instance with just the two of them could take hours and hours, and in that case, it had.

"Yeah, that was the Exceptas campaign," Zeke said. "And at the end, you had to kill the Clan Chief, Tristan Kingsbane, collect his head, and bring it back to the Sheriff of Copperton, who was also captain of the Town Militia." He gave a disapproving look. "Do you read any of the quest descriptions?"

"You mean the paragraphs of useless text that come with each task?" Gerald scoffed. "God, no. That'd take forever. Not when all I need to know is 'Collect 10 wolf pelts, Get 10 silver'. The story part is pointless."

"You're a godless heathen. And it wasn't pointless earlier when the Exceptas was raiding the town, was it?"

He winced. Zeke had a point.

The pair fell silent, and Gerald closed his eyes, hoping

sleep would come soon. His (digital?) body might not be tired, but his mind was exhausted.

"Ger? Are you asleep?"

"Jesus, Z, it's just like sleeping over when we were ten. I'm half out of it, and now you want to chat some more."

"I—sorry. I'll let you sleep."

Zeke gave him a look that might as well suggest Gerald kicked his puppy. Damn guilt. "No, I'm sorry, man. I'm just tired. Go ahead. What did you want to say?"

"Be Katie Sanders honest… what do you think is going on? Do you think any of this is real? Like, really real? "

Katie Sanders was a girl they'd had a huge crush on at the same time in the fifth grade, but neither said anything because they were awkward eleven-year-old boys who didn't know what to think about not finding a girl repulsive. They both pursued her quietly instead, with whispers and glances and secret notes that ended with the option to "Circle Yes or No."

In the end, she didn't circle anything but decided rather that she liked Bret Gough, who was both a sixth grader and captain of the basketball team. When Gerald and Zeke had their hearts broken for the first time, it was impossible to keep their secret crush secret any longer. And as they slurped extra-large, extra-thick chocolate malts together after school to ease the pain, they made an eleven-year-old's life pact to always be honest with each other and never keep secrets again.

Gerald sighed. "No, I don't think it's real. It's some kind of dream or hallucination, and that's it. My brain was all caught up in the game because we'd just been playing it, so when I got knocked out, it made this whole place up."

"So I'm not real? I'm just a figment of your imagination? A projection of how you see me?"

"That's what I think, yeah."

Zeke narrowed his football-shaped elven eyes. "How

come it's got to be your dream? Maybe it's my hallucination and you're a figment of my imagination."

"No, I *know* I'm here, seeing everything through my own eyes, just like every other dream I've ever had."

"Well, so am I, so it can't be your dream."

Of course, that was just the kind of argumentative thing Zeke would say.

"I—look, I guess we'll see. I'm still betting that when we fall asleep here, that'll be the end of it, and we'll wake up. Probably in the hospital."

"Maybe…" The word hung in the air between them, the start of an unspoken thought.

"Out with it. What?"

"That's the easy explanation. Definitely the simplest. And simple is usually better. But it ignores something."

"What?"

"The old man at the Quik Mart."

"What? That was just some guy with a thing for designer drugs and live-action role playing. He had to be high as a kite."

"How many good-timers would get all dressed up in full, *actual* heavy armor and then break into a Quik Mart? How many could or would make a reference to 'Thela' while knocking cops on the head with some kind of pyrotechnic prop? And what about whatever that glow was in the entrance to the beer cave? You saw it too, right?"

Gerald didn't say anything. He hadn't given much thought to the Quik Mart since waking up. From that moment until now, it had been one thing after another, always while he hoped that the dream or whatever would be over soon.

But the old guy. And the rippling surface in the doorway of the cooler. Plus…

"I shot him."

"What the fuck, Gerald? You shot him? When?"

"After he hit you, he came at me. I got off three shots."

"Did you hit him?"

"No. I mean, my aim was dead on. I should have hit him, center mass. He was right in front of me. But some kind of green fire, I guess, shot out of that staff, and it was like the bullets just disappeared. Then he hit me in the head, and that was about it. Except—"

"What?"

"Well, as I was blacking out, I thought to look for you."

"And?"

He hesitated, knowing what would happen if he said it. But he couldn't keep it from Zeke. "You should have been in a heap on the floor by the two-liters. But you were gone. I couldn't see you anywhere."

"See? It's because I was already here. I don't have a clue what's going on, Ger, but I'm telling you, this is real."

"I don't know," Gerald said. Some part of him wanted to agree. The rest of him, though, wasn't buying it. "Let's just see what happens when we wake up. Get some sleep."

"Okay. Right. G'night."

Gerald rolled over, glaring at his equipment belt hanging on the wall. Maybe his gun could help them figure out for sure what was happening.

But then, how much did he want to know?

For some time after that, he lay there, still as death, waiting for sleep to overtake him. The Sandman, though, was playing hard to get. Until he closed his eyes, took a deep breath, and put the whole situation out of his mind. Then, finally, he figured out how.

Sleep

CHAPTER SEVEN

THE PREPARATIONS

"GERALD. GERALD! DUDE, YOU HAVE to wake up!"

"Is he okay? Is he hurt? Is something wrong with him?" The voice was familiar.

"He's fine," Zeke replied.

"Why won't he wake up?"

Gerald tried to force his eyes open, but they were stapled shut or something. He hadn't had this much trouble waking up since the last time he had one too many dollar beers at wing night.

"Here, step back." Then, ominously, Zeke added, "Sorry, buddy."

The world exploded in a flash of colored sparks. That clacking sensation ripped through his head again five or six times.

"Jesus! What?" He bolted upright, the animal-hide blankets clinging to his chest and torso at an angle that defied both logic and physics.

Frega and Zeke stood over his pallet and beamed at him like kids waking a parent for Christmas.

So much for this all being a dream.

"Sorry, dude. You wouldn't wake up, so I tapped you across the face with my wand."

Rubbing his temple, Gerald grunted, "You didn't need to do that." The flash of pain had already subsided, though. Not even a dull ache remained. His digital body had one advantage, at least.

The clang and clatter of metal rang out from the next room. "It's just past dawn. Father's about to start work," Frega explained. "Time to get moving. Did you guys go to sleep?"

Smashing his palms against his eyes, he rubbed them hard, his everyday wake-up habit. It was a bit of familiar comfort, even if it wasn't quite the same. Not only was the pressure missing, his hands weren't as sensitive, as if he was wearing a thin pair of latex gloves. Still, he was getting used to it here. The strangeness of everything was less strange already. It wouldn't be long until it was all normal.

"Yes, we slept. It was the middle of the night, you know."

The girl shrugged. "Were you wounded from the fight? Did you need to heal or something?"

"No, I was just, I don't know, wiped out."

Zeke cocked his head. "Frega, are you saying you don't sleep every day?"

"Oh, no. Thela forbid. What a waste of time. But I'm not a Warrior yet. I don't get into fights and need healing."

Great. Just like in the "real" world, Gerald couldn't escape being labeled a layabout.

With a thought, he stacked the blankets back on the end of the pallet and stood up, reaching for his equipment belt. The peg next to it was empty. Zeke was already wearing the basic violet Mage's robe he'd "borrowed" from someone in town.

He started to wrap the belt around his waist out of habit but stopped.

"I guess I need to get some more appropriate gear first thing."

Frega held out a bundle of fabric. "These don't fit Father anymore. My mother thought you might be able to use them. There's a shirt, breeches, boots, and socks there. They aren't anything fancy, but they'll cause less talk than that." She nodded at his uniform.

Holding a hand out over the clothes, he *Took* them from her and *Dropped* them on the pallet. Then, an article at a time, he *Equipped* them onto his body, replacing his police uniform. When he was finished, his old clothes were folded in a neat stack.

"Well, that was a lot more convenient than making everyone leave the room so I could get undressed, I guess."

"What are you going to do with that?" Zeke gestured at the gun.

"What do you mean?"

"Do you think it's smart to leave it out where anyone could pick it up? Think about it. What happens to items of value just lying around in *Realm*—" With a look at the girl, he cut himself off. "What I mean is, how often have you just walked around, picking up things that looked important or worth coin?"

"Hmmm." Gerald nodded. The game world was full of objects that seemed not to belong to anyone in particular, and they often got stuffed into someone's loot bag without a second thought. The last thing they needed was for someone with a knack for crafting or weapons making to get a hold of his revolver. If they produced a recipe to make one like it, it could give birth to a new age of firearms.

"Are you still wearing the same clothes under there, or did you get some too?" he asked Zeke.

"The same, for now."

"We need to get you something more native too."

"I'm not giving up the shirt," he said, crossing his arms. For a skinny guy, he could be a stubborn ox when he wanted.

"Fine, we'll deal with that later." Gerald picked up his uniform and gun belt and crossed into the forge room. Bergan Smith was working the bellows with both hands, forcing air onto the orange coals in the furnace. "Good morning, Master Smith."

"Morning to you, Goldenshield. Those clothes look to be a better fit on you than they have been on me in some years." He patted his belly, although it wasn't much out of proportion for his generous frame.

"If you say so."

"You and your friend heading out?"

"Yes. We appreciate you offering us a place to stay last night. We owe you one."

"Nonsense," he replied, returning to work on the fire. "My family will be in your debt for as long as this shop stands. If you or your elven friend ever find yourselves in need of a helping hand, you can count on us. Anything within my power."

Gerald looked down to hide a tiny smirk. Mrs. Smith had to have given her husband a piece of her mind on the subject of gratitude last night. She was someone to keep on their side.

"Actually, since you've mentioned it, there are a couple of things we could use some help with."

The big smith stopped pumping the bellows and gave him a somber look. "Let's hear it, then, and I'll see what I can do."

"First, my, um, traveling clothes are a bit unusual for the locals. It might be best if they weren't left out where someone might happen to find them on accident. I've got some special e, too, that'd best be left alone, if you know what I

Ah, yep, I can see what you mean there."

"If you had some extra space in a safe or some other place ocked away from prying eyes, I'd be quite appreciative."

The smith rubbed his chin, considering. "Well, son, I don't know about this 'safe' thing, but I do have a chest I keep locked in my bedroom. I reckon there's room for your stuff in there. Will that do?"

"I think that'd be just fine, thank you."

"Hand 'em here, then, and I'll see to it," Bergan said, extending his hand for the bundle. Gerald *Gave* it over.

"Fine, then. Was there something else?"

"Yes, sir. We're planning to venture into the Ore Wood and collect a few hunting contracts while we're here. But, as you can see, I don't have a weapon for that kind of work." He gestured to his equipment resting on top of the pile of his clothes.

"This piece does look right strange for a weapon. Not like anything I've ever seen before, honestly. I mean, you walloped those two Exceptas with it last night just fine, but it looks lacking for reach, if you ask me. Thela's truth, when I first saw it, I took it for some kind of magic item that might throw bolts of lightning or something at an enemy."

Again, Gerald had to hide a grin. "It's got a trick or two. But it won't be much use out in the woods hunting monsters. I can only use it a handful of times."

"I'd be happy to sell you anything out of the armory. You know I'll make you a fine deal."

"Mist—uh, Master Smith, I'd love to walk inside the store and buy the sharpest thing you have. But, as we said last night, my friend and I aren't just short on money. We're lacking it."

"I see."

"Don't get me wrong. The last thing I'm looking for is a handout. But if you could find your way to letting me borrow something old and not worth putting up for sale—just for the day, mind you—I'm sure I'll make enough coin to buy something proper by nightfall."

Bergan glared and rubbed his chin while his face remained like stone. The impassive stare said Gerald was trying to sell him day-old fruit at today's price.

Gerald needed to find a way to sweeten the deal for Bergan but had nothing. All he had to bargain with was himself. An idea struck him. Maybe that would be enough.

"Hopefully," he added, "we'll come back with enough coin to get a room at one of the inns in town too. I'm sure you'd like us out of your hair, and more importantly, out of your forge house."

That was just enough to tip things into his favor. "All right, son, I've got a weapon or two I've been planning to melt down and rebuild. I don't see any reason why you can't make use of one of those for a day or so. But if it breaks and you get your face chewed off by a diseased wolf or aggressive orb spider, that's no fault of mine."

"Of course. I understand."

Nodding, the massive man said, "Behind me, there's an old forge hammer and a rusting short sword. I reckon they'd both do about the same damage, so pick the one that suits you. I'm going to go see to locking your stuff away. You'll be gone before I get back, I suspect, so I'll say good luck to you now."

"Thank you. I promise you'll have it back by the end of the day. Tomorrow at the latest."

"Fair enough."

As Bergan turned to go, the thought Gerald had had before falling asleep came back to mind. "Oh, one last thing," he added. "I just need to check my weapon there and make sure it's safe."

"Safe? Should I be worried about keeping it in the house? I've got valuables in that chest I don't want damaged."

"Oh, no, it's fine. But in case someone younger gets a hold of it, I want to be sure they can't hurt themselves by accident."

"Well, fine, check it quick, then. The day ain't going to wait on us."

Gerald held his hand over the gun, but no descriptions sprang to mind. He frowned, having gotten used to the easy transfer of items by a thought. It didn't make any sense that his clothes swapped with the others but this didn't work. Maybe the gun was just *so* foreign the game couldn't recognize it?

Whatever the reason, he unsnapped the guard and slipped the revolver into his hand. A quick flex of his thumb popped the cylinder out. Checking its load count, he frowned even deeper. Three of the chambers were full, and three were empty. Just how it should have been if he'd fired three times in the Quik Mart.

Shaking his head, Gerald slapped the cylinder back into the gun. Keeping the gun and ammo separate would have been safer, of course, but then he risked the parts getting separated. As soon as he found a place of his own to lock up the gun, he'd take it back. For now, the best he could do was hope neither Frega nor her father had a curious nature.

He placed the gun back on top of his bundle. Bergan nodded and left the forge house, heading for the rear door of the armor shop and the family's rooms on the second floor.

"So, what did he say?" Frega asked, coming up behind Gerald. "I heard you ask to borrow a weapon, but I didn't hear what he said."

Zeke followed her. "Tell me he gave you something cool. A monster two-hander or something?"

"Nope. He told me I could borrow either this marvelous old smithing hammer or, if I preferred, this lovely half-rusted short sword. But I'm not to get too attached to whichever beauty I pick, because I need to give it back to him by the end of the day or tomorrow."

"Wow, he must like you a lot," Frega said with a gasp. At first, he thought she was joking, but the longer she went without smirking, the more he realized she'd spoken with a genuine hint of awe.

"So what would he have offered someone he didn't like?"

She grinned. "That person wouldn't still be here."

Zeke clapped his hands with enthusiasm. "Which one's it gonna be, then?"

Gerald drew his brows together. Or at least he thought he did. With the way their faces worked, it was hard to be sure.

"I don't know. I mean, I should take the sword, right? Everybody always goes off on the big adventure with a sword. And if I don't practice with one, and later on there's some special holy magic artifact sword at the end of all this that we need to slay the dragon, I won't be able to use it. But, damn, that thing is crusty with rust."

"No worries, buddy," his friend offered. "There are no dragons here. Well, except for the World Dragons, but they're deep in the core of Thelaroth, sleeping where it's warm."

"And you know what? Sleeping lizards waking up to threaten the entire known world aren't my problem."

A quick assessment of both items showed that Bergan had been dead on the money when he claimed they were equivalent.

Smithing Hammer - 5 Dmg, 40% wear

Rusty Short Sword - 5 Dmg, 85% wear

Wear, though, was a different matter. The short sword was

so far gone that venturing out into the woods with it seemed a fool's dare.

"The hammer it is," he said, *Taking* it from the bench. After that, though, he wasn't sure what to do. "Where do I put this thing when I'm not using it?"

"*Release* it."

"What?"

"Don't you remember in the—" Zeke paused, looking at Frega. "Well, if you'd paid any attention before instead of just pressing buttons over and over mindlessly, you'd remember you have to *Release* a weapon when you aren't using it."

Gerald rolled his eyes. "Spare me the lecture. Who needs to remember any of that?"

"Seems like *someone* needs to know it now." Zeke crossed his arms and shot him a smug glare.

Release

The hammer vanished from his hand and reappeared hanging from a loop on his belt.

He scowled. "Fine. You made your point. Next time we have a chance to go out on that kind of adventure, I'll pay more attention." Zeke could take his self-righteousness and stuff it.

Frega coughed. "You two bicker like my mother and father. Are you finished? Can we get started now? I'd like to get some critters killed before midday. And if we'd don't hurry, we'll miss all the big ones. They pay better."

"Fine, let's go get some contracts. Lead the way."

Smiling, the girl led them out of the forge house.

Zeke brought his hands together, index fingers extended like a kid's make-believe gun, and rubbed his nose like he did when he was worried. "Do you think she's done this before? I mean, how old could she be?"

Gerald shrugged. "I don't know. Nine, maybe? Ten? What

difference does it make? She's a game character. It's not like she's a real person."

"I guess. She seems real enough to me, though."

Shrugging again, Gerald said, "To tell you the truth, I'm more worried about the 'big ones' she just mentioned. How big? These are video game monsters, right?"

His friend rubbed his nose harder. "Shit. I hadn't thought about that."

CHAPTER EIGHT

THE RANGER

"ARE YOU KIDDING ME?" JUST outside Copperton's Town Hall, Gerald glared at a vellum scroll detailing their hunter's contract. "That thing is the size of my dad's Labrador Retriever. No way I'm going after that with this piece-of-crap old hammer. It'll be like shooting at hawks with a water gun—pointless but enough to piss 'em off."

"It's not that bad," Zeke said. "I won't even let the things touch you. One fireball and I'll have it on its back. Then you can squash it."

"That's easy for you to say, Mr. Wizard," the Warrior complained, letting the scroll roll itself closed. "You won't be the one trying to attract the attention of venomous spiders the size of a full-grown hog!"

Looking from one to the other, Frega cut in, "Would you two start making sense? What's a…a…laba-door? And you can't tell me you're afraid of a little Venomous Woods Creeper? The ones around here are like pets, almost. Babies play with them. You should see the big ones in the deep woods."

Gerald and Zeke gave each other horrified looks. "Have you ever seen one of these things in person? How many hunter contracts have you brought in?"

"Well, I mean, none yet. You have to be twelve before you're allowed to take a contract. But I've heard about them."

"From where?"

"Daven—remember him? One of the kids I was with last night? His older brother is a fifteen-year-old Ranger. He told us all kinds of stories."

"Awesome. We're being led by a nine-year-old based on a teenager's stories. What could possibly go wrong?"

Taking Gerald's arm, Zeke leaned into him. "If they don't let kids go out to grind, I don't think she should go with us. We ought to send her home."

Gerald grunted but said nothing. Frega eyed them both with suspicion. "What're you two hens whispering about?"

"It's… nothing. Let's head toward the forest." Forest Road was both the direction they needed to go and the way back to Frega's home. Going that way would give Gerald some time to think about what to do with her before they reached the edge of town.

Halfway there, a familiar sign with an image of a rooster crowing from the back of a pig caught his eye, hanging motionless over the street. The Roost and Pig was one of several inns around town with a public tavern and was known for hosting a more sensible and reserved crowd than the Miner's Rest. Players went there for better reasons than to act like fools. He had to assume the same would hold true here.

"You know what? I haven't had breakfast. Let's stop in here and get a bite to eat first. We'll need our strength out there."

Zeke looked confused. After a glance at Frega and then back at Gerald, though, he got that the Warrior was stalling.

"Yes. Actually, I didn't tell you, but I did a few messenger quests this morning before you woke up. You know, 'deliver this letter to Skippy McSkipperson, the alchemist across town.' I should have enough coin for a small meal."

"Breakfast? Are you two hurt? Do you need healing?" The girl looked from one to the other in confusion.

"No, no. But, you know, breakfast is the most important meal of the day, right?"

"On a feast day, maybe. But whatever you want to do, Goldy."

He sighed again. The girl was never going to call him by name. "Come on, let's go in."

At the inn's door, his companions vanished.

"What—?" His stomach rocketed into his throat. "Where'd they go?"

Spinning in a circle, he searched for hints of Zeke and Frega. But they were gone, like smoke in the air.

Unless... Facing the door, he put a hand out. As expected, a single word whispered through his mind.

Enter?

As he thought the command, bright colors flashed, and then he was inside the Roost and Pig, standing next to Zeke and Frega.

"I swear," he muttered, "this place is going to be the death of me."

His friend patted him on the back. "Maybe, buddy. But don't worry, we'll rez you back."

"How comforting."

The Roost and Pig was dominated by a sunken common room with a long bar along the back wall. An open doorway beside it gave access into the kitchen area, and a broad staircase to the kitchen's right led up to the rooms for rent. With luck, they'd come back from the woods later with enough silver for one of them.

Gerald stepped down into the common room and picked a table near the wall on the left, just to the side of a roaring fire. It was cozy, even if a bit much for this time of day. Damn inns always had fires burning.

He dropped into a chair with his back to the wall. The other two joined him around the table.

A server with a pretty face, curly hair, low bodice, and the curves apparently requisite for the "fantasy tavern wench" mold scampered over to them. Gerald groaned. The game designers really went out of their way for her.

Zeke, on the other hand, was about a heartbeat away from drooling. His whole face had glazed over.

"Well met, strangers. I'm Nala, and don't you look like a group of thirsty travelers?" The way her voice bubbled, it was a wonder she didn't float away on it. "What can I getcha?"

"Nala," Gerald said, "we were thinking about having a nice, big breakfast before we go out in the dark woods to slay some nasty spiders. What have you got?"

She blinked in surprise. "Breakfast? I think we have a few apples and some moldy bread. If you're willing to wait for a while, we might be able to put together a Mysterious Meat Pie. Is it your Nameday or something? What are we celebrating? You don't look injured."

"Oh!" Zeke blurted, startling them all. "I… we… we'll just have two mugs of Lightning Lager and a Refreshing Spring Water for the girl."

Nala eyed him sideways for a moment, likely considering whether the elf posed some kind of threat. Apparently concluding he wasn't imminently likely to grow a tail or horns, she nodded and floated over to the bar area.

"Oh? Oh, what? What's the deal?" Gerald demanded.

"It's like sleeping. Nobody eats breakfast. Nobody eats anything. Not unless the food has healing capacity and they're hurt. Or, like they said, it's a major occasion. You know what I mean?"

"Ah… yeah, I see." In all the thousands of hours of *Realm Quest* they'd played, it never occurred to him that food and sleep were optional. Both could heal injuries, but neither was necessary. No wonder everyone had given him funny looks when he talked about a big, hearty breakfast.

"So where you're from, people eat food all the time?" Frega asked. "Wow, they must have more coin than they know what to do with. Even at Festus, Father complains about the cost of a feast that's more about being together than eating."

Gerald gave her a dopey shrug. Nala saved him from having to explain by dropping off their drinks. He reached for his cup and…

Drink

…drank heartily. A mug or two of beer before heading out to face pet-sized spiders was a better choice than a big breakfast anyway. Beer was more likely to stay down, and with luck, it would calm his nerves.

Finishing his beer, he thumped the mug to the table, belched loudly, and wiped his mouth with the back of his hand. His mother would have been appalled.

"Thela's Name, you have the manners of a dwarf, Goldenshield," Frega giggled. He couldn't help but chuckle with her.

As he waved to Nala for a second mug, a tall woman popped inside the common room. She was dressed as a Ranger, in a cloth shirt with leather breeches and a matching leather vest. She surveyed the Roost and Pig like an eagle watching for rodents.

Few other townsfolk sat at the tables dotting the common

room. Those that did were alone, nursing the mug or cup in front of them. The woman scanned over the other patrons with a dismissive look, but she stopped when her eyes fell on Gerald, Zeke, and Frega.

She hopped down the steps and strode toward them, projecting strength and confidence with every step. Instead of coming up to their table, though, she veered to the right and angled into a chair a few feet away.

Nala delivered the second round of drinks and scurried over to the new woman without a word.

"Welcome to the Roost and Pig, ma'am. What can I get you?"

"Gnome Whiskey and a Lightning Lager. And here's a start on my tab." In one deft motion, she pulled a gold coin from a vest pocket and flipped the coin up to the server, who snatched it out of the air with a healthy smile.

"Coming right up, ma'am."

The new lady's hand shot out and took Nala's in a tight grip. Fear flashed on the girl's face.

"Don't worry, we're not going to have trouble. But don't call me ma'am again, or it will cost you." The woman didn't elaborate on *what* it would cost, but by her tone, she wasn't messing around.

Nala nodded, muttered a quick apology, and scampered off back to the bar.

The Ranger turned her attention back to the three of them, pulling off a pair of leather gloves. "I am called Mehleese here. Good day and well met, travelers."

"Nice to meet you, Mehleese—" Gerald began before Zeke cut him off.

"How do you know we're travelers?" Zeke asked.

The woman—Mehleese—smiled. It was a predatory thing. Not off-putting or enough to cause shaking hands or twitching eyes but enough to remind them to stay on their toes, especially with strangers.

"Are you kidding? You stick out like a diseased wolf surrounded by turtles, what with those confused looks and your novice gear. Did you borrow those or steal them?"

Gerald felt his face flush. "Lady, I don't know who you think—"

"It was a simple question. Borrowed? Or stolen?"

Snapping his mouth shut, Gerald mumbled, "Borrowed."

"That is, borrowed without the owner's consent," Zeke added.

"On top of that, you're hanging out with a townie kid. I bet you've been letting her show you the ropes since you just got here, right?"

"How did you—?" Zeke froze, stumbling for words that would somehow negate the truth of what she'd just said.

"Let me save you the trouble, friend," Mehleese said. "You're Goldenshield"—she nodded at Gerald—"the man the town can't stop talking about. And you're his trusted elven mage buddy."

"Look, lady," Gerald replied, "I don't know where you came by your information, but my friends and I are just trying to enjoy a drink before heading out of town. So, if you don't mind—"

"I said, my name is Mehleese, and rudeness aside, I'm quite pleased to meet you. But if you think I'm going to let you stumble blind into the Ore Wood on your first day, you're a bigger fool than I imagined. I'll be accompanying you today."

"Excuse me?" Gerald scoffed. "What are you, the Welcome Amazon? No thanks. We'll be fine without any of your… help."

"No, you won't. You'll be dead. There are things out there the size of a—of a wagon. Things that can take your head and shoulders off your body in one clean swipe. Things your life never prepared you for." She paused and gave Zeke a pointed look.

"And I know you're thinking, 'Oh, we'll just rez right back. It'll be great fun.' But the thing is, no. You'll be dead. Only Thela can bring someone back from the Dark World. And she doesn't do that anymore."

"Lady, I—"

"Mehleese."

"Okay, fine, Lady Mehleese."

"Believe me, I am *no* lady."

Gerald rolled his eyes. "Fine, Mehleese, I appreciate you taking a concern—"

He stopped as Nala slipped between the tables and set the Ranger's drinks on the table. The server glanced at their mugs as well, but sensing the tension, hurried off without a word.

Before he could start again, Mehleese interjected, "Send the girl home."

"Hey!" Frega cried. "What'd I do to you?"

Gerald put his hands up, palms out. "Hold up. I don't take orders from anyone."

"The two of you following a nine-year-old girl into the forest is the very definition of a sightless cavern ogre leading an oculan missing its one eye. You'll all end up dead and then get to spend from now until Thela releases the World Dragons watching from the Dark World. Meanwhile, Fayn Smith will curse you for taking her only daughter from her. There is a very good reason they don't give hunter contracts out until someone is at least twelve. And at the moment, you two know even less than she does. So send her home. I'll teach you what you need to know. Or at least enough to survive out there on your own for a day."

"You can go suck on a crawling jelly, lady," Frega spat. "I know what I'm doing. We'll be fine."

Gerald gave the girl a disapproving look and shook his head. "Mehleese, as I was saying, we appreciate your concern but—"

"She's right," Zeke cut in. "Frega has no business going out in the forest with us. We can't protect her. And if what the lady says about dying is right…." He left the rest of that sentence unspoken.

The woman clapped. "Master Elf, you surprise me! I never expected you to be the voice of reason. But I am glad you, at least, see that I'm making sense."

Zeke glared down into his half-empty mug, flushing from the compliment while seeming ashamed for taking the woman's side.

Stroking the inches of goatee he was just getting used to, Gerald looked from one to the other of them, considering. If Zeke thought she had a point, there might be something to it. With Frega, though? Disappointed wouldn't even be in the same ZIP code of how she'd feel if they sent her away. And she had been a ton of help. Then again, if this business about dying was on the money….

"Frega," he said. "Is she right? Is that what happens when you die?"

"How should I know?" she replied, voice thick with the kind of indignation a child could produce by the barrel. "Do I look like I've ever been dead?"

"Frega," he repeated, hoping to calm her.

"Fine! Yes, she's right. You go to the Dark World and stay there. Unless Thela touches you. But that's just what people say. No one ever comes back."

"Great." That news sucked. The next part was going to suck even worse.

Drink

Setting his second empty mug down, he wiped his mouth again and sighed in contentment. At least the beer was pretty good. It didn't have that odd synthetic taste everything else did. So far, it was the one thing he liked better than home.

"As much as I hate to say it, Frega, the Ranger's right. You need to go home. Zeke and I will come by the Armory later and tell you all about it."

"But—!"

"You're just not old enough to go out on quests yet."

The girl slid off the chair and gave the three of them a look that could forge metal. "Don't be surprised when she takes you out into the middle of nowhere and cuts your throats. Don't say I didn't warn you."

"I'm sorry, Frega. We'll see you soon."

"You *hope* you will." With that, she stomped across the room and up the steps and popped out the main doors.

"There?" Gerald said, "Happy now?"

"No, I'm not happy. But I'm glad she's gone. I almost said things ears like hers shouldn't hear."

"Like what?"

"That you're living in a world now with monsters the size of Volkswagens. Terrible things, worse than you ever imagined possible. Creatures so deadly they put movie monsters to shame."

"Enough with trying to scare us—"

"Shut up, Ger," Zeke said, leaning forward. "You still aren't listening, are you?"

"What? Of course I am. Everything wants to kill us and eat our brains."

"No, dumbass. She was talking about home. Our world. The real world."

Gerald's mouth fell open. "I don't get it."

Mehleese smiled. "The Fifth World. I'm glad one of you listens, at least. Yes, I'm like you. Well, kind of. Icelandic, actually. I'm guessing you're American? It doesn't matter now. Wherever you're from, welcome to Thelaroth."

Her smile faded.

"And now you're stuck here with the rest of us."

CHAPTER NINE

THE RULES

A MILLION QUESTIONS BOUNCED IN GERALD'S head like popcorn in a popper, but all he managed to get out was, "Whoa. What?"

Zeke did a little better. "What do you mean 'stuck' here? And who are 'the rest of us'"?

A twitch of mirth danced across Mehleese's face. Saying nothing, she threw back her shot of whiskey, swallowing it in a single gulp. Eyes closed, she evidently savored whatever effect it had and sighed like Gerald had with his beer. Then she took her mug by the handle and moved to Gerald and Zeke's table.

"By 'the rest of us,' I mean the other people here who, somehow or another, have been brought from our world to this one. You're not alone in that. None of us are alone in that. And before you ask, no one knows how it works. The priests of the Temple of Thela might, but they've refused to even discuss it. Rumor has it that Thela's Shaman are more open minded. But if you ask me, that has to have more to do with the hallucinogenic mushrooms they eat when trying to commune with Her."

Gerald cocked his head. "Huh? Mushrooms? What are you saying?"

"Sorry. Point is, no one I've ever met knows anything about it."

"Okay… so how did you get here?"

"One night, after something like a thirty-six-hour marathon session online, I logged out and staggered away from my computer desk. When I turned around, the most beautiful colored light I'd ever seen was floating behind me. It looked like what I'd imagined that fairy from the movies—damn, what was her name? In the green leathers?—would have looked like to a person in real life."

"Tinkerbell?" Zeke offered.

"Yes! I always loved that one as a kid. I loved to dream of children who wouldn't want to grow up. I couldn't imagine how wonderful their lives had to have been."

Gerald shook his head. "Let's try to keep this on the rails. So you saw a multicolored Tinkerbell. Let me guess: green, blue, and magenta?"

Mehleese nodded.

"Sounds familiar. Then what?"

"As I got closer, it glowed brighter. I was mesmerized. Couldn't take my eyes off it. But then I started to wonder. Was I losing it? After a full day and a half staring at my computer screen, was I having some kind of break with reality? I had to know that it was truly there and not something I'd just made up."

"So?"

"So I touched it. A quick poke with my index finger. And that was it. I woke up here, in the loft of a barn."

Gerald waved for another beer. "That sounds a lot less

traumatic than what happened to us. An old man hit us in the head with a staff with that twinkling color thing at the end of it."

"Really?" she asked, raising her eyebrows. "I've never heard of someone from this world going to the Fifth World. That has to mean something important."

Zeke finished his first beer and switched to the second. "How long have you been here?"

"In game time or real time?"

"Is there a difference?"

She smiled. "Oh, yes. I've lived something like twenty years here. But in 'real world' time? I guess I don't know. What year was it when you left?"

After a nod from Gerald, Zeke told her.

"Wow." Mehleese whistled. "I've only been here four years."

"And you've lived over twenty years in that time?"

"More than twenty cycles from one sad, lonely Festus to the next, yes. Twenty-three to be exact."

Index fingers together, Zeke rubbed the bridge of his nose. "How old were you, in the real world, when you came here?"

"Thirty-six."

"No way!" Gerald said, too loudly. "That makes you fifty-nine? No way you're fifty-nine! You still look like you're thirty-six."

She gave him a wan smile. "That's nice of you to say. I used to worry about that. It seems aging isn't something we need to worry about now. All we have to do is focus on staying alive, and we can live forever here. All the more reason not to get killed foolishly. It would be a shame to waste the gift of near immortality languishing in the Dark World."

"You weren't kidding about that?" With his fingers, Zeke traced circular patterns around the tip of his nose.

"Thela's Name, no. If you die here, there's no quick, easy resurrection. If you get dead, you stay dead. No rez. End of story."

Gerald gave Zeke a stern look. "So, see? Don't let me die."

"Ha. Ha. Okay, so how many of 'us' are there? And how can we tell the difference?"

"I don't know how many," she replied. "Tens? Hundreds? It's hard to say. Even harder to guess how many know they aren't alone. It's not like we have a club and a summer reunion with a pig roast and a potluck dinner. That said, I do know a way to tell them apart."

"How?"

"Swearing," she said.

"What, you mean like, to Thela rather than God or whoever?"

"No, no. Before long, everyone starts taking Thela's name in vain, out of habit. It's like picking up an accent. You'll do it too. No, what I meant was actual cursing."

"You mean like saying, 'damn'? How does that even make sense?"

"The game people, the ones who belong to this world? They don't swear. At least, not that I've ever heard. It's not in their programming. And they'll look at you funny if you do. Like you've got asterisks and number signs in a balloon over your head. No, if you ever hear someone in Thelaroth get mad and throw out a tirade full of words your mom would wash your mouth out for, you know that's one of us."

"Bullshit. There has to be another way to tell."

"Not that I've ever found. Well, without coming right out and asking if they're from the Fifth World. But that can be dangerous. If you figure something else out, let me know."

Gerald shook his head. "That's crazy."

Mehleese shrugged. "I didn't make the rules here. I'm just trying to survive."

"Let's get back to that. Are you sure there's no way home?"

"No, I'm not sure. I'm no more sure of that than whether the sun will still come up tomorrow. Look around you! Does anything you see fill you with a sense of certainty or permanence? There are three rules for being one of us. First, don't let the locals know you're not one of them. Second, you worry about today. Period. There probably won't be a tomorrow, anyway. Three. Don't get dead. Nutshell. That's it. The rest of the time, keep your head down, go with the flow, and stay flexible, because you never know what the hell will happen next."

"I'll say it again," Gerald snarled. "That's bullshit. Maybe I don't want to spend the next however many years of my life pretending tomorrow isn't real. I'm not even twenty-five years old yet. I've got an entire life to live back in a world where you pick things up by using your goddamn fingers instead of having to think about something leaping into your hand. And if you or Thela or anyone else thinks I'm going to waste that life here, I'll be happy to tell you you're wrong."

"Goldenshield, I—"

"*Stop calling me that*!" he shouted, jumping up. His chair clattered to the floor behind him.

Mehleese raised her eyebrows and surveyed the room again. This time, all the other patrons looked back.

"Sit. Down. Before I make you."

"I'd like to see you try that."

In a blur of motion, before he could even flinch, Mehleese produced a dagger and laid it flat on the table, pointed at his chest. "I wouldn't have to *try*. I've got decades more experience than you. I'm countless levels above you. I can kill you without even breaking a sweat. So don't tempt me. Now... Sit. Down."

He held her eyes in a juvenile attempt to exert some control where they both knew he had none. Then he dropped backward where his seat had been, forgetting it now lay sideways on the floor. With a grunt and a loud crash, he crumpled to the ground, leading with his ass.

"Oof!"

Zeke's face went blank. Mehleese covered her mouth with her hands. They both watched him collect himself and what little remained of his dignity. He tried to fit it back into place like the chair he'd knocked over. After smoothing his breeches and adjusting his shirt, he settled onto his seat as intended.

The woman looked from him to Zeke and then back. Her mouth twitched. Then it opened in a smirk. Soon, she and the elf were smacking the table and laughing so hard they couldn't breathe.

Although trying to keep his face straight, their cackling combined with the absurdity of everything got the better of him. Gerald couldn't help but give in and was soon reduced to the deep-down, whole-body belly laughter that was typically the province of a happy toddler.

"I think he's drunk," Zeke managed between chuckles. "How strong is this Lightning Lager, Mehleese?"

When she at last caught her breath enough to answer, she said with a broad smile, "I'm sorry to make light. Are you all right?"

"Jesus, yes," Gerald said. "I'm fine. I'm giggling like a hyena just like you two. "

"Good. I'm sorry. I didn't mean to piss you off. And I wish I had more information. But Thelaroth is a big place. I'm sure the answer is here somewhere. With a little luck, you'll have plenty of time to find it."

"Right, which means we'll need to learn to fight, quickly. We need experience too. On top of that, we'll need some decent coin for traveling."

"Traveling? Where do you plan to go?"

"Yeah, where are we going?" Zeke asked, scratching a pointed ear.

"On a journey, of course. A quest across the realm. Isn't that what we're supposed to do? Journey out to find the ancient magical MacGuffin or whatever that will teleport us back to our faraway home?"

"A journey?"

"Yep." Gerald smiled, lifting his mug up to his lips. "The first place we're going is Riverglow. There has to be someone there, in the city of the king, the greatest city in Thelaroth, who can tell us something."

"That's not the worst idea I've ever heard. I've never had a chance to ask the Mages' Guild"—she cast a sidelong look at Zeke—"since they aren't very open with their knowledge of the Arcane. But they might be more willing to talk with you two."

"Either way," she went on, "if we don't get started soon, we'll never make a respectable Warrior out of you. So empty those tankards and let's get to it. We have critters to slay."

The faster they earned enough coin and experience to travel, the faster they could find someone to get them back home. Time was on his side, since it moved more slowly there, but if he wasted too much, he'd miss his chance with Brooke.

He slammed his empty mug back on the table with a belch. "Right. First, though, let's talk about those monsters that are as big as Volkswagens. Are we talking the Beetle or the Bus? Maybe just a Jetta?"

Mehleese gulped the rest of her own beer and threw the wooden mug in the nearby fire with a splintering crash. "Oh, boys, if only the Volkswagen-sized things were what you needed to worry about most."

Her laugh—a deep, throaty version of it—echoed through the common room as she made her way to the door.

CHAPTER TEN

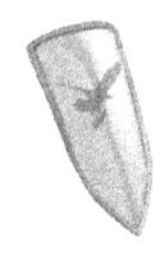

THE GRIND

GERALD LEVERED THE HEAD OF his hammer back and forth before wrenching it from the cracked carapace of the dead Venomous Woods Creeper oozing in front of him. A sulfurous, musky smell—the stink of burnt spider—filled his nose. Two of the thing's eight spiky appendages twitched and sizzled like crab legs on a grill.

He grasped the pentagon-shaped piece of shell with a white star marking on its belly and snapped it off. A greenish string of Creeper goo trailed along with it.

"Fuck me, that's nasty," he said, wiping the still-warm slime off his hands. "You didn't tell us it was going to be so godforsaken disgusting, Mehleese. It makes me want to puke."

The only redeeming thing so far was that at least the blasted creatures weren't *quite* as big as Chunky, his parents' Labrador Retriever.

Zeke strolled up from where he'd been standing behind him. "Oh, come on, Ger. It's not that bad. Plus, we've both already gone up three levels. It's almost getting easy now."

As an elven Mage, Zeke couldn't wear armor, so the

safest place for him in the midst of battle was in the rear or off to the side, someplace where he could cast high-damage spells from beyond the reach of monsters. So far, he'd been hit maybe twice while Gerald had taken all the rest of the damage. Mehleese stayed even farther back, barking instructions during combat but otherwise not interfering.

"That's easy for you to say," Gerald grumbled. "You're not dodging spider goo or, worse, fangs the size of pocketknives." He'd been bitten twice so far, and both times it felt like someone cut him open with a paring knife and poured drain cleaner into the wound. And that was considering the blunted way he felt pain here. He shuddered to think of what the Creepers' bite would feel like without the gauzy *Realm Quest* buffer.

Mehleese, thank goodness, carried a few vials of a deep-purple "Cure Lesser Poison" potion with her. She'd made him drink some after each bite to counter the effect of the Creeper's venom.

Explaining their health, though, was the single most helpful thing she'd done so far. In Thelaroth, every person could take a certain, finite amount of damage before dying. A Warrior like Gerald, who had plenty of strength and stamina, could laugh at a beating that would send a Mage like Zeke, more brains than muscle, straight to the Dark World. That finite number was their health total. Each time they got hit with an attack, they lost points, which registered as that clacking sensation Gerald had felt the night before. It was his body telling him how many points he'd lost.

Health, though, was recovered easily. It regenerated by sitting still and not fighting. Except for the pair of times the little buggers had managed to sink their nasty fangs into him, after each Creeper fight, Gerald had regenerated back to full strength by the time they'd spotted another one.

"All right, Shiny Robe, how many is that now?" He flung the shard of carapace to Zeke, who caught it and stuffed it into a bag Mehleese had given them.

"That's nine Creeper Shell Markings. We need one more. And then we can start looking for the diseased wolf tongues. Oh, and before I forget, fuck you, *Goldenshield.*"

Gerald chuckled. If he had to be covered in spider guts, at least he could get under Z's skin. Zeke spent most of the time between fights complaining about the need for a new name, one suitable for *Realm Quest*.

"What? You said you wanted a name. Do you like Glitterstaff better?"

"What I said was that if everyone is hell-bent on calling you Goldenshield, I can't very well go around being Zeke Dahlberg. I mean, how lame and ordinary is that? Nobody has a name like that here. It'll draw attention. Imagine how you'd react if a dude came into the police station and identified himself as Lothan Headcleaver."

"I'd assume that whatever Lothan called himself wasn't any of my business as long as he wasn't actively cleaving a head or carrying a previously cloven one. I'd check his pupils to make sure he wasn't on something, but let's be honest, my real concern starts and ends with the head cleaving. And I don't know why no one will call me Gerald. I'd be as happy as a cat with bacon if no one ever called me Goldenshield again. It's like the name of some freaking Gothic hero. Or a B-list superhero or something. Shit, I'm not about to be the hero of anything. I just want to go back to my police cruiser for a nap. I miss the smell of day-old double cheeseburger wrappers."

"That's gross. And you can complain about it all you want, but it's too late now. Like it or not, you're Goldenshield. No use crying over spilled milk."

Grunting, Gerald went back to surveying the green underbrush surrounding them, watching for the tell-tale twitch that meant a Creeper was waiting for dinner to scurry by. The forest didn't look much like an actual forest. It was neat and orderly, and just as he and Zeke had smoother, plasticized versions of their own faces, the trees, leaves, and bushes of the Ore Wood didn't look quite real.

Kicking at a root with Bergen Smith's worn leather boots, he sighed. "Fine. In that case, I think we should call you Ek'zae Wagonsbane. Because, man, you showed that Exceptas wagon no mercy last night. Plus, Ek'zae sounds elvish."

"Ek'zae?" Zeke groaned. "What the fuck, dude? Pig Latin is the best you can do? God, you don't have to be a dick about everything." He raised his hand, palm to the sky, and a spark crackled an inch above it. "I ought to put a fireball in the middle of your chest for that."

"Oh, did I piss off Mr. Anger Management? I bet you couldn't hit me with a fireball if you had to."

Face growing dark, Zeke sneered, "Oh yeah? How's this?"

Nothing happened. The sparks crackled but never coalesced into anything bigger. The anger melted from the elf's pale face. "Something's wrong. That should be a big-ass fireball."

Gerald patted his friend on the back. "Oh, I'm sure you're just a little worked up. Try to calm down, and everything will be fine. And really, Ek'zae, it's not all that bad. Think of the fear that will fill the thoughts of black-hearted men—not to mention innocent work wagons—upon hearing of Ek'zae Wagonsbane. Your legend is certain to spread across the Five Worlds of Thela like wildfire. Songs will be sung, and ladies will swoon at the mention of your mighty, wagon-smiting name."

Mehleese, who'd been trying to ignore the bickering as

she searched for the next Creeper, put herself between them. "I meant to ask earlier, is that rumor true? Did you two face off against Tristan Kingsbane the night you arrived?"

Shrugging, Gerald scrutinized his worn, ooze-stained smithing hammer, trying to play it cool. "Yeah. Is that a big deal? Personally, I was planning something a little stealthier than open combat, but Wagonsbane here just stood up and started lobbing fire at the Exceptas."

"I dismissed that as town gossip," she said. "Figured it had to be exaggerated. I have to say I'm impressed. It was a brave and noble thing you did, for newbies especially. You're lucky to have walked away from it. Tristan Kingsbane is one of the finest fighters in the whole of Copperton Valley. You'd have to go to Riverglow to find his equal. Most seasoned warriors would wet themselves and run off before confronting him."

"Well, it did hurt like a mother when he hit me with that axe of his," Zeke said. "I swear the damn thing was the size of a telephone pole. Almost knocked me back home by itself."

"What about you?" she asked, turning to Gerald. "Did he hit you too?"

He shook his head. "No, he sent a group of thugs to take care of me. I'd have been beaten like an egg, though, if you hadn't cast that shield spell on me, Z."

"Shielding spell? When I came to, you'd already taken care of the first two on your own. That's when I zapped the others."

"But right before the two with cudgels hit me, something covered me like an all-over shield. And their weapons just bounced off. You didn't do that?"

Raising his hands, Zeke replied, "No. I can't do anything like that. I have one or two protection spells, but they're self-casts. They only work on me. And they aren't that useful, anyway. I can encase myself in crystal for a minute, but that's about it."

Mehleese cocked her head. "Describe it."

"Something cold and static-y covered me like a blanket and then stuck like kindergarten paste and hardened."

"Steel skin."

"What? What's that?"

"Exactly what it sounds like. For a few moments, you were covered with a magical layer of shielding that adhered to you."

"Huh." He looked at Zeke. "And you can't cast anything like that?"

"Nope."

"No one can cast it," Mehleese explained. "It's not a spell. It's a Blessing. You need a Priest or a Paladin to confer it on you. So who did it?"

"God only knows." He shook his head. "I swear, this place makes less and less damned sense every minute I'm here."

"Interesting," she replied.

Then, to Zeke, she said, "I think that Ek'zae Axeblight would be a fair name, in honor of standing against the mighty axe of Tristan Kingsbane. A name worthy of remembering."

Gerald scoffed. "I'm not sure that he blighted the axe as much as it blighted him, but it does sound good."

"Shut up," Zeke shot back. "And I'd rather do without the stupid Pig Latin, but I guess if you like it, Mehleese, it can't be that bad."

"Good. It's done, then," she said, ending the debate. "Now, if we're done chatting like the washer folk, I believe that five meters to the north, there's a bush shaking unnaturally."

Palms back up into the air, Zeke smiled as balls of fire winked into existence next to his head. He looked almost...

smug. Confident. Was it because Mehleese had given him a name and said something nice about him?

He checked his friend again. Yes, he was beaming, and it wasn't just the fireballs. Sonuvabitch, the guy had a crush on their combat mentor.

Squeezing the grip of his hammer, Gerald smirked and located the spot Mehleese pointed out. Sure enough, a pair of black, pointed Creeper legs protruded from a holly bush. He strode up next to it and stopped, raising his weapon. Time for his smitten friend, Axeblight, to unleash hell.

A slash of flame shot past him and smashed into the brush hiding the Creeper. The thing squealed in pain—an ear-piercing, high-pitched noise—and scampered away from the now-burning cover on frantic, stick-like legs. Somehow drawn by instinct to the magic user of the group, it made a straight line right for Zeke. An inexperienced Mage wouldn't survive ten seconds of slashing by the spiked hooks at the end of its legs or, worse, its venomous bite. Gerald's job was to get its attention and keep it busy until their combined attacks killed it.

With a barbaric shout, he slammed his hammer down on the thing's back as it scurried past him. Combat Power—he didn't know whether it was simple adrenaline or something else, something magical in origin—flooded through him. It sent jolts of heat through his chest and a tingling sensation all the way to the tips of his ears. The Power gave him energy to perform special abilities, which included extra-powerful attacks as well as others that helped him keep a monster's attention.

After the shout, the eight-legged monster froze but only for a heartbeat. Apparently still not convinced Gerald was the guy it should attack, it continued toward Zeke instead. Gerald shouted again but this time poured his Combat Power into the War Cry.

That did it. The Creeper spun around, drawn to the Warrior.

For what had to be the fiftieth time that day, he wondered what the hell he was thinking by *trying* to attract an enormous venomous spider.

The critter reared up, flashed a pair of vicious-looking black fangs, and lunged. He'd seen that move plenty of times already, though, and swung his hammer upward into its bottom jaw. As usual, a burst of colored light erupted when he made contact, and the spider flipped backward, squealing.

Three smaller bursts of fire slammed into the creature's underside in quick succession: one, two, three. Even better, the last one caught the beast on fire, which seemed to happen with one out of every three or four.

The Creeper squealed again, trailing off as it died. The stench of charred critter filled the air.

An explosion of light surrounded Zeke at almost the exact same moment Gerald saw and felt that light radiate from him. His muscles tightened and grew, and a wave of newfound strength filled him. He felt as if someone had poured a bucket over his head and washed his fatigue away like dust. The world was sharper now, too, his senses clearer.

He'd never felt healthier or more alive.

"I think that makes nine now," Zeke said, looking at his hands.

"God, there is nothing in any world, ours included, like leveling up. It's better than sex, easy. You could get addicted to that."

"Right?" his friend agreed.

Mehleese chuckled. "Everyone gets addicted to it. Why do you think we never stop working toward the next level?

But"—she winked, looking from one to the other—"I don't know that I'd say it's better than sex. Perhaps you aren't doing it right? In need of a lesson?"

Gerald stammered to reply while Zeke stared at the Ranger, his face a shade of candy-apple red that belonged anywhere but on an elf.

Another man's voice, though, an unfamiliar one, answered. "Looky here, boys. Unless I miss my guess, these are the two townie pukes Tristan told us to be on the watch for. And here they are, delivered like a Festus gift."

CHAPTER ELEVEN

THE EXCEPTAS

THREE EXCEPTAS THUGS APPEARED FROM behind a copse of trees, each holding a short sword at the ready. They arranged themselves in a line, glaring with menace, their blue kerchiefs hanging in loose bundles around their necks.

The thug to the left was the tallest of the three and also the dirtiest, which was saying something, since they could all use a bath. His gray outfit was little more than rags, worn at the joints, frayed at the cuffs, and faded to a pale reminder of charcoal. His face was smeared with earth, and he was missing at least two teeth from a half-open, slack jaw.

The middle one was the shortest and stockiest of the trio, face and neck covered by an unkempt, uneven growth of beard. Among them, though, his eyes were the sharpest. He knew what he'd stumbled upon and was already calculating how much reward Tristan might give them. Stocky had to be the leader.

The third man, on the right, stared off into the distance,

uninterested. Like there was someplace he'd have rather been at that moment.

Tingling with the Combat Power left from fighting the Creeper and filled with the euphoria of leveling up, Gerald raised his hammer and charged. If they wanted a fight, he'd give it to them.

"Wait!" Mehleese commanded.

Gerald skidded to a stop and looked back. Her bow had appeared, with an arrow nocked and the string drawn back against her cheek. "Hold there, Goldenshield. You have to think before you go rushing into a fight. There's no reason anyone has to get hurt here. We can all just go our separate ways."

"Come on, pup," Stocky taunted. "Let's play. Or are you going to listen to that mouthy bitch? Do you take orders from a *woman*? Might as well come over here and let me cut off your balls if you ain't gonna use 'em anyway."

"Did you hear that, Ger?" Zeke said from behind him. "How can he be Exceptas if he's one of—"

"Not now," Gerald replied, dismissing whatever Z was going on about. This was *not* the time. Lowering the hammer, he laughed at the gang's leader. "I bet you enjoy getting your hands on another fella's balls, don't you, buddy?"

Stocky's face turned a fiery red. The other two, Filthy and Bored, snickered. "You gotta admit, Chaghen," Bored said, "he got you pretty good there."

"Shut up," the shorter thug hissed, shoving his companion, "or I'll put my boot so far up your backside you'll need a tree branch and help from Drank here to find it."

Filthy's eyes bulged, and his mouth snapped shut in alarm. "I'm not helping with that!"

"Both of you shut up! Tristan said he'd pay good coin for anyone bringing those two in. And I'm sure he'd pay something for the woman, even if she is old and bossy. So it's okay to hurt them, but no killing. Let's get them!"

The thugs started at Gerald, raising their worn swords.

"Last chance, Chaghen," Mehleese warned. "I don't want to have to kill you."

"If you won't shut your mouth, bitch, I'll shut it for you. Now!" Stocky shouted, urging the three Exceptas into a run. They rushed forward, hoping to overwhelm Gerald.

Setting his feet for the attack, Gerald bellowed an ear-splitting War Cry, and the warmth of Combat Power coursed through him. At the same moment, that cold, tingling electric charge washed over him again, settling like a blanket and hardening into a second skin.

No time to think about that, though. The thugs were on him. Gerald focused on Stocky first, assuming the smart one would be the most dangerous. With luck, Mehleese and Zeke would take care of the other two.

They didn't let him down. Seconds later, an arrow sprouted from Bored's unprotected throat. The man gurgled and clutched at the shaft just as another arrow struck, slipping through his hand and skewering it to his neck. He stumbled off to the side and collapsed into the forest undergrowth.

A jet of flames sprang up from the earth below Filthy's feet, who screeched in pain as the liquid orange fire enveloped him. The intense heat forced Gerald to turn away slightly, even from yards away. For the poor man in the middle of it, it must have been like standing in the core of Hell.

His rags burning, Filthy threw down his sword and dove away from the fight, startling a Creeper in the process. It scampered away from the moaning, rolling heap of burning flesh.

Stocky—or Chaghen, whatever—swung his sword in an overhead arc, leading with the flat of the blade. It wouldn't do as much damage, but if it caught Gerald in the head, it might stun him in a single blow.

As in the last fight with Exceptas thugs, Gerald threw his forearm up to block the attack. This time, though, he knew about the Blessing of Steel Skin. Stocky's sword should bounce right off.

Instead of a dull thud and glancing blow like before, the weapon drove Gerald's arm down, out of the way, and crashed against the top of his head. Half a dozen health points ticked off, and pain exploded through his skull, from his crown to the tip of his chin. He stumbled but kept his feet despite the pain and shock. Luckily, he wasn't stunned.

Stocky had only a moment to flash a look of disappointment before Gerald countered with a flurry of hammer taps up his leg, arm, and head. The thug staggered backward and reset his feet, eyes gone to fury and brimstone. He pointed his blade at the younger Warrior.

"Screw taking you to Tristan. He made it sound like you'd be as easy to catch as a hungry mouse. Well, to the Dark World with him. I'm going to put my sword through your side. See how you like that, *Goldenshield*." He lunged forward as an arrow drove all the way through his arm. A fletched tail hung from one side and an arrowhead dripping blood from the other.

Dropping the sword from his useless arm, he clutched at the wound, his eyes frantic.

Gerald brought his hammer around and whacked the man on the helmet, like gonging a church bell. Stocky crumpled to the ground.

"Well done," Mehleese said. "You took that hit like a big boy. Almost looked like a pro."

Gerald rubbed the top of his head and flexed his jaw. "I didn't feel like it. I think he might have knocked half my fillings loose."

"I'm not sure what 'fillings' are, but I dare say you knocked more loose from his head than he did yours." The woman from the night of the raid, Jehn, slipped out from behind a tree with a dancer's grace. As with the thugs, her kerchief hung around her neck. Gerald's breath caught in his throat. Her face was a perfect diamond shape, flaring at the cheekbones and tapering to a soft, pointed chin. Her eyes were sapphire blue, like almonds tilted at a slight angle, a hint of elven ancestry. She didn't wear a helmet, and her mocha-colored, shoulder-length hair bounced slightly as she stepped toward Filthy, who still rolled around in agony. "But I wouldn't worry about that. He didn't have much to knock out in any event."

Jehn knelt beside the man and put a glowing hand to his shoulder as a lock of her hair curled forward under her jaw line.

Gerald cursed himself. Sure, she was pretty, but this was no time to be paying attention to stupid things like that.

Pale-white light blazed from her overturned palm. Filthy stopped thrashing and grew quiet. Then, blinking a few times, he looked at her.

"Are you okay?" she asked, voice laden with concern.

"Yes, thank you, Lady."

"Thank blessed Thela. Now get back to camp."

"But—" he started.

"No. Not another word. Enough. Go."

Standing, he glanced at his comrades' bodies with a frown. Then, without another word, he trotted off through the forest.

The woman wiped her hand against a pair of gray breeches. "Poor thing hasn't had a proper bath in months, and it never probably occurs to him. It's tragic that gentle, decent men with good hearts like him end up out here, living in the same camp as thieves and murderers, with no one better to see to them."

"It was Jehn, right?" Gerald asked when he found his voice. "I hope you aren't planning to hit me from behind again."

The woman smiled. "I apologize for that. I was trying to keep you out of trouble during the raid. I underestimated your perseverance, though. Had I known, I might have tied you up as well."

"She's one of them, Ger. We should kill her." Zeke came up beside him, flames dancing above his hand.

"And what have I done to you to deserve a trip to the Dark World, Master Elf? Have I raised my hand against you? Or anyone else, for that matter?"

"You're Exceptas. You're all scum. Outlaw, brigand scum."

She snorted. "You have quite a clear-cut view of the world, master…." She paused, waiting for Zeke to supply a name.

After a moment, he said, "Ek'zae. Ek'zae Axeblight."

"Oh, Axeblight, is it?" Her eyes sparkled with mirth. "And how, exactly, did you come by that name? Because I don't remember you blighting the axe, exactly, when Tristan hit you with it."

"I, um—" he stammered.

"Let it go, Z," Gerald said. To Jehn, he asked, "And what is so simple about our view of the world?"

"The Exceptas are not what you think. Not all of us, anyway. Some of us had no other choice, no place to turn."

Gerald shook his head. "Everyone has a choice—"

Mehleese cut him off. "You're Outcast, aren't you?" Her voice was nearly a whisper. There was something different in it too. Something almost reverent.

Those sapphire eyes narrowed, a hint of warning. "Swear you'll never say that out loud again. They believe we're all dead. News that any of us survived would bring a wing of the king's army to Copperton Vale faster than eagles fly. And the last thing you want to see is a Purification Squad at work. They might put all of Copperton to the torch just to be thorough."

"What the fuh… freak is she talking about?" Gerald asked.

Mehleese sighed and *Released* her bow. "The King of the Western Realms, King Dalor, wasn't born royalty. He was a hunter first and then a merchant and somehow amassed a fortune large enough to raise an army capable of starting a civil war. But the old king, Rhandren Sophent, a wise man and a great king, was dying and knew it. Five years ago, then, rather than start a bloody war he knew he'd never see the end of, he abdicated the throne, gave up his claim, and fled with his family and supporters.

"Dalor took the throne and ignored Rhandren and his family for a few years. But eventually, just the threat of the old man was too much for the new king, so he had Rhandren killed. And everyone associated with the old king was named Outcast, enemy to the Realms, based on some questionable evidence and a litany of often-repeated half-truths."

"Oh, crap."

"It gets worse. The king commissioned special soldiers—bounty hunters with permission to kill in the king's name, basically—to hunt them down and kill them all. Not long after, he issued a proclamation that they'd been caught, tried, and executed for their misdeeds. That it was time for the Western Realms to move on. But apparently"—she fixed Jehn with a hard glare—"not all the Outcast were caught after all."

"Too many of us were, though. Most of us were put to the blade by Purifiers. All because a man lusted for a throne, and the Temple saw benefit to him having it. But since he took the crown, he's done nothing but let the Realms crumble."

"And the Exceptas are any better?" Gerald asked, rubbing his chin. "The other night, they nearly cleaned out Copperton's stores."

"The world is a difficult place," she replied. "We do the best we can with what's at hand. I certainly don't agree with many of Tristan's methods, but at least he isn't going to abandon the valley and leave it for the Guardians, undefended."

Zeke pinched his nose with his fingers. "What do the Guardians have to do with any of this? Or the Temple?"

"The Guardians are… well, now is not the time, Axeblight. I have to get back. We'll meet again, soon; I'm sure of it. Be careful, and avoid Tristan. He was furious with you the other night. And lady, remember what I said of mentioning the Outcast."

"Wait, Jehn—" Gerald started. But it was too late.

She'd disappeared. Again.

CHAPTER TWELVE

THE GHOST TOWN

After another hour in the woods collecting the nasty bits and pieces needed to fulfill their hunters' contracts, the trio trudged back to town with a bag nearly overflowing with Creeper shell fragments, diseased wolf tongues, and—for reasons no one wanted to speculate about—a dozen giant hare kidneys. The gruesome effort had been worth it, though. Not only were they set to collect some hard-earned coin, Gerald and Zeke had both gained significant experience and leveled up beyond novice status.

"You two might even be capable of going back out into the Ore Wood on your own without getting lost, killed, or both," Mehleese allowed as they stepped through the grand arch at the edge of town.

"Wow, careful, Mehl," Gerald muttered. "Piling such high praise on us is sure to give us big heads."

She laughed. "Don't worry, I'm sure I won't be comfortable letting you out of my sight for a while yet. I said you *might* not get killed. That's not the same as saying you're competent."

"Gee, thanks."

"What I'm not comfortable with," Zeke interjected, "is that Jehn chick dropping a reference to the Guardians and not explaining. Tristan said something about it too. What do you think is going on?"

"I don't know," Mehleese replied. "It could be nothing. Some nonsense rumor the Exceptas has hatched to further Tristan's goals, maybe?"

"But you don't say the Guardians are coming without a damned good reason. The likelihood of panic alone..."

Gerald stroked his goatee-covered chin. The Guardians were the second of the two main factions of Thelaroth's inhabitants. The first, the Favored, comprised humans, elves, dwarves, and gnomes. They shared the land making up the Western Realms and the continent of Venasier. The Sacred Scrolls spoke of the Favored as Thela's firstborn, the first races she made during the Molding of the Worlds from the Ether Clay.

The Guardians, on the other hand, came a thousand years ago, when Thela drew their home, the third continent, Akador, from the depths of Great Sea. Half-humanoid races, they were brought into the world to protect Thelaroth from the destructiveness of the Favored.

Before the Guardians, the Favored races waged almost constant war, paying little heed to the damage they did to one another and the land. Myth even held that the elven land of Venasier was once bright, beautiful, and bursting with life before a long-forgotten battle with the humans culminated in its near destruction. Now it was thought to be gray, bleak, and lifeless save for the elves themselves. Because they didn't allow other races to set foot there, though, only the elves knew for sure.

After the Blighting of Venasier, the Scrolls said, Thela

made Akador and breathed life into the seven Guardian races: the centians (half human, half horse), reptoules (half lizard, said to be descended from the World Dragons), ursals (half bear), avians (half bird), arialens (half ram), leputians (half hare), and oculans (humanoid giants with one eye).

To end the unceasing war among the Favored, the Guardians assembled a fearsome army, the Legion, and invaded the Western Realms with Thela's blessing, intent on conquering them. For the first time in their existence, the Favored allied together against the new enemy and fought the Legion to a draw. As part of the resulting treaty, the Great Bargain, the Guardians swore the Legion would remain on Akador so long as the Favored races lived and worked together to honor the land and Thela with it.

"Even I know they haven't left Akador for generations. If they came to the Western Realms, that would mean war, wouldn't it?"

"It would mean a great deal more than war," Mehleese murmured, "and none of it good."

"Something's wrong." Zeke stopped.

"That's what we're saying."

"No, there's something wrong here in Copperton. Look around."

The air was laced with hints of sulfur and char. Although the smell lacked the pungent, noxious force of real smoke, something was definitely burning. The source, though, had to be closer to the center of town. None of the buildings nearby were damaged, and there was no sign of panic. In fact, no one was around at all. A blanket of silence covered the streets.

Gerald gestured toward the armory. "Maybe the Smiths know what happened."

They checked the Smiths' home, but like the streets, the shop, their rooms, and the forge house were all empty. The hearth was still warm from the day's work, but there was no sign of struggle or any hint that the family had been taken by force. They were simply gone.

"I'm at a loss," Gerald mumbled, still stroking his chin. "What do we do?"

"Let's head to Town Hall," Mehleese suggested. "We need to turn in these critter parts and get paid anyway. With luck, someone there will be able to tell us what's going on."

They made their way across the quiet town in record time. Along the way, not a single living soul crossed their path. Not a shop-goer, a soldier, or even one of the dozens of ever-present, up-to-no-good townie kids. It was as if someone had picked up the town, shaken all the people out of it, and put it back into place while they were gone.

At last, in a tiny hut in the shadow of Town Hall on the edge of Copperton Square, they found the Keeper, who gave out quests and hunters' contracts, right where his character should be. The fastidious gnome with a dark-green bow tie and a broad, flat nose that didn't quite balance his pair of crooked eyeglasses didn't even look up at them as they handed him their scrolls and the bag of various bits and parts.

"Five contracts fulfilled," the Keeper said in a voice somehow half squeak and half grunt. "Here's your coin. The Crown thanks you for your dedication to keeping the Realms safe from dangerous wildlife, blah, blah, blah." He flipped a jingling bag to Zeke across the counter. "Are you interested in taking out additional contracts?"

"No, Master Keeper. But where is everyone?"

The gnome, still not looking up, scratched a mark in his book as he said, "I imagine they are all in the Hall, pretending to be having a town council meeting while they cower in fear and make woeful pleas to Thela in the misdirected hope that She'll make everything work itself out."

"Jesus, dude," Zeke said, "you sound like my great uncle Harold after Thanksgiving dinner and a bottle of bad scotch."

Behind them, Mehleese chuckled.

Gerald wasn't as amused. "What do you mean, 'while they cower in fear'? What are they hiding from?"

That finally earned the gnome's attention. "Don't you know?"

"Know what?"

"The Exceptas returned this afternoon. They set fire to the Trading House and kidnapped all the older children in town."

"Fuck, man. You're kidding, right?"

The gnome blinked at them. "I don't care for that tone. And do I strike you as a joke maker, Warrior?"

"I guess not. What happened to the blacksmith's daughter, Frega?"

"I am responsible for the assignment and collection of quests, not accounting for the town's population. If this Frega is an adult or a young child, you should find her inside if you can get in. If she is an older child or a teenager, though, she was almost surely taken by the Exceptas, which I believe I said once before. Please don't make me repeat myself. It's a waste of the king's valuable time."

Zeke gestured to the deserted Square. "Yeah, well, doesn't look like you're going to have much business today, Uncle Harold, so maybe lighten the fuck up some?"

"Your tone is even more hostile, Mage. Calm yourself."

"I'll show you hostile, you little...." Zeke flashed his hand, popping sparks above his flattened palm like a holiday sparkler.

Gerald waved at his friend to calm down. No use antagonizing the Contract Keeper. Shooting Gerald a disappointed frown, Zeke dropped his hands to his sides.

"Why are you out here, then? Aren't you worried? Shouldn't you take cover?"

"I am here in the name of King Dalor the Anointed as a representative of the King's Bank. Local brigands would know better than to interfere with my work. Also, my hut and I are protected by powerful shielding spells devised by the highest wizards in the king's court. Anyone attempting to accost me would learn quickly—and painfully—about regret."

"Typical," Mehleese muttered. "The king protects his money man but won't appoint a Sheriff to protect the town and its people."

The Contract Keeper ignored her and went back to whatever work he'd been doing before they showed up.

"Anything else you can tell us, buddy?" Gerald asked.

"No. Feel free to return if you'd like additional contracts."

"Yeah, I think we're done collecting spider ick for a while, sparkles. Thanks for the abundance of help."

"Then good day to you, and may you flourish in the king's peace," the gnome said as he went back to scratching at the document in front of him.

They stepped away from the contract hut and moved off to the Square just in front of Town Hall. "What a smug little prick. I kind of hate him a little," Zeke said. He paused and then added, "No, I take that back. I hate him a lot."

Mehleese shook her head. "Hating a gnome in service to the king is like hating bad weather. At best, it's pointless. At worst, it's counterproductive. Gnomes are task oriented, meticulous, and, as we've seen, dedicated to their assigned purpose with zeal. They have but the barest religious beliefs and instead funnel faith and fervor into their jobs. They are highly sought after as workers as a result. Don't blame him for his nature."

"Screw that," Zeke countered, still glaring at the oblivious, pint-sized Keeper in the hut. “A dragon’s nature is to destroy shit and horde shiny things. Everyone still hates them. So I’m going to go on hating on little Uncle Harold in there.”

“You have to admit, though,” Mehleese started, “that the difference between a dragon and—”

Gerald cut her off. “Makes no damn difference right now. We have to decide what to do.”

Zeke’s brow creased. “What do you mean? We need to go inside, find the others, and see what happened.”

Mehleese nodded in agreement. “Yes, we should see if the townspeople need our help.”

“I guess we could do that. But why? We’ve got the money we needed and enough experience to get to Riverglow City without getting hacked to pieces. The Exceptas Clan taking advantage of Copperton isn’t our problem. It’s the king’s problem. He can deal with it. We need to start looking for someone to send us home.“

“What?” Zeke spat. “That’s bullshit, Ger. We have to help these people.”

“Ek’zae is right, Goldenshield. We’ve been brought here, to this place, at this precise moment, for a reason.”

“My name is Gerald, Mehleese. And I don’t believe in any of that crap. We weren’t brought here by God or Thela or, hell, Zeus or Odin for that matter. Some old man with a theater prop hit me in the head. I’m not a hero. I just want to go home and take a nap.”

Mehleese’s face fell. “I see. Fine, then. Axeblight, would you stay with me to assist the people here?”

The question hung between them as the doors to Town Hall creaked open. Fayn Smith’s head poked out, and she spared a cautious look in both directions. Nodding, the woman slipped out of the building and rushed to cover the distance between her and the trio on the Square.

"Master Goldenshield, I have been appointed as a representative of the Town's Council to ask you to appear before the ongoing Council meeting."

Gerald sighed. "Fayn, I'm sorry, but I was just about to leave for Riverglow. Whatever the Council wants from me, I'm afraid I have to disappoint them."

The Smith's wife studied her worn boots for a moment and then turned her face up to catch his eyes. Her own were red rimmed and shiny, as if she was desperate to hold back a torrent of tears.

"You have to help us, Goldenshield. They've taken Frega. You have to get my baby girl back for me."

CHAPTER THIRTEEN

THE TOWN COUNCIL

UNCLE HAROLD THE CURMUDGEONLY GNOME hadn't exaggerated. The entire population of Copperton was gathered inside Town Hall. Once through the main doors, Gerald, Zeke, and Mehleese were surrounded by grim-faced townspeople, most with vacant, doleful expressions. The town was perched over an emotional collapse held at bay by the thinnest of shields.

"Make way, make way for Council business!" Fayn barked ahead of them, pushing through the crowd as if twice the size of her husband. She seemed to relish giving dark looks and a good shove here and there when someone didn't move out of her way fast enough. But then, Gerald couldn't pretend to understand what she was feeling. Must have been comforting to have the crowd to direct her anger toward.

After fighting through the crowd in the lobby, they entered the Council Hall, where the press of bodies was even thicker. It gave way, finally, to a small open space before a raised dais holding a long table. Seated at the table, nine grim faces, five women and four men, watched them approach.

Their escort stopped and cleared her throat. "May it please the Council Seats, the watchers were correct. Goldenshield and his friend have returned as we need them. I brought them as you requested."

Bergan Smith, sitting at the table among the other Council members, nodded to his wife. Next to him, at the center of the table, a plump woman with a weathered face and a steel-gray bun of hair said, "We thank you, Fayn. That is all for now."

The blacksmith's wife bowed her head and turned away from the table. Pausing as she passed Gerald, she took one of his hands and squeezed it before wiping at her eyes and slipping back into the mass of people.

"Lord Goldenshield," the older woman said, "as the Speaker for the Council of Copperton, we appreciate you coming. If you wouldn't mind, please ask your, um, *elf* friend to wait outside until our business is concluded." She shot Zeke a disapproving glare.

Gerald's face warmed in anger. Being led in here like a calf to slaughter was one thing, but if they thought he'd let them treat Z like a second-class citizen, they were going to learn otherwise. The hard way.

"If you want to talk to me, lady, the *elf*," he said, raising his voice to stress the word, "stays. We work together."

She sniffed and pressed her lips into a thin line. "So be it. But his kind are known for bad behavior, and I will tolerate none in this Hall."

Gerald rolled his eyes and smirked. Poor woman was delusional if she thought that Zeke was the ill-mannered one. "We can all trust he'll behave."

"Very well. As you are no doubt aware, you have come back to town to find us in crisis."

"Look, lady, I know that—"

She raised a hand to stop him. "Please, my lord, we have a few questions before you speak."

"Go ahead," he sighed. Zeke elbowed him in the ribs.

"What the hell?" Gerald whispered.

"Enough with the damn sighs all over the place," his friend said under his breath. "With all the huffing you've done today, you sound like a teenage girl mooning over a boy band poster."

He didn't sigh that much.

Did he?

"My lord," the Speaker started again, "we have already heard testimony that when you arrived in town last night, you happened across a group of those filthy Exceptas raiding the Smith's armor shop and home. Is that correct?"

"I didn't happen upon it, um—Lady Speaker?—but I did happen upon Smith's daughter, Frega, who told me her home was under attack."

"*Madam* Speaker, if it pleases my lord. I am by no means a lady."

For some reason, half the crowd chuckled at that. The Speaker flashed a smirk herself before continuing. "And when you learned of the attack, your first reaction was to intercede?"

"Well, not exactly. As Tristan and the Exceptas had the Smiths bound and gagged, I was trying to determine how best to put a stop to the Clan without getting anyone killed. But when my friend arrived—"

"Is that your… elf friend?" Again, she made the word sound like a disease.

"Yes. My friend—that is, my *elf* friend—the great Mage, Ek'zae Axeblight, came upon the raid too. And together we had the strength to prevent the Exceptas from getting away with the weapons."

"And in the course of this, you stood up to Tristan Kingsbane?"

"I'd say Ek'zae did more standing up than I did, even taking a wallop from that beast of an axe the outlaw carries. But, yes, together, we held him and the other thugs at bay and kept them from completing their haul."

"Axeblight, does he speak the truth for you? Is this a fair account of the event?"

Zeke nodded. "I swear upon the mists of my ancestors and upon on the roots of my people, may we forever be blessed to walk beneath sun and moon at Thela's wish, Goldenshield speaks the truth."

The Speaker nodded. "Thank you both. We will confer for a moment." Not waiting for a reply, she turned to Bergan at her right, already saying something the blacksmith seemed to agree with. At the same time, the other members of the Council whispered to each other. The crowd, sensing a critical decision was under debate, began to chatter as well, filling the hall with the low hum of unintelligible voices.

Giving Zeke an accusing glare, Gerald whispered, "Laying it on a bit thick there, weren't you?"

"What?"

"That freaking oath. The sun and moon, for God's sake? You forgot to mention the rivers and the butterflies."

Zeke started to reply, but Mehleese beat him to it. "For someone claiming to have played the game, you don't know very much, Goldenshield. That's the traditional Oath to Thela used by elves across Thelaroth. In an official capacity like this, if he *hadn't* answered that way, they would have thought him lying. They have little enough trust in elves as it is."

Gerald threw his hands into the air. "Jesus, of course not. Why would you trust an elf? The whole dirty, thieving race is just waiting to steal your candy and kiss your girlfriend under the maple tree."

"Well," his friend admitted, "a thousand years ago, my people *did* kidnap the king of the human realms and triggered the war that enraged Thela enough to create the Guardian races. You knew that, right?"

The Warrior shrugged.

"Did you seriously not know that? My God, how did you not? At some point, we need to sit down and go through game lore before you embarrass all of us with your ignorance. Or get us killed."

"Nope," Gerald scoffed, "no thank you. In fact, there's another reason to get the hell back home as soon as we can. I almost flunked out of high school because I couldn't pass *real* history. I'll never remember *Realm Quest* history."

"We'll argue about it later. I think they're doing something."

On the dais, the Speaker looked at each Council member one at a time and asked a noticeably short question. Each person replied with a word or two and a nod. One man in thick crimson robes on the far right of the table, shook his head and grimaced as if he'd been forced to swallow a handful of live worms.

Then the Speaker turned to Gerald. "Lord Goldenshield?"

He forced himself not to sigh again. "Madam Speaker, as I've said countless times before, I'm no lord. And I don't mean to sound rude, but if you could please explain why I've been asked to come before you?"

"For this reason: although there is still some debate among the Council Seats as to whether we have the authority to do so, we've voted by a count of seven for and two against to appoint you the acting Sheriff of Copperton Vale. At least until such a time as the king appoints a permanent one by royal decree."

The crowd erupted. Glad whoops and shouts of "hurrah" spread through the Hall and outer foyer, balanced by an equal number of boos and curses. The hum of conversation wove through both as townspeople discussed the announcement with whoever happened to be standing next to them.

Gerald, for one, was glad for the outburst. His tongue had gone slack, and his mouth felt like it contained an entire canister of sawdust. He fumbled to reply, but the words slipped from his mind as if greased. These people couldn't be serious, could they? He'd been around town less than a day, and they wanted to name him Sheriff? What did the Sheriff of Copperton Vale even do? And what insanity made them want *him* to do it? Zeke had been the one who stood up to Tristan. He should be Sheriff. Hell, he'd love the job.

From the corner of his eye, he stole a glance at his friend, who'd taken to being an elf like a fish to water. Zeke beamed back, no doubt thrilled to the tips of his pointy elf ears about the announcement.

The Speaker stood up from her seat, grabbed a nearby gavel, and began to beat it against the table. "Order! Order! The Council will have order!"

A hollow dread filled the pit of Gerald's stomach as the mob of townsfolk grew quiet. What were the odds they'd make it out of the building without being attacked, no matter what he said?

As the crowd settled to a low murmur, the Speaker dropped into her chair and set the mallet aside. "Now, then, how will you respond?"

Gerald coughed twice. "Madam Speaker, you said the vote fell seven to two. If I may ask, who voted for and who voted against me? I'd like to know why."

She gestured at the blacksmith seated next to her, whose tremendous frame more than filled the space. "Bergan Smith led those voting for you. He is a well-respected member of this community, and his account of the incident last night stood as firm proof for the votes cast in favor. By his account, you are, if nothing else, well suited for the position."

Standing up, Bergan added, "I know it's cold comfort for some of you that I nominated a man no one knows, but in the past two days, we've been raided by the Exceptas for both trade goods and our very kin, and not a single one of us has lifted a finger against them. Not a single one of us, then, myself included, is worthy to carry the Shield. And beyond that, this man came to town yesterday"—he paused and took something out of a sack on the table in front of him—"wearing what I can only reckon is a sign from Thela herself." His hand shot into the air, holding a familiar, shining golden shield.

"Oh, bloody hell," Gerald muttered to himself.

The mass of townspeople erupted at Smith's theatrics, shouting everything from "It is a sign!" and "Merciful Thela!" to "Hogwash!" The Speaker slammed her gavel over and over to bring the crowd back under control and threatened to send them all away if there was another outburst before the Council finished its business.

With control of the room once again in hand, she continued, addressing Gerald, "As you see, some here believe you were carried to us on the Breath of Thela herself to shield us in this moment of trial and the graver moments still to come."

The soft chatter of the crowd rose at that but quieted after a stern look of warning.

"And the votes against?"

She nodded at the Council member in the robes who'd given the emphatic shake of his head. "Councilman Hendel Prior, the representative for the Temple of Thela in Copperton, is opposed to the temporary appointment of *any* Sheriff, either you or someone we know better."

Nodding, the robed man on the end grumbled, "It's the king's business, and it's none of ours. We've no right to call on anyone to carry the Sheriff's Shield."

"As I told you, your objection has been noted, Lord Prior. We'll be sure King Dalor is aware that the Temple stood in his defense, even though his lack of action is a detriment to the people the Temple is committed to serve. Now, if we may continue?"

The Templeman huffed and gave the Speaker a dismissive wave.

"That's one of the votes against me, Madam," Gerald said. "The other?"

"It was my own," she announced, raising her voice enough to carry through both rooms. "Your conduct last night may have been an example to us all, but still, we don't know half as much about you as we should if we are to confer the title of Sheriff. The Sheriff is not only our protector but a lord throughout the Vale. He carries power and authority that should not be handed to a stranger. Who can say you aren't worse than that Exceptas outlaw, Kingsbane?"

"You're a wise woman, Madam Speaker. I wouldn't appoint me either. I'm too young and much too irresponsible to carry out the duties of the Sheriff of Copperton Vale."

The buzz of the crowd rose again, forcing him to raise his voice over it. "I'm deeply honored and thank the Council for their faith, but I will have to decline this appointment."

Without another word, he spun, worked his way into the thick crowd, and disappeared, leaving eight stunned faces and one smug sneer at the Council table behind him.

CHAPTER FOURTEEN

THE JOB

GERALD FIDGETED ON THE WOBBLY wooden stool, which had to be the most uncomfortable damned thing he'd ever sat on in his life. The thing might look made of wood, but it had to be chiseled out of granite or marble or diamonds or something. It had no padding or back of any kind and rocked on uneven legs like a drunk on a two-day bender. He had half a mind to stand at the bar rather than subject himself to such torture, but after the Council meeting, his nerves were guitar-string tight. He would have buckled and fallen over in less than five minutes.

He gestured to the barman, a short, stout fellow with a stained shirt a bit worse for wear than the hand-me-down Bergan had given him. "Anudder drink," Gerald muttered. Another half hour of warlock spirits—the strongest liquor the Roost and Pig carried—and he'd be falling down whether he was sitting or standing and calling *himself* Goldenshield, to boot.

The Innkeeper set a small cup of cloudy, yellowish liquid on the bar in front of him. "You should maybe go easy on that stuff, buddy. I've heard stories of it eating your brain from the inside out."

"Goot," he mustered, hiccupping in the other man's face. The barman shook his head in disgust and stomped away.

Gerald tossed back the latest shot and slammed the empty cup back on the bar with a self-satisfied nod. Something tapped him on the shoulder, and he started, almost careening off the lopsided stool. "Whazzit?"

Zeke and Mehleese stood next to him, glaring as if he was torturing kittens.

He turned away and slumped forward onto the bar. "Shouldn't sneak up," he said with a grunt. *Shudin shneek.*

"Good God," Zeke complained. "You're hammered."

"Snot true. Mostly." It came out as "moessly."

Mehleese, clicking her tongue, dug around inside her shoulder bag and pulled out a short, dark, stoppered bottle. After pulling the cork with a pop, she sniffed the contents and then poured a shot of something pine green and as thick as curdled milk into Gerald's now-empty cup. "Drink that."

"Nope, mayam. Gotta bartender already." He gestured at the Innkeeper at the other end of the bar, who was doing his best to ignore the three of them.

"Drink it," Mehleese said again, "or I'll pour it down your throat."

With an exaggerated turn of his head, Gerald squinted at her with one eye. "You're a laady, sho you're looky," he drawled, "or I'd punsh one of you. The miggle one, firs."

"Drink that," she replied. "Then you can try to hit me."

"Itsa bet!" He turned to the green drink, picked it up with a shaky hand, poured it into his mouth, and swallowed hard. In seconds, his face changed from dimwitted and slack-jawed to screwed up in revulsion.

"Hold it together," Mehleese advised. "And don't puke.

That just makes it worse. Keep it down for another ten seconds."

With both eyes open now—although still squinting against the bitter taste of whatever that was—Gerald shot her a look of unadulterated hate as he turned a pale shade close to the green hue of the liquid itself. Fire like a dragon's breath raged in his belly, and a painful, tingling sensation spread through him.

As she'd said, though, ten seconds later, the fire died out and the tingling subsided. Not that he felt *good.* He didn't, not by a long shot. His head was pounding, his tongue was dry as a creek bed in summer, and his stomach quivered in revolt. But he could think using whole words, and the room no longer spun around him.

"What the hell was that?" he asked, rubbing his temples.

"Elf liquor," she replied, a hint of a chuckle in her eye. "It's a type of savannah grass plus bark from a special tree the forest elves harvest, made into a paste and then suspended in a liquid you don't want to know any more about. It tastes like the plague and makes you feel like death for half a minute, but if you can manage that, it'll clear your body of warlock spirits."

"God, I've never had a hangover as bad as how I feel right now. I'd have been better sleeping it off."

The Ranger smiled again. "That's right, you twenty-something kids don't get hangovers, do you? Well, now you know how it's going to feel when you get older."

Waving at the bartender, Gerald mouthed the word *water*. "If this is how it's going to feel when I get older, I'll quit drinking now. Ugh. Next time, just leave me be."

"Hungover or not, we need you sober now, Ger," Zeke said. "We can't wait around for you to pass out and get over it the old-fashioned way."

"Need me? What's the rush? Riverglow will be there tomorrow."

"You can't run off to Riverglow. You have to take the Sheriff's appointment."

"What the fuck, Z? I don't *have* to do anything. All I want is a one-way ticket home, remember?"

"But these people need you!"

"Bullshit. They don't even know me! And I don't know them. Or anything about this place or what the hell is happening. What I do know is that they deserve better than me to take care of them. Hell, I could barely take care of myself in the real world, where my biggest worry was making a rent payment and not getting caught fucking around in my cruiser at three a.m. This place has a clan of bad guys who kidnap an entire town's kids and God knows what other problems. I can't be their Sheriff. I have no idea where to start."

"You can too. We'll help you."

"Fuck you. You do it, then."

Zeke clenched his jaw. "They didn't appoint me."

"Maybe they should have."

"No, they shouldn't have. I'm an elf. And a wizard on top of that. Humans don't trust elves, and nobody trusts magic users. We're either one spell away from trying to take over or one miscast away from killing ourselves and everyone in a ten-foot radius."

"Whatever. The point is, I don't want the job. I don't want anything here tying me down. I'm getting out as fast as I can. I've got stuff to do with my *real* life."

"Bullshit," Zeke spat. "Yesterday, you couldn't have cared less about much of anything back there. But now all of the sudden you think you've got a shot with a girl you've been following around like a pup—"

"Goldenshield," Mehleese cut in, "did it ever occur to you

that maybe this is happening for a reason? That maybe there's some truth to the idea that Thela brought you here?"

"*Thela*?" he shot back. "Fuck *Thela*. I didn't get stuck here by some made-up digital goddess so I could be the town's hero. Jesus, are you stupid? There. Is. No. Thela. Christ, Mehleese, or whatever your real name is, I didn't think you were as dumb as everyone else around here."

"Goddammit, Gerald, that's enough!" Zeke barked. "All you ever think about is yourself. You've done nothing but whine and mope since yesterday because there's no career path in this place that'll let you sit on your ass for forty years and not lift a goddamn finger! Does the thought of having to do something with yourself scare you that much? Are you so afraid that when faced with the idea of helping someone, your only two thoughts are to get drunk and then run away? Jesus, what happened?"

"Nothing. I got older. And smarter. And if that offends your fantasyland view of life, that's your problem, not mine. But don't stand there and give me a bunch of sanctimonious crap about how I need to live. Try living your own life for once. Fuck, there's an idea. Maybe then you'd have had something to do on Friday night besides play video games by yourself. Maybe you wouldn't have been so bored you had to get in the way of me doing my job at the Quik Mart. Maybe if you had a goddamn life, none of this shit would have happened!"

"*I* don't have a life? Fuck you, *Lord Goldenshield*! The reason I don't have a life is because of you, dipshit. You're such an immature prick. It's no wonder Robby and Derek never find time to play with us online anymore. They grew up, became adults, and probably got tired of dealing with you being a dick!"

"What do they have to do with this? Fuck them. They

graduated and changed, just like everyone else. They're assholes now, that's all."

"They aren't assholes, douche nozzle. They're getting on with their lives. They're working on families and building careers. That's what I should be doing, too, instead of wasting my time in the vain hope you'd quit being the same lazy prick you've been since middle school."

"Watch it, asshat. You keep it up and I'll knock your pointy ears flat."

"You know what? Fuck it. Let's go. It's about time somebody knocked you and your twelve-year-old's ego down a few pegs anyway."

Taking several steps back from the bar, Zeke raised his hands. The crack of sparks filled the air.

"Zeke, I am not about to—" Before he could finish, a mass of fire the size of a billiard ball slammed into his chest. Nearly a dozen health points clacked away.

"Oh, that's it. I'm done with you." Gerald stood up, knocking his barstool over with a clatter. Bergan's borrowed hammer appeared in his hand in a blink. He didn't even realize he'd thought it there. He rushed toward his red-faced friend, shouting.

Another, smaller fireball shot from Zeke's hands and exploded against the shoulder of Gerald's weapon hand in a shower of heat and light. He staggered from the blow, and another six or eight points ticked off. Worse, his arm went as limp as cooked pasta. The hammer slid through suddenly numb fingers. With a quick thought, though, it flashed from his right hand to his left, and he jabbed it into his friend's stomach.

Zeke bent at the waist and fell backward. "Oof!"

"Stop this, you idiots!" Mehleese barked.

Gerald ignored her and advanced on his friend. "Come on, get up!"

Scrambling back on the floor, the elf put a few feet between them and popped back up. Grimacing in rage, he thrust his hands forward with a shout.

But nothing happened.

Gerald froze and raised his off arm, which still tingled but was at least no longer useless. The expected gout of flames, though, didn't shoot across the room. Opposite him, Zeke stared at his hands in shocked confusion.

All of Gerald's Combat Power—as well as his anger—drained away. What the fuck were they doing? This was Zeke.

"What's wrong, Z?"

The words brought the elf back to the duel, wiping the uncertainty from his face. "Oh, *now* you give a shit about someone else?" With the wiggle of his finger, he produced a wand from the folds of his robes. Bursts of white light shot out from the wand's end, one every few seconds.

The balls of light struck Gerald in the chest and popped in a stinging jolt of energy. As he flinched, a pair of points ticked off his health with each hit, but the shots were more annoyance than serious attack.

"Zeke, seriously, quit it. It's embarrassing."

Zeke ground his teeth together and screwed his face up in a distorted scowl. The wand disappeared again, and the elf raised his hands over his head, arms wide. Swirling flames spun into existence over his head but faded to nothing. "Fuck!" he screamed. "Why doesn't anything work?" Grabbing a nearby table, he wrestled it up and over, sending it crashing sideways to the floor.

Gerald *Released* his hammer.

Zeke, gasping from the effort of overturning the table, stared at the Warrior, his face a fiery red and his eyes burning with rage. Gerald returned the look, saying nothing. He was finished acting like an idiot.

As the Mage stood, huffing for air, the torch-red fury on his face began to seem comical. The corners of Gerald's mouth twitched upward.

He looked away, trying to keep the giggles and crows of mirth that threatened to bubble out buried inside.

But he couldn't. A soft chuckle slipped from his mouth. And grew louder. And louder still until he was doubled over, laughing so hard he couldn't breathe. Eyes clouded with tears, he looked up at Zeke, half expecting him to lob a shower of molten flame across the room.

Instead, the elf had tears streaming down his delicate, no-longer-twisted face.

"What the fuck are we doing?" he asked when the cackles dwindled to throaty chuckles and, finally, a few lingering giggled breaths.

"You're both acting like Thela-forsaken children," Bergan Smith replied, glaring from the door beside Mehleese, arms folded across his barrel-shaped chest. With a great, mournful breath, he shook his head and fixed his eyes on Gerald. "I vouched for you before the whole Council, and this is the best you can do?"

The Warrior lumbered, head down, back to the bar. He righted the stool he'd knocked over and then took several long pulls from the flask of water the barman had left.

"I didn't ask you to say anything about me. I can't do the job you and your people need. As you can see, it's all I can do to get through the day without hurting the people I care about. I can't be your Sheriff."

"You may think that," the older man replied, "but a man doesn't know the fullness of his gifts until he's been tested at the anvil. And that testing can take years. You ain't been through it yet. Maybe you're right. Maybe you can't do it. But something brought you to my home when my girl told you it was being raided. You could have walked away, but deep down, you knew what had to be done."

"Master Smith, I—"

"You followed her," he repeated, ignoring Gerald's interruption, "and did what you had to. You stopped them from taking my life and my family away. Because you knew it was right, even if it wasn't easy."

"Look, maybe we did, but only because—"

"Because you knew it was right," he repeated. "And that's what we need a Sheriff for. To see to what's right to keep the town safe, even if it ain't easy. And trust me, son, this Exceptas business is just the start. The days are gonna get much darker around here before it's all over."

"Then why are you so hell-bent on putting a damned fool like me in charge? There has to be someone else. Someone with experience. Someone who believes in themselves."

Looming over him, the smith put his hand on Gerald's shoulder. "You don't get it. I don't want someone who *wants* the job. I want someone who will bring me back my girl just because that *is* the job."

"I—" He watched as a pair of tears slipped from the big man's eyes and slid silently down each cheek. He looked from Zeke to Mehleese and back again. Both waited, expectant, hanging on the momentary pause. God, he just wanted to go home. Just wanted to finally take his shot with Brooke. But then, these were kids they were talking about. Could he live with himself later, knowing he'd done nothing?

Gerald slumped onto the stool he'd just made upright. "I'm sorry. I won't do it. Can't do it. But. Because Frega needs someone to bring her back, I will do *that*. But that's it. No titles. No appointments. And if the king sends a real Sheriff before it's over, I'm off the hook."

Relief lit the three faces surrounding him. Zeke let loose a jubilant cry of "woot!"

"But Master Smith?"

"Son, my friends call me Bergan."

Gerald gave him a half grin. "Well, Bergan, if you want me to bring your daughter back, I'm in desperate need of a better weapon. I expect your shop will be happy to offer one at a substantial discount?" Then, with a mischievous wink, he added, "You know, since we're friends and all?"

CHAPTER FIFTEEN

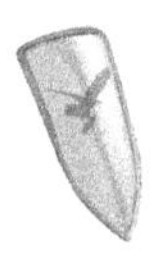

THE DEPARTURE

MEHLEESE WHISTLED AS SHE ENTERED the forge house, clapping her leather-clad hands together in appreciation. "My, my, don't you boys clean up pretty."

Gerald, startled by her arrival, spun around. Decorative spikes extending from the elbows of his shining new armor crashed against a full rack of smithy tools, knocking half of them to the floor in a jiggling chorus of metal against metal.

"Shit!"

"What is that, five times now that you've knocked everything off of a rack?" Zeke asked, a full smile beaming from beneath a new navy-blue Wizard's robe.

"All this armor crap weighs a ton, and these bracers and the shoulder pauldrons have those stupid spike details that stick out way too far. I keep forgetting how much space I need just to move without crashing into things. Why can't I just have a robe? Is it too late for me to change classes? I want to be a Thief instead of a Warrior. I think I'd rather sneak around."

Mehleese chuckled. "I don't think a Thief would make a very good Sheriff. Besides, we don't have time to retrain you. As it is, you've only learned about half of what you need to be a Warrior and not die immediately. We'll have to stick with that."

While the new armor made him feel like a turtle, it was a marked improvement over the old shirt that had been his only protection earlier. At least he wasn't wearing hand-me-downs any longer. Since they'd had no luck figuring out what was causing the occasional Steel Skin Blessing, the armor would be critical for the quest at hand.

Zeke's new robe was a stark improvement also. While the amount of protection a simple robe offered was limited, this robe was thicker and much more durable than his first one. It was also resistant to fire, ice, lightning, and some types of poison. Out of gratitude, he'd washed the one he'd "borrowed" when they arrived and returned it to the original owner's storage bin when no one was watching.

On top of their fancy new clothes and armor, when Gerald returned the borrowed hammer and started haggling over a much finer, newer one, Bergan proved that he did look out for his friends. Gerald suspected the man would have charged him a fortune for that rusty short sword the day before—when he wasn't about to go rescue the blacksmith's daughter. Today, though, Smith sold him a shiny, newly finished war hammer for barely a handful of copper.

The provisions were covered by the coin they'd made from collecting on their hunters' contracts. On top of that, Gerald had been given a small purse of gold—actual gold!—as an advance for taking on the task of going out to save the town's children. The Council had also offered him the Sheriff's office on the square opposite Town Hall to work out of, if needed, with living quarters above. Plenty of space for him and Zeke and maybe Mehleese as well, although he wasn't sure whether she needed a place to stay or not. Then again, since sleep wasn't any more necessary here than food, why would they need either the offices or the rooms?

After buying his chain mail, a new set of leather armor for Mehleese, and upgraded weapons for both at the Smiths' shop, they continued their shopping spree around town. Zeke picked out his new robe and materials for enchanting, and then, together, they gathered up the assortment of supplies that might prove essential during their quest into the Exceptas' lair.

The most expensive things on their list were mounts for Gerald and Zeke, and those were a necessity. The Clan had half a day's lead on them already. While no one could say why the Exceptas had abducted all the young people in town, most were quick to venture a guess, and they largely agreed it was the root of some sinister plot. More than half even suggested blood magic and sacrifices. Even if that was nonsense, speed was crucial.

Gerald's mount was a proud bay warhorse that towered over him. But he needed a name, and the Warrior was baffled. "We should call him something like Justice," Zeke suggested. "That's a solid name for the Sheriff's mount."

"I'm not the Sheriff. I'm just doing the Sheriff's job this one time. For Frega. And I'm not giving my horse an old TV show name. No clichés either."

"It's not clichéd."

Gerald said nothing but instead stared at the beast and shook his head. "No. Definitely not Justice. Zero. We're calling him Zero."

"Zero? Why Zero?"

"Because that's how many fucks I'll have left to give about this place after we get back with the kids."

Zeke shot him a hard glare but didn't argue.

Mehleese had a mount already, and at her summons, a filly two-thirds of Zero's size appeared. Solus, her swift, sure-footed dapple gray, nuzzled her owner's palm in contentment.

Zeke went red with embarrassment again, glancing at his own mount. Because he was an elf, just as in the digital version of *Realm Quest*, he'd be racing across the country on a unicorn. And although the animal was a beautiful ivory specimen, he had a disposition so nasty it could sour milk with one grumpy look. The creature almost bit Zeke's hand off when he joked of naming him Glitter. Conversely, the unicorn seemed to enjoy it—almost taking on a haughty sneer—when they settled on the name Demon.

Still smiling at Gerald's awkward movement, Mehleese said, "Before you knock anything else over, they're waiting for you outside, Goldenshield."

"Let's get this over with," he muttered.

The three of them filed out of the forge house, with Gerald coming last. Arrayed in a semicircle in the yard between them and the shop building, the nine members of the Town Council waited with tight mouths and solemn eyes. A crowd of townsfolk were packed in the spaces around the building, spilling out into the road behind it—not as many as had been wedged into Town Hall at the Council meeting earlier, but still, most of the population of Copperton.

"Lord Goldenshield," the Speaker began.

"I'm not—" Gerald started before the woman's sharp gesture made him freeze.

"By taking this quest, you will, whether you like it or not, represent the Town of Copperton in an attempt to save our children. At the very least, that calls for recognition of your nobility as a man. You will, then, until you prove otherwise, be addressed as lord, even by members of this Council. And

I will not hear another word about it. Do I make myself understood?"

Behind him, Zeke coughed, making a poor attempt to stifle a chuckle.

Gerald cleared his throat, and with little other choice, he said, "It looks like I have little choice, Madam Speaker. Please continue."

"Very well. You have been offered by this Council an appointment to the office of Sheriff of Copperton Vale. I will ask you again, do you accept the office?"

He almost sighed, but mindful of Zeke's warning earlier, held it back. "I refuse."

"And yet, you will still seek to return our missing family to us?"

"My friends and I will try, yes."

"So be it. Bring it forward, please?"

Fayn Smith, wearing what had to be her finest dress and with her hair piled in a formal coil, stepped forward from behind her husband. Her hands were covered in snowy gloves reaching halfway to her elbows. In those gloves, she held a burnished gold shield as tall as she was. A reflection of the sun setting behind them flashed against its surface, making it burn with a honey-colored glow unlike anything Gerald had ever seen. Set in the center of the shield was an eagle in flight carrying a scroll. It was a perfect, although much larger, version of his Simmsville Police Department badge.

Nothing else in the world existed at that moment. He heard himself gasp.

"What… what is that?" he stammered.

"The Shield carried by the Sheriff of Copperton Vale," the older woman replied. "Even if you won't accept the office, you should have every advantage possible if you're going to face the Exceptas on their ground. We offer you the Shield of the Vale, then, both to keep you safe and to demonstrate you represent the people of the Vale in standing against the Clan."

Coming to stand between the Speaker and himself, Fayn raised her hands over her head and slammed the pointed foot of the shield against the soft ground. She drove it into the earth half a foot or more and then stepped back, leaving the shield standing upright in front of Gerald. His fingers twitched with the urge to reach out and touch it, to pick it up and sling it over his arm. Something about it tugged at him, as if it were a living thing, calling out to be put to its intended use.

"Place your hands on the Shield. Normally the Sheriff would speak an oath before accepting it, but the situation here is unusual," someone—the Speaker—said.

Numb all over, he nodded and extended his hands. The metal was hot to the touch and hummed with unseen energy.

"Blessed Thela, shine your Light and bestow your Strength upon this shield and the arm that holds it. Make this man a servant of your glory and an instrument of your will. We beg of you, merciful Thela, see this man and this shield returned to us, along with our missing families and friends."

Gerald blinked, unsure what to do next. He held a hand out to shake. "Um, thanks, Madam Speaker."

The crowd held its collective breath. Expectant.

Eyes growing wide and dark, the Speaker, not daring to say anything else, ignored the offered hand and mouthed something Gerald didn't understand.

In confusion, he started to ask her to repeat whatever she'd said. Before he could, Zeke grabbed one of the spikes at his elbow. Pulling close to his ear, he whispered, "She said, 'Take the Shield.'"

Understanding lit Gerald's face. He reached forward to grasp the top of the half-buried shield with both hands.

Take Shield

It blinked, flashing up from the ground and into his outstretched hands, slamming into them as if it was shot from a cannon. The force was unlike anything he'd experienced before when *Taking* an item. That same hum of electricity now pulsed through his hands and arms, coursing through his body like a second heartbeat, pumping in harmony with his own.

Turning the shield outward to face the Council and the crowd, he held it up over his head.

He needed to say something. The occasion called for an uplifting speech, one full of promise and support. Maybe even a battle cry. But his tongue was frozen, and his head was stuffed with that rising, pulsing buzz. All he could do was hold the shield so the people around them could see it.

The feeling swelled within him, growing stronger and stronger and louder and louder. It was the hum of a plague of locusts so thick it would black out the sun, droning angrily from the dark corner just behind his eyes. The unbridled charge of an old-time locomotive racing out of control, steaming and thudding and cranking and whooshing. It was the sizzling, crackling potential of a lightning storm, struggling for release, desperate to unleash a torrent of destruction. The force of an ocean tempest, crashing wave after devastating wave headlong against a shoreline, reducing everything in its path to tiny motes of coarse sand.

When his head was certain to explode from the whirlwind of noise and vibration, when it grew to be more than he could contain, he shouted a primal, instinctive roar that shook the Town Council, the population of Copperton, and the nearby buildings on their foundations.

With the ferocious cry, he hurled a wave of power outward, from either the shield or him or both. The wave raced through the crowd in an expanding ring, an unseen blast that ruffled hair, knocked off hats, and drove the unsuspecting a step back to keep their balance. As it passed, the people let out a great cheer, clapping and hooting for Goldenshield.

Equip Shield

The heavy piece of golden plate appeared strapped to his left arm, no longer a separate piece of armor but now somehow part of him, an extension of the whole.

With a smile, the Speaker offered her right hand, grasping his arm just below the elbow.

"What the hell was that?" he asked.

Leaning in, she said, "Thela approves. She gives you her Blessing."

Eyes wide, Gerald pulled back. What had he gotten himself into?

Night fell and stretched out, testing his patience as the people of town lined up to wish him and his friends well. Although every second they wasted could be disastrous for the kids, protocol demanded he accept the congratulations of anyone wanting to take his arm and offer Thela's Blessing.

He bristled at the delay. Precious seconds, minutes, hours slipped away while he stood trapped, grinding his teeth, and trying not to lash out at the Coppertonians wasting time.

By the time the last one clapped him on the shoulder, the moon hung over them in the sky. The Council members then each took a turn to wish the party good fortune, Zeke and Mehleese included. The exception, of course, was Templeman Hendel Prior, who refused to take a step nearer than was necessary, as if either the shield or the man that bore it was somehow cursed.

Finally, after even the Council had given a word or two, Bergan Smith stepped in front of Gerald with his wife, Fayn, still wearing her snowy gloves and her best dress. The smith took his arm, and his wife, after slipping off a glove, placed her hand against the hot metal of the Shield. They said nothing but stood together—not as town leaders but as husband and wife, mother and father—heads held low and faces twisted with the searing, hollow pain of missing a daughter.

Fayn mumbled a soft prayer, too low for him to hear. When she finished, they raised their eyes to him, both with cheeks shining with tears. Releasing him, the couple took a step back.

"Lord Goldenshield," Bergan said, his deep voice little more than a croak, "I beg you, bring my girl back home."

CHAPTER SIXTEEN

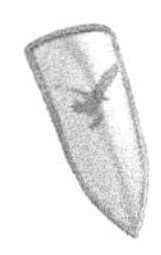

THE TRAIL

THE NARROW PATH THROUGH THE dense Ore Wood crowded the three travelers and their mounts into a tight cluster, with Mehleese at the point and Gerald and Zeke riding side by side.

"Are we sure about northeast?" Zeke cast an uncertain glance up the dark road ahead.

"Yes," Mehl muttered over her shoulder. "We don't know much else, but we do know that."

The Council had told them about rumors of an Exceptas hideout to the north, somewhere beyond the forest's reach. A torch oil–selling acquaintance of Mehleese's with nervous eyes and quick fingers whispered that they'd find the Clan somewhere in the foothills of the Iron Spikes, the mountain range that separated Copperton Vale from the Wetlands and the Coast of Dawn to the east. Another traveler—a well-dressed, capable-looking woman they'd met at the temporary Trading House—hinted that their lair was an abandoned mine that gave way to a natural cavern deep below the mountains.

All of that, pieced together with other similar hints about

the Exceptas' location, pointed them toward the mountains to the northeast. Even then, it wasn't much to go on. They'd have to pick up the actual trail along the way.

Cantering along, Gerald tried not to let the eerie quiet of the violet-tinged night weigh on him. He'd marveled since childhood at the sounds of the world after sundown, often lying in the prickly grass of his backyard long after midnight, listening to the symphony of nature and staring at the expanse of stars above. Back in Simmsville, the night would have been alive with the sounds of crickets and katydids, bullfrogs and owls. Here, though, there was nothing. No night bugs, no sudden croaks, nothing but the unnatural absence of that familiar, ambient noise. Only the rhythm of Zero's galloping hooves along the forest path provided some distraction from the quiet surrounding them.

It didn't help that no one was talking. For at least the third time in ten minutes, Gerald tried to think of something to talk about, but nothing came to mind. He gave Zeke a sidelong glance. Had he ever seen his friend this quiet? In the normal course of things, Z spoke just about every thought that came to him, often before it was fully formed. That was usually multiplied by a hundred when he got worked up about something, which made the current silence even stranger. This quest was the adventure Zeke had been dreaming of since picking up his first novel with an illustration of a dragon on the cover. The thrill of getting to live out that dream should have had him humming like a car motor.

Instead, the elf was quiet, brooding like both the others. A thick blanket of concern hung over each of them, traveling with the group through the depths of the dark wood.

To Gerald's surprise, the thing he'd expected to be the heaviest burden, the Sheriff's Shield, was anything but. Slung over one shoulder, it hung against his back, featherlight and forgotten. If it was made of pure, actual gold, as everyone seemed to think, then it had to be enchanted. Gold weighed a ton, as far as metals went, and the amount needed for something of that size would have been so heavy two hands, if not several men, would be needed to lift it. To wield it strapped to one arm should have been impossible.

The thing was also much stronger, harder, than it had any right to be. Gold was soft by nature, too, easy to dent and bend. As a test, Gerald convinced Mehleese to bludgeon the shield with the thickest, heaviest branch she could find. What she chose was as big around as his leg and so solid it might have been petrified. But not only did the wood explode in a cloud of splinters and chips, it didn't leave a single mark on the surface of the shield.

As the road through the Ore Wood led, they followed, clip-clopping along its well-traveled, hard-packed surface hour after hour after hour through the night. The same trees watched them pass, silent guardians along their way. The same short, familiar bushes quivered as they drew close, hinting of a Creeper or other some other predator hidden within, hoping to entice some prey. Pairs of shiny eyes reflected moonlight at them, floating in the dark just above the underbrush a few feet off the road.

On and on the road went, ever the same, time plodding by at a glacial pace.

At last, though, the trees thinned, and the undergrowth gave way to grass. As they crested a soft rise, the forest came to an abrupt end. In the distance, the Iron Spikes loomed, and the soft pink-orange light of dawn filtered between the sharp peaks of the mountain range.

Gerald pulled Zero up. After a few additional steps, his companions did the same. Demon, of course, was the last to stop, giving the rest of the party—mounts and people alike—a hearty sneer as he did.

"That's the end of the woods," Gerald said, "and I don't see a sign that says Exceptas Hideout This Way. So what do we do?"

Zeke shrugged and looked back toward the mountains, as if by staring they might divulge something helpful. Mehleese clucked her tongue.

"If you really want a signpost, I can make one for you. But if you'd open your fool, blind eyes instead, you'd see the signs are all around you."

Raising an eyebrow, he searched for some hint of the evidence she suggested was everywhere. Grass, trees, the road, a few lonesome rocks—nothing was out of place. Nothing looked man-made. Nothing screamed, "The Clan is this way." He shrugged.

"If I left you two alone, you'd be lost before I was out of sight," she complained. "They followed the road along here but left it about sixty yards ahead and turned due north, parallel to the mountains."

"How do you know? What do you see?"

She spurred Solus ahead and pointed down. "You can't see their actual wheel ruts in the road, but you can see how the dirt has been disturbed. It's not obvious, but by trying to conceal it, they left us something to track. And if you follow that path, you'll see that just up there"—she gestured to a spot close to where Demon stood, trying to look superior—"the grass has been churned up and, in some places, torn. That's where the wagons carrying their loot left the road."

"Huh," Gerald replied, stroking his goatee. "So, I guess we turn north too?"

Demon gave in to Zeke's urging and trotted to the others.

"Should we stick to the edge of the forest or the foothills? We don't want to be out in the open, right?"

"Maybe the forest would be better?" Gerald suggested. "If we're looking for the mouth of a cavern or mine near the mountains, we'd have a better chance of seeing it before we stumbled right on top of it."

Mehleese nodded. "I think so. But either way, be careful. Don't let your minds wander. And be ready for battle in a heartbeat."

The group turned north, stalking along the very edge of the forest, staying close enough to use it for cover. The going was much slower as they picked their way among the sparse trees and tendrils of brush that had grown just beyond Ore Wood's limit.

Shortly after, the sun rose in earnest, climbing above the mountain peaks to their right. Following that, though, nothing else changed. The foothills rolled along opposite them, crests and valleys of tan and brown, but they found nothing resembling a mine opening, abandoned or otherwise.

"Maybe we missed it," Zeke said with the sun overhead, in a cloudless, monochromatically blue sky. "For a while, earlier, the sun was in my eyes. We could have overlooked it."

"We didn't miss it," Mehleese replied. "You might have been sunblind, but I've been hunting and tracking while squinting into the sun for years."

Gerald frowned. "He does have a point, though, Mehleese. We're more than half a day's ride from town. They couldn't be much farther, could they? Not and make regular raids?"

"The longer the ride, the more complicated raiding would be, yes," she allowed. "I expected we'd find them before now."

Looking back the way they'd come, the elf said, "Maybe we should split up. One of us could double back and make sure?"

"No." The Warrior shook his head. "We may have to separate at some point but not yet. Not before we've even found the kids."

"All I'm saying is that—"

"There," Mehleese announced with a tilt of her head. A few hundred yards ahead, a slumping mine shaft stood open, cut into the face of a high hill. "Now don't point at it or go charging over there all half-cocked. There will be lookouts or sentries."

"So what do we do, then?"

Ignoring the question, she rustled through her saddle bag. "There it is," she announced, dragging out a handful of something blue.

"Is that one of their face coverings?" Zeke asked.

Gerald smiled and gave the Ranger an appreciative nod. "Very clever. And we're going to pose as…?"

"Recruits. You both look young enough to pull it off. I'll pretend to be an Exceptas recruiter, and you'll be my latest volunteers. That should get us at least part of the way in without us having to fight everyone we see. Oh, and keep your ears covered, Axeblight. I doubt they allow elves in the Clan."

Pulling his hood up to cover his face, he tsked. "Racist jerks."

She tied the navy kerchief around her neck and pulled it up over her face. "Just don't ask where I got it from. That's on a need-to-know basis."

The guys looked at each other. Zeke raised an eyebrow and said, "Well, now I'm going to have to find a reason to need to know."

Mehleese gave a soft laugh. "Follow behind me," she said and spurred her dapple gray forward. Zero let her gain half a horse length before following. Demon, for once choosing not to demonstrate his ego, matched pace with the warhorse.

They crossed the grassy land between the edge of the wood and the hills at a slow walk, scanning for movement around the mine shaft. Nothing even twitched. As expected, though, when they reached the shaft, a gruff voice called out, "Hold there if you'd keep your blood within ya." A familiar gray outfit and covered face slid out from a concealed crevice to the side of the shaft. The guard held a heavy crossbow over a round expanse of midsection.

"What you be up ta', there?" he asked. "Can't say that I know ya. Lady Ranger with a shape like yours, I'd remember to be sure. What can I do fer ya?"

Mehleese clucked again, just loud enough for her companions to hear.

"I'm Rikka," she lied, as if she'd been saying it all her life. "I've been out rustling up recruits for Kingsbane. Haven't been back this way in quite a while. Thought he'd be glad to see these two."

The guard's eyes narrowed above his kerchief. "So you come here lookin' for Tristan?"

Something at the base of Gerald's neck itched. The man's tone, maybe, or the way his hands tightened on the stock of his crossbow was wrong. As sure as the sun hung over them—video game sun or not—things were about to go badly. Perhaps very badly.

If Mehleese noticed, she didn't let on. "Of course we are," she answered with a bored sigh. "He told me he'd be here."

A flicker of motion caught Gerald's eye. Zeke had dropped Demon's reins, freeing his hands. There was only one reason Mages made sure their hands were free. He'd sensed it too.

Dismount

The crossbow came up and pointed at Gerald. "Hey, now, fella. I didn't say nothin' about anyone dismounting. Go on and get back up on that beast there."

Putting his hands up, Gerald replied, "Easy, friend. Just checking my bag for some pipe tobacco. We've been on the road for a while, and I needed to stretch my legs anyway." He turned to his saddlebag.

The guard growled. "Son, your pipe can wai—hey, what's on your back there? Is that gold? That looks like—"

Whoops. Should have thought about that.

Shield

The crossbow loosed its bolt with a loud crack. A buzzing *thwang* followed as the projectile ripped through the air between them. With the shield up and covering him, Gerald didn't see it, but his whole arm vibrated when the bolt head crashed against it with a clang. The shot dropped to the ground at his feet, the tip flattened.

Power boiled through him.

Hammer

His shiny new war hammer appeared in his right hand.

CounterCharge

Faster than he'd ever moved, he raced at the guard, kicking up a cloud of dust like that cartoon bird that always outran—and outthought—the coyote.

The Exceptas sentry inhaled a mouthful of dust in surprise, just as the massive glowing golden shield smashed into his face, chest, arms, everything. The thug grunted at the impact and flew backward. Gerald raised his hammer to finish the attack, pouring as much Power as he could hold into a strike that, with luck, would kill in a burst of colored sparks.

He swung downward, howling like an animal.

Before Gerald could strike home, though, the guard kicked upward, his boots cracking against Gerald's shin. The move disrupted his attack and knocked off a few points of health.

Incensed, the Warrior reset his feet and lifted the hammer to swing again.

Instead, Mehleese shot past him from behind and dove across the man's torso, dagger streaking his throat.

"My friend here was about to kill you, Exceptas. He's young and gets kind of hotheaded. Do you want to die?"

"N... n... no—" he stammered.

"Well, he hasn't bloodied that hammer yet, and he's itchy to do it. And my dagger hand's been known to slip anyway. If I were you, though, I'd worry more about our other friend there. He's a hateful elf necromancer. I don't even want to think about what he'd do to you. I bet you don't, either, do you?"

Zeke dropped his hood and gave his best attempt at an evil sneer. Admittedly, "evil" was rather a poor description for it. "Pained" might have been better. But to someone being held on the ground at the point of a dagger, it sufficed.

The guard tried to shake his head but stopped, remembering the blade against his throat. "No, no. Please, no."

"So talk, then. What are you doing out here?"

"Just... just trying to survive. Don't ya know? The Legion is coming."

"Why are you guarding this mineshaft?"

"Tristan took the others away. But he told me to stay. To keep the place safe and watch for anyone coming after them. Or for other Clans that missed out when he left."

"Where? Where did they go? And how long ago?"

"Weeks. Maybe a month? And I don't know where they are."

"What do you mean? Don't lie to me. You know where to find them!" She pressed the dagger's blade against his neck harder, making an indentation. "I push any deeper, you're going to bleed, old man. *Talk*!"

"I don't know! I don't know!" he squealed. "Tristan loaded everything we had, all of our supplies, onto wagons and took off to the north. Said he was going to stay ahead of the king and whatever idiot he named Sheriff. Was gonna stay ahead of the Guardians too. Then, last week, I saw them circle back down to the south. Yesterday they came through here again, with an even bigger wagon train than before. With several more wagons of supplies and some that was just cages, headed north again. And that's the last I saw anyone until I saw you! Thela's Mercy, I swear it!"

Mehleese sat back, pulling the dagger away from the man's neck. At a thought, the weapon flashed back into the sheath at her belt. "That clever son of a…"

Release

Gerald's hammer disappeared. "Who's clever?"

Mehleese waved the question away and turned to Zeke. "We need to make sure he doesn't follow. We could bind him, but that's a waste of rope. Do you have any way to…?"

His eyes widened with enthusiasm. "Oh, hell yeah. I've been dying to try this." Clasping his hands together at his chest, he stared at the wide-eyed Exceptas sentry and nodded his head.

"No! No! Don't lie—!" And then a turkey was gobbling, frantic, a foot or so from where Mehleese sat on the ground.

"Good God, Zeke," Gerald gasped. "Did you just turn him into a field turkey?"

"Ha! Yes!" his friend replied, clapping. "Awesome, right?"

"Not if you're the guy who's a turkey now. How long will that last?"

He shrugged. "An hour or two. Depends on his resistance to magic. Either way, long enough for us to get well ahead of him. Maybe even catch up to Tristan's wagon train."

"So, do we believe that? That the Exceptas has some kind of mobile camp instead of a hideout?"

"A *caravan,*" Mehleese said, "instead of a *cavern.* It's brilliant. A hell of a way to avoid the Sheriff or whoever else the king sends after them."

"But wouldn't that be way easy to track too?"

"Maybe," she allowed. "What do you say we go find out?"

CHAPTER SEVENTEEN

THE DIVERSION

"IT SEEMS," MEHLEESE MUTTERED, "KINGSBANE is more of a fool than he is brilliant after all."

The trio huddled behind a boulder among the ridged hills at the base of the Iron Spikes. They looked down into the valley below, waiting for darkness to creep over the Exceptas camp as the sun slipped behind the Everfrost mountains to the west. They'd come upon it just as evening was giving way, and they spent twilight hiding, watching the people in camp scurry about, seeing to tents and fires and the hundreds of other details that needed attention as night drew near.

The caravan was the size of a small village and then some, much larger than they'd expected. It was made up of a remarkable collection—a hundred, maybe, or more?—of mismatched wagons of every shape, size, and variety imaginable. Farmers' flatbed wagons, garish, multi-colored entertainers' wagons, high-sided cargo wagons, cloth-covered wagons, and even cage-bearing animal wagons were all represented in the formation below. And every last one of them was likely stolen or appropriated to join the Exceptas gathering.

"Yeah, they weren't so hard to find," Gerald agreed. "I can still see the benefit of keeping your outlaw clan mobile, but you'd have to be blind to be within ten miles of that and miss it."

"Still," Zeke added, "that's a whole lot more Exceptas than I figured we'd find out there. I thought there'd be maybe two or three dozen. But there are hundreds of people down there. How are we going to rescue the kids and get out of there alive?"

The kids, at least, were easy to pick out in the formation. Wagons were arrayed in two wide circles, one set inside the other, and a menagerie of small tents was set up within the second ring. Near the center of the inner circle stood a much larger tent that had to be Tristan's headquarters. Not far from that, three cage wagons held what appeared to be all of the teens and older kids abducted from Copperton.

"Shit," Gerald replied. "I don't know. With so many people, I'm not sure we can sneak in there."

Mehleese snickered. "You two aren't sneaking anywhere, anyway. You make more noise crossing a field than my horse does walking across cobblestones. You're about as stealthy as a pack of cave trolls."

Beside him, Zeke bristled.

"Don't get all worked up about it, Zeke," Gerald said. "She's right. We're not exactly experienced in the thief's arts."

"Still," the Mage said, huffing, "I bet we could sneak into camp."

"I bet we couldn't. We'd be better off walking into camp than trying to sneak our way in. We need to work to our strengths."

"And those are?" Mehleese asked.

"I'm a big guy with a shiny gold shield who should be able to take a good dose of pounding. If I show up yelling at one end of camp, I'm pretty sure just about everyone's going to come running to see."

Zeke snapped his fingers. "Classic diversion. You draw Tristan's attention away, and we set the kids free. I like it."

"That might work," the Ranger said, nodding, "but then what? How do you not end up dead, and how do we get away with a group of scared kids?"

"You two will lead them out of camp, and Zeke, you'll set fire to every wagon you see along the way. That should give them something more pressing to worry about. Once I see that half the camp is on fire, I'll turn tail and make a run for it. And we'll meet up again where the road enters the Ore Wood."

The elf's eyes narrowed. "Are you sure about this?"

"Fuck no. I don't want any part of it. I want to go back to the Roost and Pig and climb into a bottle of warlock spirits until I wake up in my room in Simmsville. But I promised I'd do what I can to get Frega back. And this is what I can do."

"Wow. How very noble of you," Mehleese droned. "You're a shining example to us all. Perhaps we should just get the Smiths' girl and leave the rest? That would make our getaway a lot easier."

"Screw you. You've been here twenty years. I've been here three days. Cut me some slack."

She eyed him before nodding. "I guess you're doing your best, all things considered. I'd be red-faced for two days if I told you how I spent my first year here."

"That sounds like a story I want to hear. You can tell us all about it over a round of lagers and spirits when we get back. First one is on me. Wish me luck!"

Her cheeks showing a hint of blush, she replied, "It'll take well more than one before I tell you that. Thela's blessings go with you, Goldenshield. We'll see you soon."

"Deal. Until we meet back up, try to keep Ek'zae there out of trouble. And don't get him pissed off. When he gets mad, he's not good for much but a light show."

"I can take care of myself," Zeke countered, face paler than usual. "You just be careful down there."

With a confident wave, Gerald slid down to the base of the hill. "Right," he murmured, "be careful. That'll be *no* problem."

He swallowed hard. The open expanse of valley between the protection of the foothills and the southernmost point of the ring of wagons looked endless. Crossing it was going to be worse than hopping mean Old Lady Winton's fence as a kid to retrieve a lost baseball. The long trek from the fence to her prize rosebushes where the ball inevitably fell was a nerve-wracking, heart-pounding exercise in mastering terror. With each footstep, you prayed she didn't notice the kid in the backyard from her kitchen window. If she did, she'd be out on the porch and shaking her cane about vandals and hoodlums faster than anyone with a cane had any right to move. And while the poor kid responsible for knocking the ball into enemy territory tried to grab it and get back over the fence, Shi-shi, her nasty little mongrel poodle, would skitter into the yard and start biting at your hands.

There was no yapping poodle here, but failure meant more than having his finger nipped. His right hand tightened on the grip of his war hammer as he took his first step into the open. His left arm, hanging at his side, itched to be burdened by that massive shield. The comfort of its protection would come at a heavy price, though. The shield's polished face drew eyes like a bug to a light. He couldn't afford risking that kind of attention yet.

Duck-walking at the same half crouch he'd used when shuffling down the hills, his first step led to a second and the second to a third, all while he felt exposed and unprotected. Naked. Gritting his teeth, one foot after another, he inched closer and closer to the spot he'd chosen to appear in, a gap between two wagons along the outer circle. Expecting to hear a shout of alarm or cry of "Intruder!" with each yard of progress, he made his cautious way across the valley.

That alarm never came. One hundred and seventy-three steps later, he stood in the grass between the wagons he'd chosen, feet set in his defensive stance. The moment had arrived.

There was no being ready for it.

"Shit," he mumbled.

Shield

A weight that was becoming much too familiar—it was, after all, just a loaner—covered his left arm. Lifting it, he positioned the shield in front of him.

Deep breath?

Gerald shook his head to clear it. "Just be Goldenshield," he whispered.

Time for a little make-believe.

WarCry

From somewhere deep within—the pit of his roiling stomach, perhaps, or maybe from some instinctive, intangible Warrior's core made out of software code and digital polygons—he unleashed an angry roar that filled the twilight air with menace. A challenge to battle for anyone brave enough to answer it.

The shouts of alarm that he'd dreaded while crossing the valley reached him at last. Word spread fast and deep into the encampment. "We're under attack! Raiders to the south!"

And then they came. With no apparent order or plan,

Exceptas after Exceptas launched themselves into battle with club, hammer, knife, sword, arrows, stone, or whatever they had on hand.

The first thug to reach him said nothing but growled, brandishing a dull, rusty dagger.

Block

The blunt edge struck the shield with a clang and a flash of sparks. The blade rebounded, ineffective.

Counter

Goldenshield slipped the vicious claw hook on the back of his hammer around the thug's ankle and ripped upward, sending his opponent to the ground. He followed with a swift boot to the head, knocking the thug out.

Two more came after that, trying to coordinate, one to each side of him. The first, to his left, was bashed with the shield and stunned. The other, on his right, managed to get a swing in, but it was knocked aside by the flash of Goldenshield's hammer. His Power-driven counterstrike caught the man in the shoulder with a sickening crunch.

He took a few steps back as more Exceptas gathered around him and let loose another shout of challenge, this time augmented by the hot flood of Combat Power swelling in him. "Tristan! Face me!" And then more Clan fighters came at him.

Time lost all meaning for Goldenshield after that, as attacker after attacker joined the fray, intent on bringing him down, on being the one to earn glory from stopping the man with that shield. He danced and parried, leaping from one Exceptas warrior to the next, never pausing for breath or a moment of respite, even as the circle of thugs and sentries grew.

Eyes in constant motion, he scanned the shifting, jeering crowd, watching for the one face he sought above the others. In its absence, he poured the rest of his focus into whichever foe was ready to assault next, staying alive by beating them, literally, to the punch.

The Exceptas attacking him were, individually, outmatched. None of them were a high enough level to defeat him one-on-one. Still, a handful did manage to land the occasional blow, knocking health points off as they did, three or four here, a half dozen there. But when he was filled with Power and in the midst of combat, his health regenerated faster than when he was at rest. In the space between the occasional attacks that did hit home, then, he regained his full complement of health.

Before long, bodies of the defeated littered the ground near the wagons, making it more and more difficult to meet the next attacker on his terms rather than his opponent's. Instead, he danced around them with a fluid grace he'd never known before. In the real world, he was a slow, plodding, larger-than-average lummox. But here, in the heat of battle and with the electric zing of Power surging through him, he'd never felt more alive—more *right*—in his life.

Soon Goldenshield lost track of everything but the next attack, the next move. The crowd of chanting Exceptas faded away, and he stopped scanning for the one face he needed to find. The world shrank to the circle of ten feet surrounding him. Nothing beyond it existed. Within it, though, he noticed, analyzed, and cataloged every sight, every smell, and every hint of motion in a fraction of an instant. The shift of his opponents' eyes gave away intentions. The sound of leather creaking behind him warned of attacks long before he needed to block or counter. The thought of combat commands ran through his mind in a steady, constant flow.

Strike

Counter

Defend

Taunt

Maim

ShieldBash

He no longer thought the words with his conscious mind; he simply acted.

At last, the thugs and sentries stopped. Standing in a wide ring, they each backed away as he approached, watching something just over his shoulder.

"Ho, now, what have we here?"

Goldenshield turned, and the rest of the world flooded back to him. He should have been exhausted, panting, and sweaty, in agony from being hit, and aching from a level of exertion he'd never experienced before. But he was none of those things. Instead, his arms, legs, hands all tingled in exhilaration. The world was more in focus, the air cleaner, and the scent of the spotty grass below his feet sharper.

When his focus shifted outside that ten-foot circle, he found what had to be the entire population of the camp surrounding him. Hundreds of pairs of angry eyes glared at him above navy-blue kerchiefs.

But only one set mattered.

"Welcome, Lord Sheriff, to the Exceptas Circus. I am Tristan Kingsbane, proprietor."

CHAPTER EIGHTEEN

THE WARNING

"WE'VE MET," GERALD SAID. "AND I'm not the Sheriff."

Tristan was dressed the same way as at their last meeting, in Exceptas grays with no kerchief and a dented breastplate that likely hadn't been polished since before Dalor was king. He took a few steps closer, moving with the casual ease of a man who knew he had unquestioned control of a situation. His massive axe hung from his back, untouched. Nothing would happen here to surprise him.

Gerald said a silent prayer that wouldn't prove true.

"Ah! I remember you. You're that strange fellow from the raid two nights ago. One of the pair that stopped us from getting the weapons we needed. Ironic that my men might have stood a better chance if they'd had some of those tonight, instead of the rusty relics we're making do with, thanks to you.

"Even so, I suppose I do owe you some gratitude. I've been saying for weeks our warriors needed more training, but no one would listen." He turned in a circle, gesturing to the bodies on the patchy ground. Raising his voice, he added, "I'd say your little display tonight has proven my point."

Many of the Exceptas lowered their heads and shifted their feet. They'd failed to stop a lone attacking Warrior.

"I didn't come here to demonstrate how ineffective your soldiers are, Kingsbane."

"No, I imagine you didn't, Sheriff. Oh, wait. That's right, you said you're not the Sheriff, didn't you? For a minute, seeing you, I thought maybe our absent king decided to do his job and manage the Vale at long last. I assumed your untimely arrival the other night was to take up your royal appointment. I guess that isn't the case?"

"I've never met the king and have no interest to. I'm here because the people of Copperton want their families back."

"Then how did you come to be carrying the Shield? I can't believe they'd have given it to just anyone. The Council is supposed to hold it until the king makes an appointment. "

"What do you care how I got the Shield? I have it. Now let's talk about what *you* have. The kids you took from Copperton? They're coming back with me."

He appraised Gerald from head to boots. "Amazing. So, the Council quit cowering in Town Hall, pulled themselves up by the breeches, and sent you out after me? You'll have to tell the old woman I'm moderately impressed. Still, I'm surprised they didn't get someone a little more… experienced. I've got breeches older than you." The Exceptas surrounding them snickered. "I'm sorry, what was your name again?"

Gerald hated to do it, but for this to work, he needed all the pomp he could muster. Shooting Tristan a defiant glare, Gerald stuck out his chin. "I am Goldenshield."

Raising an eyebrow, the barrel-chested leader of the Clan took another step closer. "Goldenshield?" he asked, lips crooking into a grin. "Bold choice. A man to be known by his work. Not quite as awe-inspiring as Kingsbane, I suppose, but not bad."

"Don't patronize me, Tristan," Gerald shot back, "and quit wasting time. Your little wagon train stops here. The Exceptas Clan is finished."

Throwing his head back, Tristan gave a full, body-shaking laugh. His followers did the same, chuckling behind navy kerchiefs.

He shook his head. "No, *Goldenshield*, you're wrong there. The only thing that's going to be finished tonight is you. Which is quite a shame. Despite how troublesome you've already proven to be, you've got real heart. I will need more brave, talented people to join the cause if we're to survive the coming attack."

That word made Gerald straighten and blink. "What attack?"

"Didn't they tell you?" The man's surprise appeared genuine.

"Tell me what?"

"Blessed Thela! I can't believe they didn't tell you. So they hung that shiny, monstrous burden on your left arm, gave you a pat on the back, and told you to do the best you could? They didn't bother to explain how deep a hole you were climbing into?"

"Tell. Me. What?" Gerald squeezed his hammer.

"Months ago, the Legion of the Guardians boarded ships and left their homes on Akador. They crossed the sea to the Western Realms, landing on two fronts. One group made landfall on the Moon Shore and the second in the Lakelands. They're heading for Kingsland, conquering everything in their path along the way. Their leader, the 'Zealot' of Thela, Atlous Bonecrusher, has pledged to take Riverglow City and unite the world under his rule before this year's Festus."

"Jesus," Gerald muttered. Moon Shore was to the west of the Everfrost Mountains. The only way to reach Kingsland from there was to march through Copperton Vale. That put Copperton right in the middle of their path. If what Tristan said was true, the town would be devastated.

"Jesus," he said again. Thinking better of it, he corrected himself. "Merciful bloody Thela."

It couldn't be true, though. This world was based on the game world, somehow. It was almost an exact copy of the world they played in *Realm Quest*. The lands were the same. The races were the same. The cities were in the same places, and the people faced the same quests. Other than how real the characters' lives here seemed, there were hardly any other differences. Nothing even half as remarkable as an army of the Legion on a campaign of conquest through the human lands had ever been teased. An event of that scale could only happen with a game expansion.

Then again, there was the matter of the king. Rhandren Sophent still ruled in the world where he and Zeke played. No one had ever heard of this Dalor character. That, too, was a pretty substantial difference.

Could this all be something coming out for the game in the future, though? Maybe an upgrade that hadn't been announced yet? Or a test server?

Possible but unlikely. There'd been no rumors of a massive war planned for Thelaroth. If anything like that had been in the works, he'd have heard about it. The hardcore game geeks would have hints plastered all over the game forums, and if nothing else, Zeke, for sure, would have mentioned it. He had been worked up into a hyperactive frenzy a few weeks ago, but that was about the return of dragons or something. Nothing at all like the Legion attacking the Western Realms.

He couldn't believe it. Wouldn't believe it. At least not until he talked to Zeke. But he'd have to worry about that later. At the moment, he had to avoid getting killed.

"Whatever your plans, Tristan, the Exceptas ends tonight. You can't just live outside the law on the fringe of society, taking whatever you think you need to survive from good, hard-working people. I'm taking the children of Copperton back with me and putting a stop to your little revolution."

Tristan laughed again, deeply, like before. "Revolution? Is that what you think this is? Hardly. This is how we plan to survive the Guardians that will very soon come swarming across the continent. King Dalor has abandoned all of us. Left us to fend for ourselves against the onslaught. We have to do something, then, because our king"—his mouth twisted in a contemptuous sneer—"is content to let us die."

"You're lying. You're gathering equipment for war."

"War? Look around you. There are families here. This is no army. It's a refugee camp. The weapons and supplies we've taken are the bare essentials needed to defend it."

Gerald looked—really looked—at the crowd around them. At first, it had been all Exceptas fighters, thugs, and sentries in those telltale grays and navy kerchiefs. Others, though, had joined them since Tristan entered the circle—men and women in plain, often ragged clothes and work aprons. People who hadn't held a weapon in years, if ever.

Maybe he wasn't lying.

"How do you plan to survive?"

"By letting the Legion do as they want and staying away from them as they pass through the Vale. The northern army has pushed through the River Plains and is on the far side of the Iron Spikes. They're in the Wetlands now. Once they secure the Coast of Dawn, they'll make for Riverglow like an arrow. The other force, the army Atlous himself leads, has already conquered the Moon Shore and is crossing the Everfrost

Mountains through the southern pass. Once they've done that, nothing will stand between Atlous and Riverglow but Copperton and a march through the Spikes along Milton's pass. That poor little town will be overrun, conquered, and occupied."

Pointing at the circle of wagons, he added, "So I'm accepting into the Exceptas Clan anyone that can be useful and wants to survive. We'll stay mobile and far to the north of the Guardians. With luck, we can avoid them altogether until after Atlous takes Riverglow. And then, well, we'll see which way the wind blows."

"I don't believe you."

"I've lived my entire life lying about one thing or another. But this? Thela's truth, I swear it. I'm just trying to keep as many people alive as I can."

"Funny, seems to me someone with such lofty goals wouldn't be kidnapping children. Stealing them from their rightful homes for God, er, Thela knows what reason."

Tristan spread his hands. "Come on, there are no real children here. The recruits we took from Copperton are all ten winters old, at least. You say they're kids? I say it's a harsh world, and it's time they saw it for what it is, a dangerous place where you have to work and fight to survive. And I never said I was a pious man or that either my heart or methods were pure. To keep these people alive, I need more workers and more fighters. There's already too much to do around this camp for the number of able-bodied workers we have, and as you've shown, we need to bulk up our defenses. If Dalor or, Thela forbid, the Legion, attacked us today, we'd be lost, and then Atlous would have a thousand more humans to butcher before claiming his prize."

Gerald hesitated. If what Tristan was saying held any truth, was it right to interfere? Maybe the people of Copperton Vale would be better off with someone like Kingsbane trying to keep them safe, never mind the "how." Gerald certainly didn't have the experience to protect thousands of people against the Legion of Guardians.

But…

No. He settled into his defensive stance and ground his teeth. The man had taken the entire town's supplies, which was bad enough on its own. Kidnapping the children was unforgivable.

"The King will defend the Vale. Or Copperton will defend itself. But you have no right to take from the town without payment. Your plan is built on a foundation of good, however misguided, intentions, so I'll let you live. But this is the end of it."

"You're a bigger fool than I thought. Or maybe just too Thela-damned stubborn. Either way, you have to give up that town. There's no hope for them. The Legion will swarm over it like a plague of locusts, and the devastation will be worse than you can imagine. Join me. Take a face mask and leave them to their fate. Or, if your conscience demands it, go back and ask them to join too. Anyone who can bring supplies, use a tool, or carry a weapon is welcome here. There's no reason to waste our energies pretending to be enemies."

Tristan pointed at the west, to the Everfrost Mountains in the distance. "Our enemy is there. And to the north, driving refugees toward us each day. Join me, and we'll find a way to survive them together."

"No, I won't. I'm leaving, and I'm taking those kids with me. And then I'm coming back for the supplies."

"Is that so? Look around. If you refuse me, you won't even leave this ring alive. My soldiers might have been dumb enough to try to take you one at a time, on your terms, before, but I promise you won't be able to fight off two dozen at the same time. So surrender that shield and get down on your knees before I have to kill you."

"Never." Thank God or Thela or whoever, he sounded more certain about that than he felt.

"If that's what you want." Turning away, the Exceptas commander started for the edge of the ring of bystanders, heading for the center of camp. "Take him," he said over his shoulder. "Alive if possible, but it doesn't really matter. Bring me the Shield when it's over."

Gerald frowned. No screaming or yelling, and nothing smelled like it was burning yet. Zeke and Mehleese needed more time. He couldn't let Tristan walk away.

"You can try to have your guards do your job for you, Kingsbane, but it will be costly. How many do you think I'll send to the Dark World before they take me down? I promise you at least the first dozen will fall. Maybe the next dozen as well. I don't need much space to bash a head in with this shield, after all."

Tristan stopped and looked at the bedraggled line of his warriors. As he turned back to Gerald with a shrug, his axe flashed from his back and to his hands. He held it in front of him, parallel to the ground, like a tightrope walker carrying a pole for balance.

"You might have a point. I very much doubt you could survive a dozen at once, but there's no point in taking the risk. At least this way, I'll get to enjoy beating you down myself and taking that blinding thing away from you."

Goldenshield smirked.

ShieldTaunt

His hammer smacked against the shield, and an ear-splitting GONG filled the air. "Bring it, Exceptas. I think you'll find I'm a little harder to knock around than that elven Mage."

With a shout, Tristan launched himself across the field,

raising his weapon overhead. He moved with unnatural, almost blinding speed and was within attack range in an instant. The wicked curve of his two-handed axe sliced through the air between the men, seeking its target, hunting like a hungry wolf.

Block

The shield came up to protect Gerald's head. With a shower of light and the clang of metal against metal, Tristan's attack met the glowing plate. Instead of rebounding, though, the axe drove forward, pressing the shield against him. He fell backward, landing hard on his back as the breath rushed out of him with a grunt. Ten or twelve health points ticked off.

Giving him no time to recover, Tristan spun the axe in a long arc behind his own head and brought it forward again in what had to be some kind of Deadly Strike. Deadly but slow.

Gerald cursed and jabbed with his hammer, thumping Tristan in the ankle through his soft boots. He didn't swing with enough Power to do any real damage but forced his opponent to sidestep, disrupting the Strike. The head of the axe fell against the soft earth, cutting into the ground beside him.

Rolling away, the younger Warrior sprang back up to his feet and lashed out with a Power-aided attack. Tristan was turned half away from him, giving him a clear shot at his kidney. The blow echoed off the man's breastplate, leaving a deep dent in it at the point of impact.

Tristan reeled, hand to his side.

"I might have misjudged you. Might have more hound than pup in you after all." As he reset his stance and brought the axe back to an attack position, his eyes twinkled. "I'm going to enjoy this more than I thought."

"I doubt you'll enjoy it half as much as you think, old man." Gerald just had to stand his ground until the fireworks started. It couldn't be much longer now.

Tristan's smile widened. "Oh, and if you're expecting your friend the elf and that Ranger woman to free my new recruits while you occupy me, I'm afraid I've got bad news. I had them captured and bound before I made my way over here. I'm not an idiot, boy."

An icy lump, heavier even than his shield, thudded into the pit of Gerald's stomach.

Shit.

CHAPTER NINETEEN

THE RESCUE

THE PLAN WAS WORKING BEAUTIFULLY, right up until it stopped working altogether.

Not long after Gerald left them on the hill, Zeke and Mehleese made their own way to the valley floor. They lay down flat at the bottom of the hill, a hundred yards from the encampment. Just hidden by the grass, they tried not to lose their minds while waiting for the bear—in this case, their gold shield-toting friend—to stir up the beehive.

He was taking his sweet time about it too. Morning would come before they'd have a chance to get off the ground and moving. Or maybe it'd started already, and they'd just missed the signal? Zeke rubbed his nose with his fingers. Should he slip closer for a better view?

He started to rise, but Mehleese placed a gloved hand over his own, stopping him. She shook her head.

Not yet.

Zeke flattened himself back down with a sigh. He'd give him a minute or two more, but that was it. The waiting was killing him.

Then again, it was nice to be touching her hand.

The thought fluttered away as a familiar battle call shattered the peace of twilight. Gerald's ferocious war cry, the enraged roar of a wild animal, rang through the Mage.

A burst of adrenalin warmed his face and neck. Time to move.

Their heads came up over the grass of the valley in unison, like prairie dogs popping out of a hole. As they'd hoped, everyone was heading in the direction of Gerald's call. Some, men and women in those gray outfits, sprinted towards him. Others, dressed in regular clothes, followed after in smaller groups, chattering together in excitement.

"Let's go," Mehleese whispered. Without waiting, she snapped up and began shuffling in a half crouch toward the edge of the wagon line. Zeke followed half a step behind.

They reached the first wagon unnoticed, slithered around it, and dashed to another one set in the inner ring. Mehleese had tied her navy bandana around her face again, just in case, but that seemed a wasted effort now. No one noticed them. The entire population of the Exceptas camp was headed away, toward Gerald's diversion.

The pair crept to the center of camp, coming up behind the first of the wagons holding Copperton's adolescents. Zeke searched for Frega among the captives and found her easily. She was staring off to the far southern edge of camp like everyone else.

"Frega," he whispered.

She turned to him, poking her small face through a pair of bars in the cage. "Zeke! What's happening?"

"Hold on. We're getting you out of here."

"Quiet!" Mehleese hissed. She gestured at the large firepit set at the center of the camp. On the far side of it stood Tristan's command tent. Shadows moved around inside.

Gerald bellowed a challenge throughout the camp. "Tristan! Face me!" The dark shapes inside the tent froze and then moved at once toward its center.

"Down!" the Ranger hissed again. Zeke dropped behind the corner of one of the wagons.

Six shapes filed out of the tent. Tristan Kingsbane was easy to pick out by the barrel chest and self-assured manner. Another four were guards or soldiers. The sixth, though, was different—tall but much slighter than the others, and impossible to tell whether a man or woman from that distance in the dark.

Whoever it was, they wore robes rather than armor. Some kind of adviser to Tristan? No way. Kingsbane was a game character, not someone like them who'd come from another world. He was software code and video graphics, nothing more. He didn't make decisions. He had programming. And the real, in-game version of the Chief of the Exceptas Clan had no need of an adviser.

Then again, it was getting harder and harder to see *this* Thelaroth in such simple terms. On that first night, Zeke had been sure this would be just like role-playing their on-screen characters but with the tastes, sounds, and smells to go with it. But their game—the actual video game—was static. Things didn't change except when the developers put out patches or upgrades. You could expect the same missions, hunters' contracts, and the like from the same characters, and they'd always be found around the same places.

Tristan was the leader of the Exceptas there, just as here, but in the game, the Exceptas hung out in the Ore Wood and annoyed newbies. Then, somewhere around Level 10, players would get a mission to go collect Kingsbane's head. After they succeeded, another Tristan would spawn for the next player.

But there were no raids on Copperton, no kidnapping, no great caravan of people and wagons.

This Tristan had moved the Exceptas out of the woods and was expanding the clan. That wasn't the only difference in this version of the world either. There was also a new king somehow. Rhandren Sophent had been the king in Riverglow City since the game came out four "real-world" years ago. And there hadn't been even a hint of rumor that he would be replaced in an update anytime soon. So what was with this Dalor guy?

None of that compared, though, to the Town Council's trying to appoint Gerald as the Sheriff of the Vale.

Yeah, whatever he'd thought when they got here, Zeke knew now that he'd been wrong. This wasn't just the same old game, following all the rules of *Realm Quest* like programming. This was a real, separate world somehow, one that had its own rules that were, believe it or not, evolving around them.

Tristan gestured at two of the guards, drawing them close. After he gave orders Zeke couldn't hear, they hurried off toward Gerald, pushing a handful of stragglers that had gotten a late start toward the excitement out of their way.

Kingsbane then turned to the person in robes, who, Zeke realized, had to be a man based on his height. Because of a stupid design trope, all the females of a given race and class in the game were shorter than their male counterparts. After dozens of online complaints and petitions, the developers of *Realm Quest* had acknowledged the problem and promised they'd address it in a future release. But this wasn't the future.

The pair had a quick exchange that ended with Robes crossing his arms and burying each hand in the wide opening of the opposite sleeve. Then, with a nod, Tristan and the two remaining guards strolled toward the commotion, which had become a steady ring of metal clashing against metal.

"Thela protect him," Zeke murmured as the trio disappeared. Gerald was on one end of all that clanging metal.

If he was going to survive—if any of them were going to survive—they needed to get started. Instead of retreating, though, Robes stood outside the tent, still as a post, facing them.

Zeke swallowed hard, trying to ignore his twitching fingers. Could he see them? Were the kids in the cages somehow giving off some kind of signal, a hint of anticipation or something, knowing that he and Mehleese had come for them?

For several gut-wrenching moments, the shadowy man waited, watching. Then, without warning, he spun and disappeared through the tent flaps.

"Okay," Mehleese said. "Let's do this and get out of here. Zeke, can you open locks?"

He shook his head. "Not yet. I'm still several levels from that spell."

She grunted. "Okay. I'm not great at it, but I can get them open with a little luck. Watch the tent. Light the place up if you see anything."

"I'm good with locks," Frega whispered. "Just get this one open, and I'll do the rest."

The Ranger nodded and started working.

Standing up and setting his hands at the ready, Zeke focused on Tristan's tent. Strange that this one person among all the others in camp didn't take the bait. Why did he hang back while the Exceptas Chief went to deal with the intruder? What *did* he do for the Clan?

The more immediate question, though, was what character class was he? If he was a magic user, they needed to get those locks free and flee from the camp as soon as possible.

Zeke was pretty sure of himself when it came to destructive magics, but dueling with another wizard, one on one, was a different animal, one that depended more on experience than strength or age. And no matter how well he knew the rules of magic in this world, he was still but a mid-level Mage at best.

Mehleese's lockpick clinked against the tumblers of the padlock, and a ring of muttered curses hung around her. She'd get it; he knew she would.

Sooner, though, would be better.

Then again, maybe Robes wasn't a magic user. He could be a Priest. They'd have a lot less to worry about in that case. Sure, a Priest alone could be a little trouble, but Priests were known for healing more than hurting. He could handle a Priest all by himself.

Zeke felt a cold tingle of dread. Something wasn't right. Or he was forgetting something. Something important. And there was no sign of any life inside the tent. Shadows had moved around in there before. But now? Nothing. No moving silhouettes, not even a ripple of the tent flap from air circulating in there. The thing seemed deserted somehow.

"Almost," Mehleese whispered, a hint of triumph in her voice. Zeke turned to see her smile as she peered on the lock. Thela, she was pretty. Especially when she smiled.

As he turned back to the tent, panic flared in his chest. The tent flaps had blown open. Robes stood outside, watching them. Darkness bloomed around him, a black aura, darker than a moonless night. As if all the light had been sucked out of the surrounding space.

Zeke threw up his hands to call the strongest fire he could command, to incinerate whoever it was on the spot. Instead, he sputtered and grunted. His tongue and mouth moved, trying to form words, but none came out.

Blessed Thela, he'd been *Silenced*. But that couldn't be. *Silence* was a skill that could only be cast by…

"What's wrong, elf? Troll got your tongue?" Bodies pressed hard to either side of him, grabbing his arms and pulling them behind his back. Soldiers. Two of them, at least. A gruff voice chuckled in his ear. "Not a troll, though. That's our Shadow Priest. He goes by Gravesire."

By the Dark World, no. Not a Shadow Priest. They were the antitheses of typical Priests. Normal ones worshiped life and would do anything to protect it. Would even let themselves be harmed in order to prevent harm to another. Shadow Priests, on the other hand, reveled in suffering, misery, and death. They were given special, sinister gifts. They could cause unbearable pain simply by speaking it. The higher-level ones could kill with just a word.

How could he have been so stupid?

"Zeke!" Frega cried out. Others in the cages started screaming too.

The two sentries shoved something filthy into his mouth and pulled his hands together behind him as his eyes searched for Mehleese. She wasn't standing by the door of the cage anymore but lay on the ground below the wagon, twitching and whimpering softly.

He pulled away, furious, almost wrenching his arms from their sockets, but the Exceptas held him tight. Mehleese cried out in agony.

"Don't struggle," the gruff voice warned. "The more you do, the more he'll hurt her. And she's got no defense right now. If you fight, she'll die."

Zeke cringed but went limp, letting them finish binding him and tying a kerchief around his mouth, pressing the gag even deeper. He thought he might choke if he swallowed hard.

"Tie her up also," a deep, rich voice from within the

depths of the hood commanded. "No need to bother with the gag, but be certain she cannot escape."

"Yes, Lord," the sentries replied. They dragged Zeke to the other side of the wagon and threw him to the ground next to the Ranger. One of the guards started binding her, hands to feet, as the other worked at wrapping his legs up as well. When they finished, they stepped back, both drawing daggers from their belts.

"Kill them, Lord?" they asked at once, much too cheerfully for Zeke's liking. Merciful Thela, what kind of people were these?

"No," the dark priest rumbled. "Not until Lord Tristan has had a chance to deal with them. He will have questions. In the meantime, you two watch over them carefully. I'm needed at our Lord's side, to assist his battle with this idiot new Sheriff. After tonight, he will at last have the Shield we need."

"Yes, Lord Gravesire, we'll guard them until you return. You can count on us."

Under the cowl of the dark robe, the Priest nodded. "I know I can. Remember what happens to those who disappoint me." With the ominous warning, he headed toward the sounds of battle in the distance, gliding away from them above the ground.

Zeke whimpered into his gag. Gerald, hands already full with Tristan by the sounds of it, didn't have a chance.

CHAPTER TWENTY

THE TURNCOAT

ZEKE CLENCHED HIS EYES SHUT. Calm. Think. Breathe.

The Priest was gone. Without him here, there had to be a way to trick the guards and get free. Maybe nudge Mehleese awake or slip a hand out of the bindings.

Off in the darkness, that familiar deep, silky voice cried out in alarm. Then came a loud thump followed by a heavy grunt.

"Did you hear that?" one of the guards said.

"Yeah, but you heard Gravesire. We're not going anywhere. Did you hear what he did to the guy who burned his breakfast?"

"That's just camp talk. You can't take all the skin off someone's hand like that. Everybody around here turns into such a baby whenever he walks by—"

"Guards, what's going on here?" A short Exceptas woman stepped out from behind a wagon. Her face was covered, but Zeke would have recognized those oval eyes anywhere. She was the same woman from their encounter in the woods. Jehn.

"Lord Gravesire caught these two trying to free the kids, er, recruits. He left to help Lord Tristan finish off the intruder."

"I see," she said. "There must be another one still stalking about the camp, then, because I just found Gravesire on the ground not twenty yards from here."

The guards gave each other anxious glances.

"Who could subdue Gravesire, Lady? What do we do?" one of them asked.

"We need to find whoever did it before they cause more harm. I'll guard these two. Go find the other one and bring him or her back."

"But Lord Gravesire told us—"

"I'll see to him. I'll explain it all when he wakes up. You have nothing to fear, I promise you. Now go, quickly, before the intruder gets away! That is, unless you'd rather wait for them to come back for the captives?"

They glanced at each other again. They might not know who or what was lurking out there in the dark, but either way, hunting was better than waiting to be a target. "Yes, Lady," they said together and hurried off.

Jehn watched them go, waiting in silence as they disappeared to another part of camp. At last, satisfied, she spun around and crouched beside Zeke.

"This was about the last way I'd have picked to do this," she said, untying the kerchief covering his mouth. "We've got to get out of here, fast."

"Thank you," he replied as soon as she removed the dirty rag from his throat. The cloth tasted like mushrooms and sweat. "And I know. This wasn't exactly our plan, either."

"You had a plan? This doesn't look like a plan to me." She worked to free his hands.

"Well, the diversion worked well enough."

"Goldenshield fighting on the other end of camp? I'd say

nearly well enough," she corrected. "If it had *truly* worked well enough, you'd be gone already with the kids. But instead, you've now made an enemy of Gravesire. Plus, I'll have to leave the Clan before I was ready."

"It could be worse," he muttered. "Wait, you were planning to leave the Exceptas?"

She nodded, moving to Mehleese. "I'll explain later. If you want 'worse,' though, I'll give it to you. You'll be lucky if your friend with the shiny shield lives another ten minutes. And by this point, Tristan won't be showing him any mercy."

A soft golden glow from Jehn's hands washed over Mehleese's face. She blinked awake, groaning. "Thela protect me, why do I feel like I just got run over by an entire stable of centians?"

"Are you okay, Mehl?" Zeke's voice was softer than he'd expected. "You had a rough fight with a Shadow Priest."

"A fight?"

"Well, it was pretty one-sided."

She pushed herself upright, taking her head in her hands. "Right, I remember now. The guy in the robes. I don't know that I've ever gotten beaten up like this before. Especially not without getting a few licks in myself. What happened?"

"That was Tristan's new advisor. We know him as Gravesire. Everything around here changed when he showed up. Before, Tristan was content to build a refugee camp and hide in that cavern, staying out of the way. But once that twisted nut got his ear, we started putting together the wagon train and kidnapping kids."

She walked over to the first cage wagon. The adolescents inside watched her with suspicion, apparently afraid to hope she might be able to release them. Jehn took a key from a pouch on her belt. They melted in relief.

Frega, the first to jump free of the wagon, made a path right to Zeke. "Where is he?"

Zeke waved toward the din of fighting to the south. "Do you hear that?"

"What's he doing? Trying to take on all the Exceptas himself?"

"Hopefully only Kingsbane."

As the other kids streamed out of the cages, Jehn joined them. "He'd have been better off with all the others. Tristan's the only Elite Warrior among the Exceptas. And your Sheriff is what, mid-level at best?"

He fidgeted, casting a nervous eye south again. "We have to help him."

Jehn shook her head. "No, we have to get out of here and put as much distance between us and camp as we can before they realize what happened and come after us."

"Us? When did you become one of us, Exceptas?"

"When the Clan started taking kids hostage and calling them recruits. I didn't sign up for this. My father would—" She cut herself off.

"What was that?" Mehleese asked.

"Doesn't matter. We have to get out of here."

Zeke scrutinized the woman. "What do you think, Mehl? Can we trust her?"

Mehleese set her hands on her hips and raised an eyebrow. After a moment's consideration, she said, "Maybe. Probably. She's had at least three opportunities to kill us but helped us out each time instead. I'll take the risk."

The shorter woman rolled her eyes. "So glad to have your vote of confidence."

"Okay," Zeke said, "you take the kids and lead them away. Get back to the road. We'll follow after we save Ger—

er, Goldenshield's bacon. Don't stop to wait for us for any reason."

"Not happening, Mage."

"What? Don't argue with me. I'm—"

"Shut up." Something in the set of her jaw or the way she stood said she expected to be obeyed. Giving orders was second nature to her. "You'll need me with you. I'm the only healer between here and Copperton. After Tristan's done with him, you'll never make it even to the Ore Wood without healing him first."

"Maybe it's not that bad."

"What if it is, elf? Are you going to bet his life and yours on that? That's a big gamble. Bigger than you know. So, instead, why don't you lead them to the road, and your lady friend and I will save Goldenshield's—what did you say?—bacon."

He gave Mehleese a nervous glance. "No. I have work to do here."

Frega forced herself between the three of them. "Quit wasting time! Somebody go save the big lummox. We know how to get to the road and back to Copperton without anyone's help, thanks. So quit bickering and go get him. We'll be fine."

The adults gave the girl a trio of blank looks.

"Uh, okay," Zeke said at last. "Sure, yeah. So, uh, do you need help rounding up…."

With a shove that knocked him back a few steps, Frega said, "*No*! Bless me, elf, you could wear out Thela herself. *Go*! My boys Daven and Blust are right over there. We'll have this lot herded back to town before you can toss a fireball."

A hearty cheer rose from the battle in the distance, and the clanging stopped. Thela, what was happening?

"Fine, then," Zeke said. "Good luck. We'll meet up with you soon."

Jehn and Mehl were already sprinting through the camp, their faces covered with navy. The elf took off after them, but after a few yards, the ring of battle started again. He stopped. Gerald must be okay—at least okay enough to put up a fight. His friend was doing his job, sticking to his part of the plan. Even if he faltered, the ladies would be there soon to take care of him.

Zeke had his own job to do. Time to get to work.

With a wicked smile, he put his hands together, rubbed them, muttered a few arcane words, and snapped his hands apart. An orange-and-blue mass of liquid flame winked into the space between them. As he spread his hands wider, the smoking orb grew to the size of a bowling ball before he turned to Tristan's tent and set his feet.

After winding up like a baseball pitcher, he tossed the orb, admiring his creation as it arced through the night air, leaving a trail of light seared into his vision. With a ground-shaking *boom*, a storm of flares and sparks, it crashed into the structure. The command tent erupted in flames.

He repeated the process, making and tossing another fireball at a nearby wagon, upending it in a blast of splinters and orange light.

"It's on, dogs!" he shouted and strode through the camp, eyes alight, casting balls of fiery destruction at anything that looked like it might aid the Clan. Wagons, tents, tools, training equipment, everything. He'd leave nothing but a smoldering reminder for anyone stupid enough to stand against Goldenshield and Ek'zae Axeblight.

CHAPTER TWENTY-ONE

THE DUEL

If his short-lived battles with the various Exceptas thugs and guards had made him feel more alive than ever before, the duel with Tristan had given Gerald a new understanding of the word "exhaustion." Before, fueled by adrenaline—or whatever his digital body used—and Combat Power, when the Clan chief came at him, he was certain he'd be ready to fight for hours into the night if necessary. However long Tristan could go, he would match.

Oh, but he'd been an idiot. The low-level fighters he'd faced before were nothing like fighting Tristan Kingsbane. Rank amateurs held up against a master. Only the Shield of the Vale and a good bit of luck had let him survive the melee so far.

Crouching on one knee while raising the shield over him, he squeezed the leather handle affixed to its back and clenched his teeth, bracing for another attack. Tristan groaned and brought the axe down, striking the face of the shield where nothing had been a second ago. A now-familiar clang filled the air, and Gerald's entire arm vibrated with the impact.

He hardly noticed. So much Power coursed through him after such a skirmish that it wasn't just tendrils of fire tickling the tips of fingers and toes. Instead, his entire body burned, head to heels, consumed by an intense, steady heat that made the world sound clearer, the air taste sweeter, the clumps of weed underfoot smell sharper.

Pushing with his left leg, he rose, leaping a step forward and to the right. Turning as he went, he brought the hammer around in a flat arc, catching Tristan in the arm as he slipped behind him. Tristan let go of his axe with that hand, spinning back around to face him, and stretched his arm out over his head.

"That didn't knock out half as many points as your first hit, Goldenshield. You're growing weak. How much longer until you can't even hold that shield?"

Gerald chuckled, belying his bone-deep weariness. "Don't you worry, Tristan. I can go all night and all day tomorrow. I'm just getting warmed up."

Launching forward, the Exceptas Chief took two short swings that Gerald evaded easily. A third, an upward slash, Gerald met with his hammer and pushed aside, smashing it back to the ground. Seeing an opportunity, the younger Warrior stomped on the flat of the axe's blade and leaned into Tristan's space. Flexing his neck, he brought his head up, smashing the other man's chin and nose with the crown of his own skull.

Tristan stumbled back, almost losing his weapon. But he clung to it and used it as a brace to right himself. Then, with a grunt, he wrenched it from under Gerald's boot. Defying his usual attack pattern of resetting his feet and hands for another heavy swing, he charged, leading with an elbow.

Gerald was caught unprepared. The assault slipped past the shield, and the point of Tristan's elbow rammed into Gerald's throat. Far too many points ticked away, and he gagged and staggered backward like a drunk after a night at the bar. Twisting away, he held the shield up to block his adversary.

Tristan was either expecting the move, was just plain faster, or some of both. He slipped his axe just inside the barrier, hooking the bottom point of the weapon's quarter-moon blade against the edge of the shield. With a firm yank, he ripped the enchanted plate away from Gerald's body but not quite out of his grip. With his opponent's defenses open, Tristan struck hard and fast.

Gerald whipped his hammer forward, hoping to parry the assault, but the axe hit the shaft of the hammer with enough force to knock it from his hand. It spun twice in the air and landed in the grass several feet to his right.

A tumultuous cheer went up from the crowd around them. From the sound of it, if the entire camp hadn't been gathered around before, they were now.

Trusting instincts he didn't know he had, Goldenshield danced sideways, again bringing the shield between him and his opponent. He had to get back around to that hammer, or this wasn't going to last much longer. Where was Zeke's blasted apocalypse, anyway?

Holding the axe parallel to the ground at his side with only his right hand, Tristan jabbed with the spike atop the curved blade, using it like a heavy spear. One-handed, though, it was a weak strike. Gerald rebuffed it, knocking it to the side with ease.

As he pushed the axe away, the realization that he'd made a grave mistake hit him like a truck. With the shield thrust to his left to deflect the spike, he'd opened up his defenses again, this time with his opponent right in front of him. Tristan, the more experienced of the two fighters, smirked and flashed forward.

Gerald tried to step back to cover the vulnerability, but it was too late. In one fluid motion, Tristan stepped within arms' reach and punched Gerald hard in the throat, forcing his head down. A shoulder strike followed, smashing into his nose and chin. More health ticked away. He had to be getting dangerously low, but luckily, his vision wasn't yet quite tinged with red, which would have meant he was Critical. Goldenshield staggered backward, desperate to keep his feet under him.

Tristan brought the head of his axe forward again, bashing with the flat of the blade. The blow caught Gerald in the chest, knocking him to the ground with a thick grunt, arms splayed out like a kid making angels in the snow. Another dozen health points rattled off.

He struggled to scramble to his feet. To bring the shield up in front of his torso. To do something, anything, to slow his opponent. But again, Tristan sprang forward before Gerald could act. This time, he slammed a foot down on the shield itself, pinning it to the ground, and drove his other foot hard against Gerald's neck, knocking even more points of health away. A crimson glow crept into his vision.

With precious few health points remaining, Gerald tried to squeeze the air out of his chest, to muster the strength to push the other man off. But it trickled out in a gurgle under the pressure of Tristan's boot. Balling up his free hand, he punched at it, but it was no use. He might as well have been trying to knock over a stone wall with a whiffle-ball bat.

"I'm sorry," Tristan said, smiling. "Is that uncomfortable? Here, maybe this will be better for you." With an evil grin, he pressed down harder.

"The bad news for you is that I need your shield. It's a symbol of authority here in the Vale that will legitimize everything I'm doing. I had hoped to get my hands on it in a more civilized manner during that raid the other night, but I couldn't find it. I suppose, though, this way will work too."

He shrugged and hefted his axe. Lining up the blade with Gerald's shoulder, he added, "It's a shame to have to lose your arm over it. You should have joined us when you had the chance."

"Fuck you," Gerald croaked. The wicked blade of the axe rose over him, silhouetted against the moon. He kicked and bucked, tried to squirm or roll, anything to throw Tristan off. Nothing worked. The blade moved forward, arcing down.

He squeezed his eyes shut.

That cold, electric sensation covered him like a blanket and snapped tight. The red in his sight disappeared.

Steel Skin.

His eyes sprang open as the axe struck. Instead of biting into his shoulder joint, it landed with a dull thud and bounced upward. A few points of health ticked off but not half as many as if the weapon had cut deep.

Tristan lurched to the side, trying to keep his balance after the axe rebounded. Free just enough to move, Gerald rolled hard to his left, stopping facedown on top of his shield arm. As he did, he tangled up in Tristan's legs, knocking the other man to the ground. Then he pushed himself up, searching among the sparse tufts of weeds for his hammer.

"I'm sick of you!" Tristan roared, having gotten back to his own feet. He sprinted forward, leading with the axe. Gerald squeezed the shield's leather handle, and the entire length of his body went rigid, preparing for the strike.

In the space between Tristan's second step and his third, the shafts of three feathered arrows sprouted from his back and neck in a starburst of varying hues. *One, two, three.* With a stunned look—as if he couldn't understand why pain was lancing up his back—the Exceptas Chief lurched forward, off balance.

Seizing the opportunity, Gerald shot forward, mustering every last drop of stamina and Combat Power available.

ShieldBash

As the two men collided, Gerald drove the shield into Tristan's head and upper body with a savage grunt, exalting at the crushing impact. After a blast of colored lights, his opponent bounded backward, spun on one heel, and crumpled to the ground, face first, at Gerald's feet.

And then the camp exploded.

CHAPTER TWENTY-TWO

THE DECISION

GERALD SAGGED IN RELIEF. OR, at least, as much as he could while surrounded by enemies. At last—at last!—Zeke must have started setting fires. Somewhere not far to the north, a glow filled the sky, and seconds later, something big—a wagon?—exploded into the air in a flower of red and orange. More came after that, blast followed by spectacular blast, as wagon after wagon erupted in spectacular flames.

Gasps that had come from the Exceptas onlookers when Tristan hit the ground became screams. The people raced away in a hundred different directions, driven in panic from the fire and destruction.

Gathering what energy he could muster and pouring all the Power that remained with him into the effort, Gerald slammed a boot into Tristan's head before the clan leader could struggle to his feet. The last thing he wanted was for Kingsbane to bring some order back to the chaos. He'd worked hard for all this disorder and was damn sure going to enjoy it.

"Goldenshield!" a woman called. Gerald tensed. Even

healed somewhat, he was still hovering near the end of his health, didn't have his hammer, and wasn't sure where it had landed. As the Combat Power faded, so did his stamina. If forced to fight any more, he wouldn't last as long as one of those Venomous Woods Creepers.

"Goldenshield!" the person called again. Then an Exceptas woman appeared out of a growing cloud of smoke, sprinting toward him.

With his heart thrumming and panic climbing into his throat, a glint on the ground caught his eye. He stumbled forward two steps and lunged, falling to his knees with his hand outstretched.

Take Hammer

Nothing happened. The hammer was inches from his reach but still too far. He had to get closer, somehow. But he couldn't move. Throwing his head back, he exhaled and brought his shield up in front of him. It wasn't much, but it would have to suffice.

The woman's hands were glowing. Great, a magic user. At least it'd be over quickly.

Reaching him, she batted his shield arm away and took his face in her hands. They were hot, scorching. How did she stand it? How could they be like that and not burn her?

With a gasp, he forgot the heat as a whiplash of chill gushed through him, from the crown of his head, down his face and his neck, and into his chest. With it came the familiar internal ticking of his health, but it ticked backward somehow, being replenished, not consumed. Memories of his grandfather teaching him to stack dominoes—one atop the other, clacking as they came together in a spiral—came to mind. He grew stronger, his senses sharper, energized with the clack of each health point returning.

She wasn't killing him. She was healing him.

The glow faded, along with the freezing chill in his chest and the searing heat of her hands. She stepped back and lowered her kerchief, revealing an angry scowl.

"Jehn?"

"You stupid ogre!" she shouted. "You should be dead. The only reason you're not is that you're too stupid, too stubborn to understand you were never a match for Tristan in the first place. Do you realize what would have happened if you'd died?" She slapped him hard across the face as a light shower of errant sparks fell around them like coarse snowflakes.

Did she just hit him hard enough to make something blow up?

Wait, no, that was silly.

Gerald stood and took a tentative step forward. He bent down and stretched out his hand.

Take Hammer

His new war hammer flashed into his grip, although it didn't look so new anymore. Scuffs and nicks marred the finish that had been shiny and perfect when they started out a day ago. Hard not to sympathize with it. He had plenty of blemishes now too.

He gave Jehn a quizzical look. "What do you mean? I'm sure I'd have died like everyone else."

Screwing up her face like she'd swallowed a ticking bomb, she stammered, "We need you, you… you… stupid ogre!"

"Goldenshield!" Another woman with her face covered by navy stepped out of the smoke, bow in hand, arrow ready. From her stance and the way she held her curved bow, he recognized her at first glance. He would have known her from a mile off.

"Mehleese!" he called back. 'Where's Ze… er, Ek'zae?"

She yanked down the kerchief. "Getting our campfire going, obviously." She gestured behind her. "Do you have the marshmallows?"

He grinned. "Did it work? Where are the kids?"

"They're on their way back. Frega and her friends are shepherding them until we catch up. Can you move?" She gave the panicked Exceptas a wary eye as they sprinted through the camp, grabbing whatever they could carry that wasn't on fire. The entire Clan was running off into the dark night, various small groups.

Gerald stood and *Released* his hammer. "Jehn fixed me up. We need to get going before Lord Exceptas there wakes up." He gestured at the unconscious form of Tristan a few feet away.

Mehleese frowned. "I hate to leave the arrows sticking out of his back."

"Afraid they're going to hurt him too much when he wakes up?"

"No." She smirked. "Arrows cost gold."

"I'm sure the Town of Copperton will reimburse you." Looking at Jehn, he said, "So what about you? What will you do?"

She took in the fires now raging around them and shrugged. "I thought I'd hang around for a while. Maybe help them put everything back together."

He couldn't help but smile at her sarcastic tone. "You don't seem too attached to the Exceptas, and you are kind of handy to have around. Want to come back with us?"

She nodded. "Yes. We'll see how things go in Copperton. I think you're going to need me anyway."

"Need who?" Zeke asked, hurrying toward them at last, trailing wisps of smoke.

"Took you long enough, Z." Gerald put his hand up to bump fists.

"Dismantling a caravan of this size is a lot of work," the elf replied, feigning hurt feelings. "I guess you could have gotten someone to do it faster, but if you want things done with a sense of artistry, you have to expect them to take some time."

Gerald laughed. "Okay, let's get out of here. Blondie over there is going to wake up soon, and I don't want to have to fight anymore tonight."

Zeke looked down. "Shouldn't we do something about him? Maybe tie him up and drag him back to town to face justice?"

"No. I think we should leave him."

The elf cocked his head. "Why? Doesn't he deserve some kind of punishment?"

"I don't know. He had decent intentions. He wants to help people, even if his approach was way screwed. So if he doesn't get fried to a crisp in the fire, maybe he'll think about that when he wakes up. He might still make something of himself. And I'm not dragging him all the way back to Copperton just to have them hang him there."

"But—"

"Look, he was a jumped-up idiot, but he was doing what he thought was best for the people of Copperton Vale. Maybe he'll learn something from his mistakes."

"He also might come back to cause more trouble later on. I mean, Ger, he can't learn. He's… well, you know." *Not real.* The unspoken words hung between then.

Gerald looked at Jehn, considering. The Exceptas had done a lot of things that had to be beyond their normal in-game programming in the past few days. And there were other game characters besides Tristan whose personalities seemed to have grown past their original boundaries. No, he wasn't so sure that they couldn't learn. Not at all. "Things aren't as black and white as all that, Z. And I think you know it too."

"Merciful Thela!" Zeke shouted. "Black! I forgot to tell you about the Shadow Priest!"

"A Shadow Priest? How the holy… whatever. How did you forget to mention that? Was it an Exceptas one? Damn, the last thing we need is to have to deal with one of them."

"Don't worry. We dealt with him already," Jehn said. "But I'd rather not be here when he wakes up. Unless you want to kill him before we leave?"

"Wakes up? And no, let's not kill anyone we don't have to. Let's just get out of here. You can tell me about it on the way back. I've got news for you too."

BOOK TWO

ACTS OF APPRENTICESHIP

CHAPTER TWENTY-THREE

THE RETURN

GERALD SIGHED TO HIMSELF, TRYING not to fidget in his saddle. His whole life he'd known that no matter how long it took to get somewhere, getting home always seemed to take no less than twice as long. The ride back to Copperton was no exception.

When they caught up to Frega and the other kids, they heard them long before they saw them. Being young, free, and caught up in the midst of the most exciting thing to happen in Copperton for as long as any of them could remember, the exuberant group filled the valley with enough noise to put a carnival to shame. At first, Gerald meant to read them the riot act, but finding them so jovial and—thankfully—unharmed, he couldn't hold on to his irritation.

Frega squealed in delight the moment the adults met them, and she ran to Zero's side, demanding Gerald get off his horse.

He slipped down from his saddle, as instructed, and crouched to eye level. The girl threw herself against him, trying, without much luck, to wrap her short arms around his armored upper body. "I knew you would come. I knew you would come," she repeated. "They said to forget it, that we were on our own, but I knew! I knew you wouldn't leave us."

Gerald's face warmed with a mix of pride and shame. He wanted it all to be for her praise, but it wasn't. Pangs of guilt clawed at him, tarnishing the shine on his ego from having been so successful—lucky, too, yes, but successful nonetheless—at the Exceptas camp. Guilt because she'd had such faith in him, even though his first inclination had been to leave them all, including her, for someone else to deal with while he made his way to Riverglow. Guilt because she'd only been taken because he'd sent her away when they left town to fulfill their hunters' contracts.

He returned the hug but said nothing. When at last they separated, he looked her in the eyes and said, "I'm sorry I wasn't there when you needed me. Thela grant me strength, I'll try to do better." Part of him actually even meant it. A little.

Frega gave him a sarcastic smile and tapped him on the breastplate. "You probably won't, but I know you mean well." And then she scampered off to rejoin Daven and Blust.

Once they got moving again, Gerald told the others about his conversation with Tristan, how the Legion was coming and that Kingsbane had planned to make the Exceptas a safe place for refugees. Zeke and Mehleese described the events of the escape that almost failed, highlighted by their meeting the Shadow Priest.

"What I don't get, Jehnilyas," Zeke asked, using her full name (probably, Gerald mused, because he liked to hint that she was of elven ancestry), "why did you knock Gravesire out instead of just letting him scurry away? Why risk it?"

"For one thing, Master Elf, if I'd let him intercede in Tristan and Goldenshield's battle, your friend wouldn't have lasted very long. He'd have been on the ground, twitching like a toad caught under a wagon wheel, in two heartbeats." She gave the Warrior an accusing glare. "He was stupid to try to take Tristan on alone as it was. If he'd died...

"Besides," she added, her tone brightening to match the twinkle in her eyes, "tell me you wouldn't have taken a shot at Old Hooded and Shadowy if you had a chance to catch him by surprise. Knocking him out was the most fun I've had in weeks."

"You should have just let him have at me," Gerald argued. "If he survives the burning camp—and let's be honest, fire probably knows better than to mess with him—it's safe to assume he'll be coming to look for us. From what you've said, he doesn't sound like the kind of guy who lets getting ambushed in the dark go without a bit of payback."

"Maybe," Jehn admitted. "Although I think he's more likely to go for a sinister, calculated revenge. He'll bide his time so he can ruin your entire life before killing you in some agonizing, preconceived manner. So you can appreciate his work. "

"Lovely thought. Either way, it's something else to worry about now. As if this business with the Legion wasn't bad enough."

No one replied to that. Tristan's story had been met with a shocked silence that hinted at disbelief. Before long, though, Zeke began to mutter, "That's impossible," every few minutes. Then Mehleese grilled him with question after question, trying to catch a mistake in the tale, like a lawyer on a TV crime drama. But Jehn corroborated every word, saying she'd even seen a few advance parties of Guardians doing reconnaissance in the southern hills of the Everfrost Mountains.

The Legion was coming. That much was certain. The only

question that mattered now was when, and could Copperton somehow prepare for it?

They fell into a somber silence after that, the four of them mulling the town's options in the face of the invasion. If not for the kids' jubilance, their journey might have seemed more like a funeral procession than a victorious return.

When the group left the Ore Wood at the outskirts of the town at midday, a series of horn blasts announced them from somewhere high in the trees above. The lookout's call brought the entire population of town running toward the forest road.

The eyes of every parent lit up like a child's on Festus morning when they caught sight of their son or daughter coming home. Smiles of relief adorned every face, and most parents shed rivers of joy-filled tears. They wrapped their children up and refused to let go, as if to keep them held in place forever, to prevent something that terrible from happening again.

The Smiths were among the first to intercept the returning party. Bergan and Fayn overwhelmed Frega with wet eyes and crushing hugs. When the blacksmith did, at last, release his daughter, he left her in the care of her mother, and came over to Gerald and the others, still sitting atop their mounts.

"Lord Goldenshield," he said, clearing a suspicious hitch in his voice. "We are all deeply in your debt. If you ever need anything, you only have to ask. Short of requesting the sun delivered in a velvet bag, anything in my power to grant is yours."

"That's generous of you, Master Smith. Although I had plenty of help." He gestured to the others. "They deserve your gratitude a great deal more than I do. All I did was try not to get killed."

"Our thanks to all of you, then. We will celebrate to honor all of you!"

"That's kind of you to say, Master Smith," Zeke added, "but you don't have to do that. We're just glad to have been able to bring the kids home where they belong."

"Thela bless you, Master Elf," he replied. "I can't tell you how much you've done to change the town's opinion of your people. You aren't at all what we expected from an elf."

Zeke beamed at the compliment.

Gerald leaned down. "I hate to mention this now, but you need to gather the Council. I have some pretty serious news to share, and the sooner we get to it, the better. I'm afraid we'll have to cut your celebrations a bit short."

Bergan gave him a solemn nod. "I'll make arrangements for the Town Council to meet at sundown. That will give us a few hours together, at least."

Twilight would have to do. With what they were facing, the sooner they met, the better.

CHAPTER TWENTY-FOUR

THE NEW SHERIFF

"WHAT DO YOU MEAN, YOU already know?" Gerald slapped the podium in front of him. The Council members, in their usual seats around the table on the dais in Council Hall, looked up, startled.

The Speaker spread her hands. "What would you have had us do? Sow the seeds of panic throughout the town when we don't even have a real Sheriff? We couldn't even keep those Exceptas outlaws at bay. News that a horde of warriors could be sweeping across the valley and coming right at us would have seen neighbors turning upon each other for every square inch of hiding space and every single stick that might be fashioned into a weapon. We discussed our options at length and voted to keep it a secret until either the king appointed a Sheriff or we chose one on our own. So we sent an urgent message to Riverglow, begging for an appointment. When *His Grace*"—her words dripped with sarcasm—"sent neither a Sheriff nor a response, we agreed this was the best course of action."

"I wouldn't say we necessarily agreed," Smith cut in. The Speaker silenced him with a glare that could slice a man open.

"For, uh, Thela's sake!" Gerald went on, toeing the line between irritation and a full-blown rant. "And you didn't think that maybe you should have mentioned it before sending us off to face the Exceptas? I shouldn't have had to learn about it from Tristan bloody Kingsbane!"

She gave him a flat look. "Perhaps if you had accepted our appointment, we might have shared more with you."

"Are you out of your mind? Only an idiot—" He growled and let the rest of his argument drop. Arguing wasn't going to help anyway.

"Does the Council have any kind of plan for dealing with the Legion?" Zeke asked from behind him.

"Lord Goldenshield," the Speaker sighed, giving a dark look to his friend, "if you insist on keeping this *elf* around, so be it. We'll withhold our opinion about it as a sign of our respect for you and for the things he's purportedly done in defense of the town. We appreciate that despite the misdeeds of his people, he seems compelled to act in a responsible way. However, that does *not* give him the right to address this Council, let alone question it. Please remind him to keep silent, or he will be barred from the chamber."

Gerald rolled his eyes. Jesus, they hated elves, didn't they? He turned to Zeke and shrugged.

Zeke's long, pale face colored in anger. "Oh, sure, I'd be happy to sit down and shut up, Ger," he hissed. "Let me know if I could maybe polish that big shiny shield for you while I'm waiting for all the smarter human folk to decide what's best for the rest of us."

Throwing up his hands, Gerald huffed. That whole thing would have to wait for another day. "He asked a good question, though, Madam Speaker. Do you have any plans?"

"Well, no," the Speaker allowed. "Our first step was to get a Sheriff. We figured we'd worry about the rest after that. But then the Exceptas came, and, well, here we are."

"Great. That's all you've got so far?"

"The Sheriff is Captain of the Town Militia. Whoever holds the position is also responsible for the town's defense. Technically, that person would also have been in charge of the king's garrison to the south of town, but the entire force of soldiers was recalled after Dalor took the crown. They haven't returned. We're assuming they won't."

"Peachy. Do you have any good news?"

"I am afraid not. Nor do I feel compelled to explain myself to you further with regard to the matter. Unless, of course, you've decided to accept the appointment we offered you? You do seem worthy of the job. I'd even vote to support you at this point."

Gerald eyed the Council members at the table, from one side to the next. Many wouldn't meet his gaze as it passed over them, no doubt ashamed at keeping the truth about the Legion quiet for so long. Only the Speaker and Templeman Prior met his eyes. She watched him expectantly, even seeming a little hopeful.

The Templeman, on the other hand, gave him a smug sneer, like a rotten kid who'd stolen someone's lunch and gotten away with it. It wasn't hard to guess who'd suggested keeping news of the Guardians secret.

"You'll have to forgive me," a man called from the empty entryway behind him, "but I wonder if I might be of some service?"

He strode the length of the lobby without hesitating, a pair of fully armored guards in the king's black-and-silver livery at his heels, one to each side. As he crossed the Hall proper, coming up beside Gerald, the Speaker smacked her gavel in front of her. "Sir! This is a closed meeting of the Town Council. I'll ask you to return for the next *public* session. Whatever your need, you will be heard then."

The man, covered from head to toe in high-quality plate armor decorated in intricate whirling designs (also in the king's colors) and ivy embroidery up and down his arms and legs, produced a scroll and unrolled it with a flourish. "If you'll forgive me, Lady, you'll need to hear this immediately."

"Sir!" she repeated. "If you do not leave *at once*—"

"By royal decree," the man began, raising his voice so it echoed in the near-empty chamber, "of his Majesty Dalor the First, the Anointed, Defender of the Western Realms, First Protector of the Temple of Thela, and Warden of Braxys the Black, Eater of Worlds, let it be known that Lord Erlas Boland, former Captain Assistant of the King's Guard, is hereby appointed Sheriff of Copperton Vale, with all accompanying rights and responsibilities. Lord Boland is to take possession of the title, including all symbols of the office, and initiate service in the name of His Royal Highness immediately upon formal presentation to the Copperton Town Council, at which time he is granted authority to act in His Majesty's name until death or full resignation of all titles and claims."

The man rolled up the scroll and handed it to the soldier on his left, who marched it up to the dais and dropped it on the table in front of an open-mouthed Speaker. She stared at the newcomer, as if afraid he might transform into a rabid animal. When she managed to wrench her gaze away, she unfurled the document. As she read, her jaw worked without making a sound while a tense silence hung over the Council chamber. When finished, she held the parchment out for the Council member to her left. He scanned it and nodded. Repeating the process, she offered it to Bergan at her right. With a glum face, he nodded as well.

At last, she managed to squeak, "The Council recognizes the royal seal and accepts the King's Proclamation with a… a… glad heart." Only Prior's face hinted at even remotely having a "glad heart." The rest of the Council wore hangdog expressions, as if someone had stolen a puppy.

"We welcome Lord Sheriff Boland to Copperton and look forward to many years of serving him as Defender of the Vale. When might we have the pleasure of his arrival?"

"You have it already," the man replied, putting a fist to his chest in salute. "I am Lord Sheriff Boland."

"Oh, uh, my lord," the Speaker stammered, "we welcome you to Copperton."

"By Thela's bloody eyeballs or whatever, would someone like to tell me what the hell is going on here?" Gerald said with more bite than he'd intended.

Boland spun and backhanded him across the cheek, forcing him back a step and knocking several points of health off in the process. "I don't for the life of me understand why you're carrying that Shield, *my shield*, boy, but I've killed better men for offering me less offense than that. I will not have Holy Thela blasphemed in my presence, and if you forget that, I will send you to meet her."

The Templeman stood up with a gleeful smile. "Forgive me for interrupting, Lord Sheriff. That boy is an uncontrolled beast, to be sure, but his bad behavior is no more his fault than an untrained dog's is for pissing on the rug. Council here, against my vote, wanted to name the fool Sheriff because they lost faith with the king, may Thela bless and protect Him. I suspect he just needs a reminder of his place."

"Yes, we heard rumors of the liberties being taken here with king's rights. Liberties His Grace is certainly not happy about." He fixed the Council with a menacing stare. "I assume there will be no more confusion on this point?"

The Speaker and the others around the table looked down at their hands in unison. Bergan Smith, though, dared to glare back at the new Lord Sheriff. But that glare was as far as he pushed his luck.

Turning back to Gerald, Boland said, "I will forgive your behavior this once. It seems that the Town Council made a series of rather poor decisions, which led to a rather egregious misunderstanding. As the rightfully appointed representative of the king in Copperton Vale, however, consider yourself duly informed of that error. You are free now to go about your business."

He gestured to the Sheriff's Shield strapped to Gerald's back. "But if you don't mind, I'll be taking my shield."

Cocking his head, Gerald said, "Begging your Lordship's pardon, but I was asked to help by the Council you seem so dismissive of. If there has been some kind of… misunderstanding, I expect *they'll* ask for the shield back."

Boland's temples clenched, and his fists curled into balls. "Berran, Thelm, take this idiot's tongue—"

The Speaker flew out of her seat, knocking it to the dais in the process. "Forgive him. And us, Lord Sheriff, I beg you. This is our fault. Templeman Prior speaks the truth. We lost faith, and this poor young man got caught up in our mistakes. Goldenshield, I regret to have to tell you that we've led you astray. Lord Boland is the rightful Lord Sheriff of the Vale. Please hand over the shield we stupidly let you borrow. We release you from any and all responsibilities."

He looked from the Speaker to the smith and back with a strange, quivering sensation gnawing in his belly. This was wrong. A terrible mistake, no matter what the "proper" thing was, no matter that he didn't even want to be Sheriff. People were going to pay for this with their lives.

But.

What could he do? He was ready to move on anyway. "Fine. I didn't take the job for a reason."

Drop Shield

The somehow unblemished golden plate dropped from his back and fell to the floor between the two men with a clang. Was it the most mature thing he'd ever done? No. But if they were going to call him "boy," he might as well act like a child.

The Lord Sheriff clenched himself up even tighter, if such a thing was possible, like an overinflated balloon about to pop. "If you ever so much as sneer at me again, boy, I will kill you, and I will take my time doing it. Now get out. I have much to discuss with my Council."

Gerald flailed for a retort, a snappy reply of some kind that would push Lord Not-Quite-Boiling over the edge into full rolling territory. But nothing better than second-grade playground retorts came to mind, and the Speaker's face pleaded, desperate, for him to go.

Snapping his mouth shut, he gestured to Zeke, who fell in beside him as they started for the doors. "Tell me I didn't want to do it anyway," he said.

Zeke hesitated. "You don't didn't want to do it anyway. You don't even want to be here."

"So why does it feel like I've got my tail between my legs?"

"Because you know they need you to do it. Also because that guy is a certifiable asshole. He's like the assistant manager for the TV place I worked at in college. He acts like he's the shit, but really, he just got his first promotion and doesn't know his ass from a hole in the ground."

Stopping, Gerald turned back to the Council dais. Bergan smirked at the same time the Speaker caught sight of him and gasped. The Lord Sheriff, golden shield now affixed to his back, glared over his shoulder and huffed. "Thela take you, boy. Get. Out. The important folk have to decide how to take care of things here."

The man whistled, and both his bodyguards reached for the hilts of their swords. With the kind of synchronization that came from hours and hours of practice, they bared an inch of cold metal of each of their respective blades. They didn't move yet, thank Thela, but stood, tense, waiting for either compliance or conflict.

"Come on," Gerald whispered to Zeke, starting again for the door.

"You're just going to leave?"

"Yep. It's time for a Lightning Lager or two. And then maybe a shot of warlock spirits. Make that a lot of warlock spirits."

"But—"

"Like you said, Zeke, that guy's a middle manager. The king sent him to shut the Council up. Sooner or later, he's gonna fuck it up. And when that happens, assuming we haven't found our way home yet, I'm going to remind him of every time he called me 'boy.'"

CHAPTER TWENTY-FIVE

THE TAVERN

GERALD SWIRLED THE AMBER-ISH—OR MAYBE brownish?—liquid around in the bottom of his mug. He lacked actual glassware, though, so the real color of Lightning Lager would have to remain a mystery. It was darker than the cheap light beers he'd spent most of his college days pounding. Heavier, too, but not unpleasant.

He shook his head and sighed. A few hours ago, he was saving the town's children from forced labor and war. Now he was relegated to debating the hue of his beer.

After setting the mug down, he picked up a smaller cup of warlock spirits and threw it back. It burned as it crept down this throat, a clean sensation that left him warmed all over. Zeke followed with his own shot, slamming the cup down on the bar and coughing hard.

"Jesus, Thela, God, what do they make that stuff out of? It tastes like paint thinner and not in a good way."

Shrugging, Gerald finished his lager and motioned for another round. "I have no idea. And I don't give two shits. It gets the job done." He already noticed a fuzzy sensation in his chest and face, the first signs of a good night. And this one was going to be epic.

They had nothing better to do anyway.

Saiyen, the now-familiar barkeep at the Roost and Pig, set down two more large mugs and a pair of smaller spirit cups in front of them. Gerald started to transfer a few coppers to him, but the bartender refused them. "I have a son again today, thanks to you, Lord Goldenshield. No matter what else has happened, you did that. Your money is no good here. Not now."

With a word of thanks, Gerald picked up his drink, glad for the man's generosity. He wouldn't have admitted it, but they were almost out of coin, having spent most of what they'd made on supplies before the raid on the Exceptas camp. And he wanted to deal with that smarmy Contract Keeper about as much as he wanted to see that asshole, Boland, again. Bad enough that they'd be back out in the woods tomorrow, grinding out contract quests by hacking at diseased mega-gophers for their spines or something just as stomach-turning.

"For real, Ger, we shouldn't get shit faced. That's not really a constructive solution."

"Fuck constructive, Ek'zae, my friend. I've been acting constructive since the moment we got here, and see what that got us? Piss on it. It's time to get a little *de*structive." He tossed back the warlock spirits and grimaced.

Zeke sighed in frustration. "Well, at the very least, we need to come up with a plan."

"I have a plan. It involves emptying cups." He winked at his friend, amused at himself.

"No, you don't get—" Sighing again, the elf picked up his own mug and took a long drink.

"Blessed Thela, what are you two doing?" They turned to find Mehleese and Jehn crossing the Roost's common room.

The pair had been out buying replacement equipment, clothing, and armor for Jehn, who'd brought little with her besides the Exceptas grays she'd been wearing.

She, at least, *did* have some coin. She was decked out in a brand-new, full set of matching mail covered by a rich blue-and-red tabard. Her armor was similar to Gerald's, but where his arm braces and shoulder pauldrons extended in hard spikes, hers were covered in much subtler wing shapes.

His breath caught in his throat. He'd thought her pretty before, but shapeless gray rags and a well-used kerchief weren't the most flattering fashions in the Realms. Plus, she'd been living in a camp for who knew how long. But now? She glimmered. And she smelled clean and pure, like soap with a hint of lilacs.

She stole the thoughts right from his head.

"We heard what happened at Council," Mehleese said. "What are you going to do?"

"Do? Well, at the moment, we're drinking. Care to join us?" Gerald grinned like a fool but couldn't make himself care. Instead, he gestured at Saiyen for drinks for the ladies. "Lady Jehnilyas, you look… striking."

"It's just an outfit. Don't forget that I can still knock you out of yours."

"Why are you in mail?" Zeke cut in. "Shouldn't you be in leather or robes?" Different classes in *Realm Quest* were limited to different types of armor. As a Warrior, Gerald could wear anything, including the heaviest sets of full plate. Mages lacked the strength to wear more than cloth but rarely fought in melee combat anyway. If Jehn could wear chain mail, that meant she had to be….

Zeke's face lit with understanding. "By Thela, you're a Paladin?"

"Why do you seem so surprised, Master Elf?"

"I'm—I'm sorry," he stammered. "I just assumed you were a Cleric or a Priest or something. I never thought. A Paladin?"

"And here I just assumed you were another diabolical elf planning to kidnap the king when no one was looking. But it seems we can all be whomever we choose, assumptions be damned. So maybe it would be best not to make them at all?"

With a snort, Gerald slapped his friend on the back. "Make some room in that elven mouth for your dainty elf feet, buddy."

Zeke gave them a sheepish shrug and fired down his warlock spirits, sputtering as before. "I'm sorry, that was stupid. Wait! That means you were the one that kept Blessing him with Steel Skin?"

"Your apology is graciously accepted, thank you. And, yes, I might have given him that particular Blessing of Thela's once or twice." Jehn winked, taking a mug of Lightning Lager and her own shot of spirits from Mehleese. With a look, both ladies drained their small cups and set them back on the bar, sighing with contentment.

Gerald started to say something, to thank her for protecting him even when they were enemies, but his tongue—and his brain—was all twisted up. Instead, he nodded and raised his mug to her. At least that mystery was solved.

"Copperton has the best warlock spirits," Mehleese said. "I think it's the hint of cinnamon. I just wish the lager around here was as good as that in the Lakelands."

Jehn sipped her own beer. "I'm partial to the Riverglow spirits myself. I like the herbs you find there better than the cinnamon. But yes, the lager here is watery at best. What do you think?" She gave Gerald a questioning look.

"Um, I'm not sure, honestly. I'm new to, um, drinking. I haven't tried the drinks from the other realms."

She winked back. "We'll have to remedy that, then."

"A shame we can't do it now," the taller woman said. "But with two armies of the Legion out there, where we can travel is limited. Maybe we should stay here for a while."

"Before our daring rescue in the Exceptas camp, I'd been planning to head to Riverglow to see if I could find—" He stopped before he mentioned their search to find a Mage who might send them home. Jehn, after all, wasn't one of *them*. "Well, to see the city. I suppose now might be a good time to try their spirits."

Mehleese drained her mug, slapped it down with a hard thump, and belched loudly. "That's an excellent plan," she said. "Since night has already fallen, what do you say we leave first thing in the morning?"

"That's fine by me. The sooner we get out of town, the better. Jehn? Ek'zae?"

"I don't know," Jehn replied. "Won't they need us here when the Legion comes? Even with the new Sheriff and the king sending soldiers to reopen the garrison?"

"Right now, they can go fu… I mean, they can forget about my help. If we get back in time, maybe we'll lend a hand. If not, we'll still be in the Legion's path at Riverglow. I bet city leaders there will be a little more appreciative."

"Come on, Ger," Zeke said. "That's not fair to the people here. You have to admit it's a bad situation."

"Whatever. It's not like I asked to be put in charge. Let's go have some fun in the city. Who's with me?"

Nodding, Mehleese said, "Good, it's settled then. We'll leave at first light." She paused and turned to Zeke in a way Gerald hadn't seen before. Her eye held a gleam he couldn't quite describe. Something almost—but not quite—predatory. "I think we still have some provisions to pick up, though. Why don't you and Jehn enjoy a few drinks, and Axeblight and I will get the rest of what we need."

Zeke gave her a confused look. "I don't think we need..." He trailed off, and his eyes grew wide. "Oh! I—I mean, I suppose we could use a few more things."

"Perfect." The Ranger snagged him by the loose arm of his robe and pulled him off his stool. She led him to the door, they flashed out of the tavern without another word.

Gerald chuckled. Lifting his mug, he asked, "You two bought everything we'd need for a trip already, didn't you?"

Jehn raised her own mug. "Why, yes, Goldenshield, now that you mention it, I believe we did. I can't for the life of me imagine what else Mehleese might need." She winked at him.

They both giggled. "In that case, here's to my friend, the Inexplicably Trustworthy Elf. May he survive the night in one piece and be able to travel tomorrow!" Knocking mugs together, they each took a deep drink of beer.

After wiping foam from his goatee with the back of his hand, Gerald said, "I couldn't find the words to say it earlier, but I owe you a ton. You've saved my life twice already, at least."

"Three, by my count," she corrected. "And you should thank Holy Thela, not me. I only ask that She bestow her Blessings. Whether She does or not is Her decision. She must be keen on you, though. She's yet to refuse."

"I have to admit, Axeblight wasn't the only one surprised to find out you're a Paladin. You're the shortest holy warrior I've ever seen."

Jehn gave him a tired smile. "The gifts of a Paladin come from Thela, not his or her stature." Face brightening, her sapphire eyes sparkled with mirth. "In fact, I'd stand toe-to-toe against you and trade hammer blows any day. Just name the hour when you're ready for a lesson in humility."

Gerald waved the challenge off. "I'm twice your size. It wouldn't be fair."

"I wouldn't judge anyone, especially your adversaries, by their size here. Someday you will meet a foe larger than you too. Would you stand aside for that reason alone?"

"I guess not." He considered his mug again for a few moments before adding, "Tell you what, next time we have a chance, I'll take you up on that offer." He drained another shot of spirits and winked. "But not today."

"Name your time and place, and I'll show you a thing or two. You might even learn something new."

"Anyway, back to you being a Paladin. You have to admit our confusion makes sense. I mean, you've done an awful lot of healing and very little mace swinging since we met."

"Oh?" she said, raising an eyebrow. "I seemed to recall hitting you pretty hard in that stable yard."

He winced at the reminder.

She continued, "Are we to act like you, the mighty—and might I add, often too brash—Warrior? No, we serve the glory of Thela, and She would rather we fight as a last resort. On top of that, when I joined the Exceptas, I swore to Her I would hurt no one but would instead try to protect innocents the Clan might harm by accident. I didn't even carry a weapon while I was with them."

"That was brave."

"It worked out better than I hoped, actually. Tristan chose me to act as an adviser, which gave me a chance to guide the Clan away from some of their more aggressive plans. As I said before, though, that only worked until Gravesire arrived. I argued against the raids on Copperton, but Gravesire was determined. That was when I realized it was time to leave."

"So why did you do it?"

"Do what?"

"Protect me. Give me that Blessing. Race to heal me after the fight with Tristan."

"Because I believe you're important to the Realms. That badge you wore the night you arrived in town was a sign that Thela sent you to protect us. And that puts me in the position of needing to keep you safe. Especially since you're either too dumb, too stubborn, or both to stay away from trouble yourself."

Gerald sighed. "I'm not the hero you want me to be. Look, the last thing I want is to get tied up in anything. I'm happy to sit around, drink some beer, and watch the sun rise and set each day. But I'm not interested in being 'important to the Realms.' Sorry, but no. Honestly, I'm not looking for reasons to hang around."

She smiled again. Joking, she said, "Careful. With such talk of commitment, you'll be fending off would-be-wives faster than Axeblight makes fireballs."

"I doubt that. But, then, you're not making long-term commitments, either, Lady. What's next for you?"

"You heard why I was with the Exceptas. For me, long-term plans aren't realistic. There aren't many places in the Western Realms I'm welcome. To be honest, I'd be safer in one of the areas held by the Legion than I would be in Riverglow."

"Maybe you shouldn't go, then. Why not stay here? I'm sure we won't be gone long. Just a few days or so."

She shook her head. "No, Thela has led me to you. I'm staying with all of you, wherever you go."

"I guess that's your call. But what's so dangerous for you in the city, anyway?"

"Well, for one thing, there's the reason Mehleese mentioned when we met in the woods."

"That's right," he blurted out, "she called you Out—"

"*Hush*!" she hissed. "If you'll remember, I also told her she was never, ever to say that word out loud."

She leaned in closer and lowered her voice. The smell of lilacs filled his nose. "I've heard stories of Purification Squads showing up to investigate with no more reason than because someone overheard that word and reported it. And when a Purification Squad does show up, people die, always. Copperton doesn't need that now. She has enough to worry about at the moment."

"Okay, so what's the other reason?"

"The Temple of Thela has put a price on my head."

Gerald blinked in surprise. "What? You're kidding, right? The Temple?"

"I wouldn't joke to you about that. In fact, it might lead all of us to danger in Riverglow."

"What did you do to make the Temple put a price on your head?"

She winked. "It's a secret. If you knew, I'd have to kill you. And that would not please Thela at all."

He huffed, frustrated. "Come on, tell me."

She gave him a conspiratorial shake of the head and sipped her beer.

"Fine," he said, dropping it. He'd get her to tell him eventually. He'd just have to take another crack at that nut later. "At any rate, Riverglow's a big place. We'll find a way to keep our visit quiet. I'm sure a good hooded cloak will help too."

Movement from the corner of his eye caught Gerald's attention. A man with a lost expression, likely from warlock spirits, staggered over to them along the bar. "Fergimme, Lurd. Heardja say Riberglow. You mebbe goin' tha way?"

"I'm not sure what you heard, friend," Gerald replied, "but it wasn't that."

The drunken man narrowed his eyes, even as it made him

sway sideways. "Oh. Fergimme den. I'll leabe—hol on. You shure? I shure I heardja say it."

"No, friend. Is there someplace we could maybe take you? You seem a bit tired. Or under the weather."

The man flung a hand up in front of his own face. "Ah jus' fine. Nowhere ta go, tho. Jus' got here a few... few... what time is it? Never min'. Thing is, Ah came from over de Er-Er-Ererfrus—"

"Everfrost Mountains?" Jehn offered.

The man nodded. "Yah. Moundins. Ah came firs. Lotsa others comin' too. The Leeshin driebin' err-ones refu... refu...."

"Refugees?"

"Uh-huh. Refushees dis way. Lots."

"Great," Gerald muttered. That was just what they needed now. Thousands of refugees fleeing the Legion, crossing the mountains, and coming to Copperton for shelter.

"So, what's that got to do with Riverglow?" Jehn asked, voice soft.

"Mah sis's farm is halfway. Need ta warm 'er."

"Warm her?"

The man huffed. "Nah. Naht warm. Warn-m her. Mus' warn-m sis. Leeshin commin'. She needta go to Riberglow. Will you teller? Teller ta get 'way?"

"Friend," Gerald said, "on the chance we happen to go to Riverglow in a week or so, I'll make this deal: if you swear to Thela to stand with the people of Copperton and fight when the Legion comes, I'll make sure your sister gets the message."

"Thas'a deal." The man gave him a jerky nod and extended a shaky hand in the space between them. Gerald shook his hand firmly enough to put the man off balance by accident. The drunk lunged forward, crying out.

Jehn murmured, "In the sight of Thela, the bond is struck. May it please her to see it fulfilled."

After propping him back up, Gerald asked, "What's your name, friend?"

"Degby, mah lohrd."

"Saiyen?" the Warrior called down the bar.

The barkeeper nodded back. "Yes, Lord Goldenshield?"

"Does that offer of a favor still stand?"

"Of course."

"My friend Degby here could use a place to sleep for a few hours. Do you have a room he could use?"

"Of course. Follow me, Master Degby, and we'll get you all sorted."

The man, his mouth hanging open, shook Gerald's hand again in a joyful silence. Then he turned, rubbed something from his eye, and stumbled after Saiyen.

Gerald returned to his stool beside Jehn. "I didn't intend to pick up a side quest. But at least it'll give us something to think about on our way to Riverglow. I guess I'm not getting a room tonight, though. I suppose we'll just have to see how many shots of warlock spirits it takes to make the sun come up around here."

Jehn smiled. "No, the real question is, how badly are you going to need healing in the morning for your hangover?"

"Are you kidding? I can handle my warlock spirits. What about you? I bet I can drink twice the spirits a little slip of a thing like you can, big, bad Paladin or not."

She gave him a wicked laugh. "If that's a challenge, Master Warrior, I accept. But don't come crying to me for healing tomorrow."

"You offend me!" he joked. "You're on."

"And what would you offer as stakes?"

Now he had her. "If I win, you have to tell me why the Temple of Thela is so pissed at you."

She gave him a long, calculating look before inclining her head slightly. "And if I win?"

"Name it."

"One favor. When I call the favor in, whatever it is I ask you to do, you will not refuse me."

He couldn't help but snicker in glee. "You're terrible at this! I'd do that already."

"It's agreed, then?"

"Absolutely."

Jehn's lips moved quickly, whispering something he couldn't quite understand. At the end of it, he thought she muttered, "to see it fulfilled."

With Saiyen off dealing with Degby, Gerald had Nala pour them another round of beer and spirits. When the server set them down, they picked up their shot cups and knocked them together. "Here's to a lazy sunrise, then, and to clear heads and a safe trip to Riverglow City."

With a laugh, they both swallowed the drinks.

CHAPTER TWENTY-SIX

THE SIDE QUEST

GERALD REMEMBERED DRAINING THE SHOT of spirits that started the contest but could not, for all the coin in the Realm Bank, recall anything about the last one. And, oh, blessed bitching Thela, his head throbbed as though an entire clan of trolls had used it for clubbing practice. Hard to believe he'd fought an Elite-level Warrior to a stalemate for who knew how long the other night without sustaining any real, lasting damage, but after only a few hours of warlock spirits, he was about ready to take a one-way trip to the Dark World if that would make the ache between his temples go away.

When Jehn woke him up with the sun peeking through the windows of the Roost's common room, he was facedown on the bar. Saiyan shook his head with a knowing smirk, but thanks to God or Thela or whomever, he said nothing. Gerald's stomach rolled like a ship in a storm, his tongue was the size of one of his gauntlets, his mouth was so dry not even cactus could have survived, and just opening his eyelids sent shivers of electric agony swirling around in his head.

Worse, he was still feeling the effects of the drinks. The world twisted in a violent spiral when he tried to sit up, and at his first attempt at Jehn's name, his mouth produced nothing but a weak, unrecognizable mewling sound.

She mocked him with a sweet smile. "Oh, does the big, strong Warrior feel not so big and strong this morning? I'm shocked! And here I am, a little slip of a thing, feeling fresh as a Planting-season rain." She rubbed the back of his neck as she said it, which, on any other day, would have been something to enjoy. As it was, though, feeling the tips of her nimble fingers against his skin was like being scraped with a garden claw.

He'd have asked her to stop if he could have.

She didn't leave him in agony for long, thank Thela. After a few minutes of making sure he'd felt the worst of it, her hands brightened with the glow of healing, and she held his head at the temples. The icy chill of healing took the sharp edges off his condition but still left him with an aching head and gurgling stomach, enough to make him glad he didn't need to eat anything.

When he could talk again, he looked up at her through a persistent but much more manageable ache. "Bless you, thank you. Thank Thela, whatever. You have no idea how bad I felt."

She gave him another wicked look. "You're lucky I took pity on you. In fact, I'd say you owe me two favors, now. One for the wager and another for the healing."

Waving a hand in agreement, he dropped his head back to the bar. "Sure, fine, yes. Heal the rest of it off and we'll make it five."

"Oh no," the Paladin laughed. "Two is plenty. And besides, if I did that, then you wouldn't learn your lesson."

His face still down on the bar, he grunted. "Oh, I learned.

I learned that they're called warlock spirits for a reason. You give them half a chance and they'll steal your rotting soul."

Through the course of the night's drinking, Gerald had made several plans for how he'd torture Zeke when the Mage and Mehleese walk-of-shamed their way back into the common room. But when they popped into the Roost and Pig—he swore Zeke was floating and the Ranger looked ready to go out and wrestle all eight legs of one of those Creepers at once—he was still in no mood to give anyone some good-natured ribbing. Instead, he grunted and tried to enjoy the relative cool of the bar surface.

"What happened to you?" The grin on Zeke's face said he knew exactly what had happened already.

"The warlock got this one last night." Jehn's voice sparkled with laughter.

"Tough break, Ger. Time to shake it off, though, if we're going to make Riverglow today."

"Degby," the Warrior groaned.

"What's that?"

"Last night," Jehn explained, "he made friends with another fan of the warlock. The man, Degby, asked if we could stop at his sister's farm and deliver a message on our way to Riverglow."

"Sis's farm," however, wasn't much to go on when it came to finding that location. The road to Riverglow City was long, after all.

"I'll get directions, and then we'll go." Gerald lurched off the barstool and straightened, thankful the room was kind enough to stay in one place.

Saiyen showed him to the man's room, where he found Degby fully clothed, lying crosswise on the bed on top of the unused covers and blankets, snoring deeply. Having a healthy dollop of sympathy for how the man must be feeling, Gerald roused him as gently as he could. After grunting in response to a few nudges, Degby woke up and moaned, peering out of one eye.

"Master Degby, do you remember me?"

"Ugh, I think. You… you're going to Riverglow?"

"We are. We've decided to go soon. Do you still want us to warn your sister that the Legion is coming?"

"Please, Lord… well, forgive me, I don't know your name, sir."

"They call me Goldenshield."

Degby's puffy eyes widened, and he tried to scramble off the bed, eliciting a heavy groan. He collapsed backward in a heap.

"Don't move," Gerald said. "I know how you feel. Believe me. I just need a moment, and then you can get back to resting up. We all have many trials ahead."

"Forgive me for my weakness, Lord Goldenshield. I'm a wretch unworthy to be in your presence."

He frowned. "Nonsense, Master Degby. I'm just a guy like you are. No more, no less."

"Begging your pardon, sir, but stories of how you thwarted the Exceptas and single-handedly defeated that villain Kingsbane are all over the Vale. You're a legend."

Gerald shook his head. "I didn't single-handedly do anything. If not for my friends, I'd be dead, and the town's children would still be in Exceptas hands. All I did was buy time for them to do the hard work. I'm not a lord and for sure shouldn't be held up as a legend."

"If you say so, my lord. Either way, I'm deeply honored that you agreed to warn my sister about the Legion."

"I'm happy to do it. But remember your part of the agreement. When the time comes for the Town to fight, you'll stand with them."

"Aye, my lord, I won't forget. It'll be an honor to stand in your name."

"Not my name. For Copperton. A man named Boland is the Sheriff. He'll lead you. And, uh, I'm sure he'll do a fine job." He almost choked saying it, but the man needed reassurance, not a litany of Gerald's dislike for the new Sheriff.

"If you say so, my lord."

"I do. Now, tell me how we can find your sister's farm."

Later that day, with his head still bearing a dull ache and his stomach continuing to protest such a volume of spirits, Gerald rode Zero at an easy walk up a dirt path. They passed an aging split-rail fence and tangles of vines heavy with pumpkins. A hundred yards in the distance, a low, log-built farmhouse stood atop a rise. The pumpkin farm, Martha's Farm according to an etched shingle hanging back where the path left Riverglow Road, matched the description Degby had muttered from his bed.

Beside him, Jehn sat her own horse, a white mare named Lineage, keeping pace. Every so often, he'd swear the corners of her mouth twitched with the ghost of a smile. She was still finding humor in his performance—or better said, failure—with the spirits the night before.

Just far enough behind to speak to each other in low voices without being heard, Mehleese and Zeke followed. Z was still aglow from the previous night, looking like the cat that ate the canary. Blasted Thela, he'd probably sport that simpering grin for a week. Even Demon, his foul-tempered unicorn, appeared to be in better spirits than usual.

Putting him out of his mind, Gerald turned to his right and pouted at Jehn. "Come on, you have to tell me how you did it."

She chuckled. "Nope."

He frowned, but it faded quickly. At least she wasn't laughing at him out loud.

"Come on, tell me. Why not?"

"What is there to tell? I matched you drink for drink until you couldn't manage to drink anymore. Or, come to think of it, even hold your head up straight. But don't feel too bad. It is a rather large head. I'm sure it must be quite tiresome to manage it all day. And I'll admit that was an impressive volume of warlock spirits. After all that, I can see how the effort alone was exhausting."

"You love messing with me, don't you?"

She winked. "How could I not? You make it so easy."

"I'll have to work on that, then."

"See that you do. I appreciate a challenge."

"Speaking of massive heads, look at that." He gestured toward the house. A woman in a wide-brimmed straw-yellow hat crouched on her hands and knees amid a collection of plants, digging in the garden. A girl, maybe ten or twelve by the look of her, was beside her in the dirt, uncovering squash from a vast tangle of stems and leaves.

As they approached, the woman leaned back on her haunches, clapping dirt from her hands and peering at them from under her hat. Even with the rendered, digital look that everyone had here, her face was worn, covered in tight, sun-darkened skin lined from hours and hours of work outdoors. Dark bags stood out beneath her eyes. The eyes, themselves, though, stood in contrast to her otherwise haggard appearance. They were cold and calculating. Sharp as a bird of prey's.

"I'd say that's far enough, friends," she said. "I've got a son ready to release our dogs the second I give him a whistle. Just so none of that becomes necessary, why don't you state your business."

Gerald cleared his throat. "Ma'am, they call me Goldenshield. Your brother, Degby, asked if we would be kind enough to pay our respects to you on your way to Riverglow. He had a message for us to deliver."

"Goldenshield? What kind of name is that?"

"It's a… long story," he replied.

"Well, Master Goldenshield, my name is Martha, and you're using up my daylight. Since these squash aren't going to tend to themselves, why don't you go ahead and give me my useless brother's message and be on your way."

"Uh, right. Sure." This reception was not what he'd expected. On the other hand, her gruff reply made it easy to be straight with her. "The Legion of Guardians has begun an invasion of the Western Realms. Degby had to flee his home in the Everfrost Mountains and is seeking refuge in Copperton, where he intends to help defend the town when the Legion arrives."

She cocked her head. "You're sure this is my brother? Skinny fellow? More than likely so drunk he couldn't talk?"

"Yes, ma'am, that's him."

"My lord, my brother hasn't done a productive thing since before Momma cut him off the apron strings. He moves from barstool to barstool, gutter to alley to gutter and back. I can't believe he even thought about me, let alone decided I needed to be warned of an army coming. Some days I wonder why Thela, bless Her, leaves men like him to make a waste of themselves while She takes fellas like my husband, Dayl, to the Dark World too soon. Thela knows I could use his help these days."

"Ma'am, um, Martha, worthless drunk or not, he did think to have us bring you the warning. And when the Legion sweeps through here, it's not going to be any place for a woman with a family to be on her own."

The lady smirked back, took off her hat, and wiped her

brow with the back of her hand, leaving a smear of dirt across her forehead. "Rosalie, why don't you run and get us the waterskin. I reckon we could use a break." The girl jumped up and ran off toward the house, not wasting time on a second look.

When Rosalie was gone, Martha shot him a scowl that could melt iron. "Son, or Golden-whatever-the-Thela-be-damned-thing-you-said, you make one more comment like that to me and you'll find this ain't no place for a young man that likes to run his mouth about things he knows nothing about, friends or not. It's been quite a few years since I opened a man from his big mouth to his jewels, but I've got half a dozen knives on me that have stolen a life, and you wouldn't see a single one of them until it was sticking out of you.

"Now, go on, tell me again how you—and my drunk brother—know what's best for me and my family. Because to be honest, son, Thela has been heaping centian droppings on us for the past three years now, and it'd be nice to get a little bloody if only to let off some steam."

Gerald shifted in his saddle. Definitely not how this was supposed to go. Beside him, Jehn coughed. Was there a hint of a chuckle in it?

"Forgive me, ma'am," he said tipping his head toward her. "Your brother led me to believe you were a little more… delicate."

"Heh," she said and then spat beside her. "Degby was always the delicate one. When he was a boy, he spent three days crying every year over the pigs when slaughter came. Now, then, I appreciate you giving me the message, but as you can see, I got a farm full of harvesting needing done, and if winter beats us to it, we'll freeze to death long before any army gets here.

"Now, if I had a few more hands to help get the harvest in,

that might make a difference. But the fact is no one will work on Martha's Farm these days, so it's up to me and my children to see to it."

"Why won't anyone work for you?" Jehn asked. "This part of Copperton Vale is usually so thick with migrant farm-hands at Harvest that you can't get your mount up to a decent run for fear of running one over."

"It's the blasted ghosts, my lady. No one'll work the farm because they think it's haunted."

"Forgive me," Zeke said, pulling Demon up alongside them. "Did you say ghosts?"

"Well, look at you there," Martha replied with a raised eyebrow. "I don't believe I've ever heard an elf talk without sneering. Will Her wonders never cease? Yes, Master Elf, I did say ghosts. At the end of my property here to the south, there's a cemetery. About a year back, a squad of Purifiers of that no-account new king came through and dug half of it up. Since then, when the sun sets every evening, a cast of soldier ghosts climbs up from the earth and goes around scaring folk half out of their minds. They don't do anything, but they stalk around the graveyard and the surrounding area, including my rear fields. Seems they don't much respect property lines. Before long, word got out, and now I have to pay double to get a hand to work my fields for a day. And I don't have double to pay."

"I'm sorry, ma'am, that sounds like—" Gerald started.

Zeke cut him off. "Lady Martha, if we could rid the place of those ghosts, send their souls to rest or on their way back to the Dark World, would that fix your problem? Could you get enough help to get the harvest in with time to make your way to Riverglow for the winter? Oh, and they call me Ek'zae Axeblight. It's my pleasure to meet you."

Rosalie returned with a waterskin and an uncertain look at Gerald, as if surprised to find him still on his horse. She handed the skin to Martha, who uncapped it and took a long drink.

When the woman finished, she wiped her mouth and corked it. Giving it back to the girl, she said, "Offer our guests a drink."

Jehn declined, but Gerald accepted the water happily, still feeling somehow dehydrated from the warlock spirits. As he drank, the woman said, "Master Axeblight, I reckon that might help me a bit, if word got around that the specters wasn't out there, apt to cause trouble. Would you be willing to do that? I mean, I ain't got anything much to give you in return. Perhaps a few loaves and some fruits for your journey."

"We'll do it!" Zeke said as soon as the words had left the woman's mouth.

Gerald sputtered on the water, dribbling half a mouthful down his front.

Now they had to deal with ghosts.

Shit.

CHAPTER TWENTY-SEVEN

THE GHOSTS

"MAYBE WE SHOULD TALK ABOUT this, you know, as a group?"

"Oh, uh, sorry, Ger—Goldenshield. I just figured we should help the nice lady out."

He looked, disbelieving, from his friend to the woman, still kneeling in her garden. Raising his hand, he held out one finger. "If you'll pardon us, ma'am. We'll discuss it for just a moment."

"Do as you will," Martha replied, giving him an amused smile that looked much like the same one Jehn was fond of flashing him.

Gerald leaned in close to his friend. On Zeke's other side, Mehleese did the same.

"What in the five bloody worlds, Zeke? We're kind of in a hurry to get to Riverglow City. We don't need to be wandering around this lady's field for half the night, trying to find ghosts, of all things!"

Zeke shrugged. "I don't know. Do we honestly need to be in such a hurry? I could stand it if we took our time a little.

Why not enjoy being in the country a bit more? And it's not like you've got a concrete plan, anyway. I mean, we were pretty much run out of Copperton on a rail by Lord High *Bland*, and we have no clue if we'll find what we're looking for in Riverglow. For that matter, do you even know who to talk to when we get there?"

"I mean, they have to have a Mages' guild or something. I figured we'd start there. Find the oldest wizard we can. They always know the secret stuff, right?"

"I'll take that as a 'No,' then. No real idea. In that case, I say what's the harm in taking a few hours to help Martha and her family out? After all, you were more than happy to lend Degby a hand and a room, and he was a stumbling drunk from what I hear. So we help the drunk but tell the lady with the farm, the responsibilities, and the family to go suck it? You're not *that* big a dick, are you, *Lord Goldenshield*?"

Before Gerald could reply, Mehleese put in, "I agree with him. If we were willing to take the man's message, I don't see why we wouldn't help his sister when she's desperate for it."

"She doesn't look desperate for anything," Gerald muttered, but deep down, did he want to be that guy? He sighed and threw his arms in the air. "Fine. We'll go pretend to be ghost hunters. Why the fuck not?"

Turning to Martha, he said, "Sure, ma'am. We'll help with your, um, ghost problem. Where can we find them?"

"Well, isn't that heartening news for an old woman's ears. I'll have my oldest boy, Turbahl, walk you out to the south end of the farm. From there, it should be pretty clear. And may Thela bless you for helping out a poor family in need."

Rosalie took a few minutes fetching Turbahl, who'd been doing some kind of work with his three other brothers in the family's wilting barn. Likely once proud and upright, the structure leaned at a frightening angle. No way it would stand for many more cycles. Turbahl, the oldest of six children—four sons and two daughters—was a ruddy-looking boy, even if too thin, approaching fifteen. He displayed none of the usual traits of a teenager, though, and took the task from his mother without a single complaint.

The boy led them beyond the farmhouse and the leaning barn and continued south along a well-worn path splitting the property down the middle longways. The farm was deeper than Gerald imagined, twice as big in the back as it was in the front, which faced Riverglow Road. They walked slowly—keeping the pace Turbahl set—past fields rich with a variety of produce including lettuces, carrots, tomatoes, peas, more squash, melons, and corn. Tall rows of it stretched out in front of them for as far as the eye could see.

"Thela's bloody prom, Zeke, why did it have to be a cornfield?" Gerald whispered as they entered the first of several sections of the tall grain.

"What's wrong with corn?"

"Are you kidding me? Next to sunflowers—and don't even get me started on those damn things; it's like they're always looking down on you, ready to eat you whole or something—corn is the creepiest plant anywhere. The stuff gets huge, and you end up wandering around in it, lost. And if that wasn't bad enough, the sun is going down, and we're going out to look for the undead. On purpose! This couldn't get any damned creepier."

"I shouldn't mention the field of sunflowers up ahead, then?"

Gerald's head whipped forward, scanning the field in panic. "What? Where?"

His friend threw his head back, laughing. "Holy Thela, Gerald," he whispered, "we're living in a damned video game. A few days ago, we spent the afternoon killing spiders the size of my car, and you're freaking out about digital sunflowers and corn? Dude, calm down. Enjoy it. Not everyone gets to live in a world of make-believe like this.

"Besides," he added, "I'm pretty sure the corn can't hurt anyone wearing mail anyway."

They rode in silence after that, Gerald considering Zeke's advice. That, by itself, was more than just a little strange. Who was this Ek'zae guy, and what had he done with his best friend? In everyday "real" life, Z would stress himself out to the point of sleeplessness when he had a new project or a deadline at work. He had once lost his temper and cussed out a grocery store cashier over a fifty-cent overcharge on a pack of energy drinks. Moderate, reasoned consideration and the easy acceptance of change weren't exactly his usual characteristic traits.

Maybe life in Thelaroth agreed with him.

Then again, maybe he was just giddy about whatever he and Mehleese had been up to last night.

As the sun slipped below the horizon, the group reached the last few rows of corn and a split-rail fence matching the one surrounding the pumpkin patch at the front of the farm. Turbahl waved at an overgrown collection of headstones just beyond it.

"Mom said to take you to the fence and come right back before the sun set." He looked to the west and the sliver of pinkish sky giving way to indigo and then black. "She said you should come on back up to the house when you're done. And if it's too late, you're welcome to the barn."

"Thank you, Master Turbahl," Jehn said. "We'll be back up in a little while. Go on, now, before your momma starts to worry."

With a curt nod, the boy turned right around and stepped quickly back up the trail. Whether because he was near the cemetery at dusk or had feelings about corn that matched Gerald's, he wasted no time making his way back toward the house. He was out of sight in no time.

Jehn and Mehleese both slid off their horses with grace. "Leave the mounts here," the Ranger said, "tied to the fence. Demon might not bolt if spirits appear, but the horses probably will. Unless they've been trained in the Darkwood, but that's time consuming and expensive. We'll walk through the gate and hang out in the graveyard until ghosts appear."

"How long will that take?" Zeke asked, dropping from his unicorn.

"Not long. If they're real, they'll show up almost immediately after the sun goes down. If we haven't seen any in an hour, it's all nonsense."

"Wait," Gerald said, "so you honestly expect to see ghosts?"

Mehleese cast an eye toward the graveyard. "We could, yes. Ghosts, banshees, skeletons, zombies, vampires—you name it, I've fought it here at some point. Don't forget where you are."

He shook his head in disbelief. Next, it'd be leprechauns and talking birds.

"So, um," Gerald said, "how do you go about killing them, seeing as they're already dead and all?"

"I'll Bless our weapons to release the tortured Dead," Jehn said. "Axeblight, do you know the Dispel Death cast?"

"Yes. But it's not easy, and there's no guarantee it'll work. We'll have to see how it goes."

"Just don't hit them with fire," Mehleese said. "They don't like that. And I'd hate to see them mess up your pretty little pointy ears."

Spots of peach colored the elf's cheeks. He gave his friend

an embarrassed shrug. Somehow, Gerald managed not to roll his eyes at them.

The group climbed over the fence, but Jehn put an arm out before they crossed into the graveyard itself. “Hold your weapons out.” Mehleese offered her bow and quiver, and Gerald followed suit with his not-so-new-looking war hammer. Jehn held up a wicked, studded mace in one hand and raised her other hand over all the weapons.

“Blessed Thela, guide our hands and eyes, and let us do Your work in releasing the tortured souls of those still bound to this World.” Her hands glowed as she spoke, and all the weapons flashed a blinding bright white.

Turning away from the searing light, Gerald blinked. “Great, now I can’t see in the dark.” His vision had become one big orange blot.

“It’ll pass soon,” Jehn said.

After he blinked hard and wiped a few tears away, his vision crept back to him. He could already see things close to the ground.

“Remind me never to look right at that again.”

“Quit complaining, Ger. Let’s check out the boneyard.”

The cemetery wasn’t a big one by any stretch, more a small collection of headstones. They were basic slabs, each with the sigil of a scroll atop a pair of crossed spears. Many were cut in half or knocked over completely, strewn in pieces across the ground.

“These graves don’t look old enough to be knocked over and crumbling.”

“They aren’t old,” Jehn said in a near whisper. “Three years, not more.”

Zeke stepped with care around the markers. “Who would do this to the recently buried?”

"Martha said a Purification Squad did it, didn't she?" Gerald asked.

Jehn gasped. "We should go," she said, ignoring the question. "Now. We need to get out of here. Right now."

"Um, guys?" Zeke pointed ahead. At the very center of the graveyard, a much larger headstone lay in a tangle of weeds, hacked into hundreds of tiny pieces. The headstone's remains carried the same sigil with the scroll, but instead of crossed spears behind it, dragons flanked it. "Isn't that—"

"Forget that, Axeblight," Mehleese said, nocking an arrow. "We have guests."

Around them, wisps of fog drew up from the ground and collected, like expanding puddles of smoke. In the span of two breaths, the pools grew upward, taking the shape of translucent men. Armored, translucent men, with full helmets and spears.

The hammer in Gerald's hand vibrated with energy.

"Back to Thela with you!" Zeke shouted and threw his hands out. Green lights swirled in spirals, growing from his open palms, building into starbursts of magic held back only by force of will. When the spinning spots of energy reached the size of small plates, he released them with a grunt and a shove. The two circles of arcane energy shot forward, coming together in a greenish beam that struck the nearest ghost-soldier in the chest. The specter threw his hands up and faded back to mist.

"One down!"

Gerald charged ahead, his ferocious *WarCry* echoing from his lips, calling the ghosts to him so Zeke could cast without interference. The call had the desired effect. The eleven remaining ghosts stalked toward him.

Shield

Nothing happened.

Shit, he hadn't thought to buy a replacement for the Shield of the Vale.

"Fuck me," he growled as the first two soldiers reached him, jabbing with see-through spears. He knocked the first aside with a clank, half surprised his hammer didn't pass through it. Spinning to his right, he avoided a second attack and countered with a head shot that would have been a Stunning blow against a normal, living being, if not a Critical Hit. Instead, the helmet smashed inward, and the spirit burst into smoke. It dissipated, floating away on the wind.

The first attacker spouted an arrow in its neck, in the one unprotected spot between the helmet and its shoulder armor. It, too, evaporated and disappeared.

Another blast of green energy sailed past Gerald and crashed into an advancing ghost, which disappeared before it took another step.

Two more fell to arrows that dropped to the ground after their targets became mist. Six down. They were halfway done.

Where was Jehn?

Before he could stop to look, a trio floated toward him, spears raised, ready to strike.

Dammit, he felt naked without a shield.

Lacking another tactical option, he jumped at them, dodging spear points and swinging his hammer at the one in the center. He caught it in the shoulder but only a glancing blow. The ghost soldier countered by sweeping his spear across Gerald's legs, knocking them out from under him.

The other two charged past him, toward Zeke.

Hitting the ground with a thud, Gerald rolled to his right, just as an eerie boot landed where his head had been a moment before. He sprang up and brought the hammer around in a flat arc, this time making a solid connection. Another cloud of flog blew away from him.

Holding the hammer over his head, he shouted again, filling it with the Combat Power. The two soldiers that had raced past him skidded to a stop and spun, coming back at him. A pair of arrows struck one of the apparitions in the side, and Zeke's green light blasted the other.

The first disappeared, but either his friend didn't charge the Dispel spell long enough or missed somehow, because the incorporeal warrior barely faltered before starting forward again. Gerald took advantage of the lapse, though, and delivered a fast strike to the chest. Power thrummed through him and his hammer, banishing the ghost.

Three shades remained, and all three raced toward Zeke. He blasted the first with that now-familiar green magic, melting it into nothing. In what was becoming a normal sight, an arrow split the gap between the second one's helmet and armor. The shade faded into fog as well, joining its brothers in the Dark World or wherever the dead were supposed to go.

Gerald intercepted the last one, planning to knock aside its spear thrust at the last second. He missed, though, and the gauzy spear struck his side in a flash of red and orange. Several health points ticked off, but it wasn't serious damage. With a shout, he swung his hammer back around, catching the specter in the same place Mehleese's arrows landed, right in the neck. It exploded into smoke and vanished.

The Warrior looked from Zeke to Mehleese, who were standing close to each other by the edge of the fence. "Are you both okay? Anyone hurt."

"Only you got hit, Goldenshield."

"Good. I'm fine. What happened to Jehn?"

His face gone somehow paler than usual, Zeke pointed a shaking finger back at the center of the cemetery.

Gerald spun, squeezing his hammer so tightly that his

hands stung with the pressure. What was wrong? Had something happened to her?

Amid the rubble of the headstones, Jehn stood near the different one, the one broken into countless pieces. Facing her, not even an arm's length away, was another, larger ghost, different from the others. His armor was enormous and covered in intricate detail work, majestic. The helmet covering his head was open at the face, revealing an older man with a full beard and determined eyes.

Eyes Gerald had seen before.

"Blessed Thela, holy God," he mumbled. "Jehn, st-step back."

She half turned to face him. Tears poured down her cheeks in a steady stream.

"Jehn, what's…"

Ignoring him, she turned back to the ghost.

Her mace dropped to the ground. She raised her other hand to the ghost's chest. A familiar golden light glowed between them. The apparition lifted a hand to her chin, frowning as it passed right through. His dark eyes filled with sadness. Pain. The look lasted barely a breath, though, before that determination replaced it once again. Then he raised a fist to his chest, in salute—not for Jehn but for Gerald. His stare was fixed on the young Warrior as the shade faded to nothing beneath the light of Jehn's holy touch.

And then he was gone.

"Gerald," Zeke said, voice filled with shock, "that was—"

Jehn dropped to her knees and buried her face in her hands.

Not turning back, Gerald replied, "I know. It was him."

"Who?" Mehleese asked.

Gerald took a step forward. "Jehn?"

"That was the man who sent us here," Zeke whispered. Mehleese gasped.

Another step. "Jehnilyas, are you okay?"

"But," the woman behind him stammered, "that was… that was… the old king. Rhandren Sophent, the king that Dalor drove out."

"Fuck," Zeke said. "You're kidding me."

Gerald reached the kneeling Paladin. Placing a gentle hand on her shoulder, he whispered, "Jehn?"

She looked up at him, her eyes red and shining with tears. "That… that was my father. I never knew where he died. Never knew where they buried him."

Her face fell into her hands again, her body shuddering with sobs.

CHAPTER TWENTY-EIGHT

THE TRUTH

AFTER SEVERAL LONG MOMENTS KNEELING beside her father's desecrated grave, Jehn stood up, shaking the stunned group into action. Together, they climbed back over the fence, untied their mounts, and started toward the farmhouse in silence. Even Zeke kept his thoughts to himself. The dark, unnatural quiet of night in Thelaroth surrounded them, oppressive. Even the tall rows of corn seemed more somber than eerie.

Reaching the farmhouse and barn, Gerald looked from one to the other. A single light burned in one of the house's windows. "Do we want to hit the road or rest here for the night? It looks like Martha is still up."

"Riverglow Road can be a dangerous place at night if you're not focused on your surroundings. We're too distracted." Mehleese scratched Solus between the ears. The horse whinnied in appreciation.

Gerald nodded, glad she hadn't named Jehn outright. Then again, he doubted the Paladin would have noticed. She had a vacant, faraway look in her eyes. Off in a world of her own.

"You're probably right. As much as I hate to lose the time, morning will bring sharper eyes and clearer heads. Let's go up to the house."

"No," Jehn rasped, startling all of them. "I can't deal with a family of strangers tonight. I'll stay out here. You go on."

"You two go on, then," Gerald said to the others. "I'll stay."

Mehleese shook her head. "Don't be a buffoon, Goldenshield. Whatever we do, we stay together. We'll shelter in the barn." She gave the slumping structure an uncertain glance. "Or maybe a simple camp out here instead."

They found a clearing free of crops not far from the barn and set out bedrolls and made a small fire. The flame added just enough light to cheer them after the grim business in the graveyard. They sat together, still silent, watching the sky above them turn from black to navy blue as the moon climbed up over the horizon.

Finally, Jehn said, "I'm sorry. I shouldn't be acting like this."

Zeke opened his mouth but snapped it shut without saying anything. Gerald, too, struggled for something appropriate to say.

Mehleese came to their rescue. "Nonsense. I can't imagine the shock of seeing that myself. I'd still be a blubbering mess down there."

"He… he sent us away. Before it got bad. He was sick. His day was coming, and we all knew it. But by then, he knew Dalor wouldn't honor his promise. Knew that the Thela-damned usurper would hunt us all down sooner or later, abdication or not. So he sent us all, what family remained—me, my older sister, and two brothers—away to find someplace safe to stay until… until the signs came. He split the Royal Guard and sent a dozen with us.

"I heard a month later that Dalor had issued a proclamation that my father was a traitor and was working with the Guardians. Days after that came another that he'd been found and put to death. I assumed that a Purification Squad found him, but I never knew where. Until today."

She scrubbed a tear from her cheek. "I can't believe that wasn't enough for him. That he had to desecrate the graves too. Dalor and the Temple will answer for that."

"So now what do we do?" Zeke murmured.

Gerald cocked his head. "What do you mean?"

"Forgive me, but Jehn, my lady, you're the rightful heir. You should be the one on the throne, even more so with the Legion coming. You need to stand up to Dalor. To fight for the crown. And we'll help you, right, Ger?"

"Who do you think you are, Ek'zae, or whatever your real name is?" she exploded, stabbing a finger at the elf. "Don't you ever tell me what I *should* do again. I don't need your help. I didn't ask for your help. I'll be damned to wander the Dark World before I let you or anyone else tell me what I'm going to do!"

Zeke flinched. "I'm… I'm sorry. I just meant—"

"I know what you meant," she cut in. She softened slightly, letting the concrete edge slip from her tone. "I'm sorry. I'm just—I'm no heir. I was never the heir. My eldest brother, Sandwin, was the heir. At least, he was until my father abdicated. After that, the line was finished. Dalor had no need to hunt down anyone, either Father or my siblings. His succession was secure. But the man has always been paranoid. He heard the name Sophent around every blind corner, in every whispered conversation. Saw it in the eyes of every sycophant in the King's Hall. I'm sure he believed we were out in the countryside rallying the people to our cause."

"Those were a hard few years, my lady, for all of us,"

Mehleese said. "What Dalor feared most of the Realms hoped for. That somehow the king or one of you, his family, would return to challenge him."

"If only. Dalor has the Temple and the Bank supporting him. Between them, those two control the nobles. We were penniless and without direction. Not exactly revolutionary."

"What did you do?"

"We moved from place to place, doing odd jobs, hunters' contracts, that sort of thing. Trying to get by unnoticed. But we failed even at that. A little over a year ago, we were camping near a fishing village in the Lakelands. I had to go into town for supplies and took one of the guards with me. Everyone else was in camp when they came."

She paused just long enough to let the hitch in her throat pass.

"I never saw them, but the village folk in the area said there were at least two groups of Purifiers, with at least one Mage and a Shadow Priest. They butchered what was left of my family and the guards. When I got back and found them…"

"Jehn, don't," Gerald whispered.

Her eyes welled up with grief and pain, but she kept going. Quiet tears cascaded down her smooth, rendered cheeks. "The two of us, the guard and I, buried everyone. And then I told him to go. I didn't want—couldn't stand the thought of—any more bloodshed in my family's name. He refused, of course, so I waited until he was asleep and snuck away. Not long after that, I found Tristan and the Exceptas. They always needed more Paladins and Mages, so they were happy to welcome me into the Clan, and they asked no questions. Most all the Exceptas have secrets, anyway, so everyone minds their own business. They did in the beginning, at any rate. It was a nice arrangement. At least, it was until Gravesire showed up and Tristan began to change.

"And that brings us here, a day's ride from my first visit to Riverglow City in three years. And to answer your question, Ek'zae Axeblight, we keep to the path Thela has laid before us."

Zeke shot Gerald a look of reproach. The Warrior winced, wracked with new pangs of guilt. They were headed to Riverglow to find a way out of here, to undo the inexplicable work that Jehn's father had done back in that Quik Mart, an entire world away from this patch of ground beside a slanted barn. Their journey wasn't the pilgrimage Jehn thought it was, directed by Almighty hands.

The guilt had to be plain on his face, but he gave his friend a slight shake of his head, dismissing the unspoken criticism. They'd deal with that another time, after they found out what they could in the city. No point in upsetting her more just yet.

"Morning will be here soon. Let's get some rest. It'll help if we're at our Max tomorrow."

Soon after, Zeke and Mehleese curled together on the soft ground, putting themselves to sleep. Jehn, however, sat up, legs crossed, staring into the night, showing no signs of wanting rest.

"You should sleep, Jehnilyas," Gerald said, whispering to avoid waking the others. Then again, he had no idea what it might take to wake someone up out of a dead sleep in Thelaroth. They might be able to snooze through a tornado and wake up only if he looked at them directly and thought, *Wake Up*.

"Sleep won't help me, Goldenshield," she replied in a low, steady voice. "For three years, I've been running away from the memory of the man that became that ghost. Three years trying not to think about what happened to my family. Three years of not asking myself, 'What if he hadn't gotten sick? What if he'd been strong enough to fight Dalor when the challenge came?' Three years of blowing like a leaf from one day to the next. Three long years, I was asleep. But now I'm awake, and I'm furious."

"Jehn, I know, but—"

"Furious that I've done nothing but hide all this time. Furious I feel so Thela-be-damned helpless in the face of the Five Worlds being torn apart." She fixed him with a hard look. "Furious that my father, the man who was king, ran away instead of fighting with every last breath to defend what was his. What was ours. What was best for the Realms."

She sighed. "And furious that I still have no idea what to do."

What was he supposed to say? That look of condemnation from Zeke hung on him like an anchor around his neck. "We'll figure something out."

"You can't fix the world for me, and I don't want you to. Now that I've found my fury, I'm going to cling to it. I'm going to forge something useful with it. And I'm not going to sleep again until I've figured out what."

He started to say… something. But even if he'd had the right skill with words, none would bring her comfort. She didn't want them. Sometimes it was best to just be upset for a while.

Instead, he slid closer to her. Settled beside her, cross-legged. Near enough to hear her breath, not quite near enough to feel it. He stretched out a hand and made a show of placing it flat on the ground between them. Still saying nothing, he stared out into the moonlit countryside.

Not turning, not looking, not speaking, she placed her hand on top of his.

Through the long hours of the night, until the horizon became a streak of flame, neither of them moved or spoke or slept.

CHAPTER TWENTY-NINE

THE CAPITAL

WHEN THE SUN ROSE OVER the mountains to the east, Martha came out from the house bearing a satchel filled with bread and fruit, as promised. On her heels, two of her children, Rosalie and a younger boy they hadn't met, brought them each a mug of minty tea spiced with cinnamon. The tea had that too-clean, almost cold, metallic taste that everything seemed to have in Thelaroth, which was even odder in a hot, spiced beverage. Still, Gerald was getting used to it.

"The animals didn't make much noise last night in fright. You managed it, then?"

"Yes, ma'am," Gerald answered. "I don't think you'll have any more trouble." He took a quick sip of the steaming tea. "How long has your family lived here?"

"My husband's people go back on the farm here four or five generations."

"So long enough to know what happened back there?"

She sipped her own mug and considered him for a moment. At last she gestured at a tall oak looming beside the squat house. Next to it was a stone grave marker. "I told Dayl not to go out there. What lords did was none of our business, and if they wanted to fight here, I thought, let 'em be done with it quick. But he'd been out talking with the old king the day before and said he wasn't about to have a dying man rousted by jumped-up rabble thugs on the edge of land his family had owned for more than a hundred years. So he strapped on his rusty old breastplate and put that two-handed sword of his on his back. Although how he managed to pick it up with his back the way it was, I'll never understand. Then he trudged out there, saying he was just going to talk. But I knew that look in his eye. He meant to stand with old King Rhandren and his guards.

"A few hours later, when the Purifiers were long gone, the boys and I wheeled him back up here on the cart and buried him beside that tree, where he used to sit in the evening and sip his cider. Took three more days to bury the others. I used to wish we could've given them nicer markers. But then the Purifiers came back, and I was glad we didn't."

"I'm sorry to hear that, ma'am. At least they'll be at rest now."

She gave him a firm nod. "I never did know what was holding all them spirits here, no matter how bad it came at the end. Whatever it was didn't bind my Dayl the same way. He's been gone to the Dark World three years now, still waiting for Thela to find a use for him, I reckon."

Casting her gaze at Jehn, she added, "I am glad you put them others to rest, though. For us, sure, but more for them. And I hope if they have any kin left, they can find some peace from it too."

"Let's hope so," Gerald agreed. "We'll be on our way now. Good luck. I hope you'll do your best to get to Riverglow before that army gets here."

The gray-haired woman gave him a grim smile and a playful smack on the cheek. “Sooner or later, son, you’re going to figure out it isn’t smart to tell women what they should do.”

“I’m sorry, Martha, I—”

“Don’t you worry your rugged face about it. We seen a lot of hard times here, and that bitter old hag Thela ain’t run us off yet. I reckon we’ll make it through the next thing, too, one way or another. Now, you all get on now.” Half turning, she squinted at Mehleese. “And you, you watch all these kids. Somebody ought to be keeping ’em outta trouble.”

The Ranger sniffed, but her eyes held a hint of a smile.

They climbed atop their respective mounts and set off for Riverglow Road, waving to Martha and the kids as they turned.

They made good time, keeping a steady, quick walk but never letting the mounts reach a trot so as to preserve stamina. At too hard a pace, they’d have needed a rest every so often. Gerald wondered if they had some kind of internal counter for that the same way he had for the health points.

The road melted past, and the peaks of the Iron Spikes rose in front of them to the east. After all the excitement at the farm—for better or worse—the rest of the journey was about as interesting as watching the patchy Thelaroth grass grow. Although it seemed for a time they weren’t getting anywhere, at last, the road led to Jordan’s Pass, the gateway through the mountains from Copperton Vale to the Realm of Kingsland beyond. On the far side, Riverglow City, capital of the Western Realms, awaited.

At dawn the following morning, they were met by the city gleaming below them. It had been built at the confluence of three rivers, and the light of the rising sun glinted off the water, giving the city its name. The light bathed it in a golden orange glow that reflected off the towers and spires climbing toward the sky from behind the city wall. Gerald's breath caught in his throat. He'd seen it before in the game but never like this.

"Awash in the light of dawn, there is no more beautiful sight in all of the Western Realms than Riverglow City," Jehn said in a husky voice. Then, more quietly, "I didn't realize how much I've missed her."

"Come on," Gerald said, spurring Zero. "I believe you promised me the best lager in the Realms."

She returned a wan smile but said nothing.

They made their way from the heights of the Pass through the foothills on the eastern faces of the Irons Spikes and toward the city itself. Not long after, they came upon a line of workers, farmers, and adventurers snaking their way up to the gate itself. The long queue of people waiting to get into Riverglow advanced at a snail's pace.

"Is it always like this?" Zeke rubbed his nose with his fingers.

"It never used to be," Jehn replied.

"No," Mehleese agreed, "a lot has changed in the past few years. Before Dalor, there was never a wait to enter the city. Now it's worse every time I visit."

She leaned in close to the others. "Watch how thorough the gate guards are. Remember when I said Dalor is paranoid? He demands an inspection of anyone entering the gates. Smugglers are levied hefty fines, and the guards on duty are docked double that when contraband slips by. As a result, the city has the most ridiculous gate checks of any I've ever entered."

"Good thing we aren't smuggling anything, then," Gerald said.

Jehn winked. "Well, anything but me, but I don't much look like the girl who left all those years ago."

Gerald fidgeted as they approached the gates, worried that wouldn't be the case. He nearly froze when they at last reached the gate and their turn for inspection. A trio of guards leered at them in suspicion, but as Jehn had said, years had passed since anyone had even thought about the disgraced king's youngest daughter. They were waved through with little more than a few uninterested questions and a handful of grunts.

Once inside the city, they were thrust into the heaving mass of citizens shuffling through the overcrowded streets. The people were packed together, not quite shoulder to shoulder, among enough mounted travelers that the crowd couldn't bother to make way for them one at a time. Instead, the pedestrians and animals all crawled along in a massive, shuffling wave.

As they made their way deeper into the city and got away from the crush of entrants, the crowd grew thinner. By the time they reached the inner wall separating the Four Wards of the city from the encircling Outer Ward, they could move at least somewhat freely.

Inner Riverglow was split into five sections built on the confluence of the three rivers. The Spikelet flowed south from the tallest peaks of the Iron Spikes, and the Souwater ran north to meet it, the only river in the Realms to do so. Those two converged at a small delta at the center of the city, just in front of the Royal Keep, and made the Freerun. From there it turned southwest, flowing beyond the walls and all the way to Kingsland Bay.

The Keep, the seat of the king's power in the Realms, was a marvel of engineering, a single castle built up from both banks of the Freerun. It was often called the "Straddling Keep," since it resembled a man straddling a creek bed, with one foot to each side of the water. The two base parts of the structure on opposite sides of the river rose high into the air, where they joined into a single, imposing fortress. Down low, the bases were connected with a hodgepodge of stone bridges and tunnels, which had been added over the years to provide access to the "leg" on the far side without requiring the high climb to the joint where they came together.

The Four Wards were split into quadrants surrounding the Keep. They included the Ward of Guilds, the Holy Ward, the Ward of Soldiers, and the Ward of Books. Centuries ago, the people living in the city observed the partitions and separated themselves based on their class and professions. That practice had ceased ages ago, though. In modern times, the wards were split more along economic lines than professional. The oldest establishments, though, could still be found in the appropriate ward, a reminder of the old ways.

Outside the inner wall, an uninterrupted ring encircled the city, a much less formal array of cart-based vendors and inexpensive shelters that were known as both the Outer Ward and, more colloquially, the Bazaar.

As they neared the inner wall, Jehn slowed Lineage and trailed behind the group. Gerald raised an eyebrow in concern. "Everything okay?"

With a burst of light, the hood of her cloak covered her head, obscuring her face with shadows, even in the bright light of morning. "You go on. I want to just walk around a bit and see some old places. Meet me at a tavern called the Drunken Rock. I'll be there by nightfall."

"Are you sure you wouldn't rather stay with us? You're less likely to be recognized in a group than alone."

"No, I'll be fine. Go ahead and do what you came here for."

"It's not safe for you to be in the city alone," Gerald grumbled.

"Relax, Goldenshield," Mehleese cut in. "I'll stay with

her." She glanced back at the younger woman. "If that's okay?"

Jehn pursed her lips but then shrugged. "Fine. We'll see if the candy store that had the best taffy in the world when I was a kid is still open. And then I'll show you where my favorite shop is for blade work."

Mehleese nodded and brushed hands with Zeke. "Keep your ears safe, elf. I'll find you soon." Then they both turned their mounts and disappeared into the Bazaar.

Zeke trotted Demon up alongside Zero, and the unicorn nipped at the warhorse as he did.

"What was that all about?" Gerald asked, frowning.

"Who knows? Women, right?"

The Warrior chuckled. "Oh, and you're an expert now?"

"Well, no, but, you know, I guess Mehl and I, um, we have a thing."

"I see. And before that, your last 'thing' was…?"

"Shut up."

"Oh, yeah, right. You and Geena Harris held hands at recess in the sixth grade. That is, until the day you showed her that toad and she broke up with you for being 'too much of a little boy.'"

"Why do you have to be such a gigantic dick? Besides, you're not exactly setting the world on fire with the lady action there, Casanova."

Ouch. As if fruitlessly mooning over Brooke for years wasn't bad enough, Gerald now had no idea what was going on between him and Jehn, if anything. He *thought* there might be something there, but then, he'd thought that same thing before. Lots of times before. Thankfully, only one of those times had ended with him being laughed at by a girl and all her friends. Even so, most of those other times, what he'd thought might have been *something* turned out to be nothing after all.

"I'm working on it. It's complicated."

The lameness of his response rang in his ears.

"Whoa, lame, Ger," Zeke shot back, echoing his thoughts. "You should just be direct. Ladies like that."

"Why do you think I want to get home? No more dancing around it with Brooke. As soon as we get back, I'm laying it all on the line." He raised an eyebrow. "And, whatever, *pot*. You don't have a lot of room to be telling the kettle to be more assertive, you know. I mean, you were basically dragged out of the tavern by the wrist the other night. Yeah, Z, you *really* know assertive."

The corners of the elf's mouth twitched in a smile. "You didn't see me fight it, did you? And I'll have you know that not long after that—"

"Nah-nah-nah-nah-nah-nah. Shut up, shut up, shut up. I don't want to hear any of the sordid details."

"Why are you such a prude? Look, when two consenting adults—"

"Jesus, Thela, God, you're killing me, Z. Can we move on, please? Let's do something constructive before I have to start looking for apothecaries selling the *Realm Quest* equivalent of brain bleach."

"You started it."

"I'll take full responsibility as long as we can get moving. I'd like to find a way home."

"Yeah, right. Home." The elf's tone held a hint of something. Disappointment? Hesitation? Whatever it was, he covered it quickly. "This is your show, Ger. Where should we start?"

Rubbing his goatee, Gerald said, "I still think the highest-level wizard we can find will be the best place. Unless you have another idea?"

"No, that makes sense."

"Okay, Master Mage, lead on."

Zeke looked confused. "Um? Lead where?"

"I don't know. You're the magic user here. I thought you'd know how to find other magic users."

"Really? How would I know that? I've been in this world, what, a minute longer than you? I mean, not a lot of free time to run off and join the Mages' Guild, you know? And besides, have you not noticed that I'm, like, the *only* magic user around? I don't know if I've seen even one other Mage."

"I did notice that, actually," the Warrior replied. "I assumed it was because there are so few of 'us' here, if you know what I mean. Think about it. In the game version, most of the magic users were players. A lot of the in-game characters were Warriors and the like. Not the more complex classes. You'd need more 'real people' to see more magic users."

"I guess that makes sense. But I still didn't join the Mages' Guild or anything."

"No," Gerald allowed. "But this city is a real-life version of the online one. Surely you knew where to find the Guild when we played the game? Just to stop in or something and say 'Hi'? It's got to be in the same place."

"No, dumbass. I never joined anything. It was you and me against everyone, remember? I didn't drop in and say anything to anyone. I have no idea where the Mages' Guild is."

"Great. So what do we do?"

The elf shrugged. "I don't know. It's probably in the Ward of Guilds. Let's start there. If we can't find it, then we'll ask a guard for directions."

Gerald spurred his mount through the archway to the inner city. "I am *not* asking a guard for directions. If we have to do that, you're doing it."

"Fuck that, Ger," Zeke replied. "We'll flip for it."

CHAPTER THIRTY

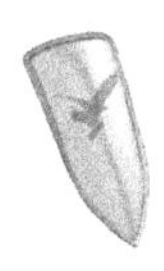

THE MAGE'S GUILD

TO THEIR MUTUAL RELIEF, DIRECTIONS weren't necessary. The pair wandered the curved streets of the Ward of Guilds for an hour before Zeke spotted a weathered shingle hanging above a tiny shop that might have been abandoned a century ago. Inscribed in the small plank with shallow, indistinct grooves was the symbol of a disembodied eye set inside a circle, all within a five-pointed star.

"That's it!" the elf exclaimed, dismounting from Demon and pointing like a child seeing a locomotive chugging off in the distance. "That's the guild sign."

"What?" Gerald asked, eyebrows arched. "How do you know?"

"Mages don't like people snooping around. Other than the obscure symbols on the sign—which is also the only sign over the place at all—the entire building says, 'nothing interesting to see here. Go on with your lives.' I bet if you try to go in, you won't be able to."

The big Warrior jumped off Zero. "No way. Some of the

other shops we've seen here in the Ward looked just as abandoned as this one."

"Go ahead, then. Try to open the door."

Rolling his eyes, Gerald climbed up a few crumbling stone steps to the warped, cobwebbed stone door. He grasped the tarnished knocker in the center and paused.

Nope, no one inside. That much was obvious. It was stupid to have thought there might be in the first place. He sauntered back down to the street.

"Why didn't you knock?" Zeke asked.

"What do you mean? Knock on what?"

"The door? Why didn't you knock on the door?"

With a glance back up the steps, Gerald frowned. "I did. There's no one there."

"You definitely didn't."

"Huh. I'm pretty sure I did."

Zeke smiled at him. "Try again."

"Why? I already—"

"Just. Please. Try again."

"Fine." Grumbling to himself, he stomped back up the stairs. Pretty stupid to do the same thing again, knowing nothing would have changed, but he didn't feel like fighting about it. When he reached the door, he grabbed the knocker again. Still, nobody home. With a satisfied nod, he thumped back down to Zeke. "See?"

"Dude, you didn't knock at all."

"What are you talking about?"

Zeke laughed. "It's the door. It's enchanted. This is definitely the Mages' Guild. Follow me." Slipping past Gerald, Zeke jumped up the steps and, rather than knocking, grabbed the rusted doorknob. It shined with a faint glow. Then, with a dull click, the door swung open. Without waiting, Zeke stepped inside and held the door open for Gerald to follow.

Grunting in suspicion, Gerald put a hesitant foot through the doorway…

…and stood in an ornate entry hall, easily twice as tall and three times as wide as the entire structure had looked from the outside. Gilded mirrors polished to a blinding gleam hung from the walls, gold-flecked tiles lined the floor, and a chandelier as big as a mid-size sedan hung above them, sparkling with a heart-stopping radiance. A marble staircase wide enough to accommodate three horses abreast spiraled up to a floor high above them.

"What the—?" He caught himself before letting rip a more modern curse as a pair of dark eyes squinted at them in disapproval from a desk at the center of the entry. A man with ash-colored hair pulled into a stubby ponytail sat at a desk with a small pot of ink, holding a quill with ink-stained fingers. He was older than they were but still quite young by the look of him. He wore a plush, flame-colored robe embroidered with ruby pentacles at its thick, padded wrists.

"Thank the Moon and Stars for lighting your way to the door of the Guild, my lord. How may I assist you?" He spoke to Zeke, hardly sparing Gerald a glance before dismissing him as unimportant.

"Do you… you know who I am?"

The man—some kind of receptionist?—gave him a patronizing smile. "I don't believe so, my lord. Should I know you?"

"Oh, no, it's just that the way you…" Zeke trailed off, embarrassed. "Well, never mind."

"No, my lord, that's how we greet all members of the Order. Are you not a member, then?"

"Uh, no. I'm afraid I was never invited to join."

"Oh my. You must forgive us, then. The recruiters rarely allow a Mage to reach your level without introductions. Please call me Sared. How may I help you? Would you like to join the Guild today? We have some lovely signing gifts."

"Uh… no. We need to see your leader."

"Oh, I'm terribly sorry, but the Lady Chancellor doesn't take walk-in appointments. Especially from nonmembers. Perhaps if you leave a token and where you'll be staying in the city, she'll contact you."

"That's not going to do it," Gerald cut in. "We need to speak to her right now."

Sared raised both eyebrows. He likely hadn't been so shocked in weeks. To Zeke, he said, "Guests are not welcome in the Guild, my lord…?"

" Axeblight. Ek'zae Axeblight."

A swift change washed over the man at the desk, like he'd been doused with cold water. "Forgive me, Lord Axeblight." Now, at last addressing Gerald, he added, "And you must be Goldenshield?"

"I am. So… what? Regular Warriors aren't allowed to talk to Mages in here, but I am?"

He shrugged. "Your reputation precedes you, Master Goldenshield. And with it come special privileges."

Special privileges. Gerald could hardly contain his excitement. "I'm not sure I want special—" he began before Zeke laid a hand on his arm.

"Sared, we need to meet the Chancellor. Today."

"I think I can spare them a few moments, Sared," said a soothing, velvet voice from the winding stairs behind the desk. A woman with honey-colored hair twisted together in a braid over one shoulder drifted down the marble steps, one delicate hand floating sensually down the unblemished white handrail. A deep navy robe that pooled in a perfect circle at her feet wasn't worn so much as it enveloped her, clinging in all the right places and opening just enough at the leg and chest to offer a hint of pale skin beneath.

Zeke gasped; Gerald forced himself not to. One of them had to act like an adult. "They call me Goldenshield, Lady. It's our pleasure to meet you."

"I am Telya Moonstruck, Chancellor of the Mages' Guild here in Riverglow. I'm delighted to make your acquaintance. How can I be of service to the two of you?" She offered Zeke a warm smile and held her hand out for him, fingers down.

"Oh, uh, yes. Yes, Lady Telya. I'm, uh, Axeblight. Ek'zae. It's my, um, pleasure to meet someone as, well, pretty as you. And enchanting too!" He took her hand but gave it an awkward shake rather than bending to kiss the back of it.

Gerald rolled his eyes. Oh, very smooth. After the Casanova conversation before, no way would he let Zeke forget about this for a long time.

A shadow of irritation flashed in her eyes, no doubt for having to endure these hayseeds in the middle of her very controlled, very impressive, very intentional presentation of grace, power, and physical allure. The look faded in an instant, though, and once again, she exuded charm.

Enchanting? More like she was *enchanted*. But Gerald kept the thought to himself. "Lady Chancellor, if we could maybe talk someplace private?"

"Of course." Turning to the receptionist, she said, "Sared, please have some refreshments sent up to my office." With that, she twirled and started back up the steps, spinning the hem of her robe. "If you'll follow me."

"What are the odds she's some kind of succubus?" Gerald whispered.

Zeke stopped, watching her almost *float* up the steps. "The odds are pretty good I don't give a shit." He hurried after her.

Gerald followed, pretending not to see Sared shaking his head.

The corridor at the top of the staircase was a physical impossibility. It ran away from them for hundreds of yards to both the right and left, and innumerable other hallways branched off from those two main passageways. Both were so long he couldn't see where they ended. Yet based on the dimensions from outside, the building couldn't have been more than twenty or thirty feet wide. It was as if relative space had no meaning.

Telya's office was just in front of them at the top of the steps, in the absolute center of the Guild house. She opened it with the wave of her hand and ushered them inside.

The room was nothing like he'd expected. In stories and movies, a wizard's office or lab was always brimming with tall stacks of yellowing spell books and shelves lined with jars containing a grotesque assortment of hands, fingers, eyeballs, and any number of other things it was better not to recognize. Arcane symbols would be scattered around the room, too, and, at minimum, a cauldron or a crystal ball had to be within a hand's reach.

This room, however, was like a mortgage broker's office. No spell books, no jars, no musty odor of *old*. And no tall pedestal topped by a crystal ball filled with swirling mists. Telya had a plush executive chair covered in Thela-only-knew what kind of fur, a stark, perfect, cherrywood desk with a few scrolls lined up to the side in a neat row, and a pair of not-quite-so-plush chairs facing it. An open window behind the desk looked out over the Royal Keep, even though that couldn't have been possible. The Mage's Guild wasn't anywhere close to the keep. It certainly didn't face the front of it.

Telya melted into her chair and gestured for him and Zeke

to take seats as well. "My Lord Goldenshield, you seem somewhat surprised."

"I… your office, it's… not what I expected."

"Oh? And what did you expect? Accessories of my craft laid out on display for everyone to see? Perhaps a polished dragon's skull?" She chuckled. "I'm afraid I'm as much administrator as I am student of the strange and arcane. And honestly, even if I were working to uncover the Lost Mysteries, do you think I'd leave evidence of it out where just anyone could see?"

Gerald laughed to himself. "Yeah, I guess not." Already, he felt more at ease. He had to admit, the woman was very good at her job.

"What brings you to my Guild house?"

He paused, uncertain. Straight-out asking about transport back to the Quik Mart seemed like a good way to get laughed out of the room.

Zeke, however, apparently didn't think so. "Lady Telya, what do you know of people claiming not to be of Thelaroth?"

Her eyes narrowed. "Everyone hears stories now and then. Usually they feature a raving lunatic, foaming at the mouth. But I don't believe they're delusional so much as they are like a plains gazelle dropped into the center of the Maelstrom Sea."

Gerald sighed. Would it kill her to make just a little sense? "What does that even mean?"

"Gazelles are made to run, not swim, my lord. Some, though, can still manage to swim, and a small number even do it well. Most, however, quickly drown."

"I'm still not following you."

"Let me ask instead, what do you know of the Five Worlds?"

The lore that accompanied *Realm Quest*, the game, was substantial and packed with references to the Five Worlds of

Thela. Gerald, though, knew next to nothing about any of it. To him, the game was just a series of quests you had to complete to move your character up the ladder of level progression. Every mission had some kind of made-up background story—which he ignored—but in the end, what mattered was doing the bulleted task detailed in your quest list. "Find Nelson, the Bee-Man," "Collect 17 Bear Snouts," or "Open the Portal of the Wind" was the limit of what he cared about. Whatever the goal of the moment happened to be, it was always marked for his convenience as an icon on the mini-map on his screen. Reading the backstory was a waste of time.

Zeke didn't agree. "Everyone knows about the Five Worlds," his friend offered. "What do you mean?"

Telya inclined her head. "Indeed, all children are taught of Thela's Five Worlds. The ones we can see and touch, of course, are the Western Realms here, Akador, the traditional home of the Guardians, and Venasier, the gray land of the elves. The Temple tells us much about the Dark World, too, where the dead linger until Thela calls for them. But that's only four. Of the Fifth World, little is known. Thela keeps it hidden from us and has given no name for it. That, not surprisingly, has led most people to say the Fifth World is nonsense. A fantasy created by Thela's fanatics."

"Is that what you think?"

She gave them a flat, plastic smile. "Master Elf, I'm a good deal older than I appear. I've walked from one tip of the Western Realms to the other and lost entire decades in the barren grasses of Akador. In that time, I've seen more wonders than you can possibly imagine. Sights that would make you tremble and cry out with joy and others that would have you gnash your teeth and question your very sanity. One of the many things I learned in all that time was never to discount legends."

"What would you say, then," Gerald said, "if we told you we'd found a man who claimed to be from there. From the Fifth World. A man brought here, through magical means."

"Then I would tell him he is lucky to have been so favored by Thela. That's what the Holy Scrolls tell us, anyway. If you believe that sort of thing."

"But what if he didn't really want to be here?"

"Then he should try to find a way back to the Fifth World."

"Is there such a way?"

"Perhaps. Is there such a man?"

"Yes."

The woman leaned back in her chair and scrutinized them. "What you're looking for won't come cheaply, you know. What you seek may be prove costly."

"What kind of price are we talking about?" Zeke asked.

Telya drummed her fingers on the smooth surface of her desk. "In the end? Only Thela can say for sure. But we'll start with a trade. Information for information. Answer me a question, and I'll answer yours."

Gerald clucked his tongue in irritation. Games like this were a waste of time, but he and Zeke needed to know. "If we have to. Shoot."

"Shoot?"

"Ask your question."

She turned a piercing glare to Zeke. "Master Elf, tell me what you saw after climbing to the peak of Mt. Orushu. What did you experience the moment you became a man?"

Zeke coughed. "I'm… I'm sorry?"

"Mt. Orushu. Tell me about it."

He swallowed hard. Mt. Orushu was the elven holy mountain in the center of their desolate, fog-covered island homeland. Folklore held that every elf, upon reaching his or her thirtieth year (which the game's programmers conveniently made coincide with achieving level 10), was called to climb to the peak of Orushu and submit to the will of Thela. Whatever happened at the top was supposed to be a very personal experience, a communion between the oldest race in Thelaroth and the world's creator.

Except Zeke had never done it. Sure, he'd done it in the game, but nothing *really* happened in the game. He saw a flash of light and heard a ding that meant the quest was completed. Then his character found a new mission in their quest log, a "pilgrimage," ostensibly from Thela herself. Coincidentally, that mission happened to be the exact same for every other elven character. It was how the game worked.

He gave Gerald a pleading look. The Warrior returned an almost imperceptible shrug. "Tell her the story. Our, uh, friend really needs that information, Ek'zae."

The elf put his hands together and rubbed at his nose. He'd picked up the implication: make something up.

"I… forgive me, Lady, but it's a deeply personal thing. I don't feel right telling you."

The Chancellor waved her hand. "Oh, no, I understand. It was in extremely bad taste for me to ask about it."

Gerald brightened. Was that it? She was going to let them off the hook that easily?

"But then," she went on, "what you're asking about is an extremely sensitive topic too. Dangerous, even. The king has been inquiring, quietly, about anyone claiming to be from or asking questions about the Fifth World for some time now. He and the Templemasters would be extremely interested in this conversation."

Nope. Still on the hook. Actually, now it was worse. That was a veiled threat if Gerald had ever heard one. "Tell her your story. We're all friends here." He gave her the best false smile he could muster. She returned a much more charming—if equally disingenuous—one.

After clearing his throat, Zeke launched into a long, fantastic tale about communing with the spirit of Thela through various woodland creatures, including a squirrel, a snake, a wolf, a bear, and an eagle. He rambled, making it up as he went, and with every new twist, Telya sat back with an amused grin and offered generic, patronizing replies like, "Oh, my!" "I can't imagine!" and "That can't be so!"

Finally, Zeke wound to the end, adding some nonsense about a gold and silver light descending through the foggy clouds to enter his body. And then he was sent on his way, to serve Thela across the Five Worlds.

"Well," Telya said when he finished, pretending to have been enthralled. "I never thought it might be like *that*. I'm sure it was a deeply… moving experience. I'll treasure that you shared that with me for the rest of my days. And rest assured, Lord Axeblight, your secret is safe with me." As she said it, she winked at Gerald.

She knew it was all bullshit. Clever woman.

"I… I…appreciate that, Lady Chancellor," he stammered, face flushing the way it always did when he'd been trying to lie and was instead just embarrassed. Gerald jumped in to save him.

"Okay, we answered your question. Now, answer ours. How do you get back to the Fifth World."

She smiled again. "I don't know."

"What? You said—"

"Just because *I* don't know doesn't mean there isn't a way. All of us with our hands in the magic of the world have heard stories of poor souls coming here from the Fifth World. Admittedly, I've never heard of anyone going back, but then, if one did, who would be left to tell that tale?"

"Look, Lady Telya, just because we maybe didn't give you exactly the story you were looking for—"

She waved him off. "You did, actually, give me a good deal more information. True, not quite what I asked for, but sometimes, when you can't be the Warrior that charges into battle with a savage *WarCry*, subtler means are your best friend."

Both men furrowed their brows. "Okay," Gerald said, "so then…?" He trailed off, hoping she'd provide a little clarity.

"You need to speak with the King's Mage, Drauwson Ice-touch. He knows much more on this subject than I do, which is why he was named the King's Mage. His dedication is to the Guild first, though. And once he knows I sent you, he will assist you in any way he can."

"Are you sure? If Dalor is on a hunt for information about Fifth Worlders, how do we know we can trust him?"

"I would gladly trust him with my life. Besides," she purred in that velvety tone, "I enjoy owing him a favor or two."

A glance between Zeke and Gerald proved they had very similar ideas about what those favors might entail. The King's Mage seemed to be a lucky guy.

CHAPTER THIRTY-ONE

THE ROYAL MAGE

COMPARED TO FINDING AND ENTERING the Mage's Guild, getting in to talk to the King's Mage, Drauwson Icetouch, was simple. Unlike capitals, castles, and people's homes in the "real world," the King's Hall was open to the whole world in *Realm Quest*. With guards at attention throughout the room and wandering the keep's halls in pairs, halberds at the ready for any sign of hostility, the king was more than safe even with his doors wide open. Beyond that, Dalor himself was an Elite warrior. Anyone stupid enough to try an assault inside the Straddling Keep was likely both a fool and soon dead.

After crossing the Melding Bridge, which spanned the confluence of the Spikelet and Souwater rivers and served as a drawbridge, the pair entered the Keep. The King's Hall, the cavernous main room used for King Dalor's court, was ten stories above, on the lowest floor where the two base structures came together. Along the way, through every door and archway, not a single guard stopped them to demand where they were going. No one even bothered to ask them their business in the keep. Instead, Gerald and Zeke strolled through the enormous structure as if lords of the place themselves. It was a striking difference from the city gate.

At last they reached the King's Hall. Dalor himself stood at its center, on the king's sigil inscribed into the marble floor, a lion flanked by a pair of torches. To his right was the Lord Bishop of the Temple of Thela, a short, slender man with a pinched nose, narrow chin, sunken cheeks, and beady eyes. On the king's left was a Mage that Gerald didn't recognize. Behind the trio, a golden glow reflected off the throne itself, situated below a magical portal in the ceiling that shone a constant light upon it. For that reason, it was known across Thelaroth as the Gleaming Throne.

The room hummed with low chatter and the undercurrent of tension. Rumors said that Dalor could be unpredictable in the best of times and that the recent events with the Legion—among others—had made things worse. No one knew what the next few months might mean for the Realms, but that war was coming to Riverglow soon was evident on nearly every face.

"I'm surprised," Gerald whispered, "that he's still just standing there, out in the open like that. I know the king always did it in the game, but that was Rhandren, and he was part of a quest chain. You had to be able to get to him. But with the things that are different here, I thought that would be too."

Zeke shrugged. "Who knows? I guess the Realms still need to have the king out in the open where the people can see him. Even more at a time like this."

"So, what do we do?"

"I don't know. I guess we just… go up to the Mage? That should be him. Drauwson Icetouch."

"I'll never understand how this place works." Shaking his

head, Gerald strolled across the room, trying to project a confidence he didn't feel. The King's Mage was a tall, well-built man, with a closely cropped beard along a strong jawline and clear, sparkling turquoise eyes. A younger man than expected, a shock of blond at his temples and at the chin of his beard stood in contrast to his otherwise jet-black hair. He wore a thick, extravagant black robe with silver trim at the cuffs and hem and down the shoulders, matching the colors of the king.

"Excuse me, Lord Icetouch?"

"Yes?" He turned to Gerald, but at seeing Zeke, he beamed. "Ah! Lord Elf! It is always good to see another member of the Arcana here at court. So few come this way. I am Drauwson Icetouch. Welcome to Riverglow and the Grand Hall!" His voice boomed, echoing throughout the chamber. They both checked around to see whose attention he might have drawn. The less the better.

"Well met, Lord Drauwson," Zeke replied. "If you don't mind, we're here on a bit of personal business. Could we maybe speak someplace more private?"

Drauwson laughed. "Private? Here is private enough." He lowered his voice a fraction, still much too loud for their liking.

"Actually," Gerald said, "we'd prefer someplace with fewer ears than the King's Hall."

The tall Mage laughed again. "No ear can hear us, and no eye can see us. Look around you."

The room surrounding them had become still and quiet. The other characters weren't quite frozen in place, but they inched along at a snail's pace as moments passed. A gray, foggy haze covered everything, dulling the people, the colorful tapestries throughout the room, and even the magic light shining down on the Gleaming Throne. It looked as if someone had thrown an enormous gauze blanket over everything.

Gerald whistled. "Wow…."

"It's a quick enchantment to give us some privacy without having to make a show of leaving. Now, then, first things first: who are you?"

"They call me Goldenshield," Gerald said, "and this is my friend, Ek'zae Axeblight."

"I thought you might be. There aren't too many pairs like you—a Warrior and an elven Mage—roaming around the Western Realms. It is my pleasure to meet you both! What brings you to me?"

"Lady Telya suggested we seek you out," Zeke said in the low, conspiratorial tone he always used when thinking he was up to something. He no doubt would have slipped on a pair of sunglasses to be more *incognito* if he'd had them. "We need information about"—he paused for effect and shot glances over both shoulders—"the Fifth World."

Drauwson guffawed. "Oh! Is that all? The way you were acting, I thought you were going to ask me to join some sort of rebel underground, determined to undermine the king." He clapped his hands and rubbed them together. "What do you need to know?"

Zeke leapt in. "Can you go ba—"

Gerald slapped his friend in the back, cutting him off. "What he meant to ask is, are stories of the Fifth World true? Is it possible to come here from there?" That wasn't what they *really* wanted to know, of course, but he'd learned something from Telya. Information had value, and there was no reason to let the Royal Mage infer that they knew anything about the Fifth World, let alone had come from it. If nothing else, his closeness to the king made that information worth keeping to themselves.

The tall Mage narrowed his eyes. "That's not the kind of question you go around asking just anyone. You might attract the wrong attention." He inclined his head at the near-motionless king beside them.

"If Telya hadn't sent you, the second you stepped away from me, I'd have arranged for you both to be detained by guards before you reached the Melding Bridge. But. She seems to trust you, which is enough for me.

"Now, I can't give an absolute yes or no, but I've done a lot of research. And even though almost all the evidence I've seen is circumstantial, there is a mountain of it lurking beneath the surface of polite conversation in Thelaroth. I'm hard pressed not to believe that yes, people do somehow get transported from the mysterious Fifth World to here. But again, I have no iron-clad proof."

Gerald stroked his whiskers. "There must be some kind of portal, then. Do you think it swings both ways? Do people come here and then someday go back?"

"Maybe. I don't know enough about the mechanics, I'm afraid. And the truth is, you'll never find out here."

Zeke cocked his head in confusion. "Why not? Telya said—"

The taller Mage waved the comment away. "Telya doesn't always listen. She's very good at telling others what to do, I'll admit. Not to mention a few other things. But all her energy goes to feeding her rather ravenous ambition. She has little time to learn about the details of something like this."

"Unlike you, right?" Gerald asked.

"Unfortunately, I know only a little more. I hate to admit it, but that kind of transfer seems possible only with the help of a Shaman of the Guardians. I suspect that, long ago, the Temple might have had information about the Fifth World as well and perhaps a way to reach it. But now, that secret is either so far buried in the Temple archives that you'd need a team of scholars digging for years to unearth it, or it's been intentionally destroyed and is lost forever. Either way, you'll never get a Templer to discuss it."

"Maybe we should ask Bishop Bob over there?"

Drauwson shook his head. "No, no, no. Absolutely do not. The Temple considers the Fifth World a blasphemous topic. If you bring it up, you'll be labeled a heretic and Purified."

"Great. So, no one knows for sure but the Guardians, who want to take over the world at the moment?"

He gave them a thin smile. "Now you see the problem I've had to deal with for the past year or so. I do have one plan in mind for learning more, but it's… ambitious. I need help to make it work and have yet to find a volunteer brave enough to accept the quest. So, the real question is, how badly do the two of you want answers?"

Zeke looked down at the hem of his robe on the marble tile floor. He shot a quick glance at Gerald out of the corner of his eye, a look just to see if he was watching, before going back to scrutinizing the floor.

Gerald frowned at Zeke's sheepish response. Didn't he understand? Whatever the cost was, they had to try. They couldn't just bury their heads in the sand and spend the rest of their lives wandering around here, lost, while time at home, in the real world, slipped by without them.

"What is it?" he asked. Then, without waiting, "We'll do it."

"You might want to hear me out first. Because to get answers about the Fifth World, we need to capture one of the Shaman traveling with the Legion."

Gerald threw his hand into the air with a groan. "Oh, sure. How hard could that be? I mean, with an entire army descending from the Everfrost mountains, it won't be hard to pick one off and sneak him back here for a little Q and A, right? No problem."

"They can be the fiercest of fighters, too, Goldenshield. I didn't say the task would be easy. But if you want answers, that is the quickest way to get them."

With a heavy sigh, the Warrior nodded. "Like I said, we'll do it. Somehow, we'll do it."

Zeke's head shot up, eyebrows raised, as if trying to figure out if his friend had lobsters crawling out of his ears. Gerald ignored it. He'd said all he intended.

Sounds flooded back into the room, the chattering hum of a hundred people talking and moving around, their sounds echoing off the chamber walls. The gray haze was gone. Drauwson had lifted his privacy enchantment.

"Come on," Gerald said to Zeke and then turned for the archway out of the room.

Before they got two steps away, someone called to them. "Ho, now, who is this, Lord Icetouch?" The voice was deep and commanding yet somehow nasal too. The kind of voice that grated on nerves but couldn't be ignored.

The voice of the king.

CHAPTER THIRTY-TWO

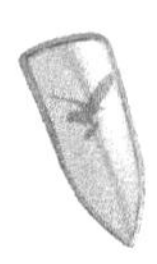

THE KING

KING DALOR THE FIRST, THE Anointed, Defender of the Western Realms, First Protector of the Temple of Thela, and Warden of Braxys the Black, Eater of Worlds, watched them, his eyes curious and his face tight, tense.

"Ah, Highness," Drauwson said, "I didn't want to bother you. I believe, though, you'll recognize my guests. Their names seem to be on the tongue of everyone with an interest in Copperton Vale these last few days. The beast of a man before you is none other than the legendary Goldenshield, and the elf is his adventuring companion, Ek'zae Axeblight."

Dalor regarded Zeke with suspicion for a moment and then puffed out his chest and raised his head. "Goldenshield, huh? I'd say it takes quite a set of brass to appear in the King's Hall—and then ignore me—after running around the countryside openly defying me for a week. I would send another to his death on the spot for carrying the Shield of the Vale without my consent. After accepting that ill-conceived appointment by those fools on Copperton's Council, it is only your rumored valor in protecting the children of the town that keeps your head connected to your shoulders. Mark me, I'll have no more disobedience from you or your *friends*."

He spat the last word and made a face as he did, as if tasting something rotten. He shifted his eyes to Zeke and back to underscore his point. They *really* didn't like elves, did they?

Gerald started to reply, but the king continued, talking over him. "Now, you will wipe that look from your eyes and lower them this instant. And I had better not ever see so much as a glance from you that hints of anything but total submission. Is that clear enough for you? Because if I ever find you staring at me as if we were equals"—he rolled his eyes—"the look of my face twisted in rage will be the last you see before the Dark World.

"If you want to continue breathing Thela's air, return to Copperton and pledge humble support to Lord Boland, the rightful Sheriff. In fact, I expect you to lick his manure-caked boots if he demands it. I am going to spare your life only because the Legion is finally on the move toward Copperton, and the Sheriff will need every hand to aid in the defense of the town. "

Fucking awesome. The king wanted him dead because, like everyone else, the man assumed he'd taken the job. Gerald ground his teeth in frustration. How could he correct the king without offending him? Clearly, "touchy" didn't even begin to describe the man.

Then again, groveling in front of him wasn't all that appealing, either; the guy seemed like a grade-A dick monkey. But even if he was a prick, he was a prick capable of having them killed on the spot.

No point in overthinking it. He'd have to give it his best shot.

Eyes to the ground, Gerald said, "Forgive me, Highness,

but someone has misinformed you. I never accepted the Council's request. I carried the Shield only to aid in saving the children of the town, not because I wanted to be Sheriff. And we wouldn't have come here. We would have stayed—as you say, to assist in the defense of the town—but your *appointed* Sheriff, Lord Boland, wasn't too keen on me when he arrived. I was afraid if we'd hung around, he'd have taken it as a challenge to his authority."

"Hmm," Dalor murmured. "You may have a point there. He can be… prickly. A bit too quick to judge. He isn't as understanding as we are here at the Keep. I suppose it might have been for the best that you left. Of course, things have changed now. Copperton has need of every battle-ready hand. If you are willing to return, submit to Lord Boland, and fight for him, I'll gladly send a proclamation with you. Something to ease his anxiety, to show you're not a threat to his authority."

Gerald hesitated. The idea of being seen as the king's trained dog made him want to crawl into bed with an angry owlbear. But the Legion was going to be at Copperton. He and Zeke needed to get back there. They'd have to be near the battlefield when the fight came to have any chance of capturing a Shaman. That would prove difficult if Lord Sheriff Erlas Boland was still being a petty pain in the ass—or if the king changed his mind and decided they might as well enjoy an extended-stay room in the dungeons of Riverglow. No doubt there were many dank cells available, and he'd bet his war hammer they all reeked of death.

Yeah, a proclamation would be helpful.

Besides, would being seen as the king's lackey matter at all when they got back home to Simmsville? Sometimes you had to do a thing you hated to get what you wanted.

The king's face was growing dark, thunderous. He'd been irritated with them to begin with, and now they were keeping him waiting despite the offered olive branch. How long until he took that as open defiance? Pretending to be subservient for a short time was better than being found defiant in a small, dank cell for a long time.

"Your Highness, that would be very much appreciated. With you to vouch for us, we'd be happy to add our hands to those defending Copperton. Thank you."

Gerald could see in Dalor's stony reaction that he somehow hadn't come across as quite subservient enough, "We are unworthy of your esteem," he added quickly.

The storm faded, but the king's eyes still fumed. Gerald might have pressed their luck too much. He caught Zeke's ragged intake of breath. The elf expected trouble.

Thela be blessed, instead of ordering to have them arrested, the king nodded and waved to a page, who hurried over. The king whispered some lengthy instructions to him and then sent the boy on his way to fulfill the order.

"It will take a few minutes for the document to be drawn up. Now that it's clear this was just a misunderstanding, I'd like to extend our thanks for the work you did for the town while Lord Boland was on his way there. There may have been some… confusion, but in matters like these, that kind of thing is unfortunately unavoidable, especially when news must travel so far to be heard. I understand the Council didn't realize I'd made an appointment and dispatched soldiers until the moment they arrived?"

Still watching the ground, Gerald was taken aback by the sudden reversal. From threats to gratitude, just like that? To say it was a misunderstanding was about as accurate as saying the surface of the sun wasn't often cool. The Town Council had voted to appoint a Sheriff in defiance of Dalor's authority, which was a tremendous slap in the face.

While inspecting his boots, though, he began to understand. To highlight that insubordination now, after Gerald had already agreed to go back to town and play toady to the new Sheriff, would only serve to show that the king's control over Copperton—and by extension the entire Vale, if not most of the Western Realms—was less absolute than he wanted people to believe. Men of Dalor's standing weren't fond of drawing attention to their weaknesses. Much easier to insinuate that the whole thing was a misunderstanding. At least until he could deal with the upstart Council members himself.

"Yes, yes, you're very wise, my lord," Gerald agreed. "No one knew what was going on at all. In fact, the Council couldn't have been happier when Lord Boland arrived with his Proclamation of Appointment." That was likely laying it on a bit thick, but so what? He'd never see the king again anyway.

A messenger wearing a burgundy-and-cream tabard embroidered with the Eye, Moon, and Pentacle of the Mages' Guild approached Drauwson. He stopped in front of the tall Mage and for the span of three or four heartbeats became blurry, out of focus, the way Gerald used to see things without his contact lenses before laser surgery. The pair snapped back into clear focus, and the messenger gave the Royal Mage a nod followed by a salute across the chest. Then he spun on his heels and left the way he came.

"I don't care how many times I see it, Mage. Your trick is Thela-damned unnerving," the king complained.

"Forgive me, sire. I know it must be hard to look at, but making discussions private through the use of that enchantment is much more convenient than wandering off to find a quiet place to receive messages. This way, I can be certain that the information I'm receiving won't be overheard. As we both know, half-heard rumors become gossip in no time. This way, I can do my job without having to leave your side several times through the course of the day."

Drauwson was good. He'd taken a complaint by the king and flipped it over on its head. Not only could Dalor hardly go on complaining, since the Mage was acting in the king's best interests, the explanation also played right into the man's overactive sense of paranoia.

"Yes, well, I still don't like it. It makes my skin itch."

"Forgive me, Highness. Next time, I'll take a few steps away first."

"You have my permission to continue using that spell, but yes, see that you do step away," the king ordered.

As they were talking, the page Dalor had dispatched came rushing back, a scroll in one hand and a tapered candle on a gold plate in the other. That proclamation for Boland hadn't taken long at all.

Gerald stepped forward to make a big fuss over the document. Surely the king would like to see a big show of appreciation. Instead, the page snatched a block of wax off the plate and held an end of it against the fire for barely a second or two. The wax melted quickly, and he mashed it down on the scroll, leaving a large glob of melted red. The page dropped the wax back on the plate and held the scroll out for the king.

Dalor raised the knuckle of the little finger on his left hand, pushing his royal signet ring out. In the same motion, he pressed it into the wax. Then he took the scroll from the page and scrutinized it. Certain that the wax had cooled, he offered the scroll to Gerald. "Here is the proclamation I promised, Master Goldenshield," Dalor said. "Let this be an end to the matter."

"Thank you, Highness," Gerald said, reaching for the sealed roll of parchment.

Take Scroll

The king held it firm, though, so both men had a hand on it. Their eyes locked together. Dalor's darkened with a hint of threat. Gerald, not remembering to avert his gaze, glared back.

"You will kneel before me, or you will be knelt for the headsman," the king said, voice gone to ice.

Submit, stupid! He dropped to one knee and examined the king's soft boots.

"Better," Dalor said. "Now get out of my city before I change my mind. Boland needs to demonstrate my authority in Copperton. If you cannot help him do so, not even Thela will be able to save you."

"Thank you, Highness." He needed something else. Something more sycophantic. "You are a beacon of patience and understanding. Your greatness is a blessing from merciful Thela." Gerald's mouth twisted at the words, but at least he didn't laugh. And with his face cast down, no one seemed to notice. "We'll leave for Copperton immediately."

The king released the scroll. Gerald stood, still averting his gaze, and backed away a few steps. He'd seen that in a movie once.

He and Zeke turned toward the grand archway and started away without a look back. The last thing he needed to do was piss the king off again by accident.

"Wait," a voice called after them. Icetouch caught up to them at the top of a long, white stone staircase running down to an arch leading out of King's Hall. In a blink, the room fell silent, and the pea-soup fog returned.

"I have a warning for you."

"What is it?" Zeke asked.

Gerald was less enthusiastic. "I've had about enough warnings today. Can we just go?"

The Royal Mage folded his hands into the sleeves of his robe. His posture became stiff, official. All traces of levity disappeared from his face. "You need this one. Two women matching the description of those entering the Spike Gate with you today are being followed by a squad of Temple Purifiers in the Outer Ward."

The two friends shared an uneasy glance. If the Temple was following Jehn….

"We entered the city alone," Zeke replied.

Drauwson shook his head in reply. "Now is not the time to play coy, Lord Axeblight. We had time for games before; no longer. And unless my information was wrong, I think one of those women would not want to be captured by the Temple. Especially since the squad is being led by a Shadow Priest I'm told is particularly… dedicated. And for that breed, that's saying something."

That couldn't be…? Gerald shot a questioning look at his friend. Zeke shrugged. Bloody Thela, Gravesire was the last thing they needed to deal with here.

They'd have to catch up with Mehleese and Jehn fast to be sure. "Thank you, Lord Mage," he replied. "We owe you one."

"If that woman is who I think, and you would repay that debt, get her out of the city immediately. There are a number of ways this can end, but that's the only one that doesn't lead to disaster for all of us," Drauwson said.

"Where are they?"

"Not far. In the second epoch of the Outer Ward. You might be able to reach them in time. Hurry. Before that Priest dooms us all."

CHAPTER THIRTY-THREE

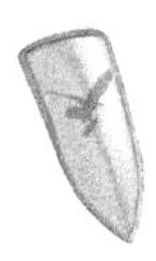

THE SHADOW PRIEST

"WE SHOULD PICK UP THE pace, Mehleese," Jehn said from the shadows of her hood. "I don't know how long it'll take the guys to find what they're looking for, but I want to get a table in the corner of the Drunken Rock before the common room fills up for the night. You can overhear just about everything going on in the city there."

Mehleese tugged at her worn leather gloves. "We need to move more quickly, then. We're just past the marker for the Second Epoch, and the Rock is in the Seventh, right?"

"Right," Jehn agreed.

The Outer Ward made a full ring around Riverglow City, separated into twelve sections, called "epochs," like the face of a clock. The twelfth epoch was the easternmost section, and the first epoch was adjacent to it to the southeast. The others followed numerically, clockwise around the ward. The seventh epoch, then, was just north of the section where they'd entered Riverglow at the Spike Gate.

"I've seen everything I wanted," Jehn added while unwrapping a green cylinder of taffy from a piece of waxed paper and flashing it into her mouth. "Everything does get smaller as you grow up, doesn't it? The Outer Ward used to seem never-ending to me. As if you could walk it for days and days and days and never see the same place twice. What I wouldn't give to have my childhood back. This time, I wouldn't spend all of it complaining about being the youngest."

Mehleese gave her an empathetic smile. "I know what you mean, but you couldn't pay me to relive my childhood." The Paladin's years in the Royal Keep as a princess couldn't have had much in common with Mehl's, moving from one place to another and living on odd jobs, trying to stay ahead of Children's Services.

"Oh? Why is that?"

"It's… I'll tell you another day. Can I have a piece of that taffy?"

Their horses side by side, they followed the steady creep of Riverglow's inhabitants through the Ward toward their destination. Time melted into the sounds and smells of the city, and before long, they were within sight of the archway to the Third Epoch. They wouldn't have long until they reached the Drunken Rock.

"What are those two up to anyway?" Jehn asked. "I thought we were coming to see the city and sample the lager. But as soon as we got here, they started looking like dogs on the scent for something. What's going on?"

Mehl hesitated. Finally, she mumbled, "I'm not sure, my lady."

The lie stung. For much of her life, lying had been as simple as breathing. She done it daily, effortlessly, as a form of self-preservation. But when she became an adult and got a real job at a technical support desk, she promised herself she'd never lie again. At least not for her own benefit. This lie may have been for a good reason—no way she could tell Jehn the guys were hunting for a way back to the "real world"—but that gave her little protection from the icy sting of failure in the pit of her stomach.

That feeling was just another log heaped on to the fire of the already growing unease in her belly. But it was hardly worth mentioning compared to the inferno of worry that she might have to face losing Zeke.

Zeke, who was so full of wonder and joy at everything. Zeke, whose enthusiasm helped her remember happiness for the first time since long before she came here. Zeke, who'd managed to make her feel something besides alone. Zeke, who she would lose if they succeeded in finding a way back.

Zeke, who, not two nights ago, had whispered that he thought he might be falling in love.

"Stay with me," she'd answered as they nuzzled together after reveling in being knotted in each other's arms and legs. It was different than how she remembered it, lying skin to skin with another flesh-and-blood human being. Then again, they weren't really flesh and blood. Their bodies were some kind of digital rendering. But it sent the same thrill through her, the same electric fire burning from the base of her spine to the nape of her neck. And in some ways, it was even better this way. Both warm and sensuous at the same time as being cool and refreshing, like the other side of the pillow.

"Gerald won't understand," he'd replied, breathing the words onto her neck more than speaking them. "I don't know that I can send him on without me. We've been friends our whole lives. Why don't you come with us.?"

"No, my elf, I cannot. I don't belong there anymore. This is my home."

"How can you say that?"

She turned her head and gave him a half smile. "I never

fit in there like I do here. I never had a purpose there like here. Why do you think I would play *Realm Quest* for 36 hours at a time?"

"Because you really liked your guild mates."

Laughter shook her. "No, my guild mates were colleagues from the office who needed a Ranger to fill out their ranks. I was a European immigrant to the middle of America. An outsider to them. My real name, my birth name, is Rakkel Sindradottir, but they couldn't even bring themselves to learn it. They nicknamed me 'Rachel' because it was easier and most of the time called me Rach. But here? Here, I'm strong and powerful. Someone to be feared, not ignored. Here, when you learn the name Mehleese Worldwalker, you remember it. No, Ek'zae, I cannot go back to the way it was."

"But you'll have me back home."

"Will I? Where will we come out if we return? Or when? I don't know."

He grunted. "I hadn't thought of that."

"And even if we come back at the same time, we'll likely be separated by thousands of miles. One of us would have to move, or we'd only see each other online. And that would be a very poor substitute for having you wrapped around me."

"I…" he stammered, "I don't know if I can stay, though."

"Don't you like this better than the life you led in the other world?"

"Yes," he admitted. "Life back home was nothing but constant stress and pressure. Always afraid of failing. Trying to live up to my parents' expectations. Trying to keep everyone happy. Struggling to get a career I didn't much care about off the ground while facing forty years of forty-hour weeks, unappreciated by pretty much everyone. It's a stark change from being told how special you were your entire life in high school and college."

"Stay with me," she repeated, stroking his chin.

"I don't know. Gerald will… I just don't know."

"Well, you haven't found a way back yet. Maybe you won't."

"No, Mehl, Jehn's father came to our world. There's a way to get there, somehow. And Gerald won't rest until he finds it."

"Just think on it, my elf. Think on it for me."

"I don't like it," Jehn said, bringing Mehleese's attention back to the present. "They're up to something. I suppose when you and your elf retire tonight, I'll have to pump Goldenshield full of lager and warlock spirits again and see what I can get him to tell me."

Leaning in close to the smaller woman, Mehleese said in a conspiratorial tone, "I think perhaps the lady is just planning to get him drunk so she can have her way with the hero of Copperton Vale."

Jehn's cheeks colored. "Mehleese! I can't believe you'd even suggest that! That's ridiculous."

Mehleese smirked. "You pretend I haven't noticed the looks you two give each other. You're like kids flirting at your first Festus ball. A blind man could see it. What's the hesitation, then? Don't you find him attractive?"

"I mean, I guess he's not *un*attractive, if you're into big Warrior types."

"Does your heart race when you look at him? Does he sometimes give you a shock or chill you didn't expect? A prickling up your spine?"

"Well, maybe. I guess."

She winked. "Sounds to me as if the important parts already know how you feel about him. I'd advise you to quit wasting time. The world is dangerous, and Thela doesn't promise us a tomorrow. Make the most of the time you have."

"I can't believe I'm even having this conversation. If Father knew…" She trailed off. Her face fell. The excited, half-embarrassed grin that had lit her eyes a moment ago vanished.

"I am sorry."

"It's… it's okay, Mehleese. Thank you."

"What a surprise to see you here, of all places, my lady," a deep voice said from behind them.

Both women whipped their heads around to face a tall, familiar figure in black robes astride a midnight-black warhorse.

Thela protect them. *Gravesire.*

"Run!" Mehleese shouted.

Before they could spur their mounts, half a dozen soldiers in half helms and plate stepped out into the street, surrounding them. They wore white tabards embroidered with towers topped by forked lightning, and each held out a long pike, trapping the horses.

Mehleese fumed, furious and terrified at once. Thela curse her, how could she have been so stupid? Here she'd been mooning over a dumb elf, chittering on about what Jehn should do like teenage girls at a slumber party. Her job was to protect Jehnilyas. To keep her safe and anonymous while they were here. Instead, she'd let them get trapped by the very Templers she was supposed to have been watching for.

Draw Bow

Her bow appeared in her hands with a flash, an arrow nocked and ready, string and fletchings drawn against her cheek. With a kick, Solus spun in a tight circle, faster than a horse had any right to in such close quarters.

"Call them off, Priest, or I'll we'll see how much Pain you can speak with an arrow through your tongue."

Gravesire laughed. "I don't think so, Ranger. Put that useless arrow away before I remind you of our last encounter." He mumbled something, and a sharp sting stabbed her in the side. Nothing like the torture he'd inflicted back at the Exceptas camp but a decent enough reminder.

Whipping Lineage around, Jehn sneered at the Shadow Priest. "I would have been pleased to go the rest of my days and not see you again, Gravesire."

"Oh," he said with a chuckle, "did I forget to mention during our time with the Exceptas that I was there in service to the Temple? I suppose I must have. Much the way you neglected to mention that you were the last living Sophent. Points to me for figuring your secret out first. I can't tell you, though, how disappointed I was when that fool, Goldenshield, disrupted months of careful planning in one night. I was days away from dragging you back to the High Bishop in chains, but he stole my prize away from me. I had hopes that His Holiness would allow me to set the fire at the base of your heretic's stake."

A wicked smile bloomed across his face. "Then again, he still might."

"I don't think fire is the tool for you, Priest." Jehn's helmet blinked into place, and her mace flashed into her hand. She spurred Lineage forward, right at Gravesire, who'd made the mistake of positioning himself inside the ring of Temple soldiers.

Exhaling, Mehleese forced her consciousness into a tight ball inside her head. Her senses narrowed. Everything around her disappeared. The noise of the streets, the crush of people, the call of vendors hawking their wares, all of it faded into a dull silence.

When everything—every thought, every fear, everything that made her *her*—was fused together, when nothing remained but that tiny ball, a crackle of energy sparked in the now-empty space. Starting as a tingle behind her eyes, it spread down the length of her spine. Then it surged into her arms and legs like a shock wave.

A heartbeat pulsed in her ears.

The tingle was her Focus made palpable. It guided her hands and eyes as arrows flew from her bow in a fluid dance. One. Two. Three. Four arrows zipped away from her, slicing through the air toward the three pikemen standing behind Gravesire.

Another heartbeat.

Her arrows sank into their targets, into the open faces of the soldiers' helmets. Two of them lost an eye apiece. The third, the unluckiest one, the one that happened to be closest to Jehn as she drove forward with her mace raised, lost both. He crumpled to the ground, a pair of arrow shafts plunged halfway through his head.

Mehleese's perception slammed back to normal as she released the Focus. Someone screamed out in fear. Mothers corralled children into their skirts and lurched away in a panic. Merchants and customers alike dove to the ground or behind carts and stalls, anywhere that looked safe from the conflict in the street. The wounded soldiers cried out, their long pikes clattering to the cobblestone street.

Mehleese inhaled.

With a chilling roar, Jehn hammered her studded mace into the Priest's shoulder. His face became a tempest of shock and surprise, and he flew backward, driven from his mount. He landed in a rolling heap of tangled robes, fallen soldiers, and forgotten pole arms.

Kicking Solus, Mehleese spun again, coming about to face the remaining three Temple guards.

She exhaled.

The world compressed around her once again, and her consciousness shrank to a pinpoint. The power of Focus raged through her.

One heartbeat.

Her targets—that was all they'd become, targets, virtual bull's-eyes painted on moving figures like paper on hay bales—tried to react. With gaping mouths and wide eyes, they dropped their weapons and began to turn. Too late.

One. Two. Three arrows flew.

The thump of another beat.

One-two-three arrows struck their respective marks, striking deep as the soldiers spun away, catching them in the neck, back, and side.

The city around her exploded in sound and motion.

"Go! Go!" Jehn screamed from behind. "I'm right behind you."

Mehleese tapped Solus on the sides with both heels. Her mount responded, racing forward in the now-open street.

And then agony.

The pain seized her everywhere at once. A thousand needles stabbed at her temples and the base of her skull. Her arms and legs had to be shattered, falling limp and useless. Her entire body was caught in a vise of the priest's Blessing of Pain, pressed together, squeezed against unseen spikes and blades. Points of health ticked off in a rapid-fire series.

She screamed and sagged against Solus, clinging desperately to the horse's neck as fire ripped through body, mind, and soul.

Jehn pulled alongside. "I've got you."

Horses racing along the now empty street, the Paladin somehow placed a steady, glowing hand atop the Ranger's head. A second of searing heat became ice, and relief washed over her, running down her neck and back like a cool shower on a hot day.

Able to sit up again, Mehleese stole a glance back. Gravesire, surrounded by a cloud of darkness, ran after them on foot, hood back and robes gaping open at the chest. His lips moved, and she cringed, steeling herself for the Pain to return. But nothing happened. Whatever he'd tried didn't work.

The Priest's features twisted in rage. He gave up the chase and faded as they pulled away.

After a hard run through the rest of the Fourth Ward, they passed into the Third, where the crowd thickened. They eased their mounts, slowing to a walk.

"Thank you," Mehleese said. "I owe you one."

"Nothing more than I owe you. You're one of the best I've ever seen handle a bow."

"Years of practice. How you handled the Priest, though? Now, that was impressive. How did you knock him off his horse?"

Jehn smiled. "It was Thela's work. For all his strength, Gravesire is arrogant. He forgot that the same power he receives from Her to bring misery, She grants me to dispel it. He can't speak Pain to me so long as I have her Blessing.

"I'm not immune or anything. It still hurts, but it's like being hit by a low-level blow. Nothing like the damage he can do to you. Certainly not enough to stop me from attacking him. Even better, because he forgot, his surprise when I didn't seize up kept him from defending himself. It was worth it to see the shock on that smug face of his. It's a shame I doubt I'll ever be able to take him by surprise like that again. If we'd been anywhere but Riverglow, the seat of the Temple's power, I would have stayed to finish him."

"We need to get out of the city. As soon as possible."

"Yes, let's find the guys—"

"Hey, are you two okay? We have to get out of here!" Goldenshield waved at them, several paces ahead. He and Zeke were on foot, weaving through the crowd at a fast clip.

The cloud of worry on Zeke's face melted away when his eyes locked with Mehleese's. She smiled back at him in reassurance that she was fine. Seeing his relief somehow filled the space in her that had been vacant for as long as she could remember.

"We have to move, fast," Goldenshield urged. "The Temple knows you're here. They're coming to arrest you."

"We've already met their welcome party. And Gravesire was with them. Yet, somehow, here we are, not in chains. Thank you for racing to our rescue, though." Jehn winked at Mehleese.

"Jesus, Thela," the Warrior muttered softly enough that Mehl could barely hear, "that guy is all we need." Louder, he added, "Thank Thela you're both fine. What's the fastest way out of the city?"

Jehn gestured ahead. "The Freerun Gate is here in the Third Epoch. We should reach it shortly. That's the quickest way out. What about you? Should we go on without you, or did you already find what you were looking for?"

Mehleese winced again at the reminder that they were keeping things from her. And that Zeke could be one step closer to leaving.

Sensing her dismay, her elf reached up and patted her hand.

"We didn't find everything we were looking for, but we did get a good tip. And we managed to meet the king. He gave us a proclamation to take back to Boland in Copperton. We're supposed to help defend the city. The Legion is on their way there, now. So let's get out of here. We need to get back to town before it's too late. Once we're out of the crowd, Ek'zae and I will summon our mounts. "

Mehl nodded in return, trying hard to ignore that damned chill in the pit of her stomach.

CHAPTER THIRTY-FOUR

THE ARGUMENT

THE LUSH GROWTH OF THE Ore Wood along the Riverglow Road followed them on their left, and the Iron Spikes loomed to the right as they made their way back to Copperton. They pressed hard, wanting to put as much distance as possible between them and the city.

The pale-yellow sun had been setting as they left Riverglow, and following a day of travel, it slipped below the crests of the Everfrost Mountains to the west. They'd been mounted and moving the whole time, and their tense expressions bore proof of it. They said little, and they hadn't shared a smile for hours.

Gerald shifted in his saddle. Damned thing wasn't designed for comfort, that was certain. Then again, being in a video game, it was probably designed by software engineers in some office in Silicon Valley or Seattle. Somehow, he'd cope. A couple more hours to go, if that, until they were back in Copperton.

And then they just had to wait for the Legion to show up.

He rode at the back of the group, with Jehn several lengths

ahead of him, keeping to herself. Zeke and Mehl, farther ahead, had been inseparable for the journey north. They were side by side as always, allowing space to come between them only when necessary to allow someone traveling the other direction to pass through.

They were a strange couple, mismatched at best given the differences between their personalities and, even more, ages. But everybody had heard of more mature ladies having an eye for young guys. Maybe that was just how she liked them. Seemed like he could have done better, though. Sure, Mehl was a great Ranger and mentor and a solid, dependable fighter to have with them in a fight. He'd be dead by now if it weren't for her. But she wasn't exactly a spring chicken. If the guy had wanted to hook up while they were stuck here in Fantasyland, why not pick someone a little… fresher? Z looked happy with her, though, which was something. He'd had few enough happy days in the real world.

Shifting his attention to Jehn, he watched her ride, marveling at the way she swayed in perfect time with Lineage's easy gait. She had more grace in her thought and movements than anyone he'd ever met, in either the real world or this one. And considering she was a Paladin, a class known more for blunt, brute force than gracefulness, that was saying something.

He tore his eyes away from her and hoped his thoughts would follow. He couldn't afford to daydream about falling for a video game princess, even if she swore she wasn't one. He had enough problems and responsibilities without getting attached to make-believe characters. Somehow, he and Zeke and Mehl would have to get a Legion Shaman alone and talking about the mysterious Fifth World. As if that wasn't challenging enough, they might have to manage it in the middle of battle and without anyone else in Copperton knowing about it.

All after, of course, making up with Lord Sheriff Prickface and signing up for defensive duty.

Easy.

As Gerald considered their options, Zeke slowed Demon's pace, separating from Mehl and letting Jehn pass him. He fell back until he was even with Gerald.

Inclining his head slightly, the elf prodded his friend. "Lord Goldenshield."

"Shut up," Gerald shot back.

Z gave him a nervous chuckle. "So, we, um, uh." He hesitated, stared at the gloves holding Demon's reins. "We should talk or something."

Gerald raised his eyebrows. "Holy bitching Thela, Zeke, you sound like you're about to ask me to prom. We've known each other since forever. You don't have to be all weird. You could tell me you were gay or an alien, or hell, planning to adopt one of those adorable little gnome people we saw building that clockwork catapult back in Riverglow, and I wouldn't give a shit. Get on with it."

His friend took a breath and cleared his throat. "Look, I'm not going home. I'll do whatever you need to help you find a Shaman and figure out how to make a portal. I mean, we know it can be done, since we saw Rhandren in our world. But, when the time comes, I'm not going with you. I'm staying."

"That's funny," Gerald replied, smiling. "Good one. Did you and Mehleese come up with that to wig me out or something? Because I'm not biting."

Zeke's face was flat and colorless. His bottom lip trembled as he looked into Gerald's eyes for the first time since Riverglow. "I'm not joking, Ger. I'm not going. And neither is Mehl. We're staying here. We… we belong here."

A streak of ice slid down the Warrior's back. "Quit fucking around. It's seriously not funny."

"I'm not fucking around, Ger."

Gerald leaned closer. "Bullshit," he hissed, cheeks warming in anger. "You can't honestly believe you belong here. What the fuck does that even mean? Nobody belongs here. It's a goddamn video game. Not even the people who live here belong here. It's all ridiculous and fucked up, and we're getting out and going back to the regular world, where things make sense. I'm not going to let you be stupid just because you never let go of some fantasy you had when you were ten years old to grow up to be a D&D character. Between that and finally finding a woman that'll give you the time of day—and apparently a lot more than that, I guess—you're not thinking right."

Zeke recoiled as if he'd gotten Goldenshield's war hammer to the face. His pale cheeks flushed with a starburst of angry red. "Fuck you, Gerald. And the fucking horse that's chafing your ass, too. This doesn't have a Thela-damned thing to do with whether I've ever been with a woman before. And no, it's not that I want to live out a kid's fantasy. You should know better than that bullshit.

"You talk like the Fifth World is some place full of joy and wonder, where your shit doesn't smell and every day is all unicorns crapping rainbows. Well, I hate to be the one to remind you, hot shot, but it isn't. You hate your life and your job, and you spend most of the latter trying to escape the former by playing this 'goddamn video game,' even while you're on duty. Your parents think you're wasting your time, you think you're wasting your time, and you don't have a single ambition beyond, 'Hey, let's drink a fuck-ton of beer tomorrow because I don't have to work.' You live like a pig, you haven't cleaned our apartment in six months, you eat take-out pizza as if it's the only food left on Earth, and in case you've forgotten, your social life isn't overflowing with dates on

Friday night either. But then, that shouldn't surprise anyone, since you're living as if every potential responsibility or commitment is radioactive.

"But *oh*! All of a sudden, now you think you've got this chance with Brooke, as if there hadn't been a thousand other chances you didn't do shit about over the past five years. Yet because of this one thing, you can't think about anyone or anything besides getting back home to maybe, finally, cough up some balls and tell her how you feel. Which likely isn't going to mean a damn thing because, dude, it's clear she loves you like a brother. But despite that, you're going to put one tiny whisper of probably pointless hope before everyone else, even though what I've got here is a real relationship with a real woman, not some bullshit ginned-up fantasy."

He exhaled. Looking away, he added, "I can't believe I came here to be straight with you—Katie fucking Sanders honest—and all you could say to me was that bullshit. Fuck you, man. If that's how you're going to be, fine. Mehl and I will just go when we get back to Copperton. You can figure out how to get home on your own."

Gerald tightened his grip on Zero's reins. "God, you can be such a whiny asshole sometimes. A selfish, whiny asshole. I mean, did you even think about me for a second? Or can you not think of anything besides jumping back into bed as soon as you can?"

Shaking his head, Zeke lowered his voice. "You've got a pair of balls to match that golden shield everyone keeps going on about if you think *I'm* the selfish asshole here, Gerald. Not a damned thing you've said surprises me. But that? What the fuck is wrong with you?"

"That's just what I'd expect a whiny assbag to say. Just… whatever. Have a nice life, elf."

Zeke hesitated as if he was going to say something else.

Instead, he muttered, “Whatever.” With a slap of his reins, he urged Demon forward. The unicorn, sensing his owner’s mood, snapped at Zero before darting ahead.

“Your mount is an asshole too!” Gerald called after him as the mage passed Jehn and joined back up with Mehleese.

“Stupid asshole unicorn,” he mumbled to himself.

Her eyebrows coming together in concern, Jehn pulled even with Gerald. “Everything okay? Sounded like you two were arguing.”

“No, everything’s not okay… I just. I don’t know. You spend your whole life thinking you’re absolute, never-ending friends with someone—brothers, really—and then you grow up, become adults, and one day, out of nowhere, they turn into someone completely different.”

“Ek’zae? Someone completely different? Are you sure? Maybe a little smitten with Mehleese, but that’s not worth crucifying him over.”

“It’s a good bit more than smitten, if you ask me,” Gerald sneered. “She got him wrapped around her little… well, whatever it is in that old saying. He’s just not being himself.”

“I don’t believe this. Are you jealous of your friend because there’s a woman showing him some attention?”

“No, no, it’s not that,” he stammered. “It’s that. You know…” He trailed off, fumbling for some way to explain that he was mad not just because of Mehleese but because Mehleese was making Zeke stay in Thelaroth. Which was a complicated enough difference on its own without also letting her know that none of them belonged in Thelaroth to begin with. Oh, and that he was getting out of here at the first available opportunity.

“Look, it’s complicated.”

She cocked her head a few degrees, just enough for the

edge of her chestnut hair to curl up under her chin. Even angry, he melted a little bit.

"How long have you known each other?"

"Since we were seven."

"Are you the same now as you were when you were seven?"

"Well, no. Apparently, he's turned into a selfish prick."

"Not him. You. Are you the same?"

"I… I mean, no. You'd have to be an idiot to say you were the same at twenty-three as you were at seven."

"Right. The thing is, I think I understand pretty well. But I'm not sure you do. Everyone changes as they grow older. And sometimes what made them friends can change too. But when someone chooses to stop being friends, you have to wonder, was it the changes themselves or that someone in the relationship was just too selfish to accept the change?"

"I… I don't get it."

"Think about it. Hopefully, it'll make some sense soon. Before it's too late for both of you. In the meantime, try to figure out how much two people have to change before they stop being brothers."

Without waiting for a reply, she whistled, and Lineage trotted back into the space between him and the others farther ahead.

With a frown, Gerald let her go and rode the rest of the way to Copperton sulking, cloaked in uncertainty.

CHAPTER THIRTY-FIVE

THE MESSAGE

By the time Copperton appeared on the horizon, Gerald's mood had grown even darker. The group had bunched closer together as they grew close to town, but neither Zeke nor Mehl would make eye contact with him. From time to time, Jehn glanced at him over her shoulder with a furrowed brow, but otherwise she left him to himself.

Upon reaching the town, though, he had to set aside his irritation. Zeke and Mehl saw them first and pulled up to a stop. Jehn stopped next, allowing Gerald to ride up beside her, just behind the elf.

"What's going on? Why'd we stop?"

"Because we're not sure what that's all about." Zeke nodded at a line of soldiers in the king's black-and-silver livery, lined up on mounts, shoulder to shoulder, across Riverglow Road. They extended beyond the width of the path itself and arced toward them in the brush to either side. The half circle was anchored with spearmen on foot, holding their spears out diagonally.

At the center of the line, Lord Sheriff Boland sat like a

statue on his warhorse, which was covered from nose to tail in elegant, ornamented plate mail. A peek of gold glinted off the shield over the man's shoulder, even in the pale light of the moon.

"I don't guess that's just a standard guard from the garrison, waiting for the Legion to arrive?"

"No," Mehl replied in a clipped voice. Safe to assume Zeke had told her what he'd said.

"Yeah," the elf agreed. "Boland doesn't really seem the type to spend all day standing a post with his men, does he?"

"Great, it's trouble, then. Do you want me to go down alone?"

Zeke and Mehl exchanged a glance. But his friend said, "No, we've been in this together so far."

"Exactly," Jehn added. "What kind of friends would it make us if we waited to see you get ripped apart by the wolves?"

He smirked. "That certainly wasn't the image I needed right now. Okay, then, let's go deliver our message from the king and see if that fixes whatever has his breeches bunched up." Spurring Zero, he moved to cut between Mehleese and Ek'zae but thought better of it at the last minute. He veered his mount to the left, instead, around Demon. To Gerald's minor relief, the surly unicorn didn't snap again.

The four took their time strolling down to meet the soldiers, tension rising as they did. Gerald took a sliver of immature pleasure from watching Boland's mouth twist in impatience. The man was doing himself no favors, watching them with a disgusted look, as if he was looking on as a family of rats approached.

Gerald pulled back on Zero's reins just inside the curve of the arcing soldiers. He did have the king's scroll, though, which counted for something.

"Good evening, Lord Sheriff. What finds you and your soldiers out on such a fine night?"

"No games, Goldenshield. I expect you know already. I have advance scouts in the woods surrounding the town. After our last meeting, I thought it would be best if you didn't spend any more time in Copperton or the Vale."

Jehn leaned close to him. "Careful here. He is loyal to the king, but we don't know how unstable he can be. And if he feels he has the grounds for it, he can make your life very difficult."

"Then I'm glad we have the proclamation," he replied.

Use King's Proclamation

Urging Zero forward, the king's order flashed out of Gerald's bag and appeared in his hand. He held the scroll out, offering it to the Sheriff. "My lord, I realized I was… rude to you during our last meeting and that you might have taken some offense. With that in mind, we spoke to the king, hoping he might vouch for us."

Boland made no effort to move but cast a wary eye from Gerald to the scroll and back. After a moment's consideration, he jerked his head a few degrees, and the soldier next to him stepped forward.

Give King's Proclamation

He took the parchment case from Gerald's hand and backed his mount up into his former space in the line. The soldier showed the wax seal to the Sheriff, who nodded and said, "Proceed." The bodyguard cracked the wax open and read the proclamation.

"It is from the king, my lord. And it's authentic. Marked by a court scribe."

"Fine." Not taking his eyes from Gerald, he said, "Give it to me."

He scanned over it and then smiled. "I must say, I'm quite impressed. The king doesn't often show an interest in the affairs of the common people."

"Maybe he thinks we aren't quite as common as you do," the Warrior replied. As an afterthought, he tacked on, "My lord."

"Yes, well, he isn't all-knowing, either, is he? Praise to Thela no one ever suggested a king was omniscient, or we'd all be in trouble. That said, though, I must say he's shown some remarkable wisdom in this case." The Sheriff nodded at the now rolled-up scroll he held across the pommel of his saddle.

Gerald shot an uncertain glance at the others. Ready acceptance wasn't something he'd expected from Boland about the proclamation. The man had led a group of soldiers here to threaten them before they even entered town. Someone willing to go to that much trouble in the middle of the night didn't seem like the sort to just go, "Oh, well, since the king says I should like you…"

At best, he'd figured they'd see some grade-A irritation over it, if the Sheriff didn't flat-out disregard it.

But this? Accepting it? With a smile?

"You see, Master Warrior, I didn't expect the king to realize and fully grasp how the situation has evolved here in the past week. Somehow, in a scant matter of days, you've become a folk hero. The 'Legend of Goldenshield' spreads like a wildfire across the Vale, to the point that most people believe you intend to ride out to meet the Legion alone and will consume them with fire from your eyes.

"As you can imagine, as the *proper* authority here, that story can be problematic. Because now every decision I make and order I give is going to be compared with what some myth carrying *my* Shield might have done."

"Truly, I am sorry about that, Sheriff. I didn't intend to be an obstacle for anyone. But look, maybe this thing the king suggested could let me dispel some of that gossip. Believe me, I'm no legend. And I'll happily take orders and be seen doing it."

Happily wasn't exactly right, but if it got him close enough to a Legion Shaman, he'd learn to fake it.

"It's 'Lord Sheriff,' and I'm afraid that won't be necessary, boy. To prove I'm the master of Copperton Vale, I'm forced to discredit you and remove you from the situation. Now, I don't know what the king *told* you he was sending with you, but this is a Royal Decree that you and your elven friend are traitors to the crown. And he sent it to me so I can post it in Town Square, where I'll be *seen* executing you for it, affirming my authority."

Turning to the soldier beside him, he said, "Capture them both. Hurt them all you want, but don't kill them. Spare the women if they don't resist, but expel them. They are not to remain in either the town or the Vale."

The sound of fireballs crackled behind Boland before he even finished speaking. Weapons flashed into the hands of the soldiers on horseback—swords and shields, axes, crossbows, longbows, and spears. The spearmen on the sides of the half circle surged forward, shouting.

Draw Hammer

As he turned to his left and raised the hammer, a spear slammed into his side, spreading fire through his torso. Health flooded away in a clicking torrent, more than he'd expected. These soldiers were good. Still, he brought the hammer down on the shaft of the man's spear, shearing it in two in a cloud of particle splinters.

That familiar sense of cold metal pulling tight across his

skin washed over him. Thank Thela for Jehn and that Steel Skin.

A fiery blast exploded amid a knot of the men somewhere on the opposite side of the circle, and screams filled the night. Zeke was finally getting better at dealing with multiples, even if he couldn't do as much damage at once that way. Arrows zipped through the air, most coming from the mounted guards.

Gerald spun Zero in a tight circle, clanging back spears as he did. Combat Power coursed through him. He shouted his barbaric *WarCry* and rushed at the one man *not* engaged in combat, Boland. The jackass sat atop his horse, his face the image of placidity, scroll still held across his saddle.

Hammer over his head, Gerald called to him in challenge.

That golden shield blinked over the Sheriff's arm, but no other weapon appeared. He gave Gerald a bored, superior look, eyes dull and half closed. Molten fury shot through the Warrior. Oh, how he wanted to leave a permanent dent in that smug face.

Closing to within a few feet, he gritted his teeth, ignoring the arrows from the surrounding mounted soldiers. He might look like a porcupine by the time this was over, but at least he'd get his shot in.

But then, those arrows weren't hitting him. Instead, they whizzed past, directed at other targets. Strange, considering he was racing toward the Sheriff.

He pushed the thought away and swung down, filling the attack with Power, visualizing how his hammer would smash through the Lord Sheriff's head.

But it didn't.

A double-edged, two-handed sword almost as long as a man intercepted the hammer, catching and turning it aside. The soldier beside Boland—one of his personal bodyguards from their meeting in the Council Hall—parried the hammer blow without so much as a grunt of effort. Goldenshield's hand and arm, on the other hand, reverberated with the shock, like he'd just crushed a fastball with an aluminum bat in little league.

A scream from somewhere he couldn't see sent a chill up his back.

"Axeblight!" a woman called, voice thick with panic.

The two-handed sword came forward again, arcing toward Goldenshield's head.

A shield would have been helpful. But he didn't have one, still hadn't thought to buy one after giving up the one on the Sheriff's arm. Instead, he raised his hammer to intercept the sword. But the soldier dipped it below his parry at the last moment, and it struck home. The massive weapon slammed into his chest just under the rib cage. He lost another flurry of points and was driven sideways from his saddle, landing on the hard, featureless ground with a thud, cracking his teeth together.

Well, at least he and Zeke would have plenty of time to make up in the Dark World. Looked like he'd be headed there soon.

"Hold!" someone commanded.

Another voice, a woman's, shouted, "Stop this! In the name of… Holy Thela, stop it! This instant!"

"Hold," the Sheriff ordered. The din of battle faded, replaced with moans and grunts of pain.

Gerald pulled himself up to his knees. Zeke lay in a heap a few feet away, with Mehl looming over him in a protective stance, bow up, arrow drawn. Jehn was several paces away, holding a shield and that wicked studded mace of hers. Seeing the elf, she took a step toward them, but she stopped when Boland hissed.

"Not an inch. Stay exactly where you are, or I'll have you so full of arrows you'll look like a tailor's pin stuffing."

"He's wounded!" the Paladin cried. "Let me heal him!"

"It's bad," Mehl added, staring down. "He's… he needs help."

Boland chuckled. "If I have any luck at all, he'll be dead before I deal with this little interruption." Then, turning around, he said, "Now, why, dare I ask, is Council interfering with my responsibilities?"

At the edge of the road, Bergan Smith and the Speaker stood bent over, with hands on their knees, panting hard, faces crimson. They had to have run all the way. Working at the forge might have made the Smith one of the strongest men in town, but he wasn't much in running shape.

"They've. Come," the smith just managed as his breathing returned to normal. "Legion. Is here!"

The Speaker surveyed the scene before saying anything. As she realized what had been happening, her eyes grew wide, and her lips pressed together in a disapproving line. "Are you a fool, Lord Boland? You were going to kill them? At a time like this!?"

"They are a threat to the peace of the Vale, Lady Speaker. Neither the king nor I can rule effectively as long as Goldenshield remains. As I have an order regarding the matter from the king himself, I hope you won't mind if I disregard your assessment. He and his elf friend are to be arrested and executed."

"My bunions know more peace than the Vale of late. May I see that?" she asked. Boland shrugged and handed it to her. Justifying himself to her seemed the last thing he was concerned about.

"Councilman Smith, what was that about the Legion?"

Having caught his breath, Bergan repeated, "They're here.

The Legion has come. They marched into range from the mountains yesterday and are setting up camp a few leagues to the west. They sent a centian with a message." He held up a smaller roll of parchment.

Boland took the scroll with a look of disdain. "I hope you had the sense to keep the flea-bitten four-legged horseman under guard while I answer this?"

Bergan curled his lip but said nothing.

After reading and rerolling the scroll, the Sheriff sighed. "It seems Thela's Zealot, Atlous Bonecrusher, requests a meeting outside their camp to discuss the terms of our submission. We'll have to finish the execution when we get back." To his bodyguard, he said, "Bind them up. Make sure the Mage is gagged and his hands are bound."

The soldier nodded. After surveying the damage of the battle and glancing at the Council members nearby, he coughed. "My lord, I'm not certain we should leave them here. If we leave enough guards to ensure they don't escape, we may not have the force to project strength in the face of the Legion. If we appear weak to them, they may attack. Our full complement is necessary to protect you."

The Sheriff tilted his head, considering. "Fine. Bind them as instructed, though. And take extra care with the Mage. Have the Paladin heal the wounded guards."

"I will not, Lord Sheriff," Jehn shot back, defiant. "Not unless you let me heal my friends first."

Boland waved at her demand. "Fine, whatever. Do it quickly." Looking down at Bergan and the Speaker, he added, "Assemble the Council. You're all coming along too. Meet me at the Everfrost Road Arch in ten minutes."

With that, he turned and headed for the interior of town, his bodyguards trailing behind.

Jehn raced forward, hands already aglow as she reached

Zeke. Mehl dropped to a knee beside her, eyes clouded with concern. Streaks of quiet tears ran down her cheeks. A few breathless seconds passed before the Paladin gave her a grim smile. He would be okay.

Gerald clenched his jaw, grinding teeth against one another. They could grind to dust for all he cared. For the first time since leaving Riverglow, he held an image in his mind of something besides a wavering portal home.

At that moment, it was the image of Erlas Boland falling before his hammer, and it was tinted red with rage.

CHAPTER THIRTY-SIX

THE LEGION

A MOTLEY CROWD GATHERED AROUND THE massive stone archway marking the edge of town limits on the west side of Copperton. Everfrost Road ran through the arch, and the town's hodgepodge delegation heading out to meet with the Legion formed an irregular column on its cobblestone surface.

The full complement of the king's soldiers that had arrived with Boland stood at attention in neat rows, with the mounted cavalry two abreast and the infantry standing four across, shoulder to shoulder. Together, though, they represented a mere three units of the Army of the Realms. Merely eighty men by Gerald's count, sixty spearmen and another twenty on horseback. That may have been enough to stoke the fires of Lord Sheriff Boland's ambition when he arrived in town, but rumors said the Legion counted better than a thousand, if not twice that. The pitiful contingent the king sent wouldn't be so much as a speed bump on their way through Copperton.

After the orderly lines of the soldiers, the members of Town Council huddled together in a pack, lacking much order of any kind. The Speaker was trying to listen to three of them at once while two others shouted at each other. Each Council member, too, seemed to have an assistant of some kind, adding to the chaos.

At the end of the column came Gerald, Zeke, Mehl, and Jehn, all mounted, along with four guards tasked with keeping spears pointed at each of them for the duration of their little field trip. The prisoners' hands were bound and tied to the pommels of their respective saddles, and their legs were lashed together through their mounts' undercarriage. Zeke, as Boland had instructed, was gagged with a piece of rope and a first aid bandage to prevent him from casting spells.

Thank Thela or God or Buddha or whoever, at least he was sitting up now, on his own, eyes bright. It had been a closer call than any of them realized before he was healed. As they were led from one side of town to the other, Jehn leaned into Gerald and whispered that the elf, after drawing the bulk of the barrage of arrows—some of which were tipped with poison—had been about as close as you could get to the Dark World without taking that one-way trip.

The townspeople of Copperton surrounded the column, chattering to each other with a mix of nervous energy and fear. The knowledge that the Legion was coming at last had spread through town like a disease. So quickly, in fact, that everyone who didn't make a habit of keeping to themselves like hermits already knew by the time Bergan and the Speaker interrupted the skirmish. When the soldiers started marching toward the Arch, then, the bulk of the town's population headed that way too.

Chaotic or not, the delegation was prepared to depart, except for the notably absent Lord Sheriff. He'd yet to make his way from his offices near Town Hall. Murmuring, the townsfolk made one of two snide suggestions: either the Sheriff was primping, making sure his beard was trimmed and oiled and his rather prodigious eyebrows were laid down with wax, or he'd soiled himself already just thinking about the Legion and had to change everything, from his breeches to his breastplate.

Gerald rolled his shoulders, trying to work out the first hitches of a cramp as he watched for signs of the Sheriff from the center of town. Boland could, of course, be packing up his things and making a run for Riverglow. After all, it was easy to *say* you'd been appointed to keep the Legion from reaching the city. Stopping them, on the other hand, was another matter. Especially when all reports indicated that the army facing them had cut a swath across the Western Realms like a hot knife running through beef tallow.

"Do you think he's coming?" On level with his left stirrup and five feet away, Frega looked up at him with one expectant eyebrow raised. "What's he waiting for? A visit from Thela to save his bacon?"

"I don't know what's keeping him. But I know you should be at home. There's no reason for you to be here, Frega. It might not be safe."

She spread her hands out. "The entire town is here, including the Town Council, which, you'll remember, includes my father. Where would I possibly be safer?"

"I don't know, but I have a bad feeling about all this."

"I do, too, Goldenshield. I have a bad feeling about you being tied up there like a common thief. *You* should be the one with the Shield."

"Look, Frega—"

"You look. You said you were going to try to be here when I needed you. We both know we're all going to need someone soon, and Thela's Blood, that someone sure isn't Erlas Boland. Who's going to watch out for me if you're not here?"

"Your parents will—"

"They can't keep me, or the town, safe, Goldenshield. They want to, but they can't. You promised, Goldenshield. You promised."

"Frega, I—"

"Forget it." She gave him a dismissive wave and turned away, disappearing into the boisterous crowd.

"Frega!" he called after her, but he was drowned out by a swell of voices. The Sheriff rounded the bend from the town square, his two bodyguards flanking him a step behind. The reason for his delay was obvious the moment he caught sight of him. That reason covered him from head to toe and forced Gerald to squint as if staring at the midday sun, even in the pale moonlight. Boland had changed every piece of his outfit and armor. He was decked out in a full set of burnished gold plate from helm to boots. The elaborate, decorative armor was a clever match for the Sheriff's golden shield, which hung on his arm, completing the extravagant ensemble.

With his customary smug smile, Boland raised his hand, seeming to expect the crowd to erupt in cheers for him. And a handful did, Templeman Prior among them, but most of the townsfolk stood with heads tilted in confusion, or worse, disgust.

Their lack of enthusiasm did little to interfere with his pompous grin.

Mehleese whistled. "That must have cost him a copper or two."

Gerald chuckled. "What an idiot. That's the most ridiculous-looking thing I've ever seen. And trust me, I've seen people do some stupid stuff."

Anger, though, burned in Jehn's eyes much more than amusement did. "More than half of these people don't know if they're going to survive the week, and he's got the audacity to strut out to meet our would-be conquerors in *that*? He is an absolute disgrace as Sheriff. My father would have had both the Shield and his head for such a display."

They fell quiet as Boland passed, somehow giving them both that self-important smile as well as a scowl of warning. He said nothing to them, but to their guards, he said, "If any one of them even twitches, raise an alarm immediately. I have a plan that might actually make these four useful to us. I will not allow any of them to hamper it."

"Yes, Lord Sheriff," the soldiers responded, saluting him as he rode forward to the head of the column. He ignored the pandemonium of the Council members, responding to calls for his attention from the Speaker and others with a wave of the hand and a dismissive sniff.

At the front of the delegation, just under the archway, he turned back to face the crowd. "I ride forth to secure the safety of Copperton and to insure our sovereignty as people of the Western Realms. For the king!" His sword—also gleaming gold—blinked into his hand, and he thrust it into the air in triumph. "For the king! Huzzah!"

The crowd slowly took up the cheer, adding applause, whistles, and huzzahs to match his own. With a flourish, and spurred on by the crowd, Boland turned west and galloped away from town, toward the awaiting Legion. The soldiers followed after him, getting the journey underway.

Gerald muttered to himself in irritation as their guards prodded their mounts to follow the column. As if capturing a Shaman somehow wouldn't have been hard enough, now he had to survive his own execution first.

Thela be thanked, the ride was short. If they'd had to travel for long with his hands and legs bound as they were, Gerald would have been so stiff and seething with anger that they might have had to kill him just to shut him up. But little more than an hour after leaving town, with the sun just creeping over the mountains behind them, they reached the top of a hill sloping down to the Legion's camp.

Boland ordered the three banners to be set beside him. The first, Copperton's, proudly showed a golden shield on a field of green placed between two mountains. Flanking it to one side was his own, a golden sword on a field of onyx, with the flag of Sheriff on the other, an eagle in flight carrying a scroll. The military units spread out in a line behind the banners, horsemen at the center flanked by the two groups of infantry. The Council members, still arguing amongst themselves, took up a position behind the line, just in case something happened and a battle broke out.

The guards responsible for Gerald and the others, while never lowering their spears, led them off to the side, where they could see what was happening. The Lord Sheriff waited with his customary pair of bodyguards, his entire body wreathed with a golden glow from the morning sun reflecting off his pompous armor.

Gerald wasn't a real military strategist, but in middle school, he'd thrilled his history teacher with a number of extra-credit research projects detailing some of the greatest armies and battles of the world's past. By the tents, cookfires, supplies, and assorted weapons racks throughout the encampment, it was clear the rumors of the Legion's size hadn't been exaggerated. At least two thousand warriors had to be in the camp, waiting for the command to attack. And they would be real soldiers, experienced fighters who'd already faced and defeated every challenger between here and where they'd made landfall along the northern beaches of Moon Shore.

By contrast, Copperton had eighty soldiers to field and

maybe a thousand townsfolk, most bearing pitchforks, hoes, and other garden implements. At best.

Gerald scoffed, trying to imagine what that idiot Boland thought he was doing. Sitting on his mount beneath a banner he'd recently had made because the king granted him a title wouldn't intimidate anyone, let alone this army. Thela's Blood, a professional army twice its size wouldn't be able to intimidate the Legion.

"It's sickening," Jehn muttered, her voice buzzing with anger. "I never thought I'd see the day there was an actual Guardian encampment on the soil of the Western Realms, in plain view of Thela and everyone."

"They aren't messing around either," Mehleese said. "Look at the arrangement of that camp. It's smart, efficient. These aren't Guardian families on a vacation."

The camp was broken into several separate sections—one for each race of the Guardian alliance—arranged around a single large tent at the center. Although each area was vastly different, as different as the seven races themselves, they were all laid out in logical, identifiable patterns. They were neat, spare, and spoke to purpose before comfort.

Zeke grunted something from behind his gag.

"What?"

He gestured toward the camp with his head.

"Yeah, we see it. What do you think we're looking at it?"

The Mage grunted again, this time with a tone of exasperation, rolling his eyes as he did so. Demon, sensing his rider's reaction, grunted a whinny in irritation and stomped his front leg against the ground several times. He stopped, waited, and then repeated the same action.

"Hold on. I've seen this before with people who said their horses could count."

Jehn clucked her tongue. "Oh, that's just ridiculous. Surely you're not saying—"

Demon stopped and started again. One. Two. Three. He continued stamping until he reached eight. After his last one, Zeke gestured again toward the camp.

What were they missing?

"Oh, I see now. That is strange," Mehl said.

"What?" Gerald and Jehn asked at the same time.

"Count the groupings in the camp. There should be seven, one for each Guardian race. But there are eight."

Gerald did a quick scan, and, beside him, Jehn muttered numbers under her breath.

She was right. Eight camps were arrayed around the center tent.

Jehn shook her head, confused. "Who could the eighth group be?"

"I don't know, but I have never been so glad I didn't accept the Sheriff's appointment as I am right now," Gerald said. "Boland's going to have his hands full, to say the least."

Jehn glared back at him. "We're all going to feel the sting of this. If we can't stop the Legion here, they'll have control of nearly all the Western Realms before the harvest ends. Only Riverglow City will remain, and all they'll have to do to claim it is set up a siege and wait. With the rest of the countryside in Legion hands, food will run short in Riverglow quickly. And I doubt the Guardians will be kind to us when we've been beaten. The Favored have a long history of being less than kind to them."

"Let's hope you're wrong about that. Because I can't see how you stop this army with what we've got."

CHAPTER THIRTY-SEVEN

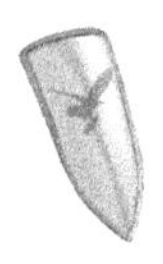

THE PARLEY

JEHN SAID NOTHING BUT WATCHED grimly as a centian—the half-horse, half-human race often used by Legion as messengers—galloped away from camp and up the hill toward Boland. She was unarmed, but still the Sheriff's bodyguards walked their mounts ahead of his and *Drew* their long two-handed swords.

The centian slowed when she reached them, inclined her head ever so slightly, and said something none of them could hear. Boland nodded in return and gave a curt reply before the horsewoman spun and raced back down the hill. She trotted past the camp boundary, weaved her way through the hustle and bustle of the military encampment, and shot into the tall tent at the center.

"I guess that's Bonesnapper's tent or whatever his name is?" Gerald asked.

"Bonecrusher," Jehn replied. "Atlous Bonecrusher, Thela's Zealot."

He arched an eyebrow. "What does that mean?"

"A zealot is someone who is fanatical about something."

The Warrior sighed. Catching Zeke's eyes over his gag, he could've sworn he noticed a glint of laughter. "I *know* what a zealot is. But why do they call him that? Is that some kind of title for people big in the Guardian church or whatever?"

"They don't have a 'church' or even a codified religion, really," Mehleese said. "Here, the Temple of Thela is as much a bureaucratic organization as it is a spiritual one. But on Akador, the Guardian's relationship with Thela, on the other hand, is purely spiritual. They have no structure, no organization, and no real religious leaders."

"How does that work? Don't they have to have rules or something? Who says what's right or wrong?"

"Thela says," Jehn explained. "The Guardians see her work and hear her breath in every facet of the world. At least, the ones who wish to can. And on the rare occasions they think they need a little extra insight with Her, they talk to a Shaman."

"That's weird."

"Is it? Or is it stranger to have a go-between who judges us in Her name?"

"I… I don't know. I never thought about it. So why do they call this guy 'the Zealot'?"

"For the past five years, he roamed the Western Realms trying to warn us that Thela was angry with us. That the Favored races had become blind to Her. He visited every city and town on the continent, some more than once, begging us to turn away from the Temple, which he claimed had been subverted. He said we should join him and the Guardians along the Shaman's Path."

"After a while," Mehl broke in, "people got tired of hearing it, and everyone started dismissing him, saying he was too much of a zealot to be reasonable."

"Not everyone," Jehn added quietly. "My father believed him."

"Yes, and look where that got both of you. The Temple put Dalor on the throne, had your family…." She stopped before adding details and instead gave the shorter woman's shoulder a squeeze. "And they're still hunting you."

"Wait, so this Atlous guy is a Shaman?"

Both women gave him disbelieving looks. Behind them, Zeke rolled his eyes and mumbled. Gerald could almost hear him saying, "Duuuuh."

On reflex, the Warrior tried to throw his hands up, pulling hard against the ropes holding them. "Well, how was I supposed to know?"

"Everyone knows," Mehl said, chuckling. "At least, anyone who's ever paid attention does."

With a sigh, he shook his head. He really should have read the mission text when taking new quests. "Okay, so I'm oblivious. Sorry. I'll pay better attention."

Zeke grunted, making his disbelief apparent.

"Whatever. What are we doing here, then? Why the big field trip out to the Legion's camp?"

"From what I've heard," Jehn said, "Atlous usually offers terms for surrender before rolling over an opposing force. I'm sure that's why he invited Boland here."

"He's not actually going to negotiate surrender and occupation, is he?" Even as big a fool as the Sheriff seemed to be, he had to have something else planned.

She nodded at the camp. "I guess we'll see. Here they come."

Down below, a group filed out of the tall white tent in a single-file line, representatives from each of the Guardian races. First came a hulking green figure, a reptoule, one of the lizard people, followed by a stout ursal, a bear-man with brown-black fur and a shaggy muzzle in the center of his face, and then a tall, long-limbed female oculan whose wide, single eye was evident even at a distance. After her came an arialen, with a ram's spiral horns on both sides of his head, an avian, a bird woman half hopping on stubby legs because she lacked the space in the tight camp to extend the wings folded on her back, and a leputian, who strutted toward the hill with an acerbic attitude, at odds with the flopping rabbit ears atop her head. Next, a massive centian horseman trotted out, followed by the smaller female centian who had delivered the message to the Sheriff. Lastly, a human stepped out, a blond, barrel-chested Warrior with a familiar swagger.

"Wait, is that—?" Gerald asked.

"Blessed Thela, it's Tristan," Jehn said. Zeke groaned.

"It… It can't be! Humans and Guardians together?"

"Actually," Mehleese countered, "it makes a kind of sense. The Exceptas must have joined with the Legion. After we destroyed Tristan's wagon train, where else would they have had to turn? No supplies, most of their numbers fled, nothing but a handful of struggling refugees. They had to get help from somewhere, and Riverglow is the last place Tristan would be looking to make an alliance."

Jehn nodded. "That must be it. You're right—Tristan loathes the king. And it explains the eighth section in camp too."

"Great," Gerald groaned. "That's just what the unstoppable army needed, Exceptas reinforcements. It *really* sucks to be Sheriff now. Which one is Bonecrusher? At least half of them seem to fit the name."

"The one leading, the reptoule," Jehn said. "Which, in a sense, is fitting for Thela's Zealot. The lizard people are said to be descendants of the World Dragons."

"Dragons? I don't remember anything—" A grunt from

Zeke interrupted him. He was staring back with wide eyes, trying to get something across. Something related to dragons? Wait, hadn't he mentioned a game expansion and dragons not long ago? If they would have to fight winged, fire-breathing lizards, Gerald was getting out of Thelaroth as soon as possible. "Never mind."

The messenger horsewoman separated from the group after leaving the tent and returned to the centian section of the camp. The rest followed Bonecrusher, making for Boland and his banners, stalking up the slope on foot.

They made the short trek without any personal guards or assistants, but weapons hung from every conceivable strap and loop among them. And unlike Boland, they didn't look as if they thought themselves too noble to use them.

At the top of the hill, they drew up into a line with Bonecrusher opposite the Sheriff. Three Guardians fanned out to each side of the reptoule leader, with the centian, avian, and oculan on his right and the ursal, arialen, and leputian on his left. Tristan hesitated but then settled beside the small, angry-looking humanoid rabbit.

After a brief exchange no one could hear, the Sheriff pointed toward the prisoners and motioned. The four guards must have expected it; they grasped the mounts' bridles right away and led them to the negotiations.

Boland wore his usual smug expression, as if bored with the whole business or somehow above it. The Guardians, though, eyed them with a mix of interest and suspicion.

"Why have you brought these humans in bindings?" Atlous asked in a rasping, rumbling growl.

Gerald couldn't take his eyes off the enormous lizard man.

When he'd first met Tristan, the Exceptas chief had seemed larger than average for a male human Warrior. Gerald couldn't be considered small himself, not with this *Realm*

Quest character body. He was broader in the shoulder and across the chest than he'd ever dreamed of being in real life, and he'd lost four inches or more of beer storage around the belt. Even so, Tristan was still half a head taller than him and as wide as a door frame.

Atlous Bonecrusher dwarfed them both. He was two heads taller than Tristan, at least, and so wide across the back and shoulders he could have been used as a roadside billboard back home. His head and face resembled one of those dragon lizards that lumbered around on nature shows, constantly tasting the air with a forked tongue. Unlike them, though, he stood upright on two massive, well-muscled legs, each as big around as a good-size tree, and balanced on a thick tail that curled at the tip behind him. He might have reminded Gerald of a *Tyrannosaurus*, but where the dinosaur had stubby, pointless arms, Atlous's were long and rippled with muscles, ending in a set of claws suited for carving a shape from solid rock.

To Gerald's disbelief, the ursal was even larger. If it came to actual battle, how could the people of Copperton ever defend against *that*?

"They are heretics, Master Bonecrusher. Betrayers of Thela. I thought you might like to see them punished yourself." He smoothed his eyebrows, trying to appear casual.

The lizard stroked his triangular chin and squinted a black marble eye at the Lord Sheriff. "Sheriff-man," he answered. "We don't care about your Temple rules for heretics. The Temple is more our enemy than your king or armies. We have no fault with these. We are here to discuss the surrender of your town and the region."

"I'm afraid we can't just surrender, Master Atlous. You know that. But we hoped we might be able to come to some terms to make it worth your while to simply pass us by and continue your advance on to Riverglow. Copperton poses no threat to you, and you could have Riverglow under siege in two days. They're banking on having time to compile resources. Imagine what you might accomplish by arriving earlier than expected."

Atlous turned first to the representatives at his left and then to the four on his right. They each gave him a slight nod.

"What do you offer?"

"I can offer you lands and titles in the Western Realms so that we might become a combined people, living and working together, rather than adversaries."

The reptoule crossed his arms. His jet-colored eyes seemed to expand as he glared, unblinking, back at the Sheriff.

Boland raised his hands. "I know, I know. You're offended by such an offer. My king suggested I try to bargain with wealth. I told him your passion could not be bought."

"You are fortunate I do not kill you for questioning my honor."

With a slight dip of his head, the Sheriff hurriedly added, "Thank you for your understanding. Please forgive my simple king. He doesn't know your people as I do."

Furrowing his eyebrow ridges, the lizard growled, "You know nothing. He knows less. Get on with it."

"Even if you aren't interested in lands or titles, or these heretics, we all know you have no Mages. You have plenty of Warriors and Rangers and even more Shamans than I'd have expected. But there are no magic-users among the Guardians. One might be helpful to you when you reach Riverglow. I'd like to give you one."

Zeke grunted in alarm.

"No!" Gerald shouted. "You can't!"

"Shut him up," the Sheriff warned. One of the guards smacked Gerald across the back of the head with the shaft of his spear.

"Stop," Atlous said. The command was a force by itself. It rumbled along the ground like an aftershock following an earthquake. The guard froze in place. "Tell me of your heretics."

Irritation burned on Boland's face. He detested not being the one in control. This was *not* how this was supposed to go. But there was little he could do about it, short of committing his eighty fighters to an immediate—and doomed—confrontation.

"The Warrior," he said, "is called Goldenshield. The Mage is his companion, Ek'zae Axeblight. The women are… well, I don't know much about them."

"They call me Mehleese Worldwalker, my lord." She lowered her head in a sign of respect.

Jehn had kept her face lowered since being led over. She still didn't raise it. "I am called Jehn."

Atlous took a few lumbering steps closer, again rubbing his chin. "Do I know you, girl?"

She lifted her head at last, eyes meeting his. "No, Master Zealot, I'm sure you don't."

Just then, Gerald thought he saw a glimmer on the lizard's face, a flash of something in his coal-black eyes. In the amount of time it took him to take a second, closer look, it was gone.

Whatever it was, Bonecrusher didn't mention it. Instead, he grunted and stomped over to the Warrior. "So, this is the mighty Goldenshield I have been hearing about? You are not what I was told to expect. And this is not how I'd imagined we'd meet, brought to me like a common prisoner. Even I would show you more respect." His lip curled in a twitch of a smile. Over his shoulder, he added, "Odd that you are the one with the golden shield, Sheriff, yet everyone calls him Goldenshield."

"Thela, it seems, has a rich sense of humor," the Sheriff replied, his voice as dry as fallen leaves. "As you can see, though, I think there's little doubt who deserves the title." He waved an empty hand over his gleaming golden armor.

"Indeed. So, you would trade your own people to me if I agreed to spare your town?"

"Yes. The heretics are of no concern to me. It would please me if you could make use of them to our mutual benefit."

"Exceptas, take the Mage and the Paladin girl."

Boland brightened. "We have an arrangement, then? You'll spare Copperton and move on to Riverglow?"

Tristan plodded over to the prisoners, wearing a twisted expression like he'd just sucked on the world's sourest lemon. Leading prisoners around must not have been what he hoped for when teaming up with the Legion. He gave the guards a caustic glare, and they backed away, leaving him access to the lead ropes. Taking Demon and Lineage's reins, he half led, half dragged them away.

"No!" Gerald shouted again. "Boland, this is wrong!" He kicked Zero, but Tristan yanked down hard on his mount's halter, holding him in place.

"Shut him up," the Sheriff hissed. Two of the guards jammed spears into his side. An electric shock exploded in Gerald's abdomen, and his health ticked down again. Mehleese, close by, shot a hateful look at the spears held against her chest.

Zeke grunted in protest. Jehn, though, her voice calm and soothing, said, "Stop. We'll be fine. Don't get yourself killed over this. Stay alive. Thela will bring us together soon. She has you in Her plans."

She nodded to Tristan, who resumed plodding toward camp. Sitting up straighter in his saddle, Gerald closed his eyes and urged his wounds to heal quickly. He and Mehl had to get out of their bindings before the delegation left.

"Do we have an arrangement?" the Sheriff repeated.

"We do, Sheriff-man. But not the one you want. I accept your prisoners and will make good use of them. In return, I will not kill you for dishonoring us with offers of coin in exchange for our salvation. Be glad."

And then chaos erupted.

Avians filled the sky behind the Guardian delegation, bows in hand. Rabbit-shaped leputians, half as tall as humans, raced up over the hill from the camp, scurrying past the Sheriff and toward the soldiers behind him. The infantrymen broke ranks without hesitation, squaring off one-on-one with the closest floppy-eared humanoid they found.

The ursal beside Bonecrusher dropped to all fours and shot forward. He sprang up from the ground at full speed, crashing into the bodyguard at Boland's right, toppling soldier and horse together. The avian on his other side jumped up, unfurled her wings, and hung suspended in the air, and she rained arrows down on the other bodyguard with precision.

Thwap! Thwap! Thwap!

At the same time, the leputian representative that had been next to the avian scampered forward and slashed the bodyguard's mount across the forelegs.

In just a handful of seconds, both of Boland's bodyguards had been taken down. The Sheriff stood alone, eyes wide in shock and horror.

Bonecrusher took one massive stride forward and swiped a vicious claw across the face of the Sheriff's mount, leaving four deep gashes. Terrified, the horse turned away, exposing the side not protected by the enchanted shield.

The four guards by Gerald and Mehleese abandoned them and ran at Atlous. The oculan, arialen, and centian representatives stepped in front to intercept them. Before any of the soldiers could react, they disarmed and incapacitated all four.

Gerald yanked and pulled against the ropes holding him.

Watching the skirmish helplessly wouldn't keep him alive for long, and he had to do something before Zeke and Jehn were secure in the camp below.

Atlous struck the Sheriff in the chest with an open hand, driving him back and throwing him from the rear of his horse. The mount raced off, wild with fear.

After a brief struggle on the ground beneath the weight of his ridiculous golden armor—like a tortoise trapped on its shell—the Sheriff managed to roll over and stand up. Behind him, his cavalry charged up to protect him, but an onslaught of arrows from the sky met them.

With one claw, the leader of the Legion lifted the Lord Sheriff into the air to meet his eyes. Boland's smug grin had vanished, and he trembled visibly.

"Please, please, don't kill me."

"Enough!" Bonecrusher roared, ending the din of battle. He pulled Boland so close that the lizard-man's breath ruffled his hair. "You are pompous and, like many of Her Favored, have no love for the Mother. You gave dishonor to me, and even worse, Her. For these offenses, you had to be bloodied. But we are not heartless. We have come to help you, to save you, not crush you beneath my heel. I will give you this day to consider. Submit to us, denounce the Temple and the puppet king, and take the true Path of Thela, which our Shamans will show you, and no harm will come to you or your people. At dawn, we will come to you. Be ready."

With that, the reptoule tossed Boland to the ground, his scratched and scraped golden armor clanging together in a thunderous racket.

Atlous turned, waved for his Legion to follow him, and stomped down the hill, leaving the humans in chaos.

CHAPTER THIRTY-EIGHT

THE DECISION

GERALD'S HANDS WERE ALMOST FREE by the time the delegation was ready to head back to Copperton. With the shock of the Guardians' attack still hanging over them, no one spared much attention to him or Mehleese. Whispered praise to Thela made its way around the humans as they regrouped, both in thanks that the Legion hadn't killed every last one of them and because none of the soldiers had been killed, except for the Sheriff's bodyguards. A few did have serious injuries, none lethal, most of which were given by the leputians. The reputation the rabbit-folk carried for being aggressive, nasty warriors—however fluffy—was well earned.

After coming to the realization that they would survive the meeting and make it back to town alive, pulling together went quickly. Retrieving Boland's mount and getting him back on top of it, however, was another story. Both were terrified beyond rationality, almost apoplectic with fear. The horse, however, responded to a measure of calm reassurance before long. The Lord Sheriff, on the other hand, looked down at the camp with wild eyes as the group prepared to depart.

Not until they were halfway back to town did he begin to recover himself, at least somewhat. With his voice still shaking, he ordered the guards to resume their watch on Gerald and Mehleese just before the young Warrior managed to free his hands. They didn't recheck them, though, as the column made somber progress through the forest. Even the Town Council was quiet; it was the first time all day they weren't arguing amongst themselves.

"What are we going to do?" Mehleese whispered.

"I don't know," Gerald said, gesturing at the same time toward his hands. If he could get his hands free by the time they arrived, they might have a chance. He could cut Mehl's ropes and together make a break for the Ore Wood. With luck, they could hide out there long enough for Boland and his soldiers to give up looking. They did, after all, have other things to worry about.

"We have to save them," she said. "Thela knows what Atlous will do with Ek'zae and Jehnilyas before he comes for the town. I can't lose him."

Gerald stared at his hands, unable to look Mehleese in the face. Her fear for Zeke was plain in the tightness around her eyes, the downward curve of her lips. Yet it wasn't only the mix of dread and anxiety for her new lover's safety he couldn't bear to look at but also the undercurrent of anger just below it all. His argument with Zeke was still a very fresh wound.

"Look, regardless of what you think, Zeke means more to me than you can ever imagine. He's been like a brother to me for the better part of fifteen years. I can't… I just can't…"

He exhaled, collecting himself.

"Mehl, I can't imagine my life without him," he said. "He's been part of it nearly every day since I was too young to even tie my own shoes. When he told me, then, that he wanted to stay with you here, I guess I lost it. I always assumed things with us would somehow stay the same forever. We'd always play games and hang out or whatever. Be there for each other. Together.

"Anyway, I said some stupid things. Hurtful things. Things I didn't mean. Things I wish I could take back. And now look at us. I didn't even get a chance to tell him I was sorry. But I *can* tell you. I'm sorry. I'm beginning to realize that a lot of the time these past few years, I've been a selfish asshole and all-around prick."

Mehleese hesitated, balancing his apology like a vendor weighing produce. Finally, though, she sniffed and gave him a thin smile. It was tentative, almost brittle, but it cooled the anger. "Growing up sucks, Gerald. Realizing that, somehow, you have to manage life's complications while your friends figure out how to face their own problems is a challenge for everyone. Change is inevitable, and we all must make our own choices. The best you can do is try to be the friend you'd want someone else to be for you. If you can't find empathy for the people you say matter to you, can they truly really matter?"

Gerald nodded. "Yeah. I'm a dumbass and a slow learner, but I'm getting there. I'm glad you found us here, Mehleese Worldwalker. Or Rakkel, or whatever your name is. This place wouldn't be the same without you."

She smiled and nodded back.

"Now that we have that out of the way," he continued in a whisper, "let's figure out what we can do. We need to get back to the Legion's camp to help Zeke. Which means we have to get free somehow, preferably before our freaking-the-fuck-out Lord Sheriff realizes he hasn't executed me yet."

"Agreed."

He cast a furtive glance around, checking the four guards

that were supposed to be watching them. Two of them hadn't looked up from their boots for the entire march. The other two were whispering between themselves. None of them paid any mind to the prisoners.

"Do you think you can control Solus even tied up like that?"

She nodded without hesitation. "Wouldn't be the first time."

"Okay, so when we reach the archway to town, as the rest of the column files through, we'll make a break for it. If they realize what's happening and send someone after us, I should have my hands free by then, so I'll swing back and keep them busy while you get away. We'll meet back up where we met the Exceptas in the woods that first day. Got it?"

Mehleese nodded again before turning away to avoid drawing attention while he worked on his bindings.

Gerald ground his teeth together to keep from sticking his tongue out while concentrating. His mother had been nagging him to break that bad habit since he was eight years old. He never would have guessed the moment would come that he'd agree with her, let alone that it would come as he tried to free his hands while on horseback. Especially considering he'd never actually ridden a horse.

Just as the archway into Copperton came into view, he slipped his right hand out of the loop holding it to his pommel. Once he could work with that one, the left was freed a few seconds later. The plan might actually work.

The townspeople had collected along the roadside near the arch like ants drawn to a forgotten piece of candy. They didn't seem to have moved in the time the delegation was gone. Unlike when the Sheriff led the column away, though, the people cheered as it returned, believing that catastrophe must have been avoided since the party looked intact. Of course, they couldn't see the half-crazed, dread-filled look in the Sheriff's eyes or the bleak faces of the soldiers who'd survived by the narrowest of margins.

Instead, in their blissful ignorance, the people of Copperton cheered with all their hearts. They hooted and huzzahed, whistled until lips were numb and applauded until hands were sore. They clamored for the returning soldiers who had marched out to defend them, the Town Council who had to have guided the negotiations, and the Lord Sheriff himself, who led their salvation.

Hearing their delight, the hope in their voices, the selfish Warrior who swore he didn't care about this town, these people, or this world felt his cold heart crack and break, shattering apart. In just over a day, an army fiercer than anything they might conjure in the bleakest depths of their nightmares would march down this very same road. With that army would come death and misery, domination and devastation. The Smiths would be among them when the Legion came. And Saiyen, the barkeep at the Pig and Roost. Nala too. How would the rest of Council fare when Atlous replaced them with a governor of his own? Would they even survive?

He found Frega among the crowd, waiting for their return, cheering the contingent as heroes. Would she or her friends, Daven and Blust, live long enough to see another Festus? Would they get any closer to someday choosing their own classes or taking on their own hunters' contracts? What did they have to look forward to, if they did survive, occupied by the Guardians?

The blacksmith's daughter caught sight of him and the cold, grave look on his face. Her smile leaked away, and her shoulders drooped. She looked at her feet and shook her head, a pitiful, disappointed motion that stole the breath from his chest.

Gerald slumped in his saddle, thoughts of free hands and potential escape driven from his mind.

The Lord Sheriff must have shared the feeling. Less than fifty yards from entering town, he put up a fist at the head of the column, halting it in its tracks. For moments, he said nothing, did nothing, but sat atop his horse in the middle of the road.

With the shake of his head, though, he turned his mount and ambled away from the arch, toward the rear of the formation. He stepped past the lines of soldiers who had come with him from Riverglow to defend the town, his head down, silent. When he reached the Town Council, milling around in their usual disorganized cluster, he pulled up beside the Council Speaker.

Boland said something to her, quiet and brief. Then the shield, that damned golden shield, flashed from where it had been slung across his back and into his hands. A second later, it flashed from his to the Speaker's. Then, his head drooping again, he turned his mount and rode into town. As he went, he tore off pieces of his opulent armor one at a time and tossed them to the ground.

He passed through the arch and the stunned mass of townspeople, now so quiet you could hear a pin drop. Boland didn't stop until he vanished from sight.

Mouths hung open. No one moved. The Sheriff of Copperton Vale had just abandoned them.

"Oh, for fuck's sake," Gerald muttered, sitting up straighter. "Change in plans," he said to Mehleese and spurred Zero hard. The horse, glad for the chance to break free, surged away from the guards and up the road. Shouting curses in surprise, they took off after him.

Looking over his shoulder, a wry smile spread across his face. Too bad he didn't have more time to lead them on a little chase. Instead, he raced up to the Council, beside the Speaker, where the Sheriff had stood just a moment ago. Several of the Council members gasped and shrank back, expecting an attack.

"Lady Speaker," he said, "unless I saw that wrong, it looks like you're up shit creek."

"I'm sorry, what was that?" She arched an eyebrow at him. "And as I've told you before, I'm not a lady."

"Uh, sorry, it's an expression. What I meant was that it seems the town has lost a key player at a bad time."

She made a face like she'd just sat on a tack. "Yes, we seem to be needing a new Sheriff in short order. Honestly, though, more of a sacrificial lamb. Do you happen to be interested in the position? It pays well, but the odds of surviving the first week aren't terribly good. And if you do manage to survive, I can't imagine King Dalor will be pleased with us at all."

Gerald looked again at the people of Copperton just beyond the archway, chattering among themselves. Somebody would have to do it. What had Mehl said? Change was inevitable. "Turns out the king's not terribly pleased with me already, so how much more damage can I do? Probably won't live past tomorrow anyway. Give me that Thela-damned shield. I'll be your lamb." He stretched his hands out.

As he said it, the guards caught up to him. Leveling spears at his side, one of them grunted, "Hands down, filth, or we'll run you through."

The other bobbed his head at the Speaker. "We're sorry, Lady Speaker. This one took us a bit by surprise in all the excitement. We'll manage from here."

"Don't call me…" She clucked her tongue and trailed off. "Oh, never mind. No, I'm afraid you won't manage him. He'll be managing you, it seems."

To Gerald she added, "But there's no halfway this time. We need a Sheriff, not a bandage. You don't get the shield unless you accept the title, swear the oath, and hold to it until She chooses to take you to the Dark World."

The condition was grim. He nodded in agreement anyway.

She held the Shield of the Vale out to him.

Take Shield

In a burst of color, it blinked from her hands to his. That same wave of power he'd felt when he took it before they left for the Exceptas camp burst away from him. Both guards were knocked from their feet by the surge.

Equip Shield

The shining plate hung from his left arm by straps that seemed made just for him, right where it belonged. The electric thrum of its enchantments pulsed through his skin, his muscles, his veins, his bones. Not that he really had any of those things.

"Thela blesses you again, Lord Sheriff. Now then, what do we do?"

"Let's hope she keeps it up. First things first. Guardsmen?" He glared down at the two men getting back to their feet. Both looked at him with a combination of fear and confusion. A prisoner didn't often become a commander in the blink of an eye.

"Uh… yes, my… my lord?" the first stammered.

The second wasn't as sturdy; he fell to his knees. "Please, Lord, mercy! We was just doing our jobs."

"What are your names?"

"I'm Felton, sir," the standing guard replied. "This wretch is Torgan."

"Well, Torgan, Felton, I don't know that I'd call it mercy, but I'm not going to punish you. Find yourselves horses.

You're going to be my personal guard from now on. And Torgan? In Thela's name, man, get up. You're embarrassing me."

Torgan clambered up off the ground. The pair shared an uncertain look.

"Lord Sheriff," the Speaker said, "are you sure you want to do that? I'm certain we can find more suitable—"

"Nah, they'll be perfect." Gerald shouldn't be messing with them, really, but he was still kind of pissed about being stuck in the side earlier. With battle coming and him now the captain of the Town's forces, being named his personal guard should make up for it. That'd have to make anyone sweat.

Mehleese rode up with the other two guards tailing behind her. "What just happened? What's going on?"

"Boland gave up the job, so I took it," Gerald explained.

She frowned. "That means you'll have to lead the defense of the town when the Legion comes. What about Ek'zae and Jehnilyas?"

He smiled. "I need them for the battle. Can you run and fetch them? I hear you're a badass with that bow."

Her sharp Ranger eyes squinted at him before she shook her head with a mix of amusement and disbelief. "You're even crazier than I thought. Cut me loose, and I'll bring them back. Somehow."

"Okay. Let's get into town," he said to the Council. "No time to settle in or see your families, though. I want the entire town called to Council Hall. Every last man, woman, and child with any kind of skill. Especially engineers and smiths. Understood? We have a lot of work to do and not much time."

The Speaker cocked her head. "What do you have in mind, Lord Sheriff?"

He winked back at her. "We're going to play a game with the Legion, Madam Speaker, a game they've never played before.

"Master Smith," he said to Bergan, "do you still have my badge and uniform tucked away safely?"

"I do, Lord Goldenshield."

"Good. Could you get them, please? We're going to need them."

They'd need a whole lot more too—including an unreasonable amount of luck—but he'd worry about that later.

CHAPTER THIRTY-NINE

THE BATTLE

With the sun warming the back of his neck and shoulders as it rose behind him, Gerald sat atop Zero at the end of a stonework bridge, awaiting their collective doom.

He leaned forward and patted the horse a few times on the neck. The poor mount deserved a better name than Zero. He'd performed every duty he'd been asked—even putting up with that blasted unicorn of Zeke's, Demon—without hesitation, and, in most cases, beyond expectations.

And today would be, without question, the greatest test either of them had faced yet.

Zero stamped and whinnied, as if sensing his rider's anticipation. Soon now. Soon.

The Everfrost Road Bridge was the only one in the area that would easily accommodate an army of the Legion's size while crossing the Ice Flow, the river running down out of the mountains. It left the mountain range a few days' ride to the north and flowed south all the way to the ocean, through the Lowland Grass realm. Here, though, in Copperton Vale, so close to the source still, the water was always within a degree or two of the same bone-chilling temperature, winter or summer, giving the river its name.

The icy river was Copperton's sole hope for survival. For reasons beyond anyone's understanding, the town had been founded right in the middle of the Ore Wood. In its early days, the town was surrounded by forest. As the logging and mining town grew, though, the road from the Everfrost Mountains to the Iron Spikes and Riverglow beyond became a well-worn path for prospectors, merchants, and adventurers. As it did, the Ore Wood opened at the town. Eventually the road bisected the forest completely. Now there were two parts to it, the North Ore and South, named for their relation to Copperton.

On the east side of town, the gap between the two was sizable—more than an hour's ride from the north part of the forest to the south. But on the western side, on the bridge along the Everfrost road, Gerald could see them both in one spot.

With luck, that would save them.

A scout, one of the cavalry riders who had volunteered for the task, approached, racing up from the west. She slowed to a stop at the end of the bridge and saluted. "Lord Sheriff, they're coming. Close behind me."

"Good, thank you. To your position now. Tell your lieutenant not to forget his orders. Hold until he receives my signal. Understand?"

"Yes, Lord Sheriff." With that, she spurred her horse past them and ran off across the bridge to the east.

Gerald returned his attention to the hill ahead of him. This was his vigil, watching the horizon, waiting for the Legion to arrive and filled with a confounding mix of apprehension, boredom, and just the slightest hint of exhilaration.

Would have been nice to have a piece of gum. A big wad of pink that came out of the wrapper as hard as a rock but yielded after a minute's exposure in the mouth and the pressure of a kid's teeth. When he used to play Little League ball, Gerald always got nervous before coming up to bat. Somehow, a hunk of bubble gum, and trying to blow the biggest bubble ever seen, helped.

There was no gum here, though. He'd have to take his mind off of what was coming on his own.

Gerald turned his head, peeking over his shoulder. "Nervous, fellas?" Even with an army of thousands mere moments away, he couldn't help but get a dig in at his "personal guard."

"No, my Lord," Torgan replied calmly. Ever since he'd realized Gerald wasn't going to have them executed, he'd been as sturdy a guardsman as a Sheriff could want.

"I'll be happy to have the sun set on today," Felton said, dodging the question. "Whatever Thela decides to do with us."

Whatever, indeed. Both men sat on horses flanking him, battle-ready mounts purchased from the stable master in Copperton. Neither looked happy about it.

"Is there any chance I could get you to change your mind about this, Lord Sheriff?" Felton asked. "I'd really rather fight on my own two feet. My training with this beast is limited to what the stable master could spare."

"No, Felton. You've gotten more horse training than the people of town have gotten battle training, but they're standing back there with weapons they don't know how to use and not complaining. I need them to see me. It's the reason I named a personal guard. They'll see you and know I'm near. You're here for morale, not to guard anything. You two are to stay mounted as long as possible and not get killed. And don't screw up the first rule unless it's going to end in screwing up the second one. Got me?"

They both gave him solemn nods. "Aye, Lord Sheriff."

Sheriff. He still couldn't believe it. How did he end up

here, in charge of the entire town's defense? Thousands of lives depended on him, hanging by the proverbial thread over the abyss. Make that the Dark World.

A week ago, he'd had his cable turned off because he couldn't remember to pay the bill. Yet just a few hours earlier, before Town Council and most of the assembled people of Copperton, he'd sworn the Sheriff's Oath for Thela and everyone present. The Speaker stood in front of him in the Council Hall, holding the Shield with him, its golden surface gleaming brighter than ever before.

"Repeat after me," she'd said. "I, Gerald of the Golden Shield, do swear in the name of Thela and King Dalor the First, the Anointed, Defender of the Western Realms, First Protector of the Temple of Thela, and Warden of Braxys the Black, Eater of Worlds..."

Blinking, he'd had to tear his attention away from the Shield. "I," he began, but then he hesitated, struck by the enormousness of it.

With a glance over his shoulder, he begged for reassurance from Mehleese just behind him. She beamed in return, conferring a sure nod of encouragement.

He exhaled. "I, Gerald of the Golden Shield, do swear in the name of Thela and... the people of Copperton Vale..."

A gasp had gone up from the bystanders close enough to hear, becoming a buzz that rolled through the rest of the crowd, front to back, as those who'd heard passed along what he'd said. The Speaker's brows shot up in surprise and then furrowed in disapproval.

Gerald shrugged. It was the best she would get. The people of Copperton meant something to him. Enough, at least, that he wasn't willing to let them flounder without a leader when the Legion came. Dalor, though? There weren't too many things he'd do in that man's name. Maybe clean out a stable. Or build a new outhouse. That was about it.

The Speaker hesitated, conflict over him changing the oath written in the scowl on her face. Realizing everyone was waiting on her, though, she huffed and shot him a look daring him not to repeat the rest of it word for word. "To accept the charge as Sheriff of the Vale, to carry this shield in defense of the Light…"

"To accept the charge as Sheriff of the Vale, to carry this shield in defense of the Light…"

"To hold it fast over the hopeless and neglected and to dispel all shadows, of man or of night, with its shining radiance."

"To hold it fast over the hopeless and neglected and to dispel all shadows, of man or of night, with its shining radiance."

"Until Blessed Thela call me to the Dark World."

"Until Blessed Thela call me to the Dark World. May that be later rather than sooner."

She released the Shield, leaving it to him, took a step back, and said, "Congratulations, Lord Sheriff. May Her Shield hold fast before you."

Waiting on the bridge astride Zero, he could hardly feel the Shield hanging over his back, but the weight of it on his heart couldn't be measured.

A horn bellowed three shrill calls, shattering the tense morning air and bringing him back to the task at hand.

"Here we go, kids." He kept his voice calm, somehow, despite the rapid-fire flutter of his heart against the walls of his video-game chest, straining to escape and skitter across the bridge to relative safety. The entire plan hinged on timing, Mehleese, and a great deal of luck. Might as well say it was up to Thela—if you believed that sort of thing.

The first line of the Legion crested the hill to the west, led by Atlous in full battle armor, a set of mail engraved with symbols of the four elements: earth, wind, fire, and water. His armor gave off a glow similar to the radiance of Gerald's own shield.

"Oh," he murmured, absently, "that's why it's so shiny. It's the enchantment, not just polish."

"My Lord?" Torgan said.

"Never mind." With that, he spurred Zero forward. Felton and Torgan followed on his heels.

Seeing him coming out alone, Atlous started toward him. They met on a grassy patch between the two armies.

"Top o' the morning to you, Zealot. Nice day for a battle, right?"

"Goldenshield? Did that spineless ooze Boland send you out to face me in his stead?"

"Something like that. He won't be joining us. Ever again."

"You surprise me. When we started to march an hour ago, I expected to find the toad quaking at me from the edge of town. And instead, I find you here, no longer bound. A day past, you were a bargaining chip—a worthless one at that—and now you're Sheriff-man. And you bring your army out to meet us. Bold, even if your army *is* only trader folk and farmers in armor. Too much to hope you've come to submit? We want to turn you back to Thela's way, not punish your town. Those I leave behind to run Copperton will rule fairly if you behave and do not question them."

"No, Master Bonecrusher. If you'd be conquerors, we're going to be sticklers about it and make you do the conquering. No free lunches in Copperton."

The mountainous green half lizard split his long, flat lizard snout in a fang-riddled smirk. "I hoped for as much, Sheriff-man. May Thela take note of your courage and spin your soul out of the Darkness as a Guardian. Such bravery is wasted on the Favored." Without waiting for a reply, he turned and stormed back up the hill to his army, shaking the ground with each thunderous step.

Gerald turned Zero in a half circle and galloped back to the bridge. He slowed at the stone span, clip-clopping across it, approaching the first squad of the king's spearmen, who stood in formation a third of the way to the Copperton side. The line parted before him, letting him pass through. A second squad of footmen was behind the first, and they split likewise. Reaching the third of the bridge closest to the eastern bank of the river, he turned again to face the Legion.

"All right, ladies and gentlemen," he called out to the soldiers in front of him. "This is going to be the hardest part of your whole day. All you have to do is hold. You don't have to kill a hundred centians; just keep the Legion from crossing this bridge until I call retreat. Whatever you do, do *not* break formation."

He frowned. Not much of a rallying speech. But blasted, bloody Thela, how he hated speeches. How, again, had he gotten himself into this?

His personal feelings aside, though, the soldiers and townsfolk needed a few words to get them going. Hadn't he read something in a literature class once that he could borrow? Shakespeare or something?

Raising his voice, he said, "Today will be remembered for as long as the Western Realms remains the home of the Favored. We few, we blessed few, will hold this bridge against lizard and bear, bird and hare! With nothing but our courage and each other, we will hold this bridge until the Dark World comes to Thelaroth, if need be. We will stop these 'unstoppable' Guardian bullies in their tracks! The bards will sing of our valor, of how we stood our ground! And every man and woman across the Realms from this day until the last will think us lucky to have been Thela-blessed enough to stand together and hold this bridge in Her name, and for all of Copperton!"

It wasn't great. It wasn't poetry. Hell, it wasn't even original. But it worked. A cheer of "Huzzah!" went up from the soldiers in front of him and the Coppertonians along the road and in the woods behind him.

The cheers ended quickly, though. The horns of the Legions sang out in reply, two long, deep notes followed by a short one. And then they started down the hill.

The arialens came first, charging at the bridge with their heads tilted forward, challenging with their ram's horns. Their snouted faces twisted in battle rage, they snorted through their wide nostrils as they ran, certain to plunge through the line of soldiers standing not quite shoulder to shoulder on the bridge.

The line of the Legion's army stretched from one side of the horizon to the other, but the bridge was narrow. Only a handful would be able to cross at a time. As they neared them, the arialens broke their ordered ranks and squeezed together, just a few warriors, two or three abreast.

His heart may have beaten rapid-fire before, but that was a gentle, precious drumbeat to the way it jackhammered with the Legion bearing down on them. The familiar feel of adrenaline coursed through him, enhanced by the tingling surge of Combat Power. Power he would need very much in the next hour.

Shouting and coughing, hooting and snorting, the arialens raced to the bridge, each one wanting the honor of having First Charge, which was said to be quite a distinction among them.

One hundred feet from the bridge.

Fifty.

Twenty feet.

"Form up!" Gerald shouted. The shoulders squeezed into a tight rectangle, the ones in front pushing their shields out toward the enemy. Pulling together, though, had created gaps between the formation and the bridge walls, and soldiers from the rear of the line swung around to fill them. In seconds, they'd gone from a standing column to a wall of shields spanning the width of the bridge.

And then the rams were upon them.

The arialens crashed into the tight formation with the power of a steam locomotive, like a force of nature. But somehow, the soldiers holding shields, supported by the ones behind them, held firm, rebuffing the crush of the ram people.

Many in the first wave of Guardians were stunned by the impact and fell on the spot. Others rebounded but were caught by the press of their own kind from behind them, forcing them against the shield wall. A look of confusion washed over them as they came, bewildered at warriors who had come to fight but instead hid behind a wall of shields, like a turtle drawing into its shell. This was not how you came to war in Thelaroth.

"Rangers!" Goldenshield called out. Behind him, dozens of bowstrings sounded a familiar twang as arrows zipped away all at once. They flew overhead and rained down on the rams at the rear of the press to cross the bridge.

"Repeat!" he called again. Another flight of arrows shadowed them overhead.

The centians came next, swords and shields at the ready. But, seeing the fate of the arialens, they pulled up instead of obliging the Coppertonian Rangers by lining up to get shot. Confusion masked their faces. Rather than charge ahead, though, they *Released* swords and *Drew* their own bows.

Atlous, standing atop the hill overlooking the bridge, shouted out something guttural. Gerald had no idea what he'd said, but the meaning was plain enough. The leputians had been lined up next on the hill, hopping in place to bring the next wave of attack. After Atlous's command, though, they stepped back wearing buck-toothed sneers of disappointment. A group of ursals, bear people with shaggy fur in a range of colors from coffee brown to midnight black, dropped to all fours and loped toward the Coppertonians' shield wall. Worse, a hundred or more avians, the bird people, unfurled their wings and launched themselves into the air, each drawing a bow and nocking arrows. They swooped down toward battle.

"Rangers, target the birds! Second squad, form up!"

The second formation of the king's soldiers raced forward, shields raised overhead. The soldiers of the first squad, leaning in behind the ones comprising the shield wall, supporting and holding back the charge, crouched as best they could while still maintaining leverage to push back. The second squad filled into the tight spaces between and over them, making an umbrella of shields just as the first volley of centian arrows showered down on the phalanx Gerald had constructed.

The Legion's missiles fell in a thunderous storm among the hodgepodge of shields mustered from the town. Some clanged against iron and clattered to the ground, while others punched into the metal, arrowheads poking through on the wrong side. Many pierced wood and leather with a hard thud, driving wicked three-pronged points inches deep into the protective canopy. Some even found gaps in the defense. Men and women cried out as they struck targets and cut through clothing, skin, muscle, and bone. But only a fraction of the barrage did any real damage.

They could hold this way. Might hold this way, for a time. But the bears lumbered at them, and the birds would soon land behind the formation and begin dismantling it from the rear. And Atlous still had a thousand more warriors to commit. Yeah, they might hold, but it wouldn't be for long.

Gerald prayed it would be long enough for Mehleese.

CHAPTER FORTY

THE ZEALOT'S GUESTS

As ordered, Tristan led Jehn and Zeke down into the Legion's camp, picking his way through into a section composed of circular firepits and simple, low-to-the-ground ridge tents. They were the same kind of angular tents with the ridge peaks along the top that Zeke had built with his dad when he was a Cub Scout. This had to be the human part of the Legion's camp. The Exceptas section.

The sullen Exceptas chief called out for two of his men to follow as they made their way toward the only tent in the area built for more than one occupant. It was a fraction as large as Atlous's at the center of camp, but it stood out in sharp contrast to the others around it.

Tristan snapped the bridles, halting the mounts. "Forgive us. We don't have adequate rooms for a princess, so I suppose you'll have to rough it for a few days, Jehnilyas. I hope you and your Mage friend like rocky ground."

"Tristan, I'm sorry—" she began.

"Tristan, I'm sorry, what?" he roared. "Tristan, I'm sorry for lying to you, maybe? Or, Tristan, I'm sorry for ruining everything you'd worked for? Go on, tell me how sorry you are that you weren't there when I needed you. How sorry you are that you knocked out my Shadow Priest just when I needed him. How sorry you are that you set this puny Mage free just so he could turn everything I'd struggled to build into a heap of ash."

Zeke growled around his gag and scowled at the Exceptas leader. He'd show that dog who the puny one was. Just as soon as he got his hands free.

Paying him no mind, Tristan took a deep breath. "Do it. Tell me how sorry you are that without you, Goldenshield's ridiculous plan to disrupt my Exceptas would have been nothing more than an evening sideshow. Tell me how bad you feel that I'm now the lowest member of Atlous's Crusade. Go ahead and try. I might even believe it."

She waited before responding, seemingly wanting to be sure his tirade was finished. When he glared back at her, gasping in frustration for something else to lay at her feet, she said, "No, Tristan, I'm not sorry for any of that. But I am sorry you started listening to Gravesire. He was using you from the moment you met him. He wanted to make the Exceptas a tool to further the Temple's plans and to turn me over to their Purifiers. I'm sorry you let him fill your head with dreams of power and ambition that you'd do anything to fulfill. Especially when you already had a worthy cause. One I was proud to support."

"That's the trick, though, isn't it, princess? Somehow figuring out how to make something of yourself without doing someone else's dirty work first. I wish you good luck with it. Most of us don't have much choice."

"We all have a choice," she shot back. "But Thela makes no promise it will be an easy one."

He shook his head and turned away, waving for his soldiers to take care of them. In short order, their ropes were cut away from their mounts, and they were half dragged, half shoved through the flaps of the tent.

The inside of the temporary structure was barren, empty. Nothing but a few pieces of cloth hanging over a dirt floor. No chairs, no beds, no tables, no personal effects, nothing. Whoever stayed in this tent had little more than the clothes on his back.

The Exceptas soldiers pushed them to the brownish ground on opposite sides of the central tent pole and tied them both to it at the hands and shoulders. Then the soldiers slipped back through the entrance and took up guard positions outside.

"This is cozy," Jehn said.

Zeke murmured in reply. The gag tasted like iron and wet dog.

"Oh, sorry. I forgot about the gag."

They waited in a sullen, forced silence for what seemed an age. The wind didn't blow in through the tent flap, no one came in to check on them or offer them a meal, and no rescue party came. Minutes plodded along, feeding into unremarkable, nearly endless hours. Zeke worried his sanity would abandon him before nightfall.

Eventually, the light seeping in through the tent walls turned from yellow to orange to pink as the sun dipped below the horizon somewhere beyond camp. Not long after, the tent was plunged into darkness, and spots of flickering orange sprang up outside as campfires spread throughout the camp. The soft, filtered light they provided was the one thing keeping shadows from surrounding the two of them.

After hours and hours that plodded by like molasses dripping through a funnel, the boots outside shuffled away, and the tent flap blew open. Rather than the wind, Atlous stormed through in a half crouch, a force of nature himself.

"Forgive the accommodations, princess. I was hoping

we'd be able to make you a bit more comfortable." Unlike when Tristan had called her "princess," Bonecrusher said it without the trace of contempt. From him, it seemed a genuine honor.

"It's fine, Atlous, thank you," she replied. "I do realize this is a military camp, after all. But do we have to be tied up, my friend?"

Friend?

Kneeling between them, Bonecrusher reached down and tugged at something, and then Jehn was free. "I trust *you.* But the Mage I'm not sure of yet. He has a decision to make still."

Decision? What the—?

She moved to where Zeke could see her, rubbing at angry red marks around her wrists. "Can you at least take out his gag? That can't be pleasant."

Blessed Thela, yes, please!

Bonecrusher lumbered around in the small space to face Zeke and squinted at him with one beady, black marble of an eye.

"I know there are limits to what you can cast without your hands, but do I have your word you will cast nothing while Jehnilyas, daughter of Rhandren, is my guest?"

Zeke nodded. Anything to get this Thela-forsaken rag out of his mouth. His jaw would be sore for a month. Well, it would have been in the Fifth World. In this one, it would, thankfully, be back to normal in moments.

Reaching forward with a green claw tipped with razor-sharp nails, Atlous flicked a finger and sheared through the rag tied around his mouth with little effort. He plucked both the gag and the rope away from Zeke's face. "Forgive me, Master Axeblight, but we have to be careful with enemies. And until I hear you say otherwise, we have to assume all humans stand with the Temple and their puppet king. Even if you are a friend of Jehnilyas."

Zeke coughed and licked his lips, trying to rid himself of the unpleasant taste and sand dune–like feeling in his mouth. With a croaking voice, he said, "The king wants me dead. I'm not with either the king or the Temple, Lord Bonecrusher. And you can assume the same of my friend Goldenshield."

A pleasant rumble rolled through the lizard-man's chest. "I am glad to hear that. You will fight with us, then? Will you, princess?"

"Wait, wait, wait," Zeke cut in. "I didn't say that. No, I won't fight my own kind."

Atlous's scaly brow furrowed. "Choose one or the other, Mage. This is where Thela has led us." Turning to Jehn, he asked, "How will you stand?"

"For now, I choose as the elf does, friend of my father. Caught somewhere between you and the Temple. You know I cannot be with them, but the course you've taken is too extreme for me to support."

"The Purge is coming, whether we wish it or not," the hulking creature warned, half growling. "Thela will release the World Dragons upon Thelaroth soon. I can feel them waking now. Soon they will grow restless. And then the skies will darken with a terrible promise of destruction. The world must be made ready, and you stubborn, arrogant Favored *will not listen*."

"Dragons?" Zeke blurted, unable to contain himself. "I knew it! I heard dragons were coming! That's going to be awesome."

"You're a fool, Mage," Bonecrusher hissed. "Thela wakes the Dragons only when she is ready to make the world anew. When she has lost faith with those to whom she entrusted it. When my ancestors climb up from their places of slumber, elf, their hunger and thirst to wreak havoc will bring an end to all the races of our worlds. And I mean *all* of the worlds, even the Fifth. The Dark World alone will remain untouched, and it will be filled to bursting with the souls of Thela's damned."

A wet chill shot down the length of Zeke's back. "You believe that?"

"She will return the souls of the worthy few back to Thelaroth, but those remaining in the Dark World will be burned in the flames of Her furious breath."

"Jehn?" Zeke asked, voice squeaking.

When she said nothing, Atlous added in an even deeper voice than usual, "We must be ready to fight the Dragons when they come. And because you Favored have chosen to be deaf to my warnings, I am forced to make you ready against your will, like a parent with a stubborn child."

Jehn sighed. "My father listened, Atlous. He believed you. And he went to the Temple with the message. The Temple replaced him and hunted him down because of it. How can you possibly think to conquer an organization so large and so powerful it can dethrone a king in his own home?"

He snorted. "Simply. Harshly. When we enter Riverglow, I will crush the Temple's forces, burn it to the ground, and put to the sword every last Templer who doesn't recant and swear to Her Path."

"But not all who follow the Temple are corrupt. The keepers of it may be, but the faithful are just that, filled with faith for Thela."

He swung his head back and forth, a massive, toothy pendulum. "Their faith may be pure, but those people are tainted by the corruption of the altar where they worship. They must recant to be redeemed. Or die."

"Friend of my father, that's too harsh. You will make a thousand martyrs and be consumed by a hidden war with the secretly faithful for years, wasting the time we need to prepare for the Awakening and Purge."

"I am a simple reptoule, princess. The direct way is the only one I know. Join us. Speak out as Rhandren's daughter. With the Temple in ruins, the people will listen to you. We can redeem your father's memory and begin work at once to ready all the Realms for the Awakening."

"I can't, Atlous. My father believed in you, and I believe you, but Rhandren gave up the throne of his own free will. I was never an heir before, and I have no claim to it now. And even if you convinced me otherwise, I can't help you in a holy war against my own faith."

The lizard hissed again in frustration. "He gave up the throne because he was pushed from it."

"No, friend of my father, he gave it up because he loved the Western Realms too much to bring civil war to its people. I have to respect his legacy."

A thunderous growl rose from deep in Bonecrusher's chest. "You disappoint me, but this isn't finished. I must prepare to squash the Sheriff-man and his paltry army as I squashed his arrogance this morning. After I've taken Copperton, we'll talk again." With that, he worked his bulk around the tiny tent and stomped out into the quiet night beyond.

As his footsteps receded, the guard's boots moved back into position in front of the tent flap. Atlous may have been willing to let Jehn walk away free inside, but that was the limit of his trust.

With an absent, faraway look, Jehn dropped onto the ground a few feet from Zeke, whose wrists started to chafe against the ropes binding him.

He said nothing, letting every comment that came to mind pass unspoken. He itched to ask a million questions, as if he might burst trying to remain quiet, especially after being silenced by the gag for hours already. But she was brooding over the conversation with Atlous; interrupting her didn't seem right.

Eventually, though, the dark of night gave way to the soft glow of morning. The boots outside—which hadn't moved all night—were replaced by a different set, and the sounds of an army mustering to march drifted through the tent's fabric walls.

The light outside was still half shadowed and pale when the shouts and footfalls of the soldiers faded. The Legion was on its way to take Copperton. How long did the town have left now? Hours? A day?

"Jehn?"

"Hmm?"

"Sounds like the army just left."

"It did."

"Shouldn't we do something? Try to help them?"

"What can we do? Could we stop them?"

"No, I guess not."

"I'm more worried about Goldenshield. Worried that Boland followed through."

"Do you think he wasted the time to execute him, even with the Legion coming?"

"I—" she stammered. "Maybe. The Lord Sheriff isn't a man of either logic or restraint. He used us as bargaining chips, for Thela's sake. Now that he knows Goldenshield has no value, well, Boland *was* ordered by the king to kill him."

Your friend, she'd said. "I didn't get to tell him I was sorry," he groaned.

She hunched down beside him and patted his shoulder tenderly. "He regretted the things he said to you."

It was little comfort when he could be dead already. But then, to hear Atlous tell it, how long before they all followed?

"Do you believe all of Bonecrusher's… uh, his tall tales??"

"Believe all of what?"

"The 'Awakening' and 'Purge' stuff. I mean, are dragons really that bad? Isn't that all kind of nuts?

"What do you mean, 'nuts'?"

"Crazy talk? Saying that Thela is going to destroy the world. Us? Her own creation?"

"Why is it so crazy?"

"That's not what gods do!"

"I don't know what the gods do where you're from, Axe-blight, but the Ancient Scrolls tell us that Thela has always been short of both patience and temper when it comes to Her children."

Zeke shook his head. "I don't buy it."

"Did you ever try to build or draw something and have a perfect image of how it should end up in your mind?"

"Sure."

"Did it always turn out perfect?"

"No."

"What did you do when it didn't?"

"If it was close, sometimes I lived with it."

"And the other times?"

He paused, not wanting to say it.

"Ek'zae?"

"I… I threw it away and started over."

"That's how it is with Thela. The Scrolls say that at some point across the ages, She will come close enough that her Creation will match what She had in mind. But until then, we are cursed to bear the cycle of the Purge."

The elf gave a slow, somber whistle. "Damn, that's depressing."

"Not really. Countless generations live between each

Purge. It's just bad timing that we happen to have been born on the cusp of one."

He fell silent again, considering what she'd said. It was impossible. Ridiculous, even. But then, if this world was just a video game, how hard would it be to wipe it clean and start again? Then again, how was his world, the Fifth World, tied to it?

And then something she'd said hit him like Gerald's hammer.

"Wait! Did you just say something about the gods from 'where I'm from'?"

She winked back at him. "I was wondering—"

Whatever she'd been about to say was cut off by a pair of sharp yelps from the tent flaps. The boots outside collapsed into a heap of Exceptas sentries.

Mehleese poked her head through the opening. "Let's go. Goldenshield—that is, Lord Sheriff Goldenshield—has need of us."

CHAPTER FORTY-ONE

THE BETRAYAL

AS JEHN UNTIED ZEKE, MEHLEESE raced through a rambling explanation of the events following Boland's ill-fated meeting with the leaders of the Legion. She was babbling, the words falling out of her like a tipped-over bucket, but she didn't care. Seeing her elf alive and in one piece made her, well, feel lighter than air. Like a teenager again. She wanted to either jump up and down in delight or attack him but couldn't choose which. Unfortunately, they had time for neither.

"And he just up and quit?" Zeke asked, rubbing his wrists.

To the Dark World with it! Overcome, she grabbed the elf and crushed him against her, trapping his hands between them. She clung to him, desperate, saying nothing, reveling in his leanness, the softness of his Wizard's Robe, the heavy, exotic spice of his arcane scent.

With a bit of wiggling, he freed his hands from between the two of them and wrapped his long arms around her, sighing almost imperceptibly as he did it. After so long here, she couldn't really remember whether this was really what it felt like to touch another human being in the "real world" or not. Then again, she didn't care. If only this moment, this feeling, could last forever, she'd stand in the tent, bound to him, saying nothing until the day of the Awakening.

But too many people depended on them. Jehn cleared her throat, bringing them back to the moment at hand.

Reluctant, Mehl pulled away. "What did you ask? Oh, yes, he just quit. No one but the Council heard what Boland said exactly, but after handing the Speaker the Shield, he tossed that ridiculous armor to the ground and rode into town. The rest of us began preparing for the Legion right away, and by the time anyone thought to look for him, he was nowhere to be found."

"Good riddance to that Thela-cursed fool," Jehn said. "So Goldenshield took the Shield?"

"Yes, and the Oath as well. He's the legitimate Sheriff of Copperton Vale now."

The Paladin smiled. "She always gets what She wants, one way or another."

"Who does?" Zeke asked.

"Never mind. Let's get moving. Why does he need us?"

"Ek'zae is a key part of his battle plan."

Jehn tilted her head. "Battle plan?"

"Yeah, he's got a plan. Something unusual in mind for the Legion."

"What does he need a plan for? He's got warriors. The Legion has warriors. Both sides send their fighters out to find someone from the other side to try to kill. Whoever's left at the end wins."

Mehleese smirked. "Yes, that's exactly how Atlous will do it. He'll commit his forces in waves to go out and find some-one to attack. But we've not even half the force, and most of our 'soldiers' are farmers more familiar with a pitchfork than a spear. But Goldenshield thinks that even with a smaller force, we can fight them off."

"I still don't get it." Jehn said, uncertain.

"Well, I do, and I never thought I'd see the day," Zeke said in wonder. "You swear that he's actually doing this? He didn't sneak away or think of somewhere else to be? He actually took the Sheriff's Oath?"

"Yes, I watched him speak the words myself. But if we don't get back soon, the only thing he'll really have committed to is suicide. Along with most of the people of town."

"Right, right," the elf said. "Let's go."

Mehl stuck her head out of the tent and scanned the area for Guardians. The camp was quiet, thank Thela. Most of the Legion had left to attend the battle. Except for the unconscious guards, the area was clear. She stepped over the bodies and waved the others to follow.

With her chest ready to burst at finding Zeke unharmed, the Ranger forced herself to breathe normally and focus, concentrating on picking a path through the deserted camp. The last thing they wanted to find out was that it wasn't deserted by stumbling into guards.

"Wow, they're all gone. There's no one here," Zeke said in his normal tone of voice.

Mehl's skin prickled, and she gasped, not quite jumping out of her boots. She spun on the elf with an angry frown. "I ought to box those pointy ears to teach you a lesson," she hissed in a whisper. "Keep it down. We can't assume we're alone."

Grimacing, Zeke dipped his head, chastened. "Sorry, I just figured… well, okay. I'll be quieter."

Nerves strung like guitar strings, Mehl led the trio through the camp. They tiptoed, shuffled, and dashed from cover to cover as they progressed, even duck-walking behind a wagon when the situation required it. Every hesitation in the open felt like a spotlight on them, and every half hint of sound they made was an uproar.

Their restraint proved worthwhile, though. Along the way, they encountered a handful of Exceptas, although most were lounging near tents, half asleep.

At last, they reached the edge of the camp unnoticed. Without a word, Mehleese pointed at the top of the hill where Boland had planted his banners just over a day ago. She started toward it at a full sprint. Once they reached the top, out of sight of the camp, they'd stop and *Summon* their mounts.

Cresting the hill with Zeke and Jehn on her heels, she let the tension leak away.

And then the color drained from her face.

Tristan and a full complement of Exceptas were waiting.

"Well, well, well. Going somewhere?" His mouth twisted in a callous scowl.

"Tristan," Jehn said, "let us pass."

The Exceptas chief threw his head back and barked a sharp laugh. "Are you out of your fool mind? It took every ounce of persuasion I could muster to convince the great and mighty Atlous Bonecrusher that he could trust us. That we would willingly submit to this Path of his. And even now he shows he doesn't trust me. Instead of bringing us to battle today, he ordered us to guard his rear, watch over the camp, and make sure you didn't try to escape.

"I'm embarrassed to report his rear is safe, and his camp is too. But then, who'd be fool enough to bother the camp of the Legion of the Guardians? But," he called to the men lined up behind him, "we appear to have escaping prisoners. How lucky are we to have something useful to do!" The Exceptas men and women behind him chuckled.

Sulfurous fireballs crackled in the air just above Ek'zae's outstretched palms. "Step aside, Exceptas dog," he snarled.

Jehn pushed the Mage's arms down, forcing him to release the flickering balls of flame. He frowned.

"Tristan, listen to me. You don't have to do this."

"Actually, we do. You've left me with little other choice, Jehnilyas."

"What if you did have another choice?"

"What else is there? There's the king and the Temple or the Guardian invaders. That's it. Those are the options. And you know I'm not about to side with that Thela-cursed king."

Jehn took a few steps toward him and lowered her voice. "Tristan, look, I understand that you blame me for this."

The cords of Tristan's neck strained as his face contorted in a sneer. "Of course I blame you!" he exploded. "You said we were going to save the Realms, all of Thelaroth. You told me to build the Exceptas into something to be feared. That all I needed was that blasted shield to challenge the king and the Temple. That they would quake in their temples when we came to stomp out their corruption."

He stepped closer to her. His great two-handed axe blinked from the harness on his back to his hands. His voice lowered, laced with a hint of threat. "You said we'd be together. You said you loved me. But then that one night came, the night we raided Copperton, and everything about you changed. You came back with a gleam in your eye I'd never seen. And just like that, you cast me aside. You accuse me of only listening to Gravesire? Yours was the one voice opposing his, and it went silent after that night."

She stood her ground, putting her hands up. "I'm sorry. I was… I was wrong. About many things. I misunderstood something my father told me before he died. And I was lost and lonely, and you were so strong. I lied to myself, and in turn, I lied to you. You have every right to be angry with me. I understand that. I do. And I'm sorry. But don't punish the whole of the Realms because *I* made a mistake. If you have to kill me to feel better, so be it. But promise me you'll fight alongside Goldenshield afterward."

Tristan turned his head and spat. "Goldenshield, Goldenshield, Goldenshield. Why the bloody fuck should I help him?"

"Because he's the 'what else' you wanted, Tristan. Thela sent him to help us stop the Purge. But if we don't help him hold the Legion here, all our hope will blow away like smoke on the wind."

"You want me to help *him*? To help the man who stole you from me?"

"He's going to need us all. Someone will have to lead his armies."

"If he's going to do what you said, he'll lead them."

She shook her head. "No, he has Thela to contend with. He'll need generals."

"Listen to yourself!" the clan chief shouted.

Looking at her boots, Jehn squeaked, "I know. But this time I'm right."

Tristan's hand squeezed the shaft of his axe, and a mix of fury and hatred glowed in his eyes. "*I hate you*!" he bellowed with an electric force that prickled Mehl's fingertips. The words became a guttural, animal roar, and he swung his axe overhead. Jehn held her ground, as if frozen in place, head lowered. The blow would kill her.

And then it fell.

The head of the axe sank into the ground just between her feet.

The Paladin met his glare. She nodded at him, a silent agreement between them.

"Harlow!" Tristan called over his shoulder.

One of the Exceptas warriors trotted up from the formation. "Sir?"

"You have five minutes to gather the men left in the camp. And then we march to help defend Copperton."

"Yes, sir!" Harlow raced down the hill without another word.

"Thank you," Jehn murmured.

"Don't thank me. It's my only choice. If I let you go, Atlous won't hesitate to kill me. And I can't bring myself to kill you, which means I can't stop you. We might as well make a battle out of it."

Leaning in close to Mehleese, Zeke said, "Whoa. Did you hear all of that?" His voice was little more than a hint of breath across her ear. She nodded.

"I can't believe they used to be a thing," he added.

Mehl struggled to keep her face neutral, to keep the shock from showing. Oh, but that was only half of it. Just wait until he figured out the rest.

CHAPTER FORTY-TWO

THE STRATEGY

THE SHIELD PHALANX BLOCKING THE bridge held against the arialens. It weathered the squalls of arrows loosed by centians and avians, turning back far more iron-tipped shafts than slipped through.

And then the ursals came.

The bear people, still running on all fours at bowel-clenching speeds, converged on the bridge and rushed headlong at the formation. They were living, breathing, fuzzy wrecking balls, their fur rippling in the wind of their charge.

The first three struck at the same moment, or close enough to have seemed to be all at once. They careened into the shields, roaring a challenge that shook the foundation of the bridge. Like bowling balls, they knocked the soldiers out of position, disrupting the tight formation. The ones that came behind the first charge leapt into the opening, slashing and tearing with great claws and mouths that brimmed with savage teeth and dripped with hot saliva.

The soldiers holding the shields overhead to form the canopy faltered. Unable to hold up under the weight and force of the ursal charge, gaps opened in the defense above the soldiers. The avians, squawking in excitement, seized the chance, pouring arrow fire on the terrified humans.

"Fill the gap!" Gerald shouted over the crash of metal on metal, the crack of bone, and the screams of the mauled. No one heard him. Or no one knew how to fill it.

"Focus on the ursals," he ordered Torgan and Felton. "Put down the ones getting through!"

Leaping down from Zero, he commanded his hammer to hand. As his boots hit the cobblestones, he flew forward, toward the rear of the failing formation.

Overflowing with Power, he swung his hammer in precise arcs, smashing into anything that resembled an animal, grunting with effort. Skulls cracked and limbs snapped beneath his ferocious attacks. A trail of bone, blood, and matted fur collected in his wake as he pressed toward the gaps.

The avians, desperate to bring him down, zipped arrows through the space around his head, some so close he felt the wind as they sailed past. A frenzy of them clanged against the shield he bore before him like a talisman.

Reaching the formation, he stepped up onto the back of a bear turned away from him and used it as a springboard to bound over the crush of bodies below. Even as he jumped, he smacked his hammer against the ursal's head, reveling in the satisfying crack as it fractured, being rent apart with his blow.

For a heartbeat, a cool, clean breeze brushed against his flushed cheeks—a brief moment of peace as he glided in a smooth arc toward the gap in the shield wall.

His feet crashed into the ground, somehow coming down on stone instead of the tangled mass of bodies surrounding him. He slammed his own shield into the gap, bashing it into the face of an unsuspecting ursal pressing through. It roared in frustration.

"Form on me!"

The other shield bearers reformed and tightened up, to more shouts and angry roars from the ursals prevented from slipping past, into the killing ground. The ones that had—not many, thank Thela—dealt a massive amount of damage in a very short time but were brought down quickly by spear and arrow. One by one, the canopy's shields rose again over the formation, protecting them from the avian rain of arrows.

They held again. But they were slipping. The press of bodies, ram and bear, against their shields drove them back on stones wet with new blood, inch by inch, together as one unit. If the wall failed again or they got pushed off the bridge, the battle would be over. Copperton would be lost.

And then the ground beneath them trembled. The tremor lasted barely a second, just long enough to give him hope. Seconds later, the bridge shook again briefly. And then again. And again, growing stronger, steadier with each wave. Howls of frustration went up from the other side of the shield wall separating him from the Legion.

Gerald smiled, and relief washed over him. Thank bloody Thela; it was about time. Shifting his shield an inch to open a gap large enough to see through, he peered out just as the bridge was rocked again with more intense rumbling.

A ball of fire lanced through the air from someplace in the woods behind them and struck the bridge on the Legion's side of the bank. The fireball exploded in a shower of sparks, flame, and stonework. A smoking, scorched divot marked where the fireballs had struck the span.

Another slammed into the center of the blackened target. Whole bricks cascaded away from the structure, falling into the freezing water below.

The press against the shields grew as the Guardians

already partially across the bridge panicked and surged to escape the rain of exploding fire.

"Hold, damn you all!" Gerald shouted to the men and women straining around him. "Just one more minute! For Thela's sake, for your own sakes, hold!"

As one, they strained forward, standing against the force of the rams and bears with nowhere else to run as the world rocked more and more violently. Airborne bombs fell in quick succession, raining gravel and stone down on top of them. And then three blasts landed in rapid succession, one after another, smashing against the bridge with the force of a high-speed train.

The world itself came apart. The ground underfoot shook, shifted, and weaved. And then, in a symphony of rumbling destruction, it pitched down like a drunk after too many cups of warlock spirits, toward the far bank. The Legion attackers fell backwards, rolling down the now-sloping path of the bridge, into the chill run of the Ice Flow below.

A cheer went up from the woods behind Gerald, but they weren't out of trouble yet. The soldiers holding the formation lurched. The entire phalanx collapsed, and shields and bodies flew forward, sliding, like the Guardians, toward the raging water, clutching at one another in a panicked frenzy to keep from falling. In front of them, a wide swath had been cut from the bridge, splitting it into two parts.

Someone snatched at Gerald's belt, and he grabbed for the shield bearer beside him as she toppled away. Like a barrel of monkeys with interlinking arms, the defenders clung to one another, keeping the next up and out of the race of water.

Shouts of "Hold on!" and "We'll get you!" came from somewhere behind them as the townspeople called out. In pairs, people sprinted out onto what remained of the bridge from the cover of the woods, one holding a shield overhead against the threat of arrow fire and the second taking a clinging soldier's arm and pulling them up to safety. Somehow, Gerald had managed to cling to his own shield, as had most of the other defenders. They held them out as cover while the rescuers worked, desperate to gain a solid foothold and scramble back up to the riverbank.

He clung to the buckling structure until his arms burned with exertion and his hands started to go numb. He hung in the open like a sitting duck for the airborne avian archers. At last, the soldier beside him was pulled to safety. Hands grabbed at Gerald and pulled him up to the riverbank and back under the cover of the woods. Familiar faces beamed as he scrambled up. Mehleese dropped the shield she'd been holding and squeezed him so hard he couldn't breathe.

Beside him, Degby clapped him on the shoulder. "That was amazing work you and the soldiers did out there, my lord. My eyes ain't never seen the like. 'Twas an honor to be the one that pulled you back up."

Gerald extricated himself from Mehleese's enthusiastic embrace and grasped the other man's forearm. "The honor was mine, Master Degby. And I think you did your sister proud today. Thank you for keeping your promise."

Degby nodded. "Thank you for keepin' yours, my lord. I'm proud to call you Lord Sheriff."

The crowd around them cheered and whooped, crying, "Goldenshield! Goldenshield! Goldenshield!"

"This isn't over yet, not by a long shot. What's Atlous doing?"

"No doubt wondering why you didn't just come out and fight them," Jehn said, slipping through the elated crowd. "What's with all the cat and mouse across the river?"

"Which way are they marching?"

She looked over the river. "South."

"*South*!" he shouted. "Reform to the south!" As his order was repeated through the crowd, soldiers and townspeople around them separated and, in loose groups, marched at a quick step in that direction.

"Ger!" Zeke ran toward them with a smile wide enough to sail a boat through. "Mehl said you needed me to destroy the bridge on the western bank. How'd I do?"

"Z!" he clasped the Mage's arm and pulled him close for a chest bump. "Fucking awesome, dude. Almost perfect."

"Almost?"

"Well, I'd have preferred not to have nearly fallen off afterward, but I won't nitpick." He couldn't help but beam. "Come on, though. We have to move. Quickly."

He trotted off behind the defenders. The others, exchanging confused looks, followed after him.

"Seriously," Jehn asked as they hustled through the woods, "what is all this about?"

"We needed cover," said Gerald. "The Everfrost Road Bridge was too open for us to hold. Those damn bird people would just fly over us and keep the arrows coming all day. We could manage to hold them at bay for a bit with arrows and shields, but arrows run out, and you can only hold shields over your head for so long. We had to keep the bridge long enough for Mehl to get, um, Ek'zae back here to destroy it."

"But how does that help? There are bridges all along the river. They'll move to the next one and cross there."

"Exactly! But all the other bridges in the area are much narrower and have plenty of woods for cover. The birdies can't kill us from above."

"But still," she said, forehead creased, "now you have to go through the whole bridge blocking again. And sooner or later, you won't be able to hold the shield formation. This just isn't how battles are fought!"

They rounded a bend in the forest path, and another bridge across the river came into view. Gerald winked at the Paladin. "No, it's not. Battles in Thelaroth are fought without any tactics to speak of. Everyone just runs out and tries to kill someone. Last one standing wins. I can promise you, princess, if we did that, the Legion would be standing last. And it wouldn't take long.

"But don't worry. There'll be no more shield formations today. That was just to kill time until you guys got here. Now we get to give them a little surprise."

"Surprise?" she muttered. "I still don't—"

"You will," he replied. "Bergan!"

"Over here, Lord Goldenshield!" The tall smith waved from near the mouth of the new bridge.

"Are we ready?"

"I think so. We're in position, and the Legion is lining up on the far side to charge again. My only problem is that I don't have anyone to act as a courier between the defenders and engineers once the battle starts. Someone will need to make deliveries."

"You don't have anyone who can do it?"

"Not quickly enough."

"We'll do it!" Several feet behind Bergan, a girl peeked out from around the trunk of a wide oak tree. Frega's friends, Daven and Blust, appeared from behind trees as well, glaring at the girl in shock.

"Why'd you say anything?" Blust cried.

Daven nodded in quick, short strokes. "Yeah! They didn't even know we were here. Now they'll make us leave!"

"By Thela's Blood, girl," Bergan roared, "you should not be out here. You get on back to the town with your mother!"

She stepped fully into the open, away from her hiding spot. "I know you want to keep me safe, Father, but if we can't stop the Legion here, there will be no safe place for me in all Five Worlds. You need fast runners, and you know the three of us outran everyone else in town last year at the Planting Festival race. Let us help."

"Under no circumstances—" he started.

"Father, please? We can help. And we only need to run to the back of the lines. They'll be plenty far away from the danger."

"No, Frega. Out of the question."

"I wouldn't tell you what to do with your own children, Bergan," Gerald cut in, "but your daughter was a tremendous help at the Exceptas camp. She kept a level head, never panicked, and knew exactly what to do. I wouldn't put her in harm's way, but she could surely handle herself as a runner."

The massive blacksmith looked from his daughter to Gerald and back and then cocked his head, considering. Slowly, a wide grin spread across his face. "Well, girl, you've apparently impressed the Lord Sheriff. So be it, then. But don't you dare tell your mother I let you within a thousand yards of this."

The three young faces lit up at the prospect. "You won't regret it, Father!" Frega said. "I promise!"

He shook his head. "Go over to the engineers' tables. They'll give you satchels to bring to the bridge. Hand them off there and get back right away. All three of you. Am I clear as Thela's Voice?"

"Yes, Father." Frega said, turning on her heel. Daven and Blust followed with a chorus of agreement. The trio dashed away toward a collection of tables nestled in a nearby clearing. After a few steps, though, Frega stopped and turned back around with a wide smile. "Thanks, Goldenshield. For everything. But most of all, for trying to keep your promise. Now knock 'em dead!" With that, she scampered away to join her friends.

"Anything else, Master Smith?" Gerald asked.

"Oh, yes," he replied. "I found this one wandering around nearby. He said he was recruited." Bergan jerked his thumbed over his shoulder at a stormy-eyed Tristan.

"And there's the surprise I got for you," Jehn said, her oval eyes twinkling. "The Exceptas want to join in the defense of Copperton."

Gerald raised an eyebrow. "Is that so?"

Crossing his arms, Tristan nodded. "So long as you swear to me you aren't doing this for the king."

"The king can kiss my—" he started to say, but he caught himself.

Tristan chuckled. "That's enough for me. The Exceptas is yours to command. At least for today."

Clapping the taller man on the shoulder, Gerald said, "You're a good man after all, Tristan Kingsbane. Copperton will owe you a great debt. Well, if any of us survive."

"You'd best not die today, then. I expect to see it paid. Oh, and this doesn't mean I like you. I don't."

"Fair enough. Are you all on foot?"

Tristan nodded.

"Okay, run north to the next bridge, cross over, and come back this way. By the time you get back, you should hear a thunder coming in waves from this side of the river. When you hear it, attack the Legion from the rear. Don't commit fully, though. Attack and fall back. Pick at them. And take the cavalry with you. That way, you can take turns harrying their reserves."

"You're giving *me* a squad of Dalor's men to command?"

"Yes. Go."

He took Gerald by the free arm and dipped his head a fraction. "Lord Sheriff, I still don't like you, but I suppose I could like you a little better." Turning north, he called out,

"Exceptas, to me!" With a wave, he gestured to the already mounted leader of the cavalry squad.

"Lord Sheriff, they're coming," Bergan said.

"Master Elf, would you be kind enough to rain destruction on the far side of the river, please? And Mehleese, if you wouldn't mind filling any Legioners who aren't already staggering around with arrows, I'd appreciate it."

"My pleasure."

He turned to Jehn. "Now here's your surprise. I'm just going to say I'm sorry now."

"What do you mean you're sorry?" she asked, but he was already on his way to the mouth of the bridge.

He took a few steps out onto the structure itself. Bonecrusher stood with his thick, scaled arms across his massive chest, scowling. Gerald allowed himself a moment of pride. Definitely not how the reptoule had expected the battle to go. From the look on his face, he thought he should already be stomping into Copperton, victorious. Points for ruining his day so far.

Goldenshield gave him a quick salute and then faced his own people, arms out. Cheers like he'd never heard before—not in a lifetime of attending high school pep rallies and Saturday-afternoon baseball games—met him, mixed with taunts for the angry Guardians.

Atlous barked an order, and a long, low horn blew. A group of oculans stepped forward from the Legion's lines. This time, they had the honor of coming first.

"Form on me!" Goldenshield shouted again. Thela be blessed, how much shouting had he done already today? And how much more did he have to go? This wasn't over by a long way yet.

Shield bearers lined up beside him, shoulder to shoulder, from one sidewall of the bridge to the other. They crouched down on one knee. Behind them, soldiers with spears came up, kneeling as well, extending their weapons over the shoulders of those bearing shields. Then the townspeople formed four lines to the rear of the spear carriers, twelve wide, each carrying a long metal tube. They set their feet in a position like an attack stance and pointed the tubes across the bridge.

Glancing from one side to the other, at the soldiers who had volunteered for this duty, he gave each a nod. "Thela be with us." They echoed it back to him in reverent whispers.

The Legion's horn called out again, this time in three sharp bleats. The oculans, impatient for their chance to show these upstart humans what the Legion did to the defiant, cheered and ran across the far mouth of the bridge, screaming. Long arms and legs churned as the creatures loped toward the humans, swords and axes ready.

"Take them in the eyes!" Goldenshield yelled. He gripped his shield tightly. If this didn't work, they were doomed.

"Now!"

Twelve deafening cracks barked out in quick succession. Smoke filled the air behind him, enveloping him and the surrounding soldiers, dragging the thick scent of sulfur and iron with it. Many of the eyes centered in the oculans' foreheads grew wide, like basketballs, and others squeezed shut in terror just before they snapped backward in a spray of bluish oculan blood. More than half a dozen of the attackers fell on the spot.

"Second volley!" Bergan shouted. In his mind, Goldenshield saw the first line of townsfolk sliding backward in a half crouch to let the second line point their weapons at the enemy, just the way they'd practiced it. Almost immediately, another thunderous barrage sounded behind, blowing more smoke into the air. More oculans fell, lifeless.

"Third volley!" Smith said. Another group of whip-crack discharges followed. Another group of oculans collapsed.

Across the bridge, Atlous coughed a curse in a guttural, foreign tongue. He had no doubt it was a curse, though. He barked another command, and the horn sounded again. In response, the avians took flight, bowstrings already singing with the thrum of arrows.

The tree canopy of the Ore Woods was thick with oak, maple, elm, and walnut trees, and the townspeople were positioned safely beneath it. A few of the bird-faced people shot arrows through in desperation, hoping for the best, but none of them found a target.

Bergan continued to call out volleys of fire as more oculans raced forward, ignoring the fallen piling up around them. The townspeople cycled through line after line of the formation in a regular pattern, falling back to reload after every shot, finding a rhythm with the cadence of the Smith's voice.

The centians rode forward, too, then, loosing arrows across the bridge with the familiar snap of bowstrings, hoping to land one in the center of the squadron of townsfolk that was destroying the oculan charges. As before, though, most of the arrows either bounced off or poked into the shields harmlessly.

Some did succeed, though, and were marked by screams of pain. But whenever a townsperson was hit, they would trade off their barrel to a backup, or if they fell, someone would rush up and take it while two others pulled the injured person to safety.

The oculans began to falter. Too many pale one-eyed bodies littered the expanse. Instead of charging, they hesitated, weary of running headlong into devastation.

With a furious growl, Atlous sent his own people, the reptoules, across the span. They snorted as they crashed forward, and Goldenshield wondered if this was the closest he would ever come to a real dinosaur attack. Stomping toward the line of soldiers and townsfolk in a thunderous demonstration of power and strength, they could take more damage than the oculans before coming down. But just the same as the cyclops people before them, they fell to volley after volley after volley of fire.

Shortly after the reptoules began to charge, another horn, one somewhere to the rear of the enemy's line, blew a single note. One long, high-pitched squeal. Three—perhaps four?—waves of attack later, the same horn blew again. And once again sometime after that.

On the third time, Atlous grunted another order. A centian standing nearby with a horn hesitated, eyeing his general in uncertainty. With a growl, Atlous repeated the command and waved his hands at the horseman. The centian raised his horn and blew four fast notes, freezing the attacking lizard people in their tracks. In the distance, another horn answered. In silence, with masks of confusion and rage in equal number, the members of the Legion fell back, reforming into orderly lines on the far bank of the river.

Cheers from the defenders filled the air. They clapped and clasped hands, shouted taunts and jeers at the bewildered Guardians, and patted Goldenshield's shoulder in congratulation. The Legion had come to Copperton and thrown their full might against the townspeople, but the townspeople had turned them back.

Gerald stood up, knees sore and his shoulders tight with tension. Zeke rushed up and gave him a high five, almost unable to form words. "We did it! We did it! Holy shit, we did it! I can't believe you showed them how to make guns!"

"They're not walking away yet. Let's not get too—"

Jehn strode up and, although smiling, smacked him across the face so hard that it cost him a few health points.

"What was that for?" he asked.

“Those smoking staffs you made. Are they magic? What are they? They scared me half to death.”

“Bergan and the master engineer worked it out. They call them ‘thunder sticks.’ I’d call it a blunderbuss.”

“I can’t believe you did that,” Zeke repeated. “And how? They made fifty of them in a day?”

“Actually, no. They made thirty-five of them in a day. It turns out that our Master Smith had already started studying my, um, other weapon days ago. He and the master engineers in town already had fifteen of them made. The hardest part, then, was getting raw material to make a lot more in such a short time. Because the iron—”

“*Goldenshield*!” Atlous thundered from the other side of the river.

Gerald turned to the west. At the very edge of the bridge, Thela’s Zealot fumed.

No, they hadn’t really turned them back. They’d only held them at bay, and this wasn’t nearly over yet.

CHAPTER FORTY-THREE

THE CHALLENGE

BONECRUSHER STOMPED ACROSS THE BRIDGE, hands in the air as a sign he was crossing to negotiate. Gerald took a deep breath and checked the straps holding the golden shield to his arm. When did he put it down last? Had he let go of it even since he'd sworn that oath?

Concentrate.

"Mehl, Jehn, Ek'zae, come with me but stay a good ten, fifteen feet behind. Keep your hands up like his until I put mine down. Master Smith, if anything goes wrong, get the townspeople out of here. The soldiers will cover your retreat as best they can."

"Begging your pardon, Lord Sheriff," Bergan said, "but if anything happens to you out there, I'm going to send as many of those motherless Guardians to the Dark World as I can before we run out of slugs. Now, go on. Thela's waiting."

Gerald squinted at the blacksmith and then took him by the arm. "Thank you, Master Smith. You're a good man."

Smith smiled back. "You're all right yourself, Lord Sheriff. I reckon you might even be okay to sleep inside the house."

Chuckling, the Warrior turned and crossed the bridge with his hands up and open, his three friends behind him, mimicking him. He stopped before reaching the center, ten feet from the Legion's leader.

"Truce?"

Atlous nodded. "Truce. For as long as we both stand here. No longer."

"Would you like to discuss terms of your surrender, Master Bonecrusher?"

The reptoule cackled, a rough, jagged sound that reminded Gerald somehow of the Hulk and Donald Duck. "You amuse me, Goldenshield, I will give you that. And that's something, with my mood today."

"Forgive us for ruining your day. But if you're not ready to give up, why call me out here?"

"You have done well with what you were given. With little but children and farmers, you managed to fight off the strongest Guardian army ever built with Thela's blessing. But you can't keep this up all day. Even with our losses, I still outnumber you at least three to one. And now my warriors are thirsty for blood. They will kill without remorse once we get a toehold on your side of the river."

"We've kept you away this long, Zealot. With Thela's blessing, we'll keep you away for hours yet before we falter. There are a lot of bodies on this bridge. Your obstacles are stacking up. And there's room for plenty more." He kept his face calm, doing the best he could to sell the lie. They'd had time to make a few more than fifty of the blunderbusses, but there was a limit to how much ammunition even an entire town's complement of engineers could make in one day. And the Coppertonians had already expended three-quarters of it. Engineers were working on more in the clearing behind him, but to survive another hour, they'd need ten times what they could make on the spot. Iron on hand was running short too.

"That is why I called you, Sheriff-man. Casualties. You are injuring too many of my soldiers. Sending too many to the Dark World."

Now it was Gerald's turn to laugh. "That's kind of what happens in battle, Master Bonecrusher."

"If we kill each other, there will be no one left to fight when the Awakening comes. But I must reach Riverglow and tear down your broken Temple and overthrow the puppet king before that time comes. Do not mistake me—I can and will take your town by force if I must. But if we have to swim the river, it will be even more costly for both of us. And Thela's truth, human, I want you and your people to survive. To fight beside us at the Purge. You have earned that honor today."

Awakening? Purge? Was he supposed to know what that all meant? Did it matter anyway? Whatever they were, they had nothing to do with the Coppertonians' limited ammunition.

"It sounds like you have a problem, Bonecrusher, not me. But, that said, I agree with you. The fewer injured here the better. I'm listening, then. If you have a suggestion, now is the time."

Atlous gave him that long, strange lizard smirk. "We decide it. You and me. Single combat."

A cold shudder rocketed up the Warrior's rendered form. Single combat? Against *him*? Was Atlous insane?

But then… Gerald *was* the Sheriff. These people were his responsibility.

Shit.

"Done," he replied, not trusting himself to say more. Thank Thela, he said that much without his voice cracking.

"We meet at the center of the bridge. First one to reach the other's side is declared victor."

"Okay. If you win?"

"The Legion will occupy Copperton and use it to stage the siege of Riverglow. But you have earned my respect. Your people will be treated as Guardians themselves."

"And if I win?"

He cackled his hulking Donald Duck laugh again. "If you win, I will agree to whatever terms you demand."

"Fair enough." Gerald extended his sword arm, and Atlous grasped it hard at the elbow.

"In the sight of Thela, the bond is struck," the Zealot intoned, eyes squeezed shut. "May it please her to see it fulfilled."

"Can I have a moment to speak to my friends?"

"Speak quickly. I will wait."

Gerald trotted back to where the trio stood. "What did you hear?"

"Enough," Mehleese said, pale as a sheet. "This is madness. I knew you were brash, Goldenshield, and young and stupid, but this? You can't face him. You're not even half his level."

"I took the Oath, Mehleese. This is what the Sheriff does."

"Dude," Zeke mumbled. "To the death or what?"

"Technically, I just have to reach the other side of the river before he reaches this one. But there's no way I'm getting through him unless he's dead. And he's a little big to try to sneak past me."

"Dude." Zeke clamped his mouth shut, cutting off whatever else he had to say. His eyes clouding, he turned away.

Mehl clucked her tongue. "I'll say it again: this is madness. But if you are committed, so be it." She wrapped her long archer's arms around him and squeezed. "Give him Hell," she whispered into his ear. "It has been a pleasure, you dolt."

"Take care of Z," he replied. "Stick together, always."

They separated, and he turned to his friend, offering his hand. "Dude, Z."

Zeke slapped it away and hugged him. "I'm sorry, man. I'm so sorry for what I said."

"No, dude. I'm sorry. I was an asshat. A selfish asshat, and I've been acting that way for a long time. Since before we came here. You guys are awesome. You need to take care of each other."

"Shut up. You'll kick his ass. Now get to it."

Lastly, he gave Jehn his best lopsided smuggler's grin. "Princess."

"Shut up." Rising on tiptoes, she leaned into him and pressed her lips to his cheek. Then she buried her head in his chest. "You owe me two favors. Remember? Because you're a terrible drinker?"

"I remember," he choked. "But now isn't exactly—"

"Come back to me. That's the first one. You come back here, do you understand?"

He backed away and nodded, his face flushed. Clearing his throat, he said, "Go on now, back to the others. I've got work to do."

The trio took a few steps backward and then turned for the woods and the other defenders. He watched until they stepped off the nameless stone bridge. Did it even have a name? He was likely to die on it; it seemed like he should know its name.

Banishing the thought and mustering his courage, he strode back to the same spot as before and set his feet for combat. Calling his hammer to hand, he raised the shield to cover the lower half of his face.

Bonecrusher dipped his head in respect. "You are big, Goldenshield. Bigger than I expected. Bigger inside than out. My friend chose well."

“What friend?”

“Rhandren, the old king. Jehn’s father. He chose you. You and your elf friend. He knew he was sick, dying. Knew he would not live to see the end of all this. But he wouldn’t leave his beloved Realms without someone to fight for the people. For that reason, he begged me to send him to the Fifth World, to bring someone back.”

Gerald’s jaw worked, but nothing came out. At last he squeaked, “*You* sent him? So you *can* send people to the Fifth World?”

“He was a good friend. One of very few Favored to show me honor when I came to live on this side of the ocean. At first, I refused him. He was old and sick by then. Too old to make the journey there and back. But he wouldn’t accept that. He was a stubborn old mule, and I eventually gave in. He knew the risks. If it killed him, I figured that was his choice. But it didn’t kill him. When he returned, he was so weak he could hardly speak. He told me and his daughter that Copperton’s golden shield was the key. To watch for it. It would mark a man of the law who would put things right.”

“Bullshit. He hit me with that glowing stick, what, just over a week ago? But he’s been dead for years.”

Atlous shrugged his massive scaled shoulders. “I sent him just before he sent his family away, years ago. The portal between worlds, like time itself, is a work of Thela. She chooses the when and how, just as she chose to put Rhandren in a place where he could find you.”

“That all-powerful god of yours sent him to a convenience store. She must have figured he needed a Thirsty Gulp and some Twizzlers.”

The reptoule twisted his head in confusion. “What do you mean? I don’t understand.”

“Thela didn’t *send* him to me. It was pure coincidence.”

"If you say so, Lawkeeper. I say She put him where he needed to be."

"Whatever. Let me make sure I've got this right, then. You can send me and the elf back to the Fifth World? You know the way?"

He nodded. "I know the rituals, yes. But as I said, it's Thela's way. She decides."

"Yeah, yeah, right. If I win, then, you'll send me back?"

Narrowing those black, marble eyes, he replied, "If you win, yes. If that is the path you choose, I will try."

"All right, then, let's do this."

"You are ready?"

"You bet. Let's go." Already he felt the surge of Combat Power welling up. He was going to give old Alligator-Face a run for his money. Time to get a ticket home.

"Begin."

Combat commands flew through his head involuntarily. *WarCry, Attack*, *Shout*, *ShieldBash.* All of those and more, dozens of them, springing to mind without conscious thought, as natural as breathing. He *was* Goldenshield, no longer a twenty-three-year-old from some other world that didn't belong here. He was the Sheriff of Copperton Vale. He was going to win this battle. And he *was* going to go home.

He leapt forward, havoc on his lips.

The Zealot of Thela, though, wasn't about to be cowed by a Warrior half his level. Bonecrusher fell back a few steps and called a Totem of Wind, which materialized, glowing, at his feet. A magical talisman, it would make his movements seem as if aided by the wind itself. Gerald had only an instant to worry over it, though. Atlous bolted forward, no longer a lumbering, stomping, hulking humanoid lizard but a graceful instrument of attack. Thela's righteous instrument.

The two met at the center of the bridge in a starburst of

sparking color. Goldenshield swung his hammer overhead, feeding Power into the attack. Bonecrusher, buoyed by the power of the wind, met the hammer mid-swing and turned it away. His mace, something more like the top post on a staircase railing than the club with studded teeth that Jehn carried, flashed out in a blur.

It cracked Gerald hard, three times in quick succession. The first clanged off the golden shield with a resounding ring, but the second smashed into his hip, claiming at least twenty health points. The third flew upward, smashing the Warrior's chin, taking a massive amount of his health away.

Half stunned, Goldenshield staggered backward, wobbling on his feet.

The Shield. He had to get his shield up. It would protect him. But a shadow was falling. Fast. Faster than he could move his arm.

Atlous struck again in a sideways arc. Gerald took the full force of the reptoule's mace in the face, a vicious, Critical hit. A killing blow. Pain exploded through his nose and mouth. The force of it snapped his head to the side and spun his whole body around. With his vision suddenly brick red at the edges, he stumbled away, following his momentum toward the bank of the river.

Faces he could no longer recognize—although he should have, shouldn't he?—alarmed, angry faces stared back at him, filled with fear. He took a step toward them. And then another, although he didn't know why. He couldn't stop moving. Something carried him farther forward. He shuffled ahead, two, three, four paces.

But it was too much; his feet didn't work with his body anymore. They dragged behind him as his head and chest surged forward. Something pulled at him, tipping him over. He leaned drunkenly. The world spun, getting darker.

With a gasp, he pitched forward. The cobblestone surface of the bridge raced up to meet him. Slammed hard against his face and shoulders.

And then, Goldenshield died.

CHAPTER FORTY-FOUR

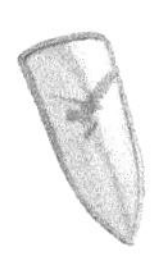

THE DARK WORLD

His eyes snapped open, but they shouldn't have worked. Did he even have eyes anymore?

Everything was dark. Not dark-like-a-six-year-old's-bedroom-at-night dark, more dark-like-an-old-time-movie dark. Dark and colorless. Black and gray. Steeped in a few dim hues of purple at best.

He heard wind, too, or the howling of it. But no breeze brushed across his skin.

Everything else around him, though, was unchanged. The bridge was below him, and those same faces watched in horror. He knew them now, of course. Zeke and Mehl and Jehn. But they were frozen, unmoving. Or at least *mostly* frozen. Zeke seemed to be trying to move, to raise his hand to shoulder level. But it was all too slow. Much too slow. As if some thick, invisible force was holding the elf's hand back.

Mehl's mouth was wide open and seemed to be screaming without making noise as her hands made slow progress toward her face. He waited, watching until they reached her mouth. It took five minutes, maybe even ten.

Jehn's head dipped low, her hands coming together. It was like watching ice melt.

But the worst part was *knowing*. There was no "probably" about it or time wasted wondering where he was. Deep down, he knew. In his core, in his bones (bones he no longer had), he knew.

This was the Dark World.

He was dead. Gerald Lawson. Officer Lawson of the Simmsville Police Department. Goldenshield. Lord Sheriff of Copperton Vale. He was all of those things here. And now, none of them. The dead, after all, were nothing.

This was his eternity. Trapped in a colorless world, alone, condemned to watch the living soldier on but in super-slow motion.

He'd been trapped maybe fifteen minutes, and already it sucked.

He turned around, coming nose to snout with the discolored, slow-motion face of his killer. The Legion's general stood with his arms stretched to the heavens and his long, flat, toothy mouth gaping in what had to be a cry of victory.

This wasn't right.

Someone had to fix it.

But who? It was too late for him. And not like he could write a congressman or a letter to the editor.

He had only one option.

"*Thela*?" His own voice rang in his ears. A drunken shout in a small, silent library. The clang of a ten-foot-tall gong in an eight-foot-wide room.

Yet, to the howl of the stagnant wind, it was nothing.

"Thela," he repeated, this time little more than a whisper, "look, I don't know if I believe in you. I didn't believe in you before. But I believed in God once, back when I was a kid. I guess I kind of always have. Are you two the same? Somehow? Or different? I don't know. But I know that this isn't what I'm supposed to do. It's not where I'm supposed to be. Why send me to Thelaroth only to bring me here? Why put me with Jehn if we can't be together? It's fucking stupid, and I can't—I refuse to—accept it. So if you're out there, somewhere, listening to me, send me back. Please. Just, please send me back to them so I can do what they need me for. So I can do what I'm supposed to do. Please."

He frowned. That wasn't quite right. Wasn't quite enough. Something was missing. Something…

"The people out there need me. And I promised to be there for them. Whether I believe in you or not, I believe in them. Help me keep my promise, and I'll work on the believing-in-you part."

A glow sparked to life in the space between Jehn's clasped hands, between the outlines of her fingers. Growing bright. A new star blazing in the surrounding darkness. He couldn't look. It stung his eyes. Blinding. Tears he shouldn't have felt streamed down his cheeks.

The howling of the windless wind grew. Louder and louder. So loud it filled his ears. It was so much, too much. Between the sound and the light, the heat of the rage building in his chest, the impotent fury of *finally* accepting he had a place in the world and not being able to do it.

All of it was too much.

And then it stopped.

CHAPTER FORTY-FIVE

THE REAL WORLD

THE SCREECHING HOWL DISAPPEARED. A faint breeze blew across his cheeks. His nose wasn't smashed, or even in pain. His chin was fine.

Could he be… alive?

Gerald scrambled to his feet. Behind him, someone screamed. Not far from that scream, someone else cheered.

His hammer, still in hand, thrummed now the same way the shield did. As if it had become enchanted on its own.

Atlous stood ten yards away, still near the center of the bridge, arms stretched to the heavens as he'd seen in the Dark World.

He dropped them, and his long lizard mouth fell open with a gasp. "Impossible," he croaked. "I killed you."

Smiling, Goldenshield gave him a cool nod. "You did."

"But… How? It can't be!"

The Warrior turned to the side of the river behind him. A ball of flame burned in Zeke's outstretched hand, just as he'd expected. Beside the elf, Mehleese's hands covered her face. She looked even more shocked than before.

Jehn was next to her, chin against her chest, hair making that swirl at her jawline that melted his heart, hands clasped together as if in prayer. But there was no golden light now. She looked at him and favored him with a wide grin. It lit up in her eyes, brightened her whole face. Her lips moved, but she said nothing. She mouthed words. Words *just* for him.

"Two favors. Now end it, for all of us."

She didn't need to ask him again.

Goldenshield flew at his adversary, hammer raised, leading with the shield that seemed to hum in his grasp—thrum, thrum, thrum—in harmony with the beat of his own heart.

Atlous Bonecrusher, Thela's Zealot, standing in shocked silence, was wholly unprepared.

The first strike caught the reptoule's mace and split the weapon in two.

The second hit was a shield bash, augmented by all the Power coursing through the Warrior—Thela's power, not his own, a hundred times more than he'd ever felt before. It was a crushing, Critical blow; Atlous gurgled in pain.

The third one came low, a smash to the thick, scaly legs, upending his opponent and sending him to the surface of the bridge with a tumultuous crash. He grunted hard, and the half of the mace he'd been holding skittered away, to the far side of the river.

Roaring in triumph, Goldenshield realized he'd been wrong. His hammer hadn't become an enchanted weapon, but rather, for the moment, he had.

He pointed it at Atlous. "Do you yield?"

"I… I…" the lizard man stammered in a throaty, wet voice, "yield."

The urge to laugh and cry and scream out all at once overwhelmed him. But not yet. First things first. Leaping over the heap of arms, legs, and green scales, Gerald sprinted to the far side of the bridge. He leapt off, landing in front of the army of the Legion, who watched him in stunned silence, the way a child at the zoo might watch a lion being fed.

Exultant, he *Released* his hammer and threw his hands into the air, shouting in challenge at the host of Guardians shying away. Each one, regardless of size, gender, or race, cast their eyes to the ground, unable to meet his glare. Those with tails drew them up, hiding them away in shame.

He spun away and crossed the bridge, returning to where Atlous was now sitting up against the sidewall.

"I believe you said any terms, Master Bonecrusher?"

Bonecrusher nodded and then gasped in pain at the movement. "I am bound by my honor. Even as I know I killed you and would swear by Thela you were dead. But you reached my side of the river first. Name your terms, then. Would you send us back to Akador? Or demand a return to the Fifth World?"

Gerald laughed again, trying not to sound like he was losing his mind. He waved at Jehn, motioning for her to join them. Atlous needed her.

"Tell you what. Let's get you healed up, and then we'll talk about that."

CHAPTER FORTY-SIX

THE BEGINNING

"THE LEGION'S ARMY WILL REMAIN camped outside of town until the Zealot and I agree how to proceed." Inside Council Hall, Gerald leaned back in his chair, boots up on the table in front of him.

The Speaker fidgeted. He'd never seen her uncomfortable like this before. "Are you sure, Lord Sheriff, that's wise?"

"You have my word, Lady Speaker," Atlous assured her in his gravelly voice, "there will be no problems during our encampment here. Anything that does happen to arise will be met with quick and harsh discipline."

"If you say so. And it's Madam Speaker. Unless you wish me to start calling you 'Lord Zealot'?"

He raised his green claws in protest. "No, madam."

Dropping his feet to the floor, Gerald sat up. He would never understand how he could possibly sit like that. That damned shield was still strapped to his back, yet somehow, he was sitting on it without feeling like he had a sled between him and the chair. Living in a video game was weird. "It's settled, then. The army will winter here while we discuss how to deal with the situation in Riverglow."

"What of your other army, Master Atlous?"

"They are camped in the Wetlands, halfway to Riverglow City. They have been notified to hold there until they receive further orders. They are under strict instructions to avoid confrontation with the locals." Atlous had dispatched an avian with the message moments after stepping off the bridge, beaten.

"I suppose that's the best that can be done for the moment," the Speaker said. Her tone suggested she'd prefer they all just went home, but she didn't say it.

"If there's nothing else, Council?" Gerald stood up and scanned the table. The eight members on hand looked back at him with warm smiles but said nothing. Bergan Smith added a conspiratorial wink. The missing member was Templeman Prior, who'd fled along with Boland. Everyone assumed they were both hiding out in Riverglow, guests in the Temple of Thela. But no one knew for certain. Or cared enough to go looking.

"I did have one additional thing, Lady Speaker."

"By all means."

Gerald turned and waved to Zeke, sitting in the far back of the room. "I'd like to officially present to Council my appointed Lieutenant Sheriff of Copperton Vale, Ek'zae Axeblight."

The Speaker frowned and gave him a sullen look. "Lord Sheriff, we've been expecting this. But I'm afraid that history—"

"Madam Speaker," he cut in, lowering his voice.

He might be a lord now, but she was still the better Speaker. "You *will* let me finish, Lord Sheriff, before you say anything."

He put his hands up in defeat.

"As I was saying, then." She cast a glare at Zeke. "I'm afraid that history has been unkind to your race, Master Elf. You have shown exemplary determination and courage since the day you arrived in Copperton, and we thank Holy Thela for sending us a much-needed Sheriff with such a strong right arm." Pausing, she held out a rolled scroll. "It is thus with the greatest pride that we offer you our deepest thanks and bestow upon you the name Ka'driel, which, to our understanding, means 'Faithful' in the Old Tongue still spoken by your people. We welcome you and your voice in this chamber any day, and Ka'driel, we accept your nomination as Lieutenant Sheriff. May Thela bless you and keep you strong."

Zeke stared at her, dumbfounded, and again struggled to find the capacity to speak. While flailing about for the right words, he approached the Council's table and took the scroll. He bowed, muttering only, "Thank you," and then backed away. The members stood up and showered him with applause.

When the clapping trailed off, the Speaker said, "Thank you, Lord Sheriff, for sitting in on our meeting today. Is there any other business?" She looked at the smiling faces to each side of her.

"Beg your pardon," Bergan Smith said. "I do have one additional thing, Madam Speaker. Lord Sheriff, my daughter instructed me to tell you that you did a fine job and she expects to see you continue it. Also, my wife and I want you to know you're welcome in our home any time."

Gerald, unable to help himself, chuckled out loud. "Thank you, Master Smith. And tell Frega I'm sure I'll be by the armory soon. I'm going to need a new war hammer before long, I imagine. I hope we can agree to a discount?"

The large man smiled and nodded.

"All right, then," the Speaker said. "Anything else?" Finding no other business, she banged her gavel against the table twice to end the session.

Tapping Atlous on his rock-like shoulder, Gerald led him out of the building behind a beaming Zeke. On the sunny steps outside Town Hall, the elf turned and said, "That's it. It's Ka'driel from now one. Next person who calls me 'Ek'zae' gets a fireball where the sun doesn't shine."

"It is a fine name, Master Ka'driel," Atlous said. "And one well earned. Now, if you'll excuse me, I need to see to finding winter provisions. Goldenshield, we will speak soon of what to do next. Preferably over several rounds of warlock spirits." He clapped the Warrior hard on the shoulder and stomped away.

Great. More warlock spirits. He would definitely have to pry the secret of how Jehn drank all night without feeling it from her.

Making a mental note, he turned to Zeke. "Congratulations, Master Ka'driel. It seems you're not the town pariah any longer."

"Yeah, it's great. Mehl's gonna be pumped. But I've been thinking, Ger."

"Wow, that is something."

"Shut up, dick."

"I'm sorry. What's on your mind?"

"Are you sure this is what you want? Bonecrusher said he'd send you back if you wanted to return to the Fifth World."

"Yeah, but I just… well, leaving doesn't feel right anymore. I belong here, at least for now. I want to—no, need to—be with my friends. We'll play it by ear and see what comes next. Besides, I'm getting used to not having to eat or sleep."

"The sex isn't bad, either, right?"

"Don't, Z. Just, don't."

The elf snickered even as the tips of his pointed ears flushed. "Which reminds me, I'm going to go show this to Mehleese and tell her that the Pig Latin bullshit is officially over. You want to come?"

Gerald shook his head. "No. I've got to go find Tristan, and Thela knows I have other things to think about. This Awakening and Purge business is terrifying."

Zeke nodded. He and Jehn had explained in detail all about Atlous's dire foretelling over a countless number of celebratory drinks following the battle. Later, after Jehnilyas called it a night, the elf shed some additional light on her and Tristan's previous relationship.

She could have mentioned that before. Not that he cared about her having a prior relationship. But he wasn't sure he could trust Kingsbane, and he worried that Tristan might try to use her to get back at him. It was an unlikely scenario, he knew, but it could linger in the back of his mind. And that might make him wary. Overly careful. He didn't want to be careful. He wanted them to be the way Zeke and Mehleese were, doe-eyed and blind to the other's shortcomings, so overwhelmed with the newness and wonder of finding that perfect someone that when they were together, the rest of the world might as well have melted into oblivion. They were wholly and completely stupid for each other.

Hard not to be at least a little bit jealous.

At the moment, though, at least his crush on Brooke had faded in the face of whatever he was building with Jehn. When he was with her, that old, familiar emptiness was filled with a soft, warm glow. It gave him a kind of reckless, delirious energy he hoped he'd never lose.

He *Entered* the Roost and Pig and somehow wasn't

shocked to find Jehn sitting at the bar. It seemed thinking of her worked as a kind of tracking beacon. There were worse problems to have. Sure, he had no shortage of stuff to deal with now that he was the official Lord Sheriff of Copperton Vale, but that could all wait. He'd done enough lately that spending an afternoon with her and a mug of lager was not unreasonable.

"My Lady Princess," he said, *Sit*-ting on the stool beside her. "What brings you here?"

"Bite your tongue, or I'll have to start calling you 'Lord Sheriff' every time I see you. And I'm having a much-belated toast to the memory of my father. Care to join me?"

With just a small gesture, Saiyen delivered a mug of foaming lager to the bar in front of him and smacked down a small cup of warlock spirits. He groaned just looking at it. "Ugh. Why the warlock spirits? Do we have to?"

"They were Rhandren Sophent's favorite toast for any celebration. Seems a fitting way to remember him and thank him for sending us a champion."

"Look, lady," he said, smirking. "I don't know what you've heard about me, but I'm lazy, have no ambition, and can be a bit of a jerk sometimes. Your dad could have picked better. I'm thinking maybe the Quik Mart wasn't the best place to look for someone willing to take on enormous, save-the-world challenges. I mean, sure, you'll find a guy with a love of nachos and cheap, leathery hot dogs there. But genuine heroes? Not so much."

She swayed, bouncing her shoulder against him. "See, that was the wisdom of my father. Even in a place filled with no-good layabouts, he found a couple of good ones."

"To the old king," he said, raising his smaller cup.

"To King Rhandren Sophent, wise and noble, the Anointed, Defender of the Western Realms, First Protector of the Temple of Thela, and Warden of Braxys the Black, Eater of Worlds," she replied. They both threw back their drinks. Gerald grimaced but managed not to cough. The spirits sent fiery tendrils spreading through his throat and belly.

"I still can't believe you knew all along and didn't say a word."

"The moment I laid eyes on you, I knew you were from the Fifth World. And that no matter what I'd thought about my father's words before, you and Zeke were what he wanted me to look out for. Everything I'd planned and arranged up until that moment was wrong. But I had to see how you would respond. Thela sends us Fifth Worlders more than anyone will admit, and often, their minds float away and never return."

He winked at her. "Well, thanks for having such confidence in me. Still," he went on, taking a serious tone, "I'm not some prophecy hero, come to redeem the whole world. I'm just this guy, you know?"

"You keep saying that. But then Thela also resurrected you yesterday in answer to my prayers. That's not a common thing. It makes you kind of a big deal."

Cringing at the reminder, he took another long drink of his beer. "We'll see, I guess. Don't get your hopes up, though. I'm almost sure to disappoint you sooner or later. It's my only real skill.

"But let's talk about something more fun. Because the Dark World? Yeah, uh, it's a messed-up place."

She raised her eyebrows. "All right, then, Lord Gerald of the Golden Shield, what would you like to discuss?"

"I suppose we could talk about the scroll on my desk asking for help with some chicken poachers in the northern part of the Vale. And if poachers weren't bad enough, someone else seems to be running from farm to farm, kicking them for no reason. I imagine I'm going to have to ride up there and see what's going on.

"But now that I think about it, I don't want to talk about that either. How about we just sit here and talk about whatever's on your mind? Or," he said, pointing at the lock of hair beneath her jaw line, "let's talk about how it makes me weak in the knees when this little guy curls up beside your face."

She slapped his hand away. "My father warned me about Warriors like you."

"You don't say. What was he like? Your father, I mean."

She launched into a series of charming old yarns about her father, stories she likely hadn't told anyone for years out of fear. He lifted his mug and drank until it was empty, then gestured for another, without the shot of warlock spirits. One was enough until Festus, at least.

Gerald smiled to himself. His future was out there somewhere, lurking, the same as it had been before, when he hid from it behind a laptop screen on dark nights in his Simmsville cruiser. But now, things were different. He was different. Finally, he was ready to stop being chased by his future and stalk *it* instead.

Through the uncertainty to come, whether merely a handful of chicken poachers or devastation wrought by world-ending dragons released by an angry goddess, he'd stand in the way of anyone or anything intent on bringing harm to this town or these people.

Because he was the Sheriff of Copperton Vale. Protecting this place was his duty.

He no longer needed to find a way home.

Home had come to him.

THE END

I hope you enjoyed following along on Gerald and Zeke's adventures as they figured out how to survive Thelaroth. As always, I'd love to hear what you thought, so be sure to leave a rating or a review wherever you picked up your copy of *Goldenshield*!.

The boys will be returning soon along with Mehleese, Jehn, and a Shadow Priest or two they'd probably prefer to avoid. For news about the next chapter in the *Realm Quest* saga and all my upcoming novels check out jrandrewsbooks.com. Don't forget to sign up for my mailing list to have updates on all my fantasy worlds delivered right to your inbox.

Follow me on Goodreads to keep up with what I've been reading, what I'm working on, what's on my mind otherwise, and to learn how to get exclusive access to shorts and sneak peaks from all the worlds living in my head.

Do you enjoy fantasy with a darker edge and a healthy dose of horror? Check out my post-apocalyptic horror fantasy, *Famine*. Tom Woodford wakes from a decade-long coma to find the world has been ravaged by an unstoppable plague, and there's nothing left but humanoid monsters that are running out of things to eat. Fans of Richard Matheson and *The Walking Dead* will love finding out if Tom can outwit the dark forces after his blood.

ABOUT THE AUTHOR

JR Andrews is the pen name for real life human Jason A. Rust. Born in Indianapolis, he has lived all but the first six months of life in Northern Kentucky, just across the Ohio River from Cincinnati, Ohio. JR has a wonderful and very tolerant wife, four very individual kids, two very lazy dogs, and a very active imagination. An avid reader and lifelong lover of Fantasy, Science Fiction, and Horror, as JR Andrews he writes stories set in fantasy worlds where the proverbial *&#% has hit the fan or is just about to do so.

Goldenshield is JR's first LitRPG fantasy novel. The next chapter in the *Realm Quest* saga is planned for release in 2021.

Twitter: @AuthorJRAndrews
Facebook: AuthorJRAndrews
Instragram: AuthorJRAndrews
Goodreads: J. R. Andrews

OTHER NOVELS BY JR ANDREWS

Famine by J. R. Andrews.
Get it now from Amazon or Kindle Unlimited, or
ask about it at your favorite local bookshop.

Lightning Source UK Ltd.
Milton Keynes UK
UKHW051324100121
376497UK00025B/419/J

9 781734 395839